PRAISE FOR *WHEN WE HAD WINGS*

"Set during WWII in the Philippines, *When We Had Wings* is the story of the first American women POWs. This is a fresh take on a very full genre of WWII retellings, and the authors do an excellent job keeping the timeline clear. If you enjoy reading about WWII, and want more than just the European front, this is a different vantage point worth reading."

—HISTORICAL NOVEL SOCIETY

"Ariel Lawhon, Kristina McMorris, and Susan Meissner have crafted a novel rich in historical detail that immerses readers in the dangers and deprivation WWII nurses suffered in the Pacific, wrapped up with a hopeful ending."

—BOOKLIST

"An illuminating story of the nurses stationed in the Philippines during WWII . . . With this fine tale, the authors succeed at bringing to readers' minds the courage and sacrifice of those who inspired it."

—PUBLISHERS WEEKLY

"A riveting novel by a trio of powerhouse authors that offers a fresh take on World War II fiction, one that is uncannily resonant today. Set in the lush tropics, *When We Had Wings* is an utterly original tale about courage, duty, and endurance."

—FIONA DAVIS, *NEW YORK TIMES* BESTSELLING
AUTHOR OF *THE MAGNOLIA PALACE*

"Three fierce women from differing backgrounds come together in the Philippines during World War II to unwillingly be thrust into the chaos of evil that will blast their worlds apart. Lawhon, McMorris, and Meissner seamlessly blend three nurses' stories and secrets with one deft and immersive storytelling voice. *When We Had Wings* asks the important question—how do we know what we can become until we must become it?—and answers it with a resounding novel of suspense, courage, and grand love. Based on the true story of the first female prisoners of World War II, *When We Had Wings* is thrilling, riveting, and deeply felt; a do-not-miss historical fiction masterwork."

—PATTI CALLAHAN, *NEW YORK TIMES* BESTSELLING
AUTHOR OF *SURVIVING SAVANNAH*

"In *When We Had Wings*, three bestselling and beloved authors deliver a story of strength and sisterhood inspired by the little-known experiences of the 'Angels of Bataan.' With gorgeous language and stunning historic detail, Lawhon, McMorris, and Meissner plunge readers into the Philippines and the epic struggles of the Pacific. Filled with heart and pathos, this is a story of hope, faith, and the power of friendship in the face of indescribable hardship."

—ALLISON PATAKI, *NEW YORK TIMES* BESTSELLING AUTHOR
OF *THE MAGNIFICENT LIVES OF MARJORIE POST*

"Three of the biggest powerhouses in historical fiction, Ariel Lawhon, Kristina McMorris, and Susan Meissner, come together to pen the breathtaking novel *When We Had Wings*, the story of three nurses serving in the Philippines during the Second World War. Combining the lush setting of the South Pacific with the unfathomable hardships of the combat theater, this book shines a light on a little-known aspect of history with a tale of unlikely friendship and the unshakable strength of the human spirit."

—PAM JENOFF, *NEW YORK TIMES* BESTSELLING
AUTHOR OF *CODE NAME SAPPHIRE*

WHEN

WE HAD

WINGS

OTHER NOVELS BY ARIEL LAWHON

The Wife, the Maid, and the Mistress

Flight of Dreams

I Was Anastasia

Code Name Hélène

OTHER NOVELS BY KRISTINA MCMORRIS

Letters from Home

Bridge of Scarlet Leaves

The Pieces We Keep

The Edge of Lost

Sold on a Monday

The Ways We Hide

OTHER NOVELS BY SUSAN MEISSNER

A Fall of Marigolds

Secrets of a Charmed Life

Stars over Sunset Boulevard

A Bridge Across the Ocean

As Bright as Heaven

The Last Year of the War

The Nature of Fragile Things

Only the Beautiful

WHEN

WE HAD

WINGS

ARIEL LAWHON

KRISTINA MCMORRIS

SUSAN MEISSNER

HARPER MUSE

When We Had Wings

Copyright © 2022 by Ariel Lawhon, Kristina McMorris, and Susan Meissner

Published by Harper Muse, an imprint of HarperCollins Focus LLC.

Any internet addresses (websites, blogs, etc.) in this book are offered as a resource. They are not intended in any way to be or imply an endorsement by HarperCollins Focus LLC, nor does HarperCollins Focus LLC vouch for the content of these sites for the life of this book.

ISBN: 978-0-7852-5304-4 (trade paper)
ISBN: 978-1-4002-4084-5 (ITPE)

Library of Congress Cataloging-in-Publication Data

Names: Lawhon, Ariel, author. | McMorris, Kristina, author. | Meissner, Susan, 1961- author.
Title: When we had wings / Ariel Lawhon, Kristina McMorris, and Susan Meissner.
Description: Nashville : Harper Muse, [2022] | Includes bibliographical references and index. | Summary: "Based on real history and alternating between three perspectives, When We Had Wings tells an amazingly moving story of heroic service, perseverance in the darkest of days, and the hope of the human spirit"-- Provided by publisher.
Identifiers: LCCN 2022014535 (print) | LCCN 2022014536 (ebook) | ISBN 9780785253341 (hardcover) | ISBN 9781400240845 (paperback) | ISBN 9780785253242 (epub) | ISBN 9780785253143
Subjects: LCSH: Nurses--Fiction. | World War, 1939-1945--Philippines--Fiction. | World War, 1939-1945--Hospitals--Fiction. | LCGFT: War fiction. | Historical fiction. | Novels.
Classification: LCC PS3601.L447 W47 2022 (print) | LCC PS3601.L447 (ebook) | DDC 813/.6--dc23/eng/20220521
LC record available at https://lccn.loc.gov/2022014535
LC ebook record available at https://lccn.loc.gov/2022014536

Printed in the United States of America
23 24 25 26 27 LBC 6 5 4 3 2

For Elisabeth, our friend and champion

When you go home
Tell them of us, and say
For your tomorrow,
We gave our today.
—PATRICK K. O'DONNELL, *INTO THE RISING SUN*

MANILA
August 1941

A sultry and sweetly fragrant breeze swept across Manila Bay as Eleanor Lindstrom walked carefully down the gangplank of the just-docked naval transport ship, mindful that her land legs might be slow in returning. A band was playing a cheerful Benny Goodman tune as she and other disembarking servicemen and women stepped onto solid ground. Filipino nationals on the other side of a rope held up by stanchions were waving hello and hawking maps of the islands or taxi rides or paper bags of sweets or bouquets of aromatic frangipani blossoms. The late-afternoon air was thick with their excitement but also with humidity that rivaled anything Eleanor had felt back home on a Minnesota midsummer's day.

The mood all around her was festive, despite the stifling heat, and she wanted to linger, to take it all in, and let the buoyant atmosphere energize her. Fortify her. Calm her. Crossing the Pacific, especially for a twenty-three-year-old Midwesterner who had never even seen the ocean before, had been challenging, yes, but it wasn't just the fatigue of travel that made her want to stop and fully embrace the novelty of her new surroundings. It was far more than that.

It was deciding on a whim to apply to the Navy and getting accepted so quickly. Leaving for training barely three weeks after signing on the dotted line. Saying goodbye to civilian life. Leaving her friends and fellow nurses at Abbott Northwestern Hospital in Minneapolis. Hugging her parents and sister farewell and knowing a three-year overseas assignment meant it would likely be several years before she saw them or the family dairy barns again.

And all this change because she'd fallen in love with a man who loved another.

1

Eleanor set down her suitcase, closed her eyes, and breathed in deep the smells and sounds and feel of her new world, a world so far from all she knew, all she loved, and the part she needed to stop loving.

It hadn't been a mistake to join the Navy Nurse Corps, she knew that. Eleanor had nursing skills they obviously needed, and she needed an abrupt change in her day-to-day life. Both she and the Corps had gotten what they desired.

She loved being a nurse, had wanted to be one since her earliest childhood memories of pretending her dolls were sick or hurt and needed her kind attention. She loved her country, too, and was proud to now be serving in the Corps. And she'd always hoped to one day travel to a foreign land and experience a vastly different culture. But she knew these were not the real reasons she was standing at that moment on an ocean pier, thousands of miles from home.

Eleanor felt a hand on her arm and opened her eyes. A fellow naval officer was standing in front of her. The single gold bar on his lapel indicated he was an ensign; the lowest ranking of officers, so fairly new to military life, like she was. He carried a clipboard in his hand.

"Hey, are you feeling alright? Do you need to sit for a moment?" Concern etched his face.

Standing with her eyes closed after just getting off the ship had surely suggested she was about to faint. "I'm fine." She laughed nervously and he withdrew his hand. "I was just . . . enjoying the fresh air."

"Oh. Okay." He peered at the name tag on her uniform. "Nurse Lindstrom. Good. I found you. I'm Ensign Mathis from Command, and I'm here to make sure you and the other new Navy arrivals get to where you're supposed to be today. You are the only new Navy medical staff on this transport, yes?"

"Yes. Just me. I was told someone would meet me dockside. Thanks for being here."

"Certainly. Headquarters has arranged a driver for you." Ensign Mathis pointed to a shiny black sedan parked just on the other side of a chain-link fence.

"What about my trunk?" Eleanor held tight to her hat as a breeze kicked up.

"It will be brought up from the hold and taken to the Yard." He referred to the Cavite Naval Yard the way all the sailors and naval officers had during her days aboard the ship. "You'll find it waiting for you when you arrive at your quarters later tonight. Right now, you're expected at the ANC for this week's welcome briefing."

He picked up her suitcase and walked toward an opening in the fence.

"The ANC?" Eleanor rushed to keep up, feeling like her legs were made of rubber.

Ensign Mathis looked back. "Sorry." He slowed his pace. "The ANC is the Army Navy Club."

"A club?"

"For officers of the U.S. Armed Forces, active and retired, and for service nurses too. And a few carefully screened American businessmen living here. It's a pretty popular place. Big. Ballrooms, bars, a tearoom, a couple restaurants, hotel rooms. Very nice. And not far."

The ensign handed her suitcase to the Filipino driver who'd stepped out of the car as they drew near. "Alright, then, you're all set. From the ANC you'll be driven to the Yard to get settled in whenever you're ready to leave the club. After the briefing a lot of people stay for drinks and dinner. The food is really good. It's pretty much a party atmosphere there."

She glanced down at her uniform. "I'm not exactly decked out for a party."

"It won't matter. A lot of people go there in uniform, so you'll be fine. Trust me."

The driver closed the trunk and then came around to open her door.

"Thanks for your help, Ensign Mathis." Eleanor turned to get into the car.

"Enjoy your tour at the Yard," he replied with an easy smile. "You being a nurse, I sort of hope I don't see you again. If you know what I mean."

She grinned in return as she got inside. "How about only at the . . . uh, ANC now and then?"

"You've got a deal."

He shut the door, waved, and then turned back for the ship, no doubt to assist other naval newcomers.

In a snap the driver was behind the wheel, then pulled the car out onto a street full of vehicles, people walking and riding bicycles, sailors milling about. Vendors in stalls were selling prepared food with names on the signage she had no idea how to pronounce. Palm trees and flowering vines abounded, and birdsong drifted in through the car's open windows, the likes of which she'd never heard before.

For a moment Eleanor wanted to hightail it back to the ship. She was out of place here, a stranger to this city, an alien to its way of life.

And yet the magical view on the other side of the window was welcoming. It was as if Manila was opening its arms to her, as if the island on which it lay yearned to soothe the ache of having lost what had never been hers, that it was already promising it would. She hadn't known a place other than home could do that. The desire to bolt evaporated as quickly as it had stolen across her.

"First time in the Philippines?" The driver cast a warm glance back at her.

"First time anywhere." Eleanor nodded.

———◆———

Punctuality had never been Lita Capel's strong suit, and sadly today was no exception. As she wove her way down the bustling sidewalk headed for the ANC, a typical chiding from her oldest sister—make that all three of her sisters—echoed through her mind: *"Daydreaming again? What a dilly-dallier you are. I swear,* bunso, *only you could make turtles seem quick."*

An endearment in Tagalog for the baby of the family, *bunso* inadvertently carried the needling reminder of where Lita, even at twenty-two, stood in the pecking order of four children. In fact, the nickname appeared at the start of every letter her sisters sent from New York, where together the siblings were building exciting new lives while working as nurses at some fancy hospital in a city called Brooklyn. Always included in their updates were assurances that their petition to the American government, requesting permission for Lita to immigrate and join them, would meet approval any day.

Of course, they'd been saying this ever since she graduated from nursing school more than a year ago. Rising tensions between America and Asia seemed to have slowed the process. Still, she prayed her sisters were right, now more than ever given the recent onslaught of headlines—like those being shouted at this very moment, in both English and Tagalog, by paperboys as Lita passed by.

"Emperor Hirohito condemns U.S. embargo!"

"Japan refuses to surrender airfields in Indochina!"

"President Quezon implores keeping peace!"

The Filipino leader, unlike Lita, was surely old enough to remember when the U.S. acquired the Philippines from Spain, setting off a bloody, three-year-long conflict with Filipino rebels.

Needing to cross the street, Lita waited anxiously for a break in the near-constant flow of motorcars. Honks punctuated the rumbling of engines and exhaust fumes choking the air. Holding her nurse cap atop her head, she dashed through an opening and away from the newsboys' warnings that intensified her brewing dread.

Over the past two weeks, as punishment for the Japanese invasion of Indochina—a reality reinforced even now by the throngs of Chinese refugees mixed within the crowd—America had not only frozen Japan's assets but also established an embargo on its oil and gasoline exports. Should the countries go to battle, a violent tug-of-war would surely ensue for control of the Philippine Islands, thanks to their strategic locations for bases, communications, and supplies.

The Great War was meant to end all wars, she'd heard since childhood. And yet with Hitler's forces wrangling for domination over all of Europe and now invading the Soviets' lands, was another world war looming? If so, would Lita be trapped here, caught in the cross fire?

"Oh, stop already," she muttered. As life had mercilessly taught her, there was no point in dwelling on things beyond her control. A social evening would serve as a fine distraction.

Plowing onward, she cut through a waft of spices from a vendor hawking empanadas and adobo. As she rounded the corner, between hats and heads she spotted the familiar three-story building, stately and elegant with its thick columns and a circular drive teeming with vehicles. Potted palms and climbing bougainvillea adorned the front, along with a sign identifying it as the Army Navy Club. Servicemembers and civilians—of which she was one, though cross-trained with U.S. Army nurses—filtered in and out of the entrance.

Finally there herself, she trailed impatiently behind a trio of American sailors. The fairest of them turned and grandly kept the door open for her. With a polite smile she stepped past him to enter. Whether from his carelessness or her own, his arm brushed the chest of her uniform, and she bristled.

"Sorry about that." He looked genuinely abashed, and Lita realized she'd flashed him a glare. Not intentional. A reflex, and for good reason.

Being a *mestiza*, the product of a Filipina mother and an American-missionary father—or "half-breed" according to the crueler girls in school—she'd learned long ago that many American boys viewed girls like her as easy. Either way, considering her future plans, there was no reason to invest in any courtship when she wouldn't be sticking around.

Thus she merely nodded at the sailor before continuing into the large foyer. Waved through by a familiar receptionist, Lita reapplied her usual cheerful veneer. It wasn't difficult in light of her surroundings.

Although beautifully appointed with fresh flowers in vases, ample sitting areas, and plush carpeting, the space's most marvelous feature was its air cooler. Despite being a good fifteen minutes late to meet her friend, she couldn't help but pause in the midst of passing an icy breeze from an overhead vent. A pleasant shiver ran the length of her back, making her aware of the sweat dampening her blouse.

A native of a fishing village on the island of Leyte, where air-conditioning was unfathomable, she couldn't imagine ever taking the luxury for granted.

"Are you lost, dear?" a woman asked, a floral dress draping her matronly form.

Lita felt a bit foolish for lingering. "Oh. I'm just heading toward Salon B."

"Well, in that case, you'll want to take this hallway to the end, make a left, and you'll run smack-dab into it."

Lita was tempted to explain that she wasn't new to the place, that since first befriending Penny, a sweet yet feisty U.S. Army nurse, a month ago at the hospital, they'd made an occasional habit of meeting here for chit-chat they didn't have time for when their paths crossed during their daily rounds. Rather, she replied simply, "Thank you."

"No, no, my dear, thank *you*."

Bewildered, Lita tilted her head.

"If it weren't for nurses like you, my husband wouldn't be up and walking about. You girls are doing the Lord's work."

At that Lita issued a grateful smile. But as they parted ways, she felt the recurrent burden that never failed to accompany such compliments. For when it came to the devotion and selflessness of her job, in all truth, she remained an imposter.

———————•———————

Penny Franklin needed a drink. She angled toward her favorite table in Salon B. It was nestled in the back corner beside an open window, a convenient distance from the watchful eye of her supervisor, Maude Davison, who was sitting near the front. Since claiming it for herself weeks earlier, Penny thought of her spot as the "bad behavior table," a place to whisper and gossip with Lita when attending a required meeting in Salon B.

She smiled at the young soldier who stepped forward to pull out her chair.

"Thank you." She tried not to laugh as a blush crept across his face.

He cleared his throat. "Ma'am." When he bobbed his head in greeting, she noticed the thin silver scar that ran through his left eyebrow, splicing it neatly in two.

The boy was sixteen if he was a day. Just another kid who lied about his age and ran off to join the Army looking for adventure. Not so different from her, perhaps. Except for the age. Penny had at least a decade on him. At this point in her life, however, sixteen felt as long ago and far away as Texas.

Three more upholstered chairs were situated around her table, and like all the others in the room, it was topped with a pressed linen tablecloth. Glinting chandeliers hung from the high ceiling. Several naval officers in day dress were arranging papers at the front of the room at a tall, carved podium. Four dozen people were already in the room in little groups, most in uniform, some sitting, some standing around and laughing as they waited for the briefing to begin.

Once settled in her seat, Penny leaned toward the vase and inhaled the scent of jasmine. A month in Manila and that rich, exotic scent still hadn't grown old. Nor had the feel of cool air against her warm skin. Her mother's patio in Houston was covered in geranium-filled terra-cotta pots, and even though she loved their wet-earth smell, they didn't compare to Philippine jasmine. So yes, perhaps the other side of the world wasn't such a bad place to lick her wounds after all.

"Franklin," came a deep, familiar voice. "Sleeping on the job again?"

Penny opened her eyes and turned to find Captain Charley Russell, quartermaster, source of unrelenting aggravation, standing in front of her. As ever, his face was unreadable and his presence unwelcome. Penny swept an imperious glance over the highball glass in his hand.

"Better than drinking on the job."

It wasn't so much a smile that danced at the corner of his mouth—he had never once smiled at her in all the weeks she'd worked with him—but acknowledgment of a barb well traded. Tit for tat. He was in civilian clothes after all, clearly off duty, so the remark could hardly be considered impertinent.

"Why bother just fighting a war when you can fight a hangover at the same time?" he said, voice so dry and humorless she couldn't tell if he was joking.

Penny scowled. "That sounds like a lot to handle at once."

He wiggled his fingers. "Ambidextrous."

Penny lifted a glass of water in a half-hearted salute and noticed that his eyes, as they had many times before, fell to her ring finger and the ghost tan line that resided there. She'd taken her wedding ring off before leaving Texas, but the truth was there for all the world to see: Lieutenant

Penny Franklin had once been married but no longer was. And oh the assumptions that always came with *that* realization. She waited for Russell to finally broach the subject. Instead he held her gaze for one long, curious second until she broke the connection and looked toward the door.

Salvation walked through in the form of Angelita Capel.

"Lita!" She waved her friend over, ignoring Captain Russell as he slipped away to join a group of fellow officers at their table near the front.

Penny had arrived in Manila thirty-seven days earlier, and Charley Russell had been a thorn in her side for thirty-six. On her first full day, Maude Davison gave her the task of submitting the hospital inventory requests to the base quartermaster. Once a week she delivered the paperwork and once a week he rejected it. It didn't matter how carefully she went over the forms; he always found an error, a typo, a misspelling and required her to resubmit them before he would sign off on the orders. Not even in nursing school had her superiors been such sticklers for immaculate handwriting and perfect spelling.

Penny was certain of very little in her life other than Charley Russell infuriating her for two hours every Friday afternoon. Was it any wonder then that she enjoyed a cocktail at the ANC every Friday evening? Sometimes, when she was lucky, Lita was able to join her.

"I'm so sorry I'm late." Lita dropped into a chair at the table, where Penny greeted her with a hug.

"Nonsense. You're precisely on 'Lita time.'"

After a wince from embarrassment, Lita joined Penny in a laugh, then asked, "Who's the fellow, by the way?" She motioned toward the back of Russell's head.

"My nemesis," Penny said.

Lita's brow arched. "*That's* the quartermaster?"

"In the flesh."

"Gee, from what you shared about his being such a grouch, I guess I thought he'd be older."

"Satan has no age." Penny broke into a wide grin when her friend laughed.

Lita glanced around the rapidly filling room. "Why are we meeting here instead of the bar?"

"Welcome briefing. There's a new Navy nurse coming in today. I volunteered to greet her. And you, my dear, are along for the ride." Penny stuck her tongue out. "Happy hour will have to wait a bit."

Lita shrugged. Then she scrunched her nose, tentative. "Dare I ask . . . any word from home yet?"

"No," Penny said. And she didn't expect it either.

Lita looked at her, those clear brown eyes filled with confusion. Though she swiftly attempted levity. "Well, it does take a while for mail to cross the Pacific. And you've only been here five weeks. Did you write to them again?"

"Once a week, every week. I even tried phoning. Since they're always home on Sunday afternoons, I got up at four o'clock in the morning because of the time difference. But when the operator said she had a call from the Philippines, my mother hung up."

Lita blinked, unable to hide her startled expression. "It . . . must have been an accident. A poor connection, maybe."

The melancholy tone of their conversation was a direct contrast to the laughter-filled buzz that radiated through the lounge. Penny was grateful that Lita didn't mind her somber mood. As a matter of fact, there seemed to be little that bothered Lita. She often appeared perfectly serene, her face the picture of untroubled waters. No frown. No pursed lips. Only acceptance and a seemingly bottomless well of patience.

"I'm sure they're not ignoring you," Lita insisted.

"Oh, that I know for certain." Penny rubbed a bead of water off the rim of her glass. She balanced it on the pad of her thumb before she flicked it onto the crisp, white tablecloth. "They're *punishing* me."

After a moment Lita's gaze fell—the way Captain Russell's had—to the ghost line on her finger. Penny had noticed Lita staring at it several times before, but her friend had never asked for an explanation and Penny had never offered. But Lita's curiosity must have finally gotten the better of her.

"Is it because you got divorced?"

And that made Penny smile because she'd known that's what everyone assumed. "I'm not divorced."

Lita's eyes darted up, widening in surprise.

"I'm widowed."

Lita's mouth fell open and she covered it with her fingertips. "They can't be angry at you for that!"

"No. Not for that. My parents won't forgive me for joining the Army and leaving them. They feel abandoned. Betrayed." Penny looked away from Lita and the sympathy pooling in her eyes. She glanced around the room. "But I couldn't stay there any longer. I . . ."

She let her words drift away when she saw the woman standing in the doorway. She was in a Navy uniform and young, like many of the other nurses in the Philippines. She had blonde hair like Penny always wished for and watchful blue eyes. The way she moved, the way she scanned the room, radiated a kind of wariness that immediately caught Penny's attention.

"What?" Lita asked.

"There's our nurse." She tipped her chin toward the door. "Poor thing looks lost."

———◆———

After handing off her purse and suitcase at the club's reception table, Eleanor stood in the salon for several seconds. Should she just snag any chair?

A uniformed Army nurse arose at a nearby table and waved to her. Seated beside the gal was a pretty Filipina, also in uniform but that of a civilian nurse.

Eleanor made her way over, grateful she'd been noticed.

The standing nurse smiled at her. "Hi there. I'm guessing you're Eleanor Lindstrom?"

"I am."

"Penny Franklin. I'm here to officially welcome you to the nursing community on Manila."

Eleanor saw that she and Penny were about the same height, but Penny's light brown hair was cut in a far more stylish bob. She also had a confident air about her that Eleanor immediately found inviting.

Penny nodded toward her tablemate, the Filipina nurse, who had also risen to her feet. "And this is my friend Angelita Capel. I offered to look out for you since all of your Navy compatriots are across the bay and we're right here."

"Everyone calls me Lita." The Filipina smiled wide and reached out to shake Eleanor's hand. She was small boned, with ebony-black hair in a low bun and graceful Asian features.

"Thanks so much for calling me over." Eleanor pulled out a chair and sat down.

"Lita's from here, as you might have guessed," Penny said. "But I asked her to come because we're getting cocktails after this. We're both at Sternberg. You'll be at Cavite of course?"

"Yes. At Cañacao Hospital."

"So where's home for you?"

"Minnesota. You?"

"Texas."

They engaged in a bit more small talk, and then the briefing began. Eleanor and the other new arrivals were informed of where everything was located, what local customs and traditions they needed to be aware of, and what sections of Manila to avoid. They were told how to engage with the territorial residents, what to say, what not to say. And then they were dismissed.

"Let's get that drink!" Penny said happily. "You will join us, won't you, Eleanor?"

"Sure. I'd love to."

Eleanor followed Penny and Lita as they made their way to an elegantly appointed bar on the main floor. It was a few minutes before five o'clock, and the room was beginning to fill with Friday after-work patrons.

Penny selected a table for three along a wall with an ample view of the rest of the room, and they ordered frothy daiquiris at Lita's suggestion. Eleanor had never tasted anything so delicious. Or strong.

For several minutes she listened as Penny told her about her arrival in

Manila and how she'd met Lita on her first day on the island. As they got to know each other better, Eleanor sensed a surprising affinity growing already for her two new friends.

A party of naval officers in dress whites entered the room along with several smartly attired young women on their arms. One of the couples, clearly in love, was being congratulated by others already at the bar. Hank and Marlene, as everyone was calling them, had just gotten married. Bottles of champagne appeared at the table the bridal party had chosen, and more congratulations were being extended by those seated nearby.

Eleanor could barely take her eyes off the couple. They looked so incredibly happy. She must have said this out loud because Penny laughed.

"Well, I should hope so! They're newlyweds."

Lita laughed lightly too.

Heat rose to Eleanor's cheeks. The strong drink must have loosened her tongue.

"So, tell us," Lita said. "Any special fellow back home you're missing already?"

Eleanor had no idea how to answer. When she didn't reply right away, Penny cocked her head in curiosity. "Come on. We're all friends now. Who is he?"

Eleanor didn't know if it was because of the excitement of being in a new place or making new friends or starting out on a great adventure, or maybe just the effect of the cocktail, but when she opened her mouth, what she hadn't shared with anyone spilled out. "There *is* someone back home, but he's not actually mine to miss. Or love. He's engaged."

Lita exchanged a look of surprise with Penny that quickly gained an overtone of sympathy, and asked, "Does he know how you feel about him?"

Eleanor laughed. "Oh, he knows. I made the mistake of telling him when I thought he might have feelings for me too. What I took for the beginnings of romantic interest was just him being nice. Reverend John Olson is an extremely nice person." She shook her head as tears sprang to her eyes. "What a fool I was."

Silence hung over the table for a moment. Then Penny laid a gentle hand on Eleanor's arm. "Clearly *he's* the fool if you ask me."

"I second that," Lita said. "A real dope." Both women smiled, and though Eleanor's heart remained in tatters, she felt the mending of a single stitch as she smiled in return.

---◆---

Through another round of drinks, Lita learned a great deal about her new friends. Eleanor shared more details about her heartbreak and John Olson, as well as about life on her family's dairy farm. Penny spoke about her parents and even a bit about the tragic loss of her husband. Lita, of course, described following in her sisters' footsteps, both in nursing and in her hopes of moving to the States. And while she rarely shared private matters, she did touch upon the passing of her parents—her father when she was a child, her mother five years ago—though, granted, not the guilt she harbored regarding the latter.

The compassion Lita received from Penny and Eleanor felt as warm and genuine as the words of comfort they continued to trade throughout their uniquely open conversation. She couldn't explain exactly why their connection felt so effortless. But in a few short hours, it seemed they had known each other for years. Lita dreaded the night ending, having found a sense of sisterhood she hadn't realized until now how much she missed.

On the other side of the room, voices burst out in celebration. A layered cake was being delivered to Hank and Marlene's table. More champagne flowed, and with it a thrilling idea.

"You know what I think?" Lita said. "The next time Eleanor is on our side of the bay, we have our own celebration—right back here for another daiquiri toast. Cake, too, for that matter," she added in jest.

"I'd love that." Eleanor smiled.

But Penny shook her head. "The way life can get away from us? I'd say we make it a standing date. How about . . . the last Saturday of every month? Assuming our duty days allow. We'll call it HAM Day!"

Lita joined Eleanor in looking at her with a puzzled expression.

"Hank and Marlene Day," she explained, as if it couldn't have been more obvious. All their smiles broadened as Penny raised her nearly empty glass. "Everyone in?"

Eleanor held up her glass. "Absolutely."

They turned expectantly to Lita, and a notion dawned on her.

She had been feeling pensive of late, a restlessness in her soul that everything about life as she knew it was about to change. But here, in this moment, she also sensed a solidifying bond in these newfound friendships.

Warming at the thought, she lifted her drink. "To HAM Day," she said, and their glasses clinked.

The sealing of a pact.

1941

Cry "Havoc" and let slip the dogs of war!
—William Shakespeare, *Julius Caesar*

ONE

ELEANOR

Cavite Navy Yard
December 1941

E leanor awoke to the sounds of rapid footsteps in the hallway outside her quarters and then heavy pounding on her door. Her room was still bathed in darkness; the day had not yet begun.

"Out of your beds!" The urgent voice belonged to Laura Cobb, the chief nurse, a longtime Navy veteran and Eleanor's direct supervisor. "Get dressed. Don't turn on any lights!"

Eleanor sat up. Something had happened. Or was happening. And it wasn't good.

The unease that came over her as she swung her legs over the side of her bed was immediate and foreign. In the four months that the naval base had been her home, she'd only experienced a sense of surprising calm. Everything she'd heard about Manila being a paradise assignment had proven true. The weekend parties in the city, the lazy afternoons on the beach, the long bicycle rides, and the HAM Days with Penny and Lita had all combined to make her off-duty hours seem as though she were on a perpetual vacation.

The same pounding fell upon the door directly opposite hers—Peg's—and with it the same pressing command. "Out of your beds. Get dressed. Don't turn on the lights."

Eleanor fumbled for her wristwatch and squinted to read it in the splash of moonlight falling across her nightstand. Four in the morning. She grabbed her uniform from yesterday with trembling hands and opened her door. Peg Nash, a fellow Navy nurse and her closest friend at the Yard, was standing outside her quarters with her uniform in her hand, too, and her curly brown hair in a tangle from sleep. Laura Cobb was moving down the hall from them, knocking on all the doors and repeating identical instructions.

"What's happened?" Peg called out to their commander.

"Japan attacked Pearl Harbor," Laura said urgently, turning to them. "It's been destroyed. Get dressed as fast as you can. The fleet surgeon has ordered us to evacuate the hospital."

Laura pivoted quickly to resume her task as a few more doors were opened, and several other nurses in their pajamas looked about in alarm in the dimly lit hallway.

Eleanor couldn't make sense of the news. She'd stopped at Pearl on her way to Manila. It was as beautiful a paradise as the Philippines. Laura's words echoed in her head as she turned to Peg. *"It's been destroyed. It's been destroyed."*

"Why are we evacuating the hospital?" Eleanor asked, somewhat dazed.

Peg began to unbutton her pajama top. "If Japan has attacked Pearl Harbor, the U.S. will declare war. You can count on it. We're going to be at war."

Again words spoken to her in clear English had defied her comprehension. *"We're going to be at war."*

"But . . . the hospital? Why are we evacuating the hospital? Hawaii is thousands of miles away."

"It's a U.S. military hospital. On a U.S. military base. No base anywhere will be safe from an attack, but especially not ours. Nothing separates us from Hawaii but water. And the Philippines are a strategic Pacific location. We wouldn't be here if they weren't. You'd better get dressed. And don't forget to modify your flashlight." Peg disappeared into the darkness of her quarters, peeling off her pajama top as she did so.

Eleanor slipped back into her own dark room, pulled off her nightgown, and donned her uniform. Her heart thumping in her chest, she wrapped a bit of blue cellophane over her flashlight to make it safe for blackout.

She stepped out into the darkness seconds later, just behind Peg and a few of the other nurses, for the short walk to the hospital. Rain had fallen while they'd been sleeping and the air was thick with a heavy, moist veil. Across the bay the pinprick lights of Manila glittered from eight miles away.

There were only eleven other Navy nurses under Laura's command at Cavite, but as they made their way quickly to the hospital, dozens of corpsmen joined them. The enlisted medics had also been awakened and were hurrying out of their barracks. Eleanor overheard two of them discussing the order to evacuate.

"How can the Japanese attack a hospital? That's against the rules of warfare in the Geneva Convention."

"Japan didn't ratify the latest agreement. They never formally agreed hospitals were off-limits."

As soon as they reached the three-story building, Laura dispersed her nurses to different positions to administrate the evacuation, while sailors got to work stacking sandbags around the building. Eleanor was assigned to help assess which patients could be safely discharged and allowed to return to duty and which would have to be transferred to a safer location. Every sailor-patient who stood in line to be evaluated, chart in hand, begged to be allowed to return to his assignment.

"It's just a little bump on the head!" one sailor pleaded. "It's nothing. Let me go. Let me defend our ships."

"You suffered a concussion yesterday," the doctor replied. "You really should be on bed rest one more day."

"I'm fine. Let me go, please. Let me help."

"I'm not convinced that's a good idea."

"But, sir. My brother's stationed at Pearl Harbor. I don't even know if he survived. The planes that bombed Pearl are surely coming here. Please release me."

The doctor sighed and then signed off on the young man's discharge order. The sailor spun away from them and headed for the exit.

Eleanor watched him go. Would she ever see that man again?

Several hours later, with the evaluations complete, a Filipino porter brought the nurses coffee and warm *pan de sal*—slightly sweet and fluffy bread rolls, and a Filipino breakfast staple—and they had their first moment to rest since being startled from sleep before dawn. It was also the first moment to hear the extent of what had happened in Hawaii. The sneak attack on the U.S. Pacific Fleet anchored at Pearl had been catastrophic. Eight battleships had been destroyed, including the USS *Arizona*, which had sunk so quickly after being torpedoed that hundreds of sailors were still trapped inside. The casualties and injuries from the attack were still being counted.

Eleanor had reached for a second pan de sal as Laura began to brief them of these details, but tears burned at her eyes and she could not eat it. As she set the roll down, she saw that all the other nurses were crying too. Hawaii was a territory just like the Philippines and full of Americans. An attack on a U.S. military installation was an attack on America. But there was little time to grieve the impact of the countless lives that had surely been lost.

An air-raid siren wailed a mournful, soulless sound. The nurses ran as one outside.

With shaking limbs Eleanor crawled under the hospital—which had been constructed with space between the ground and the building in case of flooding. While they waited in the muck for bombs to fall, an unexpected and bizarre calmness began to envelop Eleanor, even as the mud seeped into the bleached-white fabric of her uniform. She could see in her mind's eye her parents in the dairy barn in the tawny light of daybreak, the barn cats following them from stall to stall as roosters outside crowed to welcome the day. Her little sister Lizzie was riding her red bicycle down the dirt path to town, pigtails flying behind her, to get the latest copy of *Hollywood* magazine. And there was the beloved farmhouse in springtime, its porch framed by blooming forsythia and lilac and climbing clematis. She could see long summer nights dotted with firefly light, the endless golden sky in autumn, the diamond-bright first snow, and all the people she loved back home.

Before she could sweep it away in her mind, she saw John Olson in a blue flannel shirt, painting the rectory lemon yellow and humming a happy tune. That was the day she'd fallen in love with him. For the first time in months, she smiled when she thought of him. She closed her eyes and waited for whatever would come next.

The minutes ticked by and there was no drone of enemy planes, no bombs, nothing at all. Within an hour the all clear sounded, and Eleanor and the other nurses climbed out, covered in mud. The calming images faded. How many times might she have to call upon them in the days ahead?

Back inside the empty hospital, Laura dispatched two of the nurses to assist at Sternberg. As they left, Eleanor asked them to say hello to Lita and Penny if they happened to encounter them. And to tell them to stay strong and well and she'd see them on HAM Day.

"They will know what I mean," Eleanor said to her puzzled colleagues.

Laura brought out dark blue dungarees and work shirts—the male sailor's typical uniform. "Obviously our white dresses aren't practical right now. We're going to be wearing these."

One of the nurses held up a pair of dungarees. They were huge. "You could fit two of me in these!"

"They're one-size-fits-all, ladies. Make them fit. No complaints."

In the nurses' dayroom Eleanor took off her soiled dress, put on the new "uniform," and cinched the dungarees around her waist as best she could with her uniform belt. The nurses looked at each other and their oddly fitting new clothes and laughed for the first time that day. It felt good and wrong at the same time, and as they walked back into the hospital halls, the light moment slipped away as if falling upon the pile of now-useless white uniforms.

Eleanor spent the rest of the day readying the emptied patient rooms and medical stores should Cavite come under attack, her thoughts wandering every few minutes. There were nurses at Pearl. She could have been one of them. How many had survived? How many of them were hurt? How many of them had to rush to tend to the terrible wounds of bombing victims? Where in the world had they found the strength to do it?

That night she fell into her bed exhausted. The long day had been physically draining to be sure, but mentally as well. As tired as she was, though, anxiety energized her. Eleanor realized she was afraid; not of dying—she'd found a calming solace under the hospital—but that she wouldn't be able to keep her solemn word. She'd taken an oath, pledging not only to defend the United States but to bear true faith and allegiance to her country and obey every order given her. She didn't want to break that promise. With all her heart she did not want to.

But she had not considered that a Navy nurse would see war, not even when she had gotten the assignment to Cavite. She was not a warrior. She'd only wanted to escape the pain of a broken heart and chart a new purpose for her life. She hadn't really considered what she might be asked to do, only what she was asking her new life in the Navy Nurse Corp to do for her.

Eleanor prayed a simple prayer as she closed her eyes against the darkness of the blackout conditions and her own fear. "Give me strength to do what I said I would do," she whispered. "Please give me strength. And watch over Penny and Lita. Please keep them safe."

Eleanor awoke at first light to the news that the United States had declared war on the Empire of Japan.

On Wednesday the air-raid siren sounded as Eleanor was eating lunch. Several sirens had wailed since Monday's devastating news of the attack on Pearl. She rose from her chair and took her toasted salami-and-cheese sandwich with her, as did the other nurses and commissioned staff eating in the quarters' wardroom. It could be an hour or more before the all clear sounded.

The mood was slightly less than urgent as they all made their way outside, past the sandbags and then under the barracks. Even though the U.S. was now at war, Eleanor had slept better the previous night than she did on Monday when everything about their situation was new. Still, she wished she'd brought her coffee, too, as she watched one of the nurses maneuvering into the crawl space with her cup, coffee sloshing onto the dirt.

As she settled in along with corpsmen, cooks, and a few other hospital personnel, Eleanor became aware of a sound she'd not heard during the other air-raid alerts. A low and steady hum. An arrow of panic shot through her.

Planes were overhead. Lots of them.

One of the cooks still standing outside the crawl space dropped to his knees and scooted under the building, yelling, "They're coming!"

Eleanor instinctively drew her knees up to her chest, dropped her head, and covered it with her arms, the sandwich abandoned. She could hear antiaircraft guns firing from afar and the pounding of her own heart.

No bombs fell.

"What's happening?" Peg asked the cook, who was now peering out from underneath the building.

He paused before answering. "They're . . . circling back. They're coming back!" He slid underneath again and everyone waited. This time Eleanor kept her head up.

But not for long.

Bombs rained down, detonating on impact with thunderous roars. Each one seemed to fall closer to their sheltering place than the one before it. If the building took a direct hit, they would die in a flattening instant. Explosion after explosion rocked the earth, followed by a stretch of moments when the pounding ceased, only to return after the enemy planes had come back across the bay for another pass at Cavite.

The ground under Eleanor heaved as the next rounds met their targets. *Boom! Boom! Boom!* She hoped the end would be quick. She hoped there would be only one intense moment of dizzying pain, as short as a blink of an eye, and then the sweet halls of heaven. She'd see Grandma Lindstrom again. How she'd missed her.

Near Eleanor someone was whispering, "Pray for us sinners, now and at the hour of our death." A hand closed over her own. Peg's perhaps. None of them would die alone. That was a tremendous comfort. She suddenly remembered it was Eldene Paige's twenty-eighth birthday. Eleanor looked over at her.

"Happy birthday, Eldene," she said softly, strangely wanting to make sure her coworker heard these words before the end came for them.

"Thanks," Eldene replied in a hushed tone that suggested she had needed to hear it.

For an hour they waited for the bomb to fall that would kill them all. But it did not come. And then the booming ceased. The earth stopped quaking. The drone of aircraft faded.

The all clear sounded and Eleanor and her nurse comrades crawled out from underneath their shelter to see what was left of Cavite.

Acrid smoke billowed in every direction from great bulbous pillars of fire. Cavite Naval Yard had been all but obliterated. Across the bay Manila looked much the same. Torched and on fire. It made no sense to Eleanor. Manila was mostly a city of civilians.

There was no time to contemplate the destruction. Laura Cobb yelled for them to run to the hospital, which had not been hit. There would be wounded coming to them, there had to be. They needed to prepare for those arrivals. Eleanor dashed past the hulks of buildings ablaze and flattened structures, her lungs filling with a chemical smoke that made her chest burn and her eyes water as she ran to the hospital. It had not been a target. She could only hope Sternberg hadn't been either and that Penny and Lita were safe.

When she and the rest of the nurses and corpsmen arrived, the injured were already there with more soon coming. Eleanor staggered to a stop before Peg grabbed her arm and pulled her forward. She had never seen such injuries, not even in the training manuals—shattered arms and legs bent in impossible positions or missing altogether, lacerations down to the bone, blackened flesh from horrible burns. The sounds of human anguish punctuated the air.

Laura barked out instructions, sending some of them to see to the bleeders, some to the burn victims, and some to administer morphine to ease the suffering of those whose injuries were not life-threatening. Eleanor was given vials of the painkiller, all the while worried that she would run out of the drug before she'd seen to every injured person in the triage area. The nearby medical dispensary had been bombed, and nothing was left of it.

One battered sailor, whose legs were twisted at unnatural angles, grabbed Eleanor's arm as she slipped the needle into his skin.

"Is my mother alright?" His eyes were glassy, his voice weak.

"I'm sure she's fine," Eleanor soothed, as she taped a tiny piece of gauze over the injection site.

"But she's in her bedroom! How will she get downstairs? What if the stairs have been bombed?"

The poor young man thought he was back home, wherever that was, and Eleanor couldn't linger to help him understand. Too many others needed her attention.

"She is fine, I promise. Rest now."

Eleanor went on to the next wounded man who begged to know if his bunkmate had come through. They'd been together. Where was he?

Another begged for her to put him out of his misery.

Another, missing an arm, was attempting to rise from his stretcher as she reached him. Blood oozed from his tourniquet as he struggled to stand.

"You need to lie still." Eleanor eased him back down with effort.

"Let me go to my ship!" he shouted. "I outrank you. Let me go! That's an order!"

"You are wounded, sir. You are bleeding. You mustn't move about." She gave him the injection of morphine even as he threatened to inform her supervisor of her insubordination.

The next wounded sailor she sped to care for had already expired when she reached him, his wounds worse than what had been visible.

The hellish hours wore on, without electricity to sterilize the instruments or the elevator to send the most injured to surgery on the third floor. Civilians—the young, the old, men, women, children, and babies—flooded the hospital, too, and had to lay on the floor on blankets, if one could be found, because there were no available beds.

With no way to chart the care they were giving, one of the nurses had a corpsman bring her a box of morgue tags that she and Eleanor and Peg filled out with the names of the injured and what medication had been administered. They placed the grim cards meant for the dead on the wrists of the injured living.

As the day drew near its end, Eleanor and the others were tasked by Laura with recording the details of every person they had seen to, every injury they had dressed, every patient sent up to surgery, every injection they'd given, and every person who had died in their care. Family members back home needed to know what had become of their brave sailors. Wives needed to be made aware they were now widows. Mothers and fathers needed to know their sons had given their lives for their country.

"Don't think about it, just do it," Eleanor told herself repeatedly as she bent over the paperwork. She couldn't let herself consider that some of what she was writing would make its way to commanding officers who would then set about writing death notifications.

While they worked, news came down from the captain. Communication from the Japanese forces had arrived. The hospital had thirty-six hours to evacuate its wounded. If it didn't comply, it would be bombed. This news was nearly impossible to comprehend. Where were they supposed to go?

Eleanor fell to her bed that night achingly tired but unable to sleep soundly. She had seen too much suffering, too many horrific injuries, too much sadness.

———◆———

After a fitful night, morning arrived oppressively humid. At breakfast Eleanor and the other nurses were told to pack and be ready to leave for good in an hour. They were bound for Santa Scholastica, a Catholic girls' college across the bay that had been transformed into a makeshift hospital. Sixty minutes later, she was on a small transport vessel loaded with the injured from Cañacao. Eleanor stood at the bow and surveyed what had been a paradise. In every direction she looked she saw smoldering ruins.

The mood aboard the vessel was somber. U.S. Army and Navy installations all over the Philippines had been bombed or were still being bombed. Was anything still operational with which to wage war against the enemy? Even with her limited military training, Eleanor didn't see how the U.S. could continue to hold its positions. It seemed they were not so much at war as preparing to be occupied.

Eleanor wondered crazily if perhaps that would be less terrible. The occupying forces, if they came, would surely allow them to continue to see to the needs of the sick and wounded and dying, wouldn't they? Had her parents heard that Manila had been attacked? And would she be able to get word to them that she was alright? She hoped she could.

But her worst worry she hadn't allowed herself to fully ponder—not in the immediate hours after the attack and not now. No one had been able to tell her if Sternberg Army Hospital was still standing. Were Penny and Lita injured? Or worse? Would she get to Manila only to learn her friends had been killed?

Eleanor set her face against the wind as the port drew nearer, refusing to entertain the notion.

TWO

PENNY

Sternberg Hospital
December 1941

"M erry Christmas indeed," Penny muttered, but no one heard her. No one cared, their long-anticipated festivities forgotten in their desperate need to evacuate.

The Army nurses had slipped out of Manila, two dozen at a time, over the last few days. When her turn came, Penny didn't bother trying to be silent. There was no point given that the air was split with the thunder of bombs and the walls rattled so hard she couldn't hear her own thoughts, much less her footsteps. Toward the end of the line—her hand grasping the rucksack of the nurse in front of her—she stumbled through the halls and out into the night, wearing a combat helmet along with her uniform.

Out the door, down the breezeway—once draped in jasmine and dotted with ferns but now bombed and gutted and broken—then into the yard and toward a row of flatbed Army trucks that idled, waiting for them. They chose at random, tossed in their packs, and sat in two rows of four in the bed of each truck.

As usual Penny kept close to Maude Davison, and once they rolled through the entrance, she sidled closer. Still, she had to shout to be heard. "Where are we going?"

"Away from Manila."

"Not a hospital? I thought we were headed to another hospital."

Maude shook her head, then pointed to the shadowy form of Sternberg, retreating in the distance. "We'll have to make our own."

This was a possibility the nurses had never discussed. They assumed that they would be sent off to another facility like all the others. Lined with cots. Stacked with linens. All they'd known during those lazy, endless months in Manila were whitewashed walls and red-tile roofs. Until the eighth of December. Until the Japanese unleashed hell on Hawaii and then the Philippines.

"But that means . . ."

"Yes," Maude said. "Our next assignment will be a battlefield."

I didn't pack for a battlefield. Penny almost laughed because it was so ridiculous. Who cared how she packed? Nothing in the rucksack at her feet could save them if another one of those bombs fell out of the sky and onto the truck.

Penny pulled her knees against her chest and wrapped her arms around them. She leaned her head back and closed her eyes. Thought of Lita and Eleanor. Tomorrow would have been their fifth HAM Day. They'd planned to get dressed up and go dancing. Try a new cocktail. Flirt with all the handsome soldiers. But now? God only knew where her friends were.

Things had changed so quickly. For five months she'd worked in paradise, a place so pretty it might as well have been the shine on a soap bubble. Then the Japanese bombed Pearl Harbor and all hell had—literally—broken loose. Even now she could hear her mother's critical voice ringing in her ears. *"Well, what did you expect, Penny, being so stubborn and all? Why'd you have to go and be one of those career women? You should've just stayed home. Found yourself another husband."*

As an only child Penny had always known she wanted a career. She didn't like being alone and didn't like the quiet. But her options were limited. Teaching. Secretarial work. Nursing. Those were about the only career paths open to a girl from South Texas, but all of them required taking care of other people. Nursing had seemed the most exciting, so she'd gone to college looking to become an RN, as opposed to an MRS like her high school friends. The fact that she'd met Sam along the way? Well, Penny didn't let that stop her.

The truck hit a pothole and her eyes jolted open.

Maude had a system for their evacuation. It was unspoken and unacknowledged by her or anyone else. But they had all noticed. She started by removing the oldest nurses first—women in their fifties or sixties—the ones who couldn't run as fast or who had an ailment of some kind. Then came those who, as she said, "tended toward hysterics"—young girls, barely out of school, whose only real exposure to injury had been presented in the classroom. Lita and the Filipina nurses were in the second-to-last group, right before Penny. It had happened so quickly they didn't even have a chance to say goodbye.

————— ♦ —————

The trucks drove without headlights for an hour, creeping along the rough, pitted, bombed-out roads. But still they were targets—large, dark, moving objects, easily spotted from the air—and it didn't take long before the first string of Japanese Zeros could be heard rumbling toward them, dark blotches against an even darker smoke-filled sky, buzzing like furious bees searching for something to sting.

The vehicle carrying Maude, Penny, and six other nurses slammed to a stop so quickly they all tumbled to the bed of the truck like a pile of rag dolls.

"Cover!" the driver shouted, and they bolted out of the truck.

In front of them, behind them, the same scene was repeating up and down the road. Truck after truck slamming to a stop, nurse after nurse throwing herself into this ditch or that while others scrambled for the bushes or culverts or any form of protection they could find.

Penny hit the ground hard, then ran for an adjacent field. When the roar of engines and the smell of diesel fuel overwhelmed her senses, she threw herself to the grass and curled into a ball, her hands over her head, her knees tucked under her chin.

Breathing hard, she pulled in a lungful of dusty air and lay there, wracked by a coughing fit. She tensed as the Zeros roared overhead, screamed when the air was split by a sudden barrage of gunfire, and cursed herself for losing that small bit of composure.

"No crying. No screaming. No crying. No screaming," she whispered under her breath. A command. A mantra. It was an order she gave herself, and she knew how to follow orders. She was good at that, dammit.

The Zeros strafed the ground blindly, shooting at anything that looked large enough to be a vehicle. At anything that moved. Fifty feet above them, sixty max, the planes passed, leaving behind a hot *whoosh* of air and the smell of fuel. And then they were gone as quickly as they'd come, barreling off toward the horizon in search of other victims. She counted to thirty before standing up, brushing herself off, and finding her way back.

Maude leaned against the truck, massaging her lower back with her thumb, and even though she angled her face away as Penny approached, she couldn't hide the wince.

"Are you okay?"

Maude nodded. "Just a sprain. Stupid really. Tripped and fell. Could be worse."

Penny couldn't see the older woman's face very well in the dark, but something about the set of her mouth, about the tone of her voice, told Penny she was hurt.

"Be careful, a wounded nurse—"

"Can't help anyone," Maude finished. "I know. I'm the one who taught you that, remember? But I'm fine. Everything's fine. Let's go."

"We have everyone?"

"Yes," she said, climbing into the truck much slower than she had at the hospital.

"Where to now?"

"The ferry."

"And then?"

Maude Davison was not the sort of woman who flinched. But something in the sound of her voice made Penny think that if she could see her clearly right now, she wouldn't like the expression on her supervisor's face.

"To safety. I hope."

———◆———

It's not that Penny *couldn't* swim. Rather that what she did in the water wouldn't really be *called* swimming by anyone who actually possessed the skill. Flailing, perhaps. Or floundering. When asked by the officer who herded the nurses onto the ferry, she simply told him that she knew how not to drown if she fell in the water.

"That's the important thing." He handed her a life preserver, then urged her forward.

The horizon glowed with angry red fires as the ferry pulled into Manila Bay. The nurses stood at the rail and watched the city burn. Gratuitous destruction no matter where they looked. Plumes of smoke and flame. They had been given orders. Evacuate. But none of them liked the knowledge that those who needed them most were left behind.

"Boots off!" came an announcement from the officer in charge. "Minefield up ahead."

Penny grabbed Maude's arm. "What—"

"In case we end up in the water. Too heavy. We'd sink like stones."

Penny unlaced her boots and set them beside her rucksack. She didn't ask what method they had for navigating the mines but rather stood at the rail—hands gripping so tight her knuckles ached—and paid attention to every shift in speed, every change in direction as the *Mc E. Hyde* zigzagged through the bay. Fifty minutes later the officer sounded the all clear and they put their boots back on. When Penny finally let go of the rail, her forearms cramped.

"Get your bags! Follow me!" the officer ordered.

Penny, Maude, and eighteen other nurses followed him down the gangway and onto the wharf. But no sooner had they set foot on solid ground than the Zeros once again barreled into sight.

"Run!"

It was harder with the rucksacks, but they all made it across the shore and into the trees before the bombs fell. Penny watched as a dozen soldiers dove into the water. Then the angry whistling of bombs filled the air. Three in total. Two misses and one direct hit right on the deck where they'd all been standing just moments earlier. The *Mc E. Hyde* shuddered once with the impact, then exploded into a ball of fire. They watched, dumbfounded, as soldiers waded out of the water, dripping and cursing as the ferry sank, flames billowing from the starboard side.

"No time to stand around and gawk," Maude said. She led them to a string of Army trucks that idled quietly in the shadows with their head-lights off. "Get in."

Not three hours ago Penny had been asleep in bed. Now she sat, dazed and winded, in the truck as it wound through the darkened jungle. The air was thick and hot, filled with exhaust and the smell of frightened women sweating through their uniforms. Not even a suggestion of a breeze. Mosquitos buzzed her ears and Penny swatted at them in outrage.

Too much, she thought. *Too much, too fast.*

Penny rested her forehead on her knees and took long, steady breaths through her nose. She stayed there, doing all she could to hold herself together, until the truck rumbled to a stop.

"Welcome home, girls," Maude said.

When Penny lifted her head, she saw that they were parked outside the entrance to a huge cave. Above them rose a massive tree-covered hill, and before them was a set of iron gates, propped open, and a tunnel that stretched deep inside. Pale yellow bulbs hung from the stone ceiling and continued on—twenty feet apart—as far as she could see.

The driver hopped out of their truck and slammed his door shut. "Welcome to Malinta Tunnel."

Maude was wrong. They hadn't been taken to a battlefield. This was a fortress.

THREE

ELEANOR

Santa Scholastica College, Manila
December 1941

S anta Scholastica College, an all-girls academy run by a small convent of Benedictine nuns, had been left blessedly untouched during the bombing raids. The school's stucco buildings, constructed in classic Spanish architecture with an elaborate wrought-iron perimeter fence and high stone walls, had at first glance looked like a stately villa and was clearly an echo from the Philippines' long history as a colony of Spain. Inside the campus were an auditorium and two dormitories, kitchen and dining facilities, and many classrooms that had been easily converted into wards for the wounded.

The U.S. Army had quickly created the emergency medical facility out of the now-emptied school but had begun pulling its people out before the Navy evacuees from Cavite had even arrived. Eleanor had finally and happily learned upon arriving that there had been no casualties among the Army nursing staff, and she had hoped she'd see Penny or Lita there. But the majority of the Army's medical units were already gone.

One of the few remaining Army nurses had explained why as they stood in the supply room only hours after Eleanor had stepped onto the campus. "We're all headed to the jungles to field hospitals on Bataan." The

Army nurse had packed the gauze and bandages into a duffel she was taking with her.

"To the . . . jungles?" Eleanor asked, certain she'd heard wrong.

The woman nodded.

"You'll be out in the open?"

"I hear there'll be tents." The woman grinned, feigning delight.

"You'll be in harm's way," Eleanor said, thinking of Penny and Lita and not this woman whose first name she didn't even know.

"I think we're all in harm's way at this point."

"Do you know Penny Franklin or Lita Capel? They're friends of mine, and I'm starting to think it's going to be a while before I see them again. Can you tell them Eleanor says hello and not to do anything too brave?"

The Army nurse smiled. "I know who they are. If I see either one I'll pass along the message." She hiked the duffel onto her shoulder. "Good luck here, Lindstrom. It's not a bad setup. At least not right now."

The woman turned for the door and Eleanor wished her well.

"Same to you," the woman called out as she headed for a waiting truck outside.

There was no question a jungle hospital would be dangerous duty, and fresh concern for her friends had filled Eleanor.

She was still feeling it now, two weeks later.

They were supposed to have had HAM Day on Saturday. They had already made plans for it back in November. Lita had suggested they try out the new American jazz club on Rizal Avenue in downtown Manila. There would have been dancing and dinner, and the Christmas decorations still would have been strung everywhere, and they were going to drink champagne and toast the new year. Penny would have had them all laughing till tears ran down their faces because somehow she always did . . .

But there was no purpose in musing on what was supposed to have been. Word had reached them at Santa Scholastica that forty thousand Japanese troops and ninety armored tanks had landed on the eastern coast of Lingayen Gulf, only a hundred miles north of Manila. Seven thousand more Japanese soldiers had landed on Christmas Eve.

At their morning briefing on Christmas Eve, Laura had told them that American and Filipino forces were making a final stand on Bataan, a twenty-five-mile-long peanut-shaped peninsula some thirty miles across Manila Bay, as well as on Corregidor, an island fortress situated just south of the Bataan province, from which MacArthur was commanding the whole of his forces.

A mass evacuation of all U.S. Army personnel out of Manila was now under way, including the wounded soldiers at Santa Scholastica. The small naval contingent at the college was under orders to remain.

"We are also losing Ann for good," Laura said. Fellow nurse Ann Bernatitus had some days earlier been sent to Sternberg when Laura had been asked to provide two volunteers to assist there. "Ann has been assigned by one of the Army surgeons to his staff at field hospital number one. She left early this morning."

Eleanor and the others turned in surprise to look at each other. She hadn't had the opportunity to get to know Ann well, but she still found it difficult to imagine her gone from them completely. There were so few Navy nurses in comparison to the Army, and the dozen of them had already experienced so much together.

"Why did he take her?" Eleanor asked.

Disappointment and frustration flashed in Laura's eyes for a moment, and Eleanor could tell their commander had also questioned this decision. Laura was a veteran of the Corps and, at nearly fifty years old, a respected officer who surely had earned the right to make logistical decisions regarding her own staff.

"Her surgical experience is needed on Bataan," the chief nurse said flatly, as though the answer she'd also been given for losing one of her staff wasn't sufficient for her either.

When the last Army detail was gone, the skeleton crew of naval officers, nurses, and corpsmen at the college and their patients appeared to be the only American military left in a city soon to be occupied by the enemy.

"I don't understand why they're leaving us here," Eleanor said that evening to a young Navy lieutenant, a public affairs officer with a shattered right leg who'd been evacuated out of Cavite like she had.

"I can tell you why the Army is leaving, but I can't tell you why the

Navy's medical team isn't joining that effort now since Cavite is gone. It doesn't make a whole lot of sense to me."

"Why are they leaving, then?"

"There has always been a strategy in place should the Philippines come under attack. All the commanders from all the services here know about it—us, the Army, the Marines, the Filipino military. It's part of WPO-3. War Plan Orange. It's been in place for several years. If the Japanese were to attack, the Army was always going to pull out of Manila and take up better positions on the Bataan Peninsula and Corregidor. The Japanese Navy would have to sail right past them to get to Manila and the rest of Luzon."

"So it will work? Our Army forces can stop the Japanese Navy?"

"I don't know. I'm sure that's the goal. But if the Army can't get fresh supplies, especially food and artillery, I don't see how they can pull it off. I'm not a logistics officer, so I don't know what they know. But if the Japanese are anchored off the coast, how will our supply ships get to them?"

"You're scaring me," Eleanor said.

"I'm sorry. I don't mean to. I'm just saying it like I see it."

"So what are we supposed to do here in Manila, alone, in the meantime?"

"Pray that I'm wrong."

1942

I would rather walk with a friend in the dark, than alone in the light.
—HELEN KELLER

FOUR

LITA

Bataan Peninsula
January 1942

A gasp pulled Lita from her thoughts. She couldn't pinpoint who of the twenty or so nurses packed around her, a mix of Americans and Filipinas, had expelled the sound. But as they rumbled down the road in the back of an open-air truck, all those seated across from Lita were staring gravely at something behind her.

Against a surge of dread and through whirling yellow dust, she twisted toward the sight.

White crosses. A sea of them. Dozens upon dozens, row upon jagged row, the markers of death stretched out beneath the morning sun.

The existence of a hospital cemetery was hardly a secret to the medical staff. Since arriving at Camp Limay on Christmas Eve to set up Hospital One, they had treated well over a thousand casualties. Naturally, not all of them survived. Yet the unexpected visual, collective evidence of Allied soldiers—just boys, most of them—whose bodies would never make it home, pricked Lita's eyes with tears.

She wasn't the only one.

Still as statues in their tropical khakis and combat boots, heads topped with helmets, a good number of the other women in the truck were staving off a rise of emotion. Perhaps it was the crosses, or maybe it was simply their first chance to relinquish their guard after twenty-nine days of hell. Near double that if counting the three weeks in Manila following the start of the Japanese attacks. Three weeks of watching her fears of impending war become reality, the heart of her homeland reduced largely to ruins. She could only hope that the village she'd grown up in, and the kind residents who had supported her after her mother's death had left her on her own, were being spared the worst of the battles.

Now once again, Lita was among the fifty-some nurses ordered to evacuate, half of them Filipina, their civilian status a mere technicality. This time, however, rather than heading south along the eastern coastline of the Bataan Peninsula, the convoy was bound inland and deeper into the jungle, where the entire hospital was being moved. The enemy's "big-gun" assaults and strafing runs had been hitting much too close, and with General Homma breaking through the Allies' defenses at the neck of the peninsula, Japanese ground troops were inching ever closer. Only thirteen miles from here, battles were raging at the Abucay barrio.

Lita turned back in her seat and strove to mute her surroundings. Over the truck's bumping and rattling came the intermittent roars of bombs and blasts of artillery. The smell and taste of incendiary smoke clung to the humid air. She swore she could even feel the ground's concussions reverberate through the vehicle. While Hospital One's structures—long bamboo sheds topped with thatched nipa grass—had provided but a semblance of protection, traveling openly through daylight in a military convoy seemed a beckoning target.

"How about a sing-along?" Cassie chimed in, a blatant attempt to reduce the tension. Around Lita's age, the American Army nurse of Italian lineage—Helen Cassiani being her Christian name—had a round face and an infectious smile. A farm girl from Massachusetts, she possessed a tomboyishness reminiscent of many girls Lita had grown up with on Leyte. "'She'll Be Coming 'Round the Mountain,' girls? What do you say?"

No immediate answer followed. The majority of the nurses looked as tired as Lita felt, exhaustion having seeped into the marrow of her bones. She supposed two hundred procedures a day would do that to even the heartiest of medical teams.

Cassie wasn't deterred. She launched straight in, at a carefree volume that caused Lita to cringe. The last thing they needed was to draw more attention from the Japanese!

But then Lita acknowledged the foolishness of the notion: revving motors from the string of trucks and buses-turned-ambulances—transports for the patients—were anything but stealthy. She relaxed slightly in her seat.

The other American nurses gradually joined in, energy returning, mood lifting. The Filipinas all spoke English fluently but appeared unfamiliar with the tune. Their smiles crept upward all the same. Before long, Lita found herself softly singing. She'd learned the lyrics from her father at some point, before he died in a boating accident when she was four.

Or had her sisters taught her? In the line of siblings, two years separated each, save for Lita who trailed by a gap of six. Rarely had a day passed when their house wasn't filled with music. Singing, after all, cost nothing. Same for their frequent laughter.

Lita's lips went still, and an ache pulsed within her. It had been five years since the last of her sisters left for the States. She'd be lying if she said she hadn't reveled in being the only child for once, a chance to be her own person—whoever that was. Meanwhile, they were off building their lives full of new loves: one with a beau, the other married just last fall, and the oldest married with little ones whom Lita knew through photos and stories.

Oh, how worried her sisters must be over her safety now. She'd dashed off a letter in Manila, though she had little confidence posts would be getting through for some time. She wished she could be with them at this very moment, far away in New York, where war would exist only in newspapers and on the airwaves. Where her nails wouldn't be stained daily with blood, nor her mind seared with the moans and cries and images from an endless assembly line of patients shredded by war.

Would she ever divulge to them all she'd experienced? How could they ever fully understand?

Unlike Penny and Eleanor. Wherever they were.

At the uncertainty, the ache inside Lita swelled.

November's HAM Day was the last she had seen of Eleanor, and Penny was still stationed in Manila when Lita had been corralled onto a truck, much like the one in which she was currently riding. Perhaps her dear friends were stationed at Hospital Two. Twenty miles farther south, nurses had apparently helped establish the outdoor facility roofed by a dense jungle canopy. Word also had it that some nurses were assigned to Corregidor.

Whatever the case, Lita prayed her friends were alive and safe and that one day soon they'd all be together again, laughing and dancing and chatting the night away.

———◆———

The new Hospital One swiftly acquired a nickname. For its resemblance to a cool, lush, mountainous retreat north of Manila called Baguio, the place was dubbed "Little Baguio." Military engineers had already begun to carve out the area for a camp, so three sizable wooden buildings equipped with running water were primed for the taking. They were divvied up into wards, operating rooms, and staff quarters, each of their roofs painted white, then topped with giant red crosses, while huts were converted into the likes of pharmacies and laboratories.

Though direct threats from the Japanese felt lessened this far inland, there was no rest to be had over the following week. Casualties continued to amass as fast as trucks and buses and mule carts could deliver them. Armies of mosquitos from Bataan's nearby swamps were just as ruthless. Pairing those with malnutrition from a dwindling food supply, staff and troops alike were being walloped by tropical diseases—as was proven by yet another soldier Lita was now caring for, this one Filipino.

On a table near his cot, she used a bowl of water to remoisten his rag. After spending much of the day assisting with ghastly surgeries, to be back to her assigned ward was a relief, though only partially.

As she bent down, placing the washcloth upon the fellow's forehead, a pain pinched her lower back, a consequence of regularly hovering over beds and low cots. She gritted against the nuisance and said in Tagalog, "There you go now. Does that feel better?"

He didn't reply, just continued to shiver from the malaria wracking his body. Heat emanated from his skin, as strongly as it had for days. The room's kerosene lamps flickered shadows over his face.

Righting herself, Lita couldn't help but contemplate the extreme threats of the disease: the clogging of capillaries and internal organs that could lead to coma or death for the poor man. At merely thirty, she'd guess. Was he married, a father? How much had he given up to join the battle?

She could easily guess at his motivation, matching those of so many guerrilla fighters up in the mountains, unyielding for valid reason. A grand deal had been struck with America's Congress. After the Philippines' long history of being conquered and colonized, the country would gain independence in just four more years.

If the Japanese didn't thwart those plans by taking full control.

"You keep strong, you hear me?" Lita told the man and gently squeezed his arm. She opened her mouth to say more—how she had full faith that he'd pull through—but the acidity of the lie, told too many times, dissolved the words on her tongue.

She gathered her bearings with a deep breath, the air thick with disinfectant. Given the short supply of quinine, as with all their medications, illnesses like his would continue to mount. All she could do was perform her duties as best as she was able.

Eager to finish her rounds, she regarded her watch. Past nine. The two hours beyond her official shift made it another fourteen-hour stretch.

Feet throbbing, she proceeded with her tasks. She paused only to rub her eyes that were lightly blurring from even less sleep than usual—thanks to a bothersome gecko.

Some might find the little creatures cute or charming. This wasn't so for Lita. Not after one startled her awake last night by sprinting through her hair.

A grip tugged her hand, a GI reaching from his cot. He was blond with a sweet, young face, slightly flushed from days of fighting dengue fever.

"Everything alright, Private?" Lita had learned not to offer, *Is there something I can do for you?* Not unless she was prepared for a soldier's innuendo and consequent chuckles from his ward mates. Male patients were still male, even in war. Especially so.

"Got a favor . . . ," he began, voice raspy and dry, "to ask."

She waited for the rest.

Slowly he pulled the chain of his dog tags from the collar of his undershirt. Between his thumb and forefinger he held a class ring, which he glanced at before meeting Lita's eyes.

"My folks gotta have this . . . case I don't make it." The slight tremble in his words spurred a tightening in Lita's throat. But as he went to unclasp the necklace by feel, she laid her hand over his.

"If it comes to that, we'll take care of that ring. But there's no need for anything now but for you to focus on getting well. Understood?" She pressed him with her gaze, allowing but a single answer.

A faint spark of hope entered his eyes, a beautiful thing, then he nodded, hair rustling against his pillow.

Lita smiled genuinely. It was a response she would have otherwise needed to muster. The expectations were drilled into her since nursing school: She was to raise spirits to aid in mending. No looking glum regardless of diagnosis; no look of shock or revulsion at any wound. Moreover, she was to maintain a gay and ladylike composure, hair and face primped—complete with rouge, powder, and lipstick—even, rather ridiculously, here in the jungle.

"How about some water?" she asked. "Would you like that?"

"Sure," he breathed. "That'd be swell."

When she discovered the closest pitcher empty, she told him, "I'll be right back. No sneaking away and getting into mischief now, or you just might get me fired."

His lips hinted at a smile, and Lita's couldn't help but widen. It was always nice to make a difference, even if a small one.

Pitcher in hand, she headed out of the ward. She would revel in the cool nighttime air if not for the blasted mosquitos. From a canvas Lister bag hanging from a pole, she refilled the pitcher with warm water that smelled of chlorine—and tasted just as bad—then reentered the ward.

"Who the Sam Hill did this? Who dressed these burns?"

Lita stopped midstride and traced the gruff tone to Dr. Thomson. Nearby at a patient's bedside he stood facing the other way, his fringe of gray hair toward Lita. As a family doctor back in the States, he was typically kind and unflappable but suddenly appeared, like many, to be reaching his breaking point.

The human brain simply wasn't built for these conditions, for the relentless attempts to save limbs and lives. To feel responsible for the flurry of telegrams sent to loved ones, decimating worlds with a measly piece of paper.

"I said, *who*?" he demanded when no immediate answer came.

The three other nurses and lone corpsman in the room traded glances that ricocheted like pinballs. Lita surveyed the patient in question. She realized then that the dressing on the fellow's arm was hers, though she had no inkling how she'd erred.

Bracing herself, she stepped forward, clutching the pitcher. "I-I did, sir."

The doctor spun toward her and spoke through clenched teeth. "Come here. Now."

She swallowed hard, feeling the pressure of surrounding stares, and dared to move closer. His six-foot height towered acutely over her petite stature of five two.

"Did you, or did you not, remember to apply Vaseline under this man's gauze?"

She was about to reply that she had, because she always did, but then noticed an absence of ointment bordering the bandage. In her tired state she must have forgotten. Her stomach sank as Dr. Thomson charged on.

"Had it gone another day, the gauze would've melded with the wound. Clearly you think we have morphine to waste. Do your job right or don't bother at all." The rebuke sliced straight through her pride.

He turned to an adjacent figure. "Nurse Delos Santos, fix this."

The Filipina replied agreeably, "Yes, Doctor."

Of all the people here to choose, of really anyone in the world, why did it have to be her?

The doctor marched past Lita to the exit, and Reyna Delos Santos slid in. Her eyes—ever contrasting with her gentle, round face—glinted with smugness.

Since the start of nursing school, she'd derided Lita with snide looks and flips of her bobbed hair, always insinuating her superiority over those she didn't care for. Lita, in particular. Their stationing at Sternberg together was bad enough, but to have her here, in this instant, made Lita feel smaller than ever before.

Though desperate to flee, she managed to keep her head up and pushed herself to finish delivering the water. She approached the young soldier's cot just as an American nurse was scrambling to locate his pulse. Lita stopped cold.

"He's gone into shock," the nurse reported.

It was a symptom of a severe dengue infection, a sign of blood pressure plummeting. A corpsman rushed to help revive him despite the obvious, well learned from experience.

He was gone.

In just minutes.

Frozen in place, numb, Lita simply watched him being covered with a sheet. Then the nurse walked over and gently took the pitcher from Lita's stiffened hands. "I've got this."

Still, Lita couldn't move. "His ring . . ." The words drifted out as if formed by another. "On his necklace. It's for his parents."

Empathy rode the nurse's brow. "I'll take care of it," she promised. "It's hours past your shift. Go on and rest." She patted Lita's arm and returned to her work.

The ward had turned impossibly quiet.

Robotically, only vaguely aware of the gazes still trailing her, Lita followed the instruction and retreated outside to reach the nurses' quarters. She made it halfway there before her sense of detachment waned and, without warning, the dam within her broke. A rush of grief and helplessness burst through, an unleashing of pressure from the day, the week, the endless month of horrors. Another life she couldn't save.

Legs threatening to buckle, she pressed her hand to the backside of a hut and crumpled to her knees. For the first time since her mother's death, she cried, weeping alone in the dark until fully spent of tears.

FIVE

PENNY

Malinta Tunnel, Corregidor Island
February 1942

A re the straps secure?" Dr. Cooper asked.

Penny stood beside him, ready to assist with the amputation. She tugged on the thick canvas straps holding the young man's lower legs to the operating table. "Yes."

Of the dozen or so Army surgeons assigned to the Malinta Tunnel compound, Dr. Cooper was Penny's favorite. He reminded her of the grandfather she'd lost at ten years old. That loss had stayed close her entire life and left in its void a deep and abiding fondness for old men—particularly those who used a gruff exterior to mask a molten-chocolate core. The habit of seeking out their company had played no small part in her decision to focus on surgery rather than recovery or childbirth during nursing school. The older surgeons, the ones nearing retirement, were typically the teaching surgeons, men eager to pass on what they knew before drifting off toward a future on the golf course or a hobby farm. Penny learned early on that a seasoned doctor could take a crisis and—using little more than a calm voice and a scalpel—put an entire surgical team at ease.

Dr. Cooper had crow's feet so pronounced, they stretched from the corners of his dark eyes all the way to his hairline. More salt than pepper, it remained thick despite the fact he was nearing sixty. His voice was filled with good humor, his eyes were kind, and he had a penchant for delivering philosophical lessons during surgery.

"There are some things that are only moral in an operating room," he told Penny. "At no other time could I tell a person to lie down on a table and allow me to knock them unconscious so I can remove their clothing and cut into their body."

"Nor would you want to, I hope." A wry smile curled the corner of Penny's mouth.

"Indeed, I would not." He lifted a wicked-looking handsaw and its sharp, serrated teeth glinted beneath the lamp that hung above the table. "Remember, the mandate to do no harm often requires a kind of harm never allowed outside a room such as this."

Their patient lay on the table, anesthetized and limp, oblivious to what was about to happen. Since being in the tunnels, Penny had assisted with hundreds of surgeries, sometimes a dozen or more a day, and all the faces had started to run together, an unending stream of broken young men splayed before her long, slender fingers.

I used to play piano with these hands, she thought. Penny had grown accustomed to such random thoughts in the nearly two months since leaving Manila and was no longer alarmed by them. Now her fingers were tucked inside rubber gloves and smeared with blood. This, too, was a new reality of the strange situation in which she found herself. Rare were the moments that she *wasn't* covered in blood.

She stared at the boy's face, searching for signs of looming consciousness, and was startled to realize that he looked familiar. Young, *so* young. And then the memory snapped into place, like a rubber glove popping against her wrist. A thin scar ran through the middle of his left eyebrow. This was the boy from the Army Navy Club in Manila, the boy who had jumped up to pull out her chair the night she and Lita met Eleanor. And now he was just another busted rag doll about to lose his foot. He'd been brought in an hour earlier, after being fired on by the Japanese while patrolling one of the beaches. Dr. Cooper said there was no saving the appendage.

"Ready?" he asked.

She set her gloved finger against the boy's scar, smearing blood across his brow. Too young for a beard. He shouldn't be here.

"Yes."

Blood didn't scare her. Nor did the inherent sights and smells common to every operating room. It wasn't until Corregidor, however, that she discovered the only part of her profession that truly upset her were the *sounds*.

Nothing could weaken her resolve like a grown man crying for his mother. Thankfully the boy on the table was lost in a fog of anesthesia, but that only made the *zzz-zzz-zzz* noise of Dr. Cooper's handsaw all the clearer. It sounded like a zipper being yanked up and down as he worked his way through what was left of the boy's ankle.

Penny rarely knew the names of her patients, but it felt like a tragedy at that moment, as she swabbed the steady flow of blood from the newly severed veins and flesh. She swallowed hard, blinked twice, and held his lower leg steady. The foot was already dead, and the tarsus had been shattered, along with the lower part of his tibia, so Dr. Cooper made quick work of the amputation. But it was the *thud* of the boy's mangled foot dropping into a bucket beside the table that made Penny wince.

She'd never assisted with a surgery like *this* in nursing school. She'd never heard a sound like *that*. And during those first languid months in Manila, the worst injuries she'd treated were sunburns and splinters and once a broken nose after a soldier drunkenly fell down three steps and caught himself on the pavement with his face. Until Corregidor she'd felt as though she had been a nurse in name only.

"Prepare for cauterization," Dr. Cooper ordered, and though they performed this procedure together several times a day, she still was not prepared. The *crack* and *sizzle* were far worse to her than the accompanying scent of burned flesh.

Penny knew these sounds would stay with her for the rest of her life. And they weren't just emanating from her operating table. The surgery was filled with doctors and nurses, medics and patients—most of whom were still awake. They rarely screamed anymore—the boys had figured out that didn't help anyone—but they did whimper and curse and hiss. Hissing filled the surgery: the lukewarm air moving through the ventilation system, the sterilizer blowing off plumes of boiling steam, desperate prayers streaming through clenched teeth.

There were other noises as well—less disturbing but still able to work their way into Penny's every dream and wandering thought. The constant, quiet patter of feet as nurses moved from one bed to another. Their whispers. To each other. To the surgeons. To the patients. Those whispers filled the room and her mind like the flutter of small wings. The metallic *snip* of scissors cutting clothing, cutting muscle, cutting sutures. The wet slop of a mop hitting the floor and the *swish-swish* as it slid back and forth across the stained concrete, cleaning the never-ending puddles of blood. So much blood. The *drip* of blood from table to floor. And the endless dripping of IVs. The only drips she could *not* hear were those of sweat trickling down the small of her back after hours in the hot, cramped surgery. So many long hours. So many lost soldiers.

Penny worked silently beside Dr. Cooper as they stabilized the boy. Finally he stepped away from the table and stretched his neck to the side with a loud *crack*. Another sound she logged in her growing inventory and filed under exhaustion.

"Good work, Franklin. We'll see you tomorrow, then."

She glanced from his face to the clock on the wall above the door that led to the north entrance. Six thirty. Her shift had ended two hours ago, but she'd been so focused on her work she hadn't noticed.

She blinked heavily, overcome with a weariness she'd refused to acknowledge until dismissed. "Yes. Tomorrow."

Penny pulled off her rubber gloves, dropped them into a pan at the foot of the bed, and set her hand on the boy's cheek one last time. Soft as a peach. She couldn't help but think about his mother. And that made her think about her own mother, so she slammed the mental door shut.

"Do you know his name?" she asked.

Dr. Cooper pulled the dog tags out from under the boy's shirt. He leaned close, squinting at the tiny embossed print. "James R. Moody."

"I bet his parents call him Jimmy."

"Why do you say that?"

"He's Texan. I talked to him once, in Manila. Heard it in his voice."

Dr. Cooper studied her face, lifted one dark eyebrow above the rim of his spectacles. It made him look like Groucho Marx and she almost laughed. Almost.

"No one can drag out an *a* like a Texan," she said by way of explanation, then added, "*Ma'am*. Every *a* becomes two syllables."

He did laugh then, and she was glad to hear it. A handful of surrounding nurses and patients looked up at them curiously.

Penny was exhausted and hungry, but she hadn't been outside in days. So if she cleaned her workstation and showered quickly, she might be able to make it to the tunnel entrance before the sun set. Few pleasures existed on Corregidor, but the sky lit up like a Maxfield Parrish painting at the end of every day, and Penny didn't miss any opportunity to watch it.

She dropped her filthy apron into the wash basket, took her tools to the sterilizer, and made one last pass through her row of patients—checking foreheads and pulses. Six were stable enough to be moved to the recovery ward. Penny gave instructions to the enlisted men assigned to this task and, after glancing around one last time, removed her cap. Rituals were important in this place, she'd learned. Do certain things in a certain order, and it gave you a sense of normalcy.

Routine complete, Penny heaved a sigh and closed her eyes. She arched her back and rolled her neck—this way and that—but when she opened her eyes again, Maude Davison was standing in front of her, returned from her survey of the field hospitals on Bataan.

"You're back!" Penny cried, and, before she could think, threw her arms around the older woman.

Penny expected Maude to flinch. To stay reserved, as always. But she wrapped her arms around Penny's back and pulled her tight, the way a mother would. For three long seconds they stood there—Penny covered with blood and Maude covered in dirt, clearly exhausted—in the middle of the operating room.

"How was it?" Penny asked.

"Worse than we'd imagined. They're like no hospitals I've ever seen.

Open to the elements. Overrun with mosquitos. Overcrowded. Overwhelmed. Underfed. Understaffed. They're taking the brunt of the assault on Bataan. Both hospitals need more nurses than I can spare."

"You're transferring some of us?"

"I'll have to. There's no way around it. We're hard pressed, but they're underwater."

"How are things at Hospital One? How are the Filipina nurses?" Penny couldn't help but think of Lita, sent off to Bataan and the jungle hospital in December.

"They were taking so much fire they had to move locations. It's called Little Baguio now. The nurses are almost as bad off as the patients. Most have malaria, I think. Or at least they look like they do, but it's hard to tell with food rations so tight. Everyone has lost weight."

Penny made her decision without giving it a second thought. "You can send me. I'll go."

"No."

"But—"

"No." Her voice was tight as a drum. Maude Davison was a stern, immovable old warhorse of a woman who brooked no argument.

But that didn't stop Penny. She took a step back, angry. "I know those women. What kind of friend would I be if I just left them out there?"

"Lieutenant Franklin, I don't give a rip about what kind of *friend* you are." Penny opened her mouth to argue, but Maude continued. "I do, however, care a great deal about what kind of *nurse* you are. And by all accounts, if these surgeons are to be trusted—Cooper in particular—you are irreplaceable. So I need you to carry on, as you are, right here."

The hope of seeing Lita again had been as slight and ephemeral as gauze, and Penny could feel it slipping away.

Seeing the dismay on her face, Maude stepped closer. "The truth is, Franklin, *I* need you as well. I'm not . . ." She paused, and Penny could see her wince, the reaction to some fleeting pain. "My back . . ."

"It still hurts?"

"It's *worse*. I've been on my feet for days. I could barely make the hike from Little Baguio to Hospital Two."

Ever since their escape from Manila, Maude's back hadn't been right. Something in her lumbar spine was either broken or bruised, and she now lived with a lingering pain that grew as the day progressed, ebbing only while she slept.

"Surely there's something we can do?"

Maude straightened as much as possible and glared at Penny. "Cooper said you helped with a foot amputation earlier?"

"Yes?"

"Then you know my back is the least of anyone's concerns. Certainly not mine."

Penny gave up. "Who will you send?"

"Some of the younger girls, I think. I can only part with five and hope that it's enough." Maude patted her on the shoulder. "Now go get cleaned up and try to sleep."

"I thought I'd catch the sunset first."

Maude laughed then, loud and clear. "Do you know what time it is?"

Penny looked at the clock above the door. Not much time had passed since she'd finished surgery. "Almost seven."

"In the *morning*, Franklin. If you don't hurry with that shower, you won't even see the sunrise."

———◆———

In many ways the escape from Manila prepared Penny for life on Corregidor. The bombings had not stopped. Not on their journey to the island, nor any day since. The thunderous crash now seemed an inevitable part of her life, the rattle of walls and the whispering sound of dust sliding to the floor as normal as rainfall or birdsong. In the confines of the Malinta Tunnel, however, daylight was replaced by either harsh electric bulbs or the flashing red lights that indicated a topside bombing raid. They hung in the tunnel doorways, a macabre warning system that gave the corridors an apocalyptic glow. Not that anyone needed the warning, of course. They could all hear and feel the unrelenting Japanese shelling that assailed the island.

The Army's retreat to Corregidor Island and the Bataan Peninsula was a blow. After the attack on Manila, they were surrounded by Japanese forces and fled to the jungles and this underground fortress. It couldn't last indefinitely. Everyone knew that. But the choice had been retreat or surrender, and MacArthur wasn't ready to wave the white flag yet.

Now, after almost two months in the tunnels, Penny could not say the place felt like home, but at least it was familiar. Buried seventy feet beneath solid stone, the complex of tunnels was situated in the middle of the island directly beneath its highest point. At first the sprawling underground complex of Corregidor—the Rock, as it was called—seemed like a safe harbor. An impregnable stronghold. However, Penny had to force her mind not to think of its similarities to the other Rock—Alcatraz—also an island fortress that kept its inhabitants locked inside.

Although far safer than they'd been in Manila, the nurses had started to feel as though escape was impossible. Always, even in her dreams, Penny could hear a distant *boom* and the rattle of falling bombs.

She and the other nurses were assigned a portion of the complex inside the tunnels by General MacArthur, Corregidor's commanding officer. The fortified complex served as his headquarters, and from here he directed the war effort throughout the Pacific theater.

Instead of a hospital with white walls and starched linens, the nurses' domain was now a one-hundred-yard-long corridor with eight smaller passageways that branched off at regular intervals. The nurses used these hallways as designated wards for surgery, recovery, convalescence, medical dispensary, mess hall, and sleeping quarters. As with the entirety of the complex, each smaller corridor was connected to other passages, turning the inside of the fortress into a meandering warren. It was easy to take a wrong turn, to get lost, to end up in the armory or the men's barracks. To take a left instead of a right and find herself in the middle of an officers' meeting.

Beyond the layout of the tunnel itself, the systems that kept it running were also unreliable. The generators were touchy. Any aggressive bombing topside could cause them to sputter and fail, leaving everyone in utter darkness. More than once Penny had found herself in surgery with a bleeding patient beneath her hands when the power went out. It became such a nuisance that Maude Davison put in a request for soldiers to be assigned to the operating room around the clock so they could hold flashlights during surgery in the event of a power outage. It happened at least once a day. They'd learned to count, slowly, until the distant whine of generators resumed. Penny had never made it past 452. Seven minutes, thirty-two seconds to work on a wounded man beneath the narrow beam of a flashlight.

All she cared about now was a shower, however. Penny was half asleep as she maneuvered toward the nurses' quarters. They'd each been allowed a single rucksack when they left Manila, barely large enough to hold a change of clothes, a blanket, toiletries, and a few personal items. Penny grabbed her things from beneath the bed and made her way to the shower. She stripped down, wearing nothing but a gold chain with a small pendant at the bottom in the form of a gold nugget. Her father had found it in a stream in Colorado when she was a child and gave it to her as a graduation present. Now with oceans—literal and figurative—between them, it was the only connection she had to him.

The tunnels had cured Penny of both modesty and her addiction to long, hot showers. In all the weeks she'd lived on Corregidor, she had never showered alone. There was only a single spigot protruding from the ceiling in the middle of a ten-by-ten room, and the water was never warm, much less hot. In and out was the name of the game, and she didn't complain about the temperature or the inevitable company. Two other girls rotated beneath the weak spray, taking turns dousing their hair and body, when Penny stepped into the shower. The girls shifted, making room, and they all went about their ablutions, passing the soap back and forth. Penny was the last one out and she turned off the spigot.

In addition to showers the nurses also had flushing latrines, cots, and adequate linens—a sheet and a pillow with a case. Penny knew that compared to her friends in the jungle hospitals, she was fortunate. She wasn't at the mercy of the elements or the insects. Yet it often felt as though she'd been buried alive. Never a fan of enclosed spaces, she had to make a concerted effort not to panic those first days underground. As a result, whenever possible, she ended a shift by getting a breath of fresh air at the main entrance and—when she was lucky—watching the sun set.

Penny yanked on her khaki coveralls and buttoned them up the front.

She rolled her sleeves above her elbows and plucked the fabric away from where it clung to her damp skin. Even though she had civilian clothes in her pack, she stayed in uniform most of the time. It was practical. She felt unladylike, but she also felt capable and uninhibited, and that mattered too. Especially now when all hell could break loose at any moment. She never wanted to find herself in a position where she was running for her life through the jungle in a party dress and a pair of heels.

Her hair was still wet, dripping onto her collar, when she made her way back through the surgical ward and into the lateral tunnel that led to the entrance.

Maude was right.

Sunrise, not sunset.

It was amazing how she could lose all sense of time underground. Day became night. Up became down. All her circadian rhythms were gone, replaced by some frantic fight-or-flight sensation she could never really tame, not even in the deepest reservoir of sleep. Penny lived in a revolving door in which the realities of time meant nothing. But at least the tunnel entrances were protected from the heaviest shelling. They were neither near the beaches nor the top of the hill, so they rarely attracted fire.

The sky was lit up like a furnace, a rim of bright ochre along the horizon that caught the clouds and cast them in bronze. And above that, a deep, inky blue—almost purple—and a smattering of stubborn stars not ready to give up their glory to their daytime counterpart.

A sunrise indeed.

"Well, hell," Penny muttered, leaning against the wall as she cocked one hip to the side and rested her hand in the dip of her waistline. "What do you know?"

"Any number of things," came a deep, familiar voice behind her. "But what in particular are you curious about?"

She hadn't heard that voice since Manila, but it still made her entire body tense, like she'd just been sent to the principal's office. Penny straightened her spine and looked back over her shoulder. Charley Russell stood there, looking every bit as weary as she felt, but he wasn't glowering and that was something at least.

"Captain," she said.

"Lieutenant."

They nodded their greetings, and both turned back to the horizon.

"Pretty morning," he said.

"Until a few minutes ago I was under the impression that it was evening."

He shrugged. "Happens." Then he reached into one pocket for a pack of cigarettes and another for a lighter. He tipped the pack toward her, offering a cigarette—and, she thought, a conversation. "Want one?"

On a whim Penny decided to accept both. "Sure. Why not."

Charley Russell pulled a smoke from the pack, lit it with expert precision, and handed it to her. She lifted the cigarette, tipped it toward him in thanks, and set it against her lips. The entire exchange felt so *normal*—her first normal in months. Two professionals on break, sharing a cigarette. Penny inhaled deeply, the way she'd learned in college. The nicotine hit her system with bright, explosive fury.

She coughed.

Then spluttered.

Penny bent at the waist and hacked up smoke for a moment but turned from Charley when he tried to retrieve the cigarette.

"Oh God," he said. "I'm sorry. I just assumed—"

"Haven't smoked since . . ." Penny caught herself, lied, ". . . college."

Since I got pregnant, she thought, and turned to the rising sun, blinking hard, letting him assume it was the smoke that made her eyes water.

"You okay?"

"Fine. Just . . . too much, too fast."

He nodded but didn't ask questions or seem concerned.

Penny cleared her throat and tried again. Her second inhale was smaller, more manageable, and she blew the smoke out her pursed lips and turned back to him.

"What are you doing here?"

"I came in December, with everyone else. Each post has a quartermaster. One at Little Baguio. One at Hospital Two. And"—he bowed—"one here."

"I actually meant what are you doing *out* here, now, but it's good to know the other sites aren't left unmanned."

He caught the teasing note in her voice and watched her quietly for a moment. "Saw you pass through. Came to ask if you need anything. For old times' sake."

"You'll have to ask Maude. I haven't seen a request form in months. She assigned that task to some other unfortunate soul."

"So I've noticed," he said, and Penny thought she heard bitterness in his voice. "But I'm not asking Maude. I'm asking you."

Charley Russell turned to her, and Penny had to tilt her chin upward to meet his gaze. His hair was dark—not quite black—and rumpled, like he'd been pulling at it. He needed a trim and a shave. Probably a good night's sleep as well. The cool, stern, unyielding quartermaster from Manila was gone, replaced by a man with sad gray eyes that held a question. She just couldn't figure out what they were asking.

The moment stretched out longer than it should have, and finally Penny realized she was standing in the tunnel entrance, a smoldering cigarette between her fingers and her gaze locked on a man who—until seconds ago—she had assumed despised her.

Penny could typically recite the surgery inventory the way she could recite all the counties in Texas. But her mind was blank now, devoid of all relevant information. She cleared her throat. "I'm sure the surgery needs something. It always does."

Charley Russell smiled, then plucked the cigarette from her fingers and took a long draw. She could not help but notice that his cheeks hollowed, casting the bones in shadow as though they'd been chiseled out of marble. He blew the smoke out his nose in two thin streams, and she watched it dissipate into the breeze. Then his other hand rose cautiously to her face, paused, and tucked one errant, damp curl behind her ear. The edge of his finger brushed her cheekbone—the *faintest* whisper of a touch—and, stunned, she held her breath.

"I wasn't asking about the surgery either," he said, then turned and walked back into the tunnel.

SIX

LITA

Little Baguio Field Hospital
February 1942

L ita wasn't at the dance ten minutes before regret crept in.
  She wrapped her arms over her chest, aiming to appear casual
despite feeling awkward and, above all, bare. The flared skirt of the black-
and-white polka-dotted dress Cassie had insisted she borrow was all fine
and good, but just how much its sweetheart neckline accentuated Lita's
cleavage wasn't clear until she arrived tonight—specifically when a corpsman whistled in passing, his eyes flitting toward her bosom.

With no mirror but a cosmetic compact, she'd lacked a gauge of how
brazen she looked, save for her own current downward view, which now
made her wish she'd remained in her khakis. That had been her plan, in
fact—since an infuriating rat had shredded the one civilian dress she'd
packed—yet Cassie intervened.

"*You simply must get dolled up,*" she'd contended in their shared quarters. "*It's my twenty-fifth birthday, after all! For a single night we're going to
forget all about this blessed war. We'll pretend we're back in dazzling Manila
without a care in the world.*"

The escape of it did sound dreamy, reminding Lita of nights when she,
Eleanor, and Penny would dance and laugh and gallivant until sunrise.
Plus, the recent lull in battles, though undoubtedly temporary, provided

one more reason to celebrate. Lita had thus wrangled her hair into a fancy French twist and even borrowed Victory Red lipstick, then set off for the makeshift dance hall nestled outdoors, away from the hospital in an area cleared of jungle.

Now, though, standing at the edge of the party illuminated with posted torches, she was slammed by second thoughts. Not the least for her being the sole Filipina here. Of the only other two Filipinas who'd opted not to transfer from Little Baguio, one was on night shift and the other was an introvert averse to large social events. At a glance it appeared all eleven American nurses, who likewise hadn't transferred to Hospital Two, were in attendance and busily engaged in laughter and chitchat with the twenty or so other staff members.

Would anyone really notice if Lita slipped away?

Tempted to do just that, she was ebbing back when an arm hooked her elbow. It was Cassie, stunning in an A-line turquoise dress, her dark brown hair stylishly pinned. "Golly, don't you look sublime? I said that you would! Like a right Jean Harlow."

More like Harlot, Lita refrained from adding, not wanting to insult the garment.

"Now then." Cassie turned serious. "Any idea what time it is?"

Lita went to check her watch, but Cassie supplied the answer with a grin. "Time for a cocktail!"

With that she whisked Lita off, briefly pausing to hook the elbow of another straggling nurse. As if serving as a human shuttle bus, Cassie delivered the pair to a circle of nurses near the dance floor, which consisted of old Army blankets stretched and tacked to bamboo flooring. There, Cassie snagged her canvas satchel and with a flourish produced a bottle of Johnnie Walker Red. "Bottoms up, ladies!"

Lita wasn't the only one gaping in disbelief. How the devil had the gal managed to hoard a full bottle of booze through bombs and bullets and two evacuations?

The conundrum fell away the second the cap came off. *Gulp, breathe, giggle, pass along.* These were the actions of every nurse in the circle as the booze made several rounds.

The flames in Lita's chest lessened with each of her subsequent swallows, her head lightening with her mood, any worries over her appearance subsiding.

As the male guests, too, indulged in the whiskey, below a sky speckled with stars, music floated on the soft breeze. Set on an adjacent table, a vintage phonograph was playing an instrumental tune Lita didn't recognize, but it was soothing and melodious and prompted fellows to ask ladies to dance. One pair after the other funneled onto the dance floor. Lita suspected she would soon be the last girl left.

It was definitely time to sneak out.

"Care to cut a rug, Nurse Capel?"

She turned to find Dr. Thomson, who held out his hand in a friendly manner. Orange flickers from the torches highlighted his facial wrinkles. Save for a few brief medical exchanges, this was their first run-in since his reprimand over the gauze, an outburst fueled by a reason she had since come to learn.

And so, overriding her urge to leave, she tendered a smile. "I'd be delighted."

With a flash of relief in his eyes, he led her to the dance floor, and together they rocked to the rhythm. From the feel of his aged, callused hand, somehow pleasantly comforting, she thought of the father-daughter dances she'd never attended in school and imagined it would have felt much like this.

"Now, aren't you glad you stayed? You would've missed all this fun."

She wondered how he knew her intent, then realized he was referring not to the party but to Little Baguio.

"Oh, for certain I am." An honest answer.

When Josie Nesbit, the CO of Hospital Two, recently requested any nurses who could be spared, Reyna clearly aimed to gain accolades by rallying most of the Filipinas to volunteer for the transfer. She was a charming natural leader when she wanted to be. The location was said to be no more dangerous than here, though a flood of casualties to the area had left the staff shorthanded. The idea of Reyna stationed elsewhere gave Lita ample motivation to stay put.

"You know, it's occurred to me," the doctor said tentatively. "I never did apologize for coming down on you so harshly." If this was the reason he asked her to dance—to make amends—she was glad to have attended the party after all. "That night, I'd been altogether worn thin, but . . . well, I could've handled myself far better."

"It's quite alright," she assured him, and truly it was. According to scuttlebutt, which understandably he wasn't mentioning, he'd lost a patient in surgery earlier that same day. Not just any patient, but the son of a lifelong friend. All to say, he was human.

"You were right to correct me about the dressing. On account of that, it's a mistake I'll never make again."

He smiled softly and lowered his shoulders, his burden eased by her offering of grace.

"So, tell me," Lita said, "what's the latest word from the betting pool?"

It was a detour to a lighter topic, though she was also curious. Among the staff, predictions over the arrival of rescues and reinforcements helped sustain hope, even for those like Lita who'd refrained from placing a wager.

"Don't know the current pot, I'm afraid, but I do have ten buckaroos riding on the twenty-seventh of this month."

"In that case, I'll get a welcome mat ready on the twenty-sixth."

Beyond his grin, she sensed he wasn't convinced it would be all that soon. Regardless, they discussed things from back home they couldn't wait to revisit. He spoke of his favorite foods, as did everyone since rations had been cut to two monotonous meals a day—mostly carabao, canned tomatoes, and rice. He also described his rose garden and, with a touch of emotion, his beloved wife.

All along, Lita pretended to believe what so many American staff and soldiers insisted, that the whole war would be over in just months. A year at most. She, of course, feared otherwise. The Philippines had a history of long conflicts, and small countries comprised of islands, Japan in this case, were often underestimated.

As one song gave way to another, the doctor sighed and released Lita's hands. "Having bent your ear plenty, I suppose it's time for these ancient feet of mine to retire for the night."

"I think that makes two of us—minus the ancient part," she teased, covering her worries with a smile.

He chuckled just as a finger tapped his shoulder.

"May I, Doc?"

Dr. Thomson angled back, revealing a fellow with a medium build, eyes the color of amber, and hair a shade darker. Called "Gibs" by others, he carried a quiet, almost mysterious air about him. Lita had yet to encounter him personally but knew him to be a medic.

"That, Corporal McGibbons, is entirely up to the lady." Although the doctor delivered this with an assertive voice, he sent her a stealthy raise of his brow, signaling encouragement as a father would about a well-approved choice.

As it felt wrong to decline, she obliged, and Dr. Thomson slid away and disappeared into the night.

Clasping Gibs's hand and shoulder, Lita swayed with the slow tune while surveying the nuzzling couples surrounding them. The liquor, paired with the life-is-short view that wartime evoked, appeared to have forged several sets of sweethearts, at least for the night. She only hoped her dance partner, regardless of his pleasing looks, wasn't expecting the same.

"Real nice to finally meet you, miss."

"Lita is fine," she offered. "And you're Gibs?"

"Lon, officially."

She smiled politely before a silence fell between them that did nothing to reduce the awkwardness.

"So . . . your back's giving you fits?"

His sudden question confounded her. "I'm sorry?"

"I just noticed you rubbing it the other day."

"Oh. Oh, right. Just knotted from work is all."

Silence again. "Well, if it keeps bothering ya, I'd be happy to massage it out—if you'd like."

Her feet stopped. Whether inspired by other couples—or sure, perhaps by the dress—or because he pegged her as an easy mestiza, the fellow had some gall.

Her face must have said as much based on his stammered response.

"I-I didn't mean to imply— It's just that I've massaged loads of farm animals before, and—"

Lita cut him off with a humorless laugh and pulled clear away.

"That's not to say you're a farm animal," he hastened to correct. But then he seemed to acknowledge he needed to simply quit.

As if on cue, the music ceased.

Dancing couples complained with groans until discovering the reason: a nurse was carrying out a mango adorned with a single lit match. The crowd broke out into singing "Happy Birthday" to Cassie, and out of nowhere a wave of nausea rolled through Lita. Her mind swirled and a flush scaled her neck. Apparently the booze was taking full effect.

Not bothering with parting words for Lon, she proceeded to do what she should have from the start: turned around and made her way back to her quarters.

Only on the brink of dawn did she learn the whiskey wasn't entirely to blame, if at all, for her sickly condition. When she awoke from a raging fever, her body hot as the sun, the true, frightening cause became evident.

Just how badly she was off, with malaria or dengue fever, she didn't yet know but would soon find out.

SEVEN

ELEANOR

Santa Scholastica College, Manila
February 1942

When the new year had dawned, the American and Filipino militaries who'd long been the defense arm of the Philippine Islands had been replaced overnight with exultant Japanese troops. The ranking Navy captain at Santa Scholastica ordered that none under his command venture outside the gate, but Filipino nationals who did said the American flag had disappeared and the red-orbed Japanese flag was now flying everywhere instead. In its front-page news story on New Year's Day, the *Manila Tribune*—now under Japanese control—instructed all civilians to carry on with normal, peaceful life, to be respectful of the incoming occupying forces, and to obey every order given to them.

"But we're not civilians," Peg said to Eleanor, as they'd read the article together. "Are they thinking *we're* going to be able to carry on with normal, peaceful life?"

"We're noncombatants," Eleanor said quickly, wishing to quell the fear that had immediately spiked within her.

"We are uniformed nurses in the U.S. Navy. That's what we are."

Eleanor had left the paper with Peg and gone to check on her few remaining patients. *"Don't borrow trouble from tomorrow,"* she heard her father saying from within the folds of her memory. If he were here, this was what he would say to her, no doubt. She repeated his oft-spoken advice under her breath, over and over as she moved from bed to bed.

The next day, Eleanor and a few of the other off-duty nurses were sitting outside while one smoked a cigarette, when they heard and then saw between the fence poles a parade of marching soldiers and trucks and flag-flying cars. Japanese civilians up and down the street yelled, *"Banzai! Banzai!"*—a rallying cry that meant "Long live His Majesty the Emperor!"

Eleanor wondered for a tense moment if the marching soldiers would demand entrance onto the campus, but the parade stomped past as if the school were not there.

"They have to know there are people in here," Peg said warily as the sound of the marchers faded.

"They know," said the nurse with the cigarette.

But did the Japanese know what *kind* of people were behind the gate? Did they know there were naval officers, and Navy nurses, and 100 enlisted corpsmen inside? Would they care that there were also 160 wounded, both American and Filipino? If the Japanese didn't know today who was sheltering in the school, surely they would not fail to be apprised of these details. It was only a matter of time.

"What do you think they will do with us?" Eleanor had asked Laura the next evening when Japanese revelers could be heard in the streets several blocks away.

"We don't know." Laura's tone was surprisingly confident. "We don't know what they will do, but we know what we will do, don't we? We will honor our country, our oath to the Navy, and our pledge to minister to the sick and hurting. That's what *we* will do."

She smiled at Eleanor and squeezed her shoulder before walking away.

Her superior's words were so inspiring and inviting, Eleanor decided then and there to latch onto them and emulate them as best she could and for as long as she could. She knew her parents would be proud of her if she did. She wondered for a scant moment if John would be proud of her. Of course he would be. And it did not feel wrong to imagine that he would.

Eleanor did not have to wait long to begin to live each day by Laura's words. The next day a contingent of armed Japanese soldiers pounded on the doors of the college. Their declaration via the aid of an interpreter was immediate and decisive: everyone at the school was now a prisoner of war.

A bolt of fear zipped through Eleanor at this proclamation. Her military training had included a condensed unit on warfare, but she'd not expected she'd be called to act on it. Women in uniform didn't have combat roles in the U.S. military. The specter of war had been in the realm of possibility, but not this. "What does that mean for us?" Eleanor had whispered to Laura as the inhabitants of Santa Scholastica stood in tight rows to listen to the announcement.

"Hush. It means we continue to do what we've trained to do. We just keep doing it."

Eleanor had so many other questions; her apprehension was growing by the second. Would they be incarcerated? Separated? Chained up? How long would it take for her parents to be advised of what had happened?

But this was not the time for questions. Nor was it the time for answers. None of them, not even Laura, knew what they could expect. All that the nurses were sure of was that Japan hadn't ratified the 1929 Geneva Convention—the international rule of law regarding warfare, which included the treatment of enemy prisoners.

Within hours everything about life at the school-turned-hospital had been turned upside down. The MPs were relieved of their guns and their jobs and Japanese guards took their places. Every cabinet, every closet, every duffel, every issued footlocker was inspected. If a Japanese soldier saw something he liked, he took it.

The prisoners' knives and flashlights and radios were confiscated, which Eleanor had expected. But she did not think the occupiers would rummage through the food stores to cart away whatever looked interesting or walk off with any mattress that didn't have someone lying on it or loot the medicine cabinets and dispensary.

"They took the quinine!" Eleanor whispered to Peg two days later during *tenko*—their now twice-daily roll call. Quinine was the nurses' best defense against malaria, which could now easily run rampant through the hospital.

"That's not the worst. They took the mosquito nets too," Peg whispered back. "All of them. They may as well just shoot us all dead now."

Several times over the next few days Eleanor saw the Navy captains—highly respected officers with years of service—slapped hard across the face for the most mundane of reasons, like not answering a question quickly enough or failing to bow deeply enough or speaking too fast for the interpreter to understand. It was humiliating to watch.

Laura Cobb instructed her nurses to say nothing, do nothing to attract their captors' attention. Not even to appear appalled at the treatment being suffered by the male prisoners.

"The Japanese don't know what to make of us," she said. "Women don't serve in their military. At least they don't want to acknowledge our presence here. I think they believe it is beneath them. But I'm afraid it won't last. For now keep a low profile."

Eleanor had never experienced such a bizarre and constricting life as the one she was now living. She was not just a prisoner; she was the enemy. And not just an ordinary American foe, but a member of the reviled United States military. She could tell by the way the Japanese soldiers regarded her—now that they were finally acknowledging the military nurses' existence—that they found her presence as an officer in the Navy distasteful. Females did not belong in the rank and file. Who was she to think she did? It was unseemly. Dishonorable. She should be at home preparing for the takeover of her country by a superior nation.

Eleanor was surprised by how intentional and sure her captors were as they assumed their control over the last occupants of Santa Scholastica; nothing seemed to surprise them. Only a small number of patients remained. As soon as a wounded or sick POW recovered, he was transferred to a labor camp. There were increasingly fewer reasons for the Navy nurses to remain incarcerated there, but this didn't seem to figure into their captors' thinking as the nurses waited to see what would be done with them.

One February morning after roll call, Laura asked one of the guards who spoke some English if the nurses could be relocated to another hospital or infirmary where they could be of better use. The guard frowned at her.

"Your use to us not your concern. Your use *our* concern." He pointed a finger at her and wagged it.

"I am only saying we have skills to offer you. We are nurses, not soldiers. If there are people who are sick or wounded, we can help."

The guard shook his head as if Laura were a simpleton. "You don't tell us what to do with you. We tell you. You think we don't have plan for you?"

"That's not what I meant. I only—"

"No more question. You women go to your place." He shooed Laura and the other nurses toward the wards.

As the meaningless days slid by, Eleanor was beginning to understand that the Japanese had surely spent as much time studying Manila as she'd learned they had Pearl Harbor. They'd no doubt planned to use Santa Scholastica from the beginning. With that high wall and fence, it had served well as a hospital for the wounded. And now it was serving as their jail.

Despite strutting about like victors of a war instead of men still engaged in one, as the days marched on the Japanese guards began to lose their patience with the prisoners seemingly every minute of every hour. In the beginning their captors had meted out punishments only to the men for failure to obey to their standard. But now, if the nurses angered them, they were also slapped.

Eleanor had learned fast to bow deeply and keep her eyes averted. She could still feel the sting on her cheek from when the guard to whom she'd tried to sufficiently bow one morning before tenko was affronted by her attempt and struck her hard with the flat of his hand. Her eyes had burned with ready tears at the pain and the embarrassment, but Laura, standing a few feet away, had caught her eye, shook her head slightly, and smiled at her.

"You are strong. The pain will pass. You did nothing wrong," her expression seemed to say.

Eleanor had willed the tears away and nodded.

She hoped—they all did—that the tense mood of their captors was because the Japanese were losing the battle on Bataan. There was no way of knowing how the battle was going.

The empty days wore on, each like the one before it. She wanted to write to her parents and let them know she was okay, but there was no way to post a letter. No mail was going out and none was coming in, and any question regarding when that might change was ignored. With no news on when they might be relocated, she looked for ways to occupy her time.

One of the priests taught Eleanor to play cribbage, and in the evenings she joined discussions that had to be conducted in library-quiet voices. The one time the prisoners tried an evening sing-along, guards rushed in with fixed bayonets and screamed for silence. The few books and magazines the nurses had between them were spread round, read and reread and reread again.

What they all wanted more than anything was news from the outside. Were additional troops coming to rescue them? Were the Army and Filipino forces regaining control of the islands?

And Eleanor desperately wanted news about Penny and Lita at those jungle hospitals.

"I didn't think being a prisoner would feel like this," Eleanor told Peg one night in late February as they lay on their cots after a long day of doing nothing. "I didn't think I would be so . . . bored."

"I think they want us to feel this way. They want us to feel like we're nothing. That we have no good reason to be alive."

That this could be true sent a shiver down Eleanor's back, despite the clammy heat in the room. "I wish I'd brought more books," she said a moment later, needing to redirect her thoughts away from the notion that she was expendable. That they all were. "I had room in my trunk. I could have brought more."

Peg sighed. "You and me both."

———◆———

Santo Tomas Internment Camp, Manila

The first week of March Eleanor and the other nurses were ordered into the courtyard after breakfast, and well after normal tenko. The announcement from the Japanese lieutenant standing in front of them was swift.

"Pack what belong to you. Tomorrow you go to Santo Tomas Internment Camp. That is all. Go." He pivoted from them. There were to be no questions.

But Eleanor didn't care. She didn't have any questions and she didn't want to get slapped for asking one. This news after eight weeks of monotony was a welcome interruption, and she returned to her sleeping quarters eager to comply.

Eleanor had walked past the campus of Santo Tomas once, with Penny and Lita. The Dominican academy was located in a busy section of Manila near the port. Lita had told them the university had been around since the seventeenth century and was named for the well-known friar and philosopher Thomas Aquinas. Just like Scholastica, Santo Tomas had a high concrete-and-stone fence, but its grounds had seemed to Eleanor to be much larger. She had peeked through the iron gates that day and seen the grounds. It was a pretty campus and not a bad choice for an internment camp. And now that it was one, that meant there would be an infirmary. Her days would have meaning again.

After the noon meal the following day, Eleanor stepped onto a bus that idled at the gate next to a truck loaded with their belongings. The transfer to Santo Tomas began.

As the vehicles took to the streets, Eleanor got her first glimpse of everyday life in the now-occupied city. The difference between the Manila at which she'd arrived in August and this one was startling. Americans strolling the sidewalks were nowhere to be found. Instead the boulevards were full of Filipinos chauffeuring Japanese officials. The burned-out reminders that the city had been bombed in the days leading up to its surrender were everywhere. The bus ambled through the Escolta shopping district, looking quiet and deserted now, and turned finally onto Calle España where the university stood.

The unending yards of barbed wire topping the high fence were the first thing Eleanor saw, and her heart gave a little shudder. The barbed wire was new. The school already looked like it was no longer a place of loveliness and knowledge.

The bus approached the gate, and Main Building, as the primary structure on the campus was known, already looked tired and abused despite its three stories and brilliantly white cross high atop the tower. Dirty mattresses and blankets draped over the windowsills of Main Building as far as they could hang without falling, as if to beg the sun to warm them.

"Bedbugs!" Peg shook her head as she stared at the sills and what was flung over them. "That's the only reason I can think of for bedding hanging out the window like that."

They passed through the gate and Eleanor immediately saw the beautiful grounds were now a trampled mess. The once-manicured lawns were torn through to the dirt from both vehicle and foot traffic. The bus chuffed to a stop in front of Main Building and three American men came out to greet them.

When the nurses all disembarked the bus, one of the men stepped forward and spoke.

"We're from the executive committee. My name's Jim Hobbs. You must be the nurses from Santa Scholastica. I'm sorry to say we just found out you were coming today. We will need to speak to Mr. Tsurumi, our new commandant, to see where to put you. I'm afraid all the women's sleeping quarters are full."

"Shall we, then?" Laura Cobb said in a slightly peeved voice, motioning to the building behind him.

She went inside with the three men, and Eleanor and the others moved to the shade of a nearby tree to wait for her. Two internees were tasked with unloading their belongings and medical equipment from the truck.

Now out of the sun's glare, Eleanor could see that the campus was full of other internees, some in groups talking to each other. Some looking for glimpses of life outside the gate. Some just milling about as if bored and hungering for something to do. All appeared as though they'd been here awhile. Along the interior side of the perimeter wall, from one end of it to the other, ramshackle shanties had sprung up that hadn't been there before. Eleanor wondered who lived in them.

"Why do you suppose the new commandant is a mister?" Eleanor asked Peg. "And not a lieutenant or something?"

"I heard Laura telling Dorothy this camp is commanded by Japanese civilians who were already here on the island when the troops arrived," Peg replied.

"A civilian-run camp!" Eleanor exclaimed. "That already sounds like a huge improvement."

"No kidding. I'm guessing most Japanese civilians haven't been trained on making the most of a face slap."

"I won't miss those." Eleanor surveyed the campus. "There seem to be a lot of people here already. I thought maybe this camp was just initiated and that's why we had to wait so long to get transferred."

"There's actually more than three thousand of us at this hellhole," said a nearby woman in a faded gray dress. She was American and perhaps in her late forties. She came closer to them. "Sorry. I couldn't help overhearing. The Japanese army just dumped us here. Men, women, little kids. All of us citizen civilians of Allied countries. They told the friars here to figure out where to put us all because they couldn't have cared less. There's only sixty-two classrooms. We were supposed to be here only until we registered as civilians from enemy nations. But we're still here."

"I'm so sorry to hear that. I'm Eleanor. This is Peg. We're Navy nurses. We were at Cavite before all of this."

The woman thrust out her hand. "Loretta Harris. I worked for an American-based company helping Manila city planners improve their infrastructure. I was an executive secretary, handling correspondence and scheduling golf rounds, and now I'm a prisoner. Can you believe it?"

"I can believe anything these days," Peg said.

"So do you know that man who came out to speak to us?" Eleanor asked.

"Jim's the current chairman of the internees' executive committee. There are ten fellas on it. He was picked to lead it because he was a leader in a businessman's organization or something like that. The Japs don't want us bothering them, so if you need something or want to complain about something, you go to the committee. And I'm sorry to tell you there's a lot to complain about. The camp hospital, if you want to call it that and where I guess you'll probably be working, is in the engineering building of all places. It's a place no one wants to get sent."

"That bad?" Peg said.

"There's just too many people here and not enough supplies if you ask me. And none of us were trained for this kind of life like maybe you were. We're just office workers and ballet dancers and bankers and the like."

"And you said there are children here?" Eleanor asked.

"Hundreds of them if I had to wager a guess. I can't imagine how hard this is for their parents, seeing their little ones in a place like this."

"And those shanties?" Eleanor nodded toward the dilapidated structures, some of them roofless. All of them open to the elements in some way.

"Internees are living in those. All the buildings are full. They've got seven hundred men bunking in the gym alone, most of them elderly."

Laura Cobb came out of the building and motioned for the nurses to gather. With her were half a dozen internees, all American. Eleanor thanked Loretta for talking with them, and she and Peg joined the other nurses.

"We're being billeted, at least for now, on the second floor of Main Building," Laura said. "Gather what you can for your quarters and the rest will be carried in by these fellows." She nodded to the young men who had unloaded the truck. "Our hospital equipment will be headed elsewhere, so for now just leave it. One of these men will watch over it so it doesn't disappear. Let's move."

Eleanor hoisted her duffel onto her shoulder and followed Laura through the mahogany doors and into the building. The first floor was a sea of makeshift sleeping and sitting areas and thrown-together administrative offices, all of which seemed immensely out of place in a building with so much architectural character. The view was more like an evacuation center to which residents had fled to wait out a bad storm, except the people hunkering down had obviously been here for weeks, not hours or days.

The second floor of former classrooms was nothing short of chaos. Sleeping areas had been cobbled together from double beds, bunk beds, cots, bamboo mats, and even boards on blocks. Mosquito netting of all levels of repair and disrepair was slung from wall to wall on drooping wires. Kitchen items and suitcases and crates were strewn everywhere. And there were people everywhere, in every room and in all the hallways. Young and old and every age in between. Men were in some of the classrooms-turned-dormitories, and women in the others.

Eleanor could feel the hopelessness of so many people in so small a space and in ninety-degree heat. A bit farther down the hall was surely an overworked restroom. Eleanor could smell its stink, knew it was there without even seeing it.

Santo Tomas was quickly proving to be nothing like she had expected it would be, but then, she was learning the hard way that it was best to expect nothing. Expectations were of no help now. If anything, they were the opposite of help. But she was sure of one thing. She didn't know how long she could live this way. They would have to find a way to improve these living conditions or disease would flourish.

"Is it always so crowded in here?" Eleanor turned to the internee behind her who'd been tasked with helping to bring in their mattresses.

"Ha," he said with a humorless laugh. "Wait until it rains."

EIGHT

LITA

Little Baguio Field Hospital
March 1942

T he world was a blur of confusion. Lita strained to clear her vision, her focus improving with each waking blink. Gradually she registered the blanket upon her as Army-issue. The smell of disinfectant placed her in a hospital, her cot in the ward being the last in the row.

"You're awake." A woman sighed, pausing her steps. "Thank heavens." She lowered her clipboard and smiled, pronouncing her dimples. The senior nurse in charge, Rosemary Hogan, was an easygoing American with dark hair that matched her perfectly arched brows, and hailed from some city with a silly name—Chattachooga, was it?

The thought dissipated upon Lita's recognition of sunlight slanting through the windows, a sign of morning.

Wait—why was she here? Had she nodded off at the end of her shift?

Angst stirred in her gut.

She attempted to push herself up. "My rounds, am I late for them?" Her voice emerged hoarse.

"Now, now." Rosemary waved, motioning her downward. "Plenty of chances for all that. You had us all worried till your fever broke last night. I'm ordering you to rest a smidge longer this time."

This time . . .

Then Lita remembered. She'd been diagnosed with malaria. After several days of a fever, nausea, and chills, she'd recovered enough to return to work, doing her best to conceal her headache and fatigue. Never wanting to justify her babyish nickname of bunso from her sisters, and still troubled by the soldier's sudden death from dengue fever, she had switched her role of "patient" back to that of "nurse" as rapidly as possible, only to relapse a few weeks later. The second bout had left her worse off than before.

At least she presumed as much, based on the snippets of memories floating back to her now: of feeling feverish while assisting a surgery, of the room tilting before everything went black, of a nurse lifting her head from a pillow to offer sips of water.

"Soon as I hand off this paperwork," Rosemary said, "I'll be circling back to check your vitals." She threw a glance down the ward. "Meanwhile, it appears your usual visitor can keep you company."

Lita reached through the fogginess of her thoughts, befuddled by the reference, until a uniformed figure moved closer and his features gained clarity. "Lon . . . ?"

"Lita—gosh, do you look better." Relief filled his voice as Rosemary strode away, leaving a spot for him near the foot of the cot. "How you feeling?"

"Okay. I think. A tad achy."

"Can I get you something? Some water?" he said. "Food?"

The suggestion triggered a vision too tantalizing not to voice, implausibility aside. "A plate of *lumpia*?"

He chuckled, as if he should have guessed. "Your ma's specialty."

Perplexed again, she stared. "How . . . did you . . ."

He hesitated before replying. "You told me as much. Quite a few times, actually." He smiled.

If it weren't for her lingering grogginess, she might have been embarrassed over rambling while delirious. Although, her mother's signature dish, equating to "Filipino egg rolls" according to the American nurses, did warrant repetition.

"Apparently I've been hungry."

"You're definitely not alone in that department." He again flashed a smile, spurring her own, before he pulled a chair from the nearby corner. As he settled in to face her bedside, she noted for the first time green flecks in his amber eyes and a small scar along his jawline.

"Did I . . . say anything else?" She was almost afraid to ask.

"About other foods mostly. Also some phrases in Tagalog, it sounded like. Oh—and you were pretty insistent I talk to some villagers." He leaned forward with elbows on his knees, his forehead scrunching. "Evidently you wanted to give *'everything* back to 'em'?"

She absorbed this, then murmured as if at a loss, "Just the fever talking."

He seemed to detect she wasn't being forthright but didn't prod. After a brief stretch, they both went to speak, then stopped. "You first," he encouraged.

"I was wondering how long I've been here."

"Four days, thereabouts."

It felt like forty—or a blink.

"And the fighting?"

"Still enjoying a lull."

She cast her gaze across the room and, sure enough, discovered a decent number of vacant cots. Another nurse, taking a patient's temperature a short way down, sent Lita a knowing wink. That's when Rosemary's comment boomeranged back, about Lita having a usual visitor.

Returning her attention to Lon, she struggled to connect the pieces. "You've been coming to see me . . . Why?" She caught the brashness of the question. "Only to say, you scarcely know me."

He didn't appear offended. "When I heard about your collapsing, I got worried. Besides"—he shrugged and sat back in his chair, his mouth curving upward—"I was kinda hoping for a chance to make a better impression."

She recalled a snip of their awkward discussion. "So . . . without comparing me to farm animals?" she said lightly.

He winced. "You remember that already, huh?" Not needing an answer, he at last explained himself. "Thing is, my pop is a farm vet back in Illinois. I've been lending a hand since I was a kid, gearing up to take over the practice. Clearly more time around people would've been helpful in keeping my foot out of my mouth."

A soft laugh slipped out of Lita. He was forgiven. "Makes sense," she said, gradually comprehending, "about your being assigned as a medic."

"Yeah, well. When I enlisted, truth be told, I'd hoped to get away from it all—working in medicine, that is. Army had other ideas." He said that with a bit of a grumble. "After the war, though, with the GI Bill? I'll be heading straight to school for finance. Then it's off to Chicago and a banker's life all the way." His face brightened, as if their current wartime predicament could only meet a favorable end.

Lita savored the notion, while also feeling a sting of envy over the surety of his path, his purpose.

"Sorry," he said when she went quiet. "I'm rattling on, and you've got to be dog-tired. I ought to leave you be."

She opened her mouth while he rose, to assure him that wasn't the problem, but then it dawned on her how exhausted she indeed was. As Rosemary pointed out, a smidge more rest this time would be wise.

Once he returned the chair to the corner, readying to depart, she told him, "Thank you, Lon. For being here."

The warmth in his eyes said he understood she was referring to more than just today.

Given how little they knew of each other, some might find it odd that throughout her delirium he'd paid her regular visits, even chatting at her bedside.

Rather, Lita found it comforting to know that while teetering on the verge of death she hadn't been alone.

———◆———

Through the following week, Lita's health continued to improve. Enough so, she returned to her daily rounds, though at a slower speed while battling fatigue and occasional nausea. At times a headache. By the fourth Sunday of March, save for tightening her belt loop by another notch, she felt increasingly like her old self. Thanks to the ongoing break in fighting, one could almost remember how life felt before the war. Particularly when attending an event as normal as a wedding.

Granted, Lita wouldn't typically have donned tropical khakis for such a special occasion. But no polka-dotted number would doll her up this time around. Only her regulation rouge and lipstick and hair pinned in a low bun.

Still, from Lon's subtle intake of breath when she arrived that evening at the outdoor dance hall, against a backdrop of an orange-pink sunset, she felt as radiant as a bride herself.

He offered her his elbow, a gesture he'd made a habit of these past few weeks when greeting her for nighttime strolls as their duties and her energy allowed. On their walks they'd speak of their hometowns and families and childhoods. Much like she missed doing with Eleanor and Penny. In this instance Lon simply escorted her to where the guests were standing, a gathering made smaller due to several nurses recovering from moderate illnesses. At the front awaited the chaplain and the groom, an artillery officer stationed near Hospital Two who'd hitchhiked to wed his sweetheart.

Just then, a Filipino man with a guitar played a *kundiman*, a Philippine love song. On a pathway dividing the guests came the bride, a nurse from Oregon, wearing a skirt stitched from khakis and gripping a bouquet of mostly leaves with a sprinkling of tropical flowers.

As the couple declared their devotion to each other, Lita realized she hadn't yet released Lon's arm. Her gaze drifted over the profile of his face. Surely amplified by the equally romantic melody and vows, she couldn't help envisioning herself with Lon at an altar. The thought was nonsensical considering the circumstances, never mind the length of their relationship—if it even constituted such a term.

Then he glanced her way, catching her staring. She snapped forward and her cheeks flamed. Out of the corner of her eye, she noted his gentle smile before he refocused on the featured couple. Upon their official marital kiss, the guests burst into applause and whoops and whistles.

There was no standard reception, as the groom soon needed to depart for his station, and no doubt the newlyweds preferred privacy in the time they had left.

As Lon escorted Lita along the perimeter of the grounds to reach her quarters, of the many topics they had covered, she realized one she'd been unconsciously avoiding. She said after a quiet stint, "May I ask you something?"

"Anything," he insisted. And she knew he meant it.

"How did you know you wanted to be a banker?"

He laughed under his breath, as if he'd rightly predicted her diverting to a benign topic—meaning not involving the formality of a courtship. "A baseball game."

He subjected her to only a second of confoundment before clarifying. "For my twelfth birthday, Pop drove me and my best pal over to St. Louis to see the Cardinals play. Man sitting next to me had a bombshell of a date and spent half the game chatting her up, raving about his important work at the bank."

Lita's jaw slackened and her feet stalled. "So that's the reason? You wanted a bombshell date?"

"Nah, it wasn't that." He slowed his pace. "Well—maybe a little. I mean, I *was* twelve." When he smirked, she pushed his arm away and laughed, then they resumed walking.

"Point is"—his tone leveled—"I got a load of that dapper fella's pin-striped suit, fancy hat, and polished wing tips. A barber's close shave. Fingernails trimmed and shiny as all get-out. And then there was my pop, with his old suit and scuffed shoes, his dirty nails and stained collar—not that I don't admire him to heaven and back. He's a real good man, the best, and helps a whole lotta folks. It's just that . . . I just . . ."

"Wanted something different."

His gaze connected with hers. From the tenderness of his smile, he appeared to know that the words applied as easily to her own life. "Yeah," he said.

Their common understanding was one more element supporting a closeness she'd never experienced with another fellow, a sense of being truly seen. In that moment she yearned to impart more, a confession she'd yet to bring herself to utter. The night's residual air of romance assuredly magnified the compulsion. Still, she dove in before she could lose her nerve.

"You remember how I told you about my sisters, how they always wanted to be nurses?"

"Sure. Saw it as a ticket out of your village for a better life, you said."

She gave a nod. "Well, what I didn't share is that one day, toward the end of senior year, my mother and I got into an argument. I told her that in spite of her wishes, I wouldn't be going to nursing school, that I was old enough to make my own decisions."

Lon cocked his head at her. "What'd you want to do instead?"

"That's the thing. I had no idea. She said I was acting like a spoiled child, which I suppose I was, especially when . . ." The rest trailed off as tears rose in her eyes.

"Lita." He grasped her hand, guiding her to a stop. "What is it? What happened?"

She looked away, undeserving of his concern, and pushed out words long weighted by shame. "A day later, my mother fell ill. Rheumatic fever. I should've apologized right then, but I was being stubborn. And really, I think part of me believed that somehow, if I didn't say I was sorry, she couldn't die. Because how could she possibly before we made up?" Her voice broke on the words.

"Come here." He pulled her into his arms. A tear slid from each of her eyes as he held her tight. It was the closest they'd been since they first danced. Now absent of any awkwardness, there was only deep-seated care and comfort. "Lita, she was your mother. You've got to know she understood. And hey, you obviously became a nurse in the end. For her."

He was offering the observation to alleviate her guilt. The truth of the story, however, wasn't so tidy, nor flattering.

But before she could divulge as much, he drew his head back to face her and wiped her cheek with his thumb. The touch sent a humming through her skin. Slowly, he leaned in for what, at last, would be their first kiss. As her guard receded, a yearning within her grew. The warmth of his breath had just brushed her lips when a blast roared in the distance. His hand jolted on her face and the ground faintly shook.

They turned and scanned the heavens. More roars, accompanied by rumbles. Miles away smoke plumed in all directions—from the beach, the mountains, the jungle. Dots moved through the sky—Japanese Zeros and bombers. Explosions from antiaircraft shells and incendiaries ripped holes in the fading sunset.

The lull in fighting was over.

Casualties were coming.

———◆———

Eighteen-hour workdays made the next week feel like a decade.

With General Homma's reinforced troops making a tremendous push southward, wounded Allies rolled in by the hundreds, soaring the patient count to at least fifteen hundred. At times some cots held two soldiers apiece; in a bind, blankets on the floor served as beds. Litter bearers' arms visibly shook from the constant strain of toting bodies. The surgeries were never ending, the gap between them so minimal linens often went unchanged. There were bullets and shrapnel to remove, limbs to amputate, infections and concussions to treat, knife and bayonet wounds to close.

There were deaths.

All the while, nature and malnutrition continued their assaults with common ailments like dysentery and beriberi, an illness caused by a lack of thiamine in the body, not to mention emergency procedures not usually thought of during wartime: appendectomies, kidney stones, even root canals.

Midafternoon on an endless day, Lita dropped off blood samples at the lab hut. She stretched her stiffened hands while returning to the surgical ward. Almost there, she took a moment to stand and breathe. If only she could mute the squealing brakes from trucks traveling the steep road behind the hospital, their gears and axles incessantly grinding.

She arched her back, her lower spine aching, and thought how nice it would be to finally take Lon up on his offer of a massage. She smiled solemnly to herself, missing their nightly strolls, their talks.

As if conjured from the notion, she glanced up and spotted him across the way. He was kneeling beside a Filipino soldier who bore a bandaged head and cigarette in hand while seated on the dirt. Lon had presumably just returned from another ambulance run. As he stood to check on the next patient, his gaze swept past Lita but then promptly doubled back. And he sent her a weary smile.

That image was the final one in her mind before all at once she felt herself floating. Time and space stretched into something inconceivable. There were no sights or sounds. Just an indescribable void until reality snapped back and slammed her to the ground. Every fiber in her body felt instantly swollen. Pressure bulged through her skull, her eyes, her ears. She heard only gasping, someone starved for air.

It was her—her own lungs clambering to breathe.

Dizzy, confused, she managed to push herself to sit upright. She had cuts on the backs of her hands but otherwise, somehow, thankfully, she appeared intact.

A bomb. They'd been hit by a bomb.

Or were there several?

Smoke hazed the air and flames boiled from what only a moment ago was a fully functioning operating ward. The mess hall and officers' quarters were no longer standing. Tin roofs were blown off, leaving shells of structures.

There was blood. So much blood. And screaming.

Mangled bodies were sprawled across the area. Limbs and cots had been launched high into trees. People were rushing this way and that. Giant branches through the jungle were splitting and falling, cracking like so many bones now broken. It was a tornado of chaos and terror.

Hell couldn't be worse.

Lon—where was he? Where did he go?

She scrambled to her feet, coughing through the smoke, and strained to find him. Panic coursed through her veins as she worked her way over to where he'd last stood. The soldier with the bandaged head—he lay on the ground with his neck at an odd angle. His eyes stared toward the sky, lifeless. She knew he was gone without having to check.

Just up ahead, a man lay beneath a pile of wreckage, his forearm outstretched. The wristwatch, it was Lon's . . .

No—please. God, no!

She rushed forward and fell onto her knees. "Be alive, please be alive," she begged, tossing away pieces of wood and debris. Uncovering his face darkened with grime, she confirmed it was him. Body still, eyes closed.

Fear gripped her chest. Through the sting of tears, she cradled his cheek with trembling hands. "Lon? Lon, can you hear me?"

His eyelids rose a fraction and his hand moved. Lita's breath caught. His blinks continued, his consciousness returning. She frantically searched for visible injuries, incredibly finding none. "What hurts?"

"I'm fine . . . yeah, I'm fine." He pushed himself up, grimacing. "And you—you're okay?"

She managed a nod, then wrapped him with her arms. Her tears fell from relief. Only then did she glimpse a slice in his sleeve, a bloody cut on the back of his upper arm.

She pulled away. "Lon, you're bleeding."

He traced her gaze over his shoulder but shook his head. "It's nothing—it can wait." He glanced past her. "We've got to help the others."

Her universe had shrunk to a tunnel-like view and now suddenly expanded.

They climbed to their feet with effort and joined the frenzied stream of workers in saving any lives they could.

———◆———

Unintentional. That's how the Japanese announcer over the Manila radio waves framed the bombing that killed twenty-three and injured close to a hundred, the majority Filipino workers. Even the CO of Little Baguio claimed to believe the assertion, or maybe he was merely trying to balance the rage of his staff. That or he simply struggled to fathom a cruelty great enough to lead any pilot—any human—to drop a payload on a neutral compound marked with a red cross, fully aware it housed the sick, wounded, and dying. A small number of them even Japanese.

Lita herself was tempted to believe so.

Until exactly seven days later.

For that's when a Japanese pilot ravaged the hospital with a deadlier direct hit.

———◆———

"As a missioner of health, I will dedicate myself to devoted service to human welfare."

The last line of the Nightingale Pledge, a nurse's credo of care for her patients—one Lita was being abruptly commanded to discard—looped through her mind as she scoured the hospital grounds in search of Lon.

"Have you seen Gibs, either of you?" she demanded without preamble.

Slightly shadowed on the verge of dusk, the two corpsmen glanced up from their task of plundering supplies from what little was left of the pharmacy hut. She'd asked the same of a half dozen other people, starting at Lon's quarters. The common response consisted of head shakes or suggestions directing her elsewhere, which the stocky corpsman was now doing by jerking his thumb over his shoulder.

"Up at the gangrene ward, last I saw."

Running out of time, she neglected to thank him while hurrying away. The distance felt twice as long to her still-recovering body. On a low hill, the ward designated for treating gas gangrene was deliberately set apart from the main hospital. The putrid stench, repulsive wounds, and patients' cries of agony made it a spot to avoid whenever possible, unless you were Lon, who regularly volunteered for the detail.

That fact should have occurred to Lita sooner, but she wasn't thinking clearly. How could she possibly after the CO's announcement?

On her way the distant blasts of explosions echoed through the night air, each one causing her to wince. Same for the *pop-popping* of small-arms fire that grew ever closer. Since the second direct hit just two nights earlier, noises to which she'd otherwise become accustomed were making her jittery.

She was rounding a bend to reach the ward when she saw him. Standing thirty yards ahead, Lon was speaking to another medic.

"Lon!" He turned. She broke into a lumbering run, and his expression tightened with alarm. As the other medic departed for the ward, Lon raced toward her. Meeting her halfway, he looked straight down at her uniform. She realized she was still wearing an apron tainted with blood from her shift.

"An order just came through," she told him, clarifying. "They're evacuating the nurses."

He relaxed, if a margin. "Where?"

"Corregidor."

"How soon?"

"Thirty minutes—or must be twenty by now. A bus is coming."

His response rode a sigh. "Thank God."

She straightened, tensing. "Lon, it means Bataan must be falling. They're gearing up to surrender."

"What it *means* is you'll soon be safe."

Frustration rose within her; he was supposed to tell her what to do, how to stay. Yes, she had spent many a night since the start of the war wishing to be with her sisters in the comforts of New York, a haven free of the jungle and constant battles. But the thought of abandoning almost two thousand soldiers, wounded and defenseless, to an encroaching, ruthless enemy— and Lon along with them—wrenched her gut.

"What about the patients?" she insisted. "What about you? What about everyone here?"

"It'll be okay. We'll be fine."

At the hint of doubt underlying his words, it dawned on her that she could simply hide for the night. Surely the transport wouldn't wait for a single person.

As if reading her thoughts, Lon cupped her face with both hands, his tone turning to steel. "You can't be here when the Japs arrive. As a woman, especially a Filipina, you know what they might do to you. And if I'm not able to stop 'em . . ." A mix of fear and anger strained his voice. He paused, leveling himself. "Please. For me, Lita. Go grab your things, and I'll meet you at the bus."

She squeezed her eyes closed, knowing he was right. Hating it.

"We'll be together again," he whispered, and touched his forehead to hers. "I swear it."

Looking back at him then, she found a certainty in his eyes she couldn't help but trust.

"Promise me you'll go," he said, "that you'll do everything to keep yourself safe."

She conceded with a nod, and his lips, at long last, pressed to hers. While indeed filled with longing, it was a kiss that brimmed just as much with hope, a feeling she suspected she would need through whatever lay ahead.

———— ◆ ————

From behind a dusty window, Lita watched the shadowed figures grow smaller as the bus rumbled away. Among those who'd gathered to send the women off were Lon, Dr. Thomson, and many other fellows the fourteen nurses had worked and laughed and survived beside. Each of those men would soon be prisoners of war.

There would be no singing of folk songs to brighten this particular transport. Even Cassie was silent this go-around, same for all the passengers. Taken so off guard by the evacuation, a couple of nurses were wearing pajamas, their hair set in curlers. Another nurse had managed to grab only a toothbrush and comb. Two others had been forced to walk out midsurgery.

In less than a minute the small crowd they'd left behind vanished entirely from Lita's view, though not the mental images of patients waiting in pain, yearning for a nurse's help that wouldn't be coming.

As the bus continued down the main road toward Mariveles, guilt blanketed the air, dark as a shroud. Rosemary, who two nights ago had emerged injured yet remarkably cheerful from her just-decimated ward, only now appeared to shed a tear. Along for the ride was a rather young chaplain with a cleft chin and downturned eyes. Responsible for guiding them all to the docks, he recited a prayer for strength, courage, and safety.

Lita couldn't say how much time had passed before the pounding struck. Literal pounding. Civilians on the road were hitting the bus as it lumbered past. They were begging to be let on, terrified of the coming Japanese forces.

"Take it easy, girls," the driver, a transportation officer, hollered back to the nurses. "I feel terrible for them too. But unless we can fit them all, we can't take a single one."

A feeling of helplessness squeezed Lita's heart. She tried not to look, but the faces in the windows could so easily have been her mother. Her sisters.

Her.

Once finally at the harbor, she clutched her rucksack while staying close behind the chaplain. Through the moonlit bedlam of panicked evacuees, he guided the nurses toward the dock.

A blast roared and shook the ground. Lita instinctively ducked her head and gripped the chaplain's sleeve.

"Ammo dumps," he explained loud enough to be heard over the din. "Allies are blowin' them all. Navy tunnels too. Trying to keep them out of enemy—"

Another explosion cut off his words. The thunderous sound echoed off the cliffs surrounding the harbor, making it seem as if attacks were coming from every which way. It didn't help that Lita couldn't imagine an easier target than the docks.

Her eagerness to clear out of the area ratcheted with every step—until reaching the guarded vessel. In truth, she hadn't afforded it much thought but assumed some sort of hearty, if not large, ship would be ferrying them across the bay, likely with other military folks deemed worth saving. She hadn't envisioned a meager motorboat that the chaplain was now waiting for her to board.

"On we go." He offered a guiding hand.

Her feet refused to budge. A sudden fear stemming from her father's death, a night-fishing accident in a small boat, seized hold. "Are there life preservers?" She scanned the launch.

"It's a short trip. Just a few miles."

In other words, *no.*

Her lungs hollowed and pulse raced. Averse to open water, she'd never become a strong swimmer. In her village, where kids swam as much as they walked, it was one more thing that had made her "different." And now the white smear of moonlight on the blackened water seemed a pit ready to swallow her whole.

"Lita, what's wrong?" a nurse asked from behind.

She glanced back at the group, their concerns but also restlessness evident, especially in those worn from illness. "I'd just prefer to go last." She edged out of the way to let the others file on. As each one found a spot to squeeze into, whether on a seat or on the floor or atop their bags, an alternative glared in Lita's mind.

If the bus was still here, perhaps she could catch it and head back to Little Baguio. She could help the staff care for patients, ones who'd likely need her even more when the Japanese came.

But then she recalled her promise to Lon and, even more so, what he would do to any enemy soldier—or commander—who dared lay a hand on her.

She had no choice.

Several ladies in the launch stared at her expectantly. Being the last nurse on the dock, she worked to slow her quickened breaths, summoned the strength the chaplain had prayed for, and took his hand to board.

———◆———

In the end Lita stayed behind—in the mess hall, that is. After gobbling down a late-night snack in the underground compound on Corregidor, the other nurses from the boat ambled toward the sleeping quarters to rest for the few hours left until morning. Despite the water crossing being relatively uneventful, Lita's stomach remained too knotted to eat. So she sat alone with her food—more canned tomatoes and rice—and sought to reset her nerves.

There was so much to process from the day, the week, she wasn't sure where to begin. She needed to wrangle her emotions, tuck them deep inside.

She needed to stave off thoughts of the lights flashing Morse code from across the bay.

Dot-dot-dot. Dash-dash-dash. Dot-dot-dot.

S.O.S. A plea for help.

All the guesses in the betting pool, it seemed, had been wrong. There would be no reinforcements. No rescues.

Nobody was coming to save them.

"Lita? Lita, is it really you?"

The familiar voice turned her toward the room's entrance, where the presence of her friend nearly stole her breath.

"Penny?" The word barely eked out.

Penny's face, though thinner than before, beamed with a smile that never failed to fill Lita with joy. She had just managed to rise when, quick as a snap, Penny bounded across the mess hall and threw her arms around Lita.

"I was so hopeful when I saw the other nurses settling in. Then I got worried when I didn't see you. One of the girls told me you were here."

"Well, you know me," Lita replied lightly, "always on 'Lita time.'"

Penny drew her head back and laughed. "Figures."

Lita started to laugh, yet without warning, the dividers separating her emotions crumbled, and what came out instead was a half-stifled sob.

"Oh, honey, come here." Penny pulled her into another hug. From a beloved friend, that gesture of comfort caused Lita's well of pent-up tears to overflow. "Trust me, I understand," Penny soothed, and indeed, Lita believed that she did.

NINE

PENNY

Malinta Tunnel, Corregidor Island
April 1942

Penny woke each day to the distant *boom* of aerial bombardment. She worked to the cacophony as well—that cannon-like thunder always above her, in the distance. Ominous, as though a malicious giant were stomping around the island, pounding out his fury right above their heads. She ate every meal to the sounds of war. Showered. Rested. And then, at the end of each grueling day, she slid into her cot and listened as the Japanese warships battered the island again from their posts in Corregidor Bay.

The Japanese were "softening up" the island for invasion. That's what the generals said. The assault was a way of weakening their defenses and their resolve. Sometimes the shelling would go on for hours at a time. Three, four, five. An unrelenting barrage of rumbles and rattles. Then suddenly there would be silence. But instead of relief, it brought a hushed sort of suspicion among the fortress inhabitants.

What was going on out there?

Why did they stop?

The shelling made them anxious and the silence made them paranoid. During those long weeks in April, a malaise settled into the tunnels, like a foul mist that dragged on their spirits and festered into a kind of oppression that divided the tunnel rats—as they'd come to think of themselves—into two distinct camps: those who were afraid to leave the tunnels at all and those who became reckless in their pursuit of fresh air.

It was no surprise, then, that the entrance to the north tunnel was more and more crowded at the end of every shift. Some of the soldiers and nurses—Penny among them—stayed just inside the heavy iron gates, safely within the shadows. They smoked their cigarettes and talked with one another in hushed tones. But others gathered outside, faces turned to the sky, laughing and shouting brazenly in the open air of that spring sunset, as though daring the Japanese to come for them. Had they been on the other side of the island, closest to the bay and the heaviest shelling, she knew they wouldn't be so bold.

Penny watched the crowd of men and a handful of nurses mingle with one another and did her best not to make eye contact with Charley Russell. He leaned against the opposite wall, twenty feet away, deep in his own conversation, but he glanced toward her occasionally.

Lita was still in surgery, or Penny would have dragged her along to act as a buffer, as she'd done most nights since they had been reunited. It wasn't that Charley was overt. All he ever did was offer her a cigarette and ask if she needed anything. She always accepted the first offer and refused the second, while wondering if he would once again find an excuse to touch her. A strand of hair tucked behind her ear. A smudge of dirt wiped off her cheek with his thumb. Perhaps the brush of his fingers against hers while handing her a cigarette. He'd done all of that since their first meeting in February.

It was innocent.

And she was reading too much into it.

But it had been a long time since Penny was touched by a man, and she was not immune to the effects. Even if her feelings toward this particular one were ambivalent.

That's what she told herself as she watched the last sliver of sun dip below the horizon like an orange dropping below the surface of a pond. *Plop.* Gone again for another ten hours.

The fact that Lita liked Charley was a problem. It had taken less than a day in the tunnels for Lita to notice the way they watched each other. She thought Charley was nice. Funny. And she goaded Penny into spending more time with him. Sometimes Lita tried to slip away and give them time alone. Sometimes her plan worked and—when Penny went looking for her later—she would grin.

"*Still hate him?*" she'd ask when Penny got back to the nurses' quarters.

"*Shut up.*"

God, it felt good to laugh. Even over something silly, like a boy.

No. Captain Charley Russell was most certainly a man.

The crowd that night was larger than usual, nearing one hundred, if she had to guess. Out in the bay the *boom* of artillery guns rang out. It wasn't the sound itself that made the crowd flinch and look at the sky—they were far too accustomed to it by now—but how *close* it seemed. Penny's first thought was that the shells were so much louder out here in the open air. Her second thought—as she instinctively moved backward into the safety of the tunnel—was that she could hear whistling.

And then all of her senses shattered with concussive force. It was as though she could see the *BOOM* and taste the pain of being thrown backward into the wall of the tunnel—tangy and iron-tinged, like blood on her tongue—while smelling the shock waves that sent people tumbling to the ground. She could almost feel their shouts of pain, hear the dust that filled the tunnel, her nose, her mouth. Everything out of order, happening at once, nonsensical.

Penny lay there, people scrambling all around her, gasping for breath. Slowly her senses returned, righting themselves to their proper alignment, and she wrapped herself in a ball to avoid being trampled by those scrambling back into the tunnel. She was too dizzy to stand; try and she might get knocked down again anyway.

There *was* blood in her mouth—she'd bitten her tongue—and her ears were ringing, but other than that nothing hurt. Nothing was broken.

"Penny! Are you alright? God, are you okay?" Someone knelt over her, running hands along her back and scalp.

"Yes. I think so. What happened?"

She was lifted to her feet and found herself once more face-to-face with Charley Russell. Bedlam surrounded them, but he ran his hands over her arms, her face, looking for injuries.

"Two shells landed at the tunnel entrance. One was a dud. But the other a direct hit. It smashed the entrance gates shut. That was half the noise. They just slammed together. No"—he set a palm on each of her cheeks and forced her eyes back to his face—"don't look. Two guys were standing there. I mean, *you* were standing there a few seconds before it happened. I thought . . . I . . . you were . . ."

Charley cupped her face as he lowered his forehead and pressed it against hers. She could feel his hands shaking, could hear his ragged breath. And then other things registered as well. Screaming. Shouting. People running.

"I'm going to look now. I have to. It's my *job*."

Charley didn't argue, but neither did he release her face. He simply held it beneath callused fingers as she turned toward the gate. Penny could feel his gaze on her face as she took in the carnage. Two men had been in the way when it crashed together, and now parts of them were on either side. At least a dozen people lay sprawled beyond the gates, tangled and broken and missing various appendages.

Her knees buckled and Charley shifted his weight so he held her up, one arm around her waist.

"Oh God," she said. "I have to get out there. I have to help."

"How?"

Penny turned to him, offended, and tried to push him away. "How I always do!"

"The gate." He pointed with his free hand as his other arm locked tighter around her waist. "You have to wait until they open the gate."

It didn't take long. Even as those nearest the explosion ran back into the mountain, others in the lateral tunnels were running toward the entrance. It took five men to push the gate open, and she was already moving toward the entrance when Charley grabbed her hand.

"*Penny*—"

She knew what he was about to ask, could see that now-familiar expression in his pleading eyes. "What I need right now you can't give me." She yanked her hand free, then ran out into the melee.

———◆———

Fourteen men died outside the entrance that night, but it was the additional seventy wounded that kept Penny and her colleagues up until dawn. Every nurse was yanked from her bed or pulled from her dinner. No one slept. They worked nonstop in the surgery, elbow-to-elbow with one another and the doctors. By that point they had all seen their fair share of war, but this was grueling in a way that most of their other shifts had not been. These were familiar faces, sometimes even friends.

Before long Penny's apron was drenched in blood. It was smeared across her face and the back of her neck where she pushed away clumps of sweaty hair with her gloved hands. At one point she and Lita ended up beside each other. From her time in the jungle, Lita continued to endure fluctuating effects of malaria. She'd grown thin and often tired quickly, as though operating on a drained battery. Lita didn't complain, but her left eye was watering as it always did at the onset of a headache.

"You okay?" Penny asked.

"Yes. Why?"

"Your eye. Another headache?"

Lita shrugged and lifted her shoulder to wipe her eye. "I'm used to it."

"What about your hands?"

She lifted them and curled her fingers into a fist. "Starting to ache. But I'll be fine for a bit longer."

It was astonishing to Penny that something as tiny as a mosquito could bring an illness so terrible that her friend would likely battle dizziness, headaches, nausea, and joint pain for the rest of her life. It was another item on a long list of things she found unfair about their situation.

They worked silently, snipping tattered clothing away from gaping wounds. Snipping the ends of sutures. Snipping off the tips of mutilated fingers and toes. The soft *thud* of amputated digits landing in the bucket between them made Penny woozy. She paused for a moment and grabbed the edge of the table to steady herself.

"Look at him, not the bucket," Lita said, directing her attention back to a middle-aged man on the table before them. He was a civilian contractor—an accountant, she'd been told. Just another innocent man caught up in the awful business of war.

"What's his name?"

"I don't know. But he's wearing a wedding ring. So there's someone waiting for him to come home. Let's make sure he does."

And with that, Penny was back to herself, no longer overwhelmed by concern for her friend or the carnage before them. Together they sewed up the eight-inch gash in his thigh and bandaged his hand, now two fingers short.

"Thank you," Penny whispered when their patient was carted off to recovery.

"For what?" Lita asked, face lifted.

"For not making me feel stupid that I couldn't hold it together just then."

"No one can hold it together all the time." She smiled gently. "Not even you."

Penny blinked hard. Cleared her throat. And turned to another table, another wounded man.

It was well after dawn by the time the final patient was treated. Penny and Lita were the last nurses to leave the surgery. Shattered with exhaustion, hungry, and stiff from being on their feet all night, they stumbled toward the nurses' quarters.

Maude called her name. "Franklin!"

Penny turned. "Yes?"

"Get cleaned up. Get some sleep. But I need you back here by noon to help me with the schedule."

"Yes, ma'am." She used the last of her energy to propel her answer across the room. Then she submitted herself to a crowded, freezing shower and fell into bed with wet hair dripping down the back of her neck.

———◆———

General Jonathan M. Wainwright had—as Penny's father would say—a "face for radio." It wasn't that he was unattractive, per se, but rather that the sum total of his parts, once assembled, was too *long*. As though he'd been stretched out in the hot sun. Long legs. Long arms. Long torso. Long neck. Long nose. Penny looked up in surprise—then jumped to her feet—when he marched his long body into the cordoned-off area that Maude used as a makeshift office.

She and Penny had been going over the week's schedule, assigning the various nurses to their shifts. Since the girls from Little Baguio and Hospital Two had been evacuated to Corregidor, there were extra hands on deck. But after last night's bombing there was even more need for them in the recovery ward—which was now so crowded they were using triple-decker beds.

Josie Nesbit was back on Corregidor and Penny expected her own place as Maude's right-hand woman would be revoked, but her role had simply shifted. She stepped aside for Josie in matters of leadership but continued on in matters of administration as though nothing had changed.

"I want you to assist Josie during the night shift for the rest of the week," Maude had said, just before General Wainwright shoved aside the curtain and ducked into her office.

Penny, already on her feet, looked at Maude with some dismay as she slowly struggled to rise. Her lingering back pain had morphed into a stiffness that plagued her every movement.

"General," they said in unison, saluting.

"Please"—he motioned them to sit—"as you were."

Maude's office was a ten-by-ten area at the end of the lateral hallway used as a medical dispensary. Rather than connecting to one of the larger tunnels, this one ended in a U-shaped bend that led to the tunnel next to it, like the curve at the top of a hairpin. Inside was little more than a folding table, an overhead light, a stack of filing crates, and three chairs. But it was the closest Maude could arrange to having headquarters of her own, and she guarded the space zealously.

Wainwright lowered himself into the third chair and looked directly at Maude. "There's something we need to discuss."

She nodded at Penny. "You can go. I'll finish the schedule later."

"No." Wainwright shook his head. "You're going to need help on this one."

"Should we get Josie?"

Again he shook his head. "She's in surgery. Saw her on the way through. You'll have to fill her in later. And you"—he looked directly at Penny—"are forbidden to speak of this with anyone other than the two of them. That's a direct order."

The urge to swallow was so strong that Penny had to grind her teeth together. "Yes, sir."

He turned back to Maude, then leaned forward so his elbows rested on his knees. "I've received word that two Navy PBY seaplanes are going to slip through the Japanese blockade and reach Corregidor. They have two primary objectives: deliver a load of supplies—mostly weapons and ammunition—and evacuate a small group of passengers."

Maude nodded but said nothing, waiting for Wainwright to continue.

He watched her, performing some silent assessment that Penny didn't understand, then finally sighed. "There will be no wounded among the evacuees."

Maude deflated, as if someone had let the air out of her lungs. She shrank in her chair, withered at the news. "Why not?"

"General MacArthur has given me a list. He's ordering the immediate evacuation of all American civilian dependents, a group of staff experts vital to the war effort, and a few cryptographers. Apart from that he has given me latitude to send a handful of others."

MacArthur himself had been ordered by Washington to leave Corregidor the month before, and he had taken his staff to safety by PT boat and then later on a B-17 to Darwin, Australia. He'd left General Wainwright in command, and the two remained in close communication.

"I see. And who are *you* sending?"

"My oldest officers, those in no condition to endure captivity. I've identified ten. Which brings me to eighty evacuees. We have room for one hundred."

"And you want me to help identify twenty more?"

"Specifically," he said, "I want you to choose twenty of your nurses."

Penny could see the realization wash over Maude's face. "You're sending the women away."

"Yes. As many as I can get off this rock before the Japanese invade."

"My girls know what they signed up for."

"Maybe. Perhaps. Years ago, when they first signed their papers, they might have. But not now that they are serving under combat conditions." His jaw clenched and Penny could hear the steel in his voice. "Not since Nanking."

The Japanese invasion of China and the subsequent sacking of Nanking were well known among the American forces. Five years prior, the Japanese army had taken the city in less than two days and, on direct orders from Tokyo, the soldiers had gone through and executed every man—regardless of age or infirmity—then gone house to house and methodically raped every single woman. Many of them repeatedly.

Looking at him, Penny knew Corregidor would fall. If whispers of Nanking were circulating among the generals, then they had done the math and come up short. She could hear the resignation in Wainwright's voice.

"How long do I have to decide?" Maude brushed the back of her hand across her forehead, shoving aside a section of gray hair that had slipped out of her braid.

"Days at most. Probably less. But you are not to notify them until I give you word that the seaplanes are ready to depart. I need to get them out as quickly and silently as I can. Your nurses will have thirty minutes to collect their belongings and depart. There will be no prolonged farewells. I am trusting you to get your girls out the door with as little fuss as possible. Who you choose is your purview entirely, but if I may . . . ?"

Maude squinted, suspicious of a caveat. "Of course."

"I suggest you send those who are older. Or ill. Or wounded. Those who are already showing signs of distress or mental breakdown. I do not know what is coming for us or how long it will last, but I can tell you from experience who you will need at your side. Those with emotional fortitude and physical stamina. Those who can withstand deprivation." Wainwright looked at Penny again. "Those who are not given over to fear."

Penny wanted to argue that she was *terrified*. She wanted to tell him how she'd nearly fallen apart during surgery last night. That his words— particularly the mention of Nanking—filled her with the kind of empty dread she'd known only twice in her life. But she knew that any mention of the real and tangible fear that gripped her heart might be construed as her asking to be among the evacuees.

In response to her silence Wainwright gave her a single approving nod. "Maude speaks highly of you. I can see why."

"I do have one question," Maude said. "What of my Filipina nurses? Can any of them be included? All of them have malaria. Several are wounded. Two are older than me."

Wainwright did look sorry when he answered. "No. The seaplanes are bound for Australia. It makes no sense to evacuate Philippine nationals to another continent."

Maude was careful with her next words. "But if Corregidor falls and we are taken captive, the Japanese won't just see them as enemies; they will see them as traitors. We cannot protect them here."

"I understand your concern. And it is one that has been considered. But that is an order, Lieutenant Davison. Your Filipina nurses do not get on those planes."

Penny was determined not to let them see her cry, but it was a struggle. Lita had given so much already. It was unfair to exclude her from the chance of rescue for such an arbitrary reason. The idea of her remaining on this wretched island to be left at the mercy of the Japanese horrified Penny. Hot, angry tears pressed at the back of her eyes. They made her throat itch. But she breathed slowly and blinked slower, and neither Maude nor Wainwright were the wiser.

"I'll need your list by tomorrow." He rose to his feet.

Maude stood and saluted, as did Penny.

"Yes, sir," Maude said.

Wainwright paused. "I am sorry."

"For what?"

"That I can't get every one of you out of here." He turned on his heel, swept the curtain aside, and disappeared into the U-shaped curve at the end of the tunnel.

"Not a word of this to *anyone*," Maude said. "Especially Lita. I know you two are thick as thieves. But if you care for your friend, you won't burden her with this."

Penny nodded. "Yes, ma'am."

"I will tell Josie. And the three of us will meet back here in the morning.

Keep an eye on the nurses' quarters. I want to know who is sicker than they let on. I want to know who is barely holding it together. Understand?"

"Yes."

Maude dragged fingers down her face. It was the closest Penny had ever come to seeing her overwhelmed.

"Back to work, then."

When Penny left the office, she went the opposite direction from Wainwright, back through the dispensary, into the main tunnel, and then to the nurses' quarters. It was instinct, Penny told herself, this desire to locate her friend. She would have done the same if Eleanor had been in the tunnels with them instead of God knows where.

Eleanor.

Her foot paused briefly in midair. She had no idea where her friend was or what she faced.

No. Penny shook her head, forcing the thought away. She had too much to deal with. She could *not* add another burden to her mind right now.

Penny found Lita exactly where she expected her to be: still asleep, one arm thrown over her face, ebony hair spread across her pillow. She looked so young, smaller than usual. It wasn't fair. None of this was fair.

—————•—————

The seaplanes came in fast and low across Corregidor Bay just after sunset, when visibility was slight and the engines couldn't be heard by the Japanese warships above the booming thunder of their own cannons. Penny and Josie were assigned to gather six girls each while Maude took eight.

"Maude needs you in the dining room," Penny said to each of them.

"Why?" they asked. "When?"

"Because," she answered. "And *now.*"

As usual the hospital ward was buzzing with activity. It was easy to deliver the order without causing a scene. Penny followed the last of her nurses to the dining room. Once there, she found six women scattered throughout the room who met none of Wainwright's suggested criteria.

All of them young, healthy, and—she could not help but note—romantically involved with high-ranking officers on the island. The other fourteen were all injured, ill, or older.

Penny sidled up to Josie at the back of the room. She tilted her chin toward the pretty young nurses. "How'd they get on the list?"

Josie, inscrutable as ever, merely shrugged. "Maude said she drew the last few names out of a hat."

"Meaning she got vetoed?"

"No, honey, she got *orders*."

Penny couldn't help but wonder who had been left off the evacuation list so that these girlfriends could get on. Rosemary Hogan wasn't present. She had been seriously injured on Bataan when Hospital One took a direct hit. Surgery removed the debris from her hip and shoulder but left scars and debilities she'd carry for a lifetime. If anyone needed off this island, it was Rosemary.

Maude gave a single sharp clap at the front of the room to get the nurses' attention. She held up a stack of papers. "These are orders that state each of you is being reassigned from your current duty. You will take the next available transportation"—she looked at her watch—"in roughly one hour to Melbourne, Australia, where you will await news of your next assignment."

Maude held up a single finger—high—before the unanimous gasp could turn into a gaggle of comments or questions. "You will tell *no one*. You will not say *any* goodbyes. You will pack your things and report back here in thirty minutes. If you are not here, you will not get on those planes. Understood?"

The women nodded, eyes wide, hands over their hearts.

"Good," Maude said. "Go."

Penny waited until the room was empty before she approached Maude. Her cheeks were flushed with some mix of shame and anger.

"Don't say it, Franklin. I didn't have a choice."

"I know," she said. "But they were smiling when you gave them the news."

"So?"

"I'm guessing some of them already knew. Which means their guys told them. And if I know anything about those girls . . ."

Maude sighed. "They'll blab."

General Wainwright, for all of his brilliance, could not anticipate one thing: the nurses had grown close during their time together, and leaving without any kind of goodbye felt like cowardice and betrayal to them. They were friends and comrades and—until that evening—they were in this together, dammit.

Within five minutes other nurses started pouring into the mess hall, pelting Maude with questions. "What's going on? Why not me? Can I go too? Why did you pick her?" And then, of course, came the accusations. "It's not fair! She's only getting off this island because she's pretty! Because she's going steady with that captain. Apparently it's all in who you know," they complained.

Penny watched this chaos from the back of the dining hall, then turned when someone squeezed her hand. Confusion filled Lita's eyes.

"Did you know?" she asked.

Penny nodded. "I was ordered not to tell. Both Maude and Wainwright made me swear."

"There were no Filipina nurses on the list."

"Maude tried. Please believe me. She did try. Wainwright forbade her from including any of you."

She nodded slowly, her lips forming a firm line. Penny wished she could comfort her with reasons that made sense. As none seemed to exist, she simply held tight to Lita's hand while the remaining nurses came to offer their protests.

Maude stuck with her established story as she answered each of the questions and accusations. "I drew the names out of a hat."

Twenty-five minutes later, the group of nurses, along with the rest of the evacuees, were rowed out to an island and boarded onto the seaplanes. Those who dared to go outside stood and watched as the aircraft lifted into the sky and disappeared without a single shot fired by the Japanese.

———◦———

Several days later Penny found herself face-to-face with Charley Russell again, but this time it was in Maude's office instead of their usual rendez-vous spot at the tunnel entrance.

"I didn't mean to eavesdrop!" Penny threw her hands up the moment he stepped around the curtain. She sat behind her supervisor's desk, pretending to finalize the shift schedule for that week. The task was already done, but her mind raced, and she needed a quiet place to think.

His hands were behind his back and his face was flushed, angry. "What are you talking about?"

They stared at each other for several tense seconds before Penny rose from her chair and moved to the other side of the desk. She lifted herself and scooted back so she was sitting on the edge, feet dangling several inches off the floor. No point in lying. It didn't matter now. She was in trouble anyway.

Penny dropped her head and stared at her feet. "I heard you and Wainwright talking a few minutes ago. I took a wrong turn out of the hospital and, instead of going right on the main tunnel into the storage laterals, I accidentally went left and ended up on the other side of the compound, in the quartermaster's area. By the time I realized where I was, I heard your voice and I . . ." She looked up, winced.

Charley tilted his head to the side. "You what?"

"I stopped. And listened."

He took a step closer. "Why?"

Because she was glad to stumble upon him. Because she liked the sound of his voice. Because—even though she was never alone—she was *lonely*. She would never admit that to him, of course. Being a fool and feeling like one were different matters entirely.

"I was curious." She tilted her chin defiantly.

He eased forward another step until Penny's knees brushed against the front of his trousers. His voice dropped, a whisper. "About?"

Penny remembered this feeling. How the air could crackle with sexual tension when a man stepped close. She remembered it. And she missed it. And it scared the ever-loving daylights out of her.

"Why Wainwright sounded so scared."

That wasn't a lie. She *had* gotten lost and found herself steps away from a conversation she had no business hearing.

"Do you have my list?" Wainwright had asked Charley not fifteen minutes ago as she stood in that tunnel, and then, a moment later, she could hear the crinkle of paper being unfolded.

She might have turned on her heel then if not for Charley's voice. Instead of walking away, she pressed herself to the wall and listened. Damn him and his sudden about-face. Why couldn't he have remained cantankerous like he'd been in Manila?

"Having one hundred fewer mouths to feed will help," Charley had said. *"But you can expect additional food shortages starting this week. Beyond that, the situation is grim. We have no helmets. No towels. Blankets, rain-coats, and tarpaulins are gone as well. But that's not the worst of it. The Japanese blockades have been ruthlessly effective. We have thirty days."*

"Before what?" Wainwright asked.

She heard the agitation in his voice. Charley prided himself on being able to distribute what was needed. *"Before Corregidor runs out of power and water."*

"Then we prepare for invasion," Wainwright said. *"We can probably hold off one wave—maybe two—but they will keep dropping troops on the island. And once we lose the beaches, it's only a matter of time."*

Some look must have passed between them because Charley spoke again after a moment. *"Yes. Ammunition for our short-range artillery is limited. A few days' worth once the fighting gets closer."*

"When we lose that, it's surrender or retreat. And if we choose the latter, they will drive us into the tunnels and seal us in. Poison gas. Fire. Starvation. They have a thousand ways to kill us then."

Despair filled Charley's voice. *"Are you telling me this is over, General?"*

Wainwright cleared his throat. *"No. I'm simply telling you we must pre-pare for the worst."*

Penny had taken that opportunity to slip away. If there was more bad news, she didn't want to hear it. But now here Charley was, bad news per-sonified, and she had no escape.

He closed the gap between them and set a finger under her chin. He tilted her face upward. "What did you hear, Penny?"

She told him.

And then she collapsed against him, forehead pressed to his chest. The shirt of his uniform smelled of dust and storage and supplies, exactly the way a quartermaster should. He smelled of stability and provision and she hated herself for liking it.

"I didn't know you overheard. And I'm not here to scold you." He ran his fingers through her curls.

"Why did you come, then?" she asked, her voice muffled against his shirt.

"To ask a favor."

"What?" She lifted her head.

He brought his other hand out from behind his back, and in it was a piece of silk, folded into a neat triangle. He held it out and she took it, curious. She carefully unfolded it and found that she held an American battle flag for the Twelfth Regimental Quartermaster Corps. Emblazoned on it was the insignia of a bald eagle with arrows in its claws set against a background of red and gold.

"This is your flag."

"Yes."

"Why are you giving it to me?"

"Because it's important to me." Charley placed his hands on her forearms. "And because I want you to smuggle it out of here."

"I heard Wainwright," she said. "None of us are getting out of here."

He shook his head. "No. Not the men. Not for a while at least. But you—"

"Don't you dare pretend that it will be different for us! Not when all of the officers whisper about Nanking behind our backs."

"That won't happen. It *cannot* happen. They will send you somewhere, but it won't be to your death. Keep this for me. *Please.*"

"Why?"

"So that I can come find you when this is all over and get it back," he said. Then, much to her astonishment, he kissed her.

It had been years since Penny Franklin had a first kiss, but never had one come so out of the blue.

She froze.

Then she melted.

After that, Penny might as well have been lit on fire for all her inability to keep from kissing him back. Before she knew it, one of his hands pressed into the small of her back and the other was in her hair.

Several long, intoxicating seconds later, she pulled back and stared at him in shock. "I thought you hated me."

"*What?*" he asked, and she was more than a little gratified to see that his eyes were glazed.

"Those damn *forms*! You made me redo them *every* week. You were merciless."

Charley threw his head back and roared. "Is *that* what you thought?"

Penny had never heard him laugh before. "Can't fathom what else I was supposed to think," she said, and crossed her arms over her chest.

"That I wanted to see you again. And the only way to do that was to add typos to the forms myself after you handed them in so you'd have to come back sooner than the following week. I thought it was *obvious*."

"The only obvious thing about any of it was that you were being an ass." He shrugged and Penny felt an irrational impulse to strangle the man she'd just kissed senseless. "You could have simply asked me out."

"You would have said no."

She couldn't deny that, so she said nothing.

After a moment Charley slid his hand from her hair down her left arm, over her hand, and lifted it. He gripped her ring finger between two of his own, then tapped the ghost line where her wedding ring used to be. "I don't know what happened here, and I don't care."

She stiffened. "I'm *always* going to care. One kiss from you doesn't change that."

"That's fine too." He bent his head closer. "But it won't be just one kiss."

It took that long to gain her senses, but Penny finally pulled away. "Yes, it will. Until you prove something to me."

"What?"

"That this"—she waved a finger between them—"isn't some silly wartime crush."

Charley gave her a crooked smile. "How am I supposed to do that?"

Penny hopped off the table and stood to her full five feet seven inches. She glared at him, imperious. "Don't die."

He inched closer and set a hand on each of her hips. "I won't die."

"You have to *promise*."

He bent his head until there was only a breath of air between his lips and hers. The tip of his nose brushed hers, back and forth. "I *promise* I won't die."

He stole the next kiss, quick and certain, then left her standing alone in Maude's office.

Later that night, Penny lay in her cot, wide awake, listening to the artillery shells fall overhead, worried that she'd forced a man to make a promise he couldn't keep. And then she laughed, thinking of that kiss, and what he'd told her all those months ago in Manila.

"Ambidextrous indeed."

———◆———

By the following day Penny could tell that Wainwright and his quartermaster had relayed their orders throughout the tunnels. Dinner that night was a simple concoction of stewed tomatoes, rice, canned meat, and coconut. "Casserole" the cooks called it and denied everyone a second helping. By the next morning drinking water was rationed. And within forty-eight hours, the nurses were told bathwater would be limited to what they could hold in their helmets.

The Malinta Tunnel had once felt like a sanctuary, but now it began to feel like a tomb. Damp. Dark. Suffocating. It smelled of fear and mold and a kind of inevitable despair.

And still, always, ever, the bombs fell overhead.

The nurses were pulled from bed the next morning well before dawn. Those on shift in the hospital were temporarily dismissed as well, leaving the surgeons to hold down the fort. They all sat together watching Maude, waiting for the inevitable. The choice was simple, Wainwright had told her: surrender now, or have the Japanese drive up to the tunnel entrances with their tanks and blow them all to hell.

After the beach landings the night before, eight hundred men lay dead and another thousand wounded, most of them out in the open, away from the hospital where the doctors and nurses could help. Over the last five days, the gunships had dropped tens of thousands of artillery shells on them—sometimes as many as twelve per minute. The United States Army no longer held the island of Corregidor.

In the mess hall now, the nurses knew what to expect, but still, the news hit them hard.

"You were the first group of American and Filipina women to serve under combat conditions. And now you will be our first female prisoners of war. Prepare yourselves accordingly."

"How?" one of the girls choked out. "How do we prepare for that?"

They sat around the tables, huddled together, eyes large, hands in their laps.

"By doing exactly as I say." Maude held out her hand and began to count off the rules, one finger at a time. "First, you will wear your uniforms at all times and you will not take them off to eat or sleep. Your gas masks will remain with you always. I suggest you affix them to your belt.

"Second, make sure your Red Cross armband is visible on your sleeve. We can only hope that the Japanese will recognize the emblem and treat you as noncombatants."

"That didn't stop them in Nanking," another nurse said. Her voice was low and fearful, but it still carried across the room. "None of those women were combatants."

Maude didn't argue with her. "That is why you will—*third*—remain in the sleeping laterals or in the hospital ward at all times. You will not wander through the compound and you will not go outside. Stay in groups. Do not put yourself in any situation where you could be caught alone."

"But are you certain we will be safe *inside*?"

"No." Maude shook her head. "I am not. Once we leave this room, I am not certain of anything."

———•———

At ten o'clock—three hours after the nurses' meeting—General Wainwright took to the tunnel intercom and announced his intention to surrender to the Japanese.

"With broken heart and head bowed in sadness, but not in shame, I report that today I must arrange terms for surrender of the fortified islands of Manila Bay," he began, and Penny watched as her friends and colleagues wept.

But not her. Penny's tears were hardwired not to sadness but to anger, and she did not yet feel the kind of white-hot fury that would unleash them.

Lita sat beside her, their hands once again entwined, knuckles white from the force of holding on to each other. But her hand didn't shake, and when Penny looked at Lita, she saw merely resolve on her face. If only that deep well of calm was something Penny could draw from with a touch.

"We have accomplished all that is humanly possible," Wainwright went on, "and we have upheld the best traditions of the United States and its Army. It is with profound regret and with continued pride in my gallant troops that I go to meet the Japanese commander. Goodbye."

By noon Wainwright had sent Charley Russell and another officer to lower the American flag from the pole outside the main entrance into the Malinta Tunnel. They replaced it with a white bedsheet. The task took a full five minutes to complete, and a bugler played "Taps" through the intercom system the entire time.

Two hours later Wainwright went to meet with General Homma and the Japanese assumed control of the island. Thousands of enemy soldiers—outnumbering the Americans six to one—amassed on the beaches, in the forest, and on ships in Corregidor Bay, providing no means of escape.

The officers marched into Malinta Tunnel, boots stomping in unison against the concrete floors. Several American officers—Charley included—summoned the nurses and had them line up in formation in the mess hall. Maude, Josie, Penny, and seven others were at the front, and behind them were nurses stacked six deep, with the Filipinas at the back, out of view. The less attention directed to them, the better. It took every ounce of self-control Penny had not to turn and look at her friend.

They stood at attention, silent and tense, as the Japanese marched in. Penny dared a glance at Charley, but he stared resolutely at the entrance, jaw clenched, as the five officers gaped in astonishment at the assembled nurses. They had no shame in surveying the women from head to foot, to breasts, to bare calves, up and down, quietly for several seconds.

The commanding officer stepped forward and tilted his head to the side. Another man joined him, slightly behind, and the officer fired off a series of questions in Japanese.

"General Tanaka demands to know who these women are," the interpreter said in perfect English. "Why are they here?"

He looked to Charley for an answer.

"We are nurses." Maude Davison stepped forward. "Noncombatant officers in the United States Army."

The translator relayed this, and they stared in confusion for a moment, then began to laugh, a couple at first, then all five.

"Women have no place in war," the translator said. "It is a man's domain."

Maude gave a tight-lipped smile. "And yet it comes for us regardless."

"Where are you from?" he demanded.

"America."

"*Where* in America?"

They had been briefed about this. The Geneva Convention stated clearly that no prisoner of war had to give any information to their captors beyond name, rank, and country of origin.

"America," Maude repeated.

The translator whispered her response to his commander, then stepped forward. "You are no longer in America. You are prisoners of the Imperial Japanese Army."

The officers moved along the line of nurses, sizing them up again. The translator brought up the rear, and when he got to Penny, he stopped. They were the same height and she stiffened as his eyes locked onto hers. Penny said nothing, didn't so much as budge an inch or avert her gaze, but her heart hammered so hard in her chest that she could hear the blood rushing through her ears.

He bent over slightly and reached for the hem of her skirt, then ran the material through thumb and forefinger, rubbing it softly back and forth.

Only then did she cast a terrified glance at Charley. He appeared angry enough to explode right out of his skin, but she shook her head slightly, warning him to do nothing.

After several long, excruciating seconds, the translator stood upright and pinched the fabric of his collar between thumb and forefinger. He was a slight man, narrow of shoulder with a shaved head. But his eyebrows were full and dark, and they pinched together in confusion. "The same fabric." He shrugged. "A uniform."

Of all the things to convince him! She cleared her throat. "Yes."

"What is your name?" he demanded.

She looked at Maude for permission and, after getting a nod, squared her shoulders and said, "Lieutenant Franklin, United States Army Nurse Corps."

"I am Lieutenant Akibo. And you," he said, "along with ten others, will come with us."

Maude stepped between them. "Where?"

"Outside."

"Why?"

"We have a message to send to your General MacArthur. Like a coward he has abandoned you, and we mean to let him know who is in control of this island now."

———◆———

Penny, Maude, and nine others followed the Japanese out of the room. Charley and the other officers were ordered to stay in the mess hall. She caught his eye as they passed through the door and the glance they exchanged was filled with both longing and terror.

When he took half a step forward, she mouthed the words, *Don't die,* then turned her face away. They were led, single file, into the main tunnel, through the hospital, and outside the tunnel entrance. There the women stopped short, horrified. The ground was littered with bodies. At least a dozen dead, bloated soldiers. They were covered in flies and stank so badly the smell cloyed in their nostrils and made their eyes water.

"Line up," Akibo told them.

As they did so, another Japanese officer stepped forward with a camera in his hand. An armed guard with a bayonet affixed to his rifle was placed on each end, and they were told to smile. None of them did.

"We are going to send this picture to MacArthur to prove that you are alive." Akibo paced in front of them.

"Sounds like a hostage photo," one of the girls whispered.

As he passed Penny said, "You speak very good English."

"I graduated from one of your universities."

"Which one?"

"Harvard," he said, then moved on.

The nurses were forced to stand in the hot sun for ten minutes while the photographer took an entire roll of film. He took individual and group shots, sometimes getting close enough that Penny could smell his breath. The nurses barely moved and never smiled, and when it was over, they were told to go back inside the tunnels.

"And now," the translator said, "you will do exactly as you're told."

Penny woke with a knife to her throat.

The nurses were startling awake all around her, gasping in fright at the nearly two dozen Japanese soldiers spread throughout their quarters. They leaned over beds, leering. They pawed through bags and trunks, plucking what they wanted and scattering the rest around wantonly.

No screaming, no crying. Her mantra returned in full force, and Penny repeated it silently as her heart thudded in her chest.

She tried to scoot back, but the soldier—she now recognized the bald head and dark brows of Lieutenant Akibo—stood above her. He stepped closer and pressed his blade a little harder against her skin. She froze, paralyzed by the reality of what was happening.

"No," she whispered.

He laughed quietly. "Who are you to give orders to a lieutenant in the Japanese Imperial Army?"

She tensed and drew back. The fact that they were of equal rank seemed irrelevant to him. "Do not touch me."

He leaned closer, inch by inch, until she could feel the warmth of his breath on her face. "Ask nicely. Say, '*Please*, Lieutenant Akibo.'"

Penny could not think of a single time in her life when she had ever begged for anything. Instead she ground her teeth together and glared at him. "Do. Not. Touch. Me."

Slowly, Akibo reached down with his free hand and undid the first button of her shirt, then he dragged the tip of his knife down the skin of her neck, her clavicle, and dipped it under the gold chain of her necklace. He could have flicked the blade upward and ripped it off her body, but instead he ran his fingers around her neck and unclasped the lock with thumb and forefinger. Penny shrank from his touch.

All around her, guards were rifling through the nurses' belongings, taking what they wanted, laughing, pulling rings from fingers and personal tokens from bags. But Penny scooted back on her elbows, horrified as Akibo clenched his knife between his teeth and then strung her necklace around his throat. She watched the golden nugget disappear beneath his shirt.

"It is mine now." Akibo leaned over her again, knife held casually at his side. "And before long, you will be as well."

TEN

ELEANOR

Santo Tomas Internment Camp, Manila
May 1942

W hen Eleanor had first arrived at Santo Tomas Internment Camp—
everyone called it the STIC—the tumbledown shanties all along
the perimeter of the university grounds seemed the worst possible way to
be housed, but within a few weeks Eleanor and all the other Navy nurses
were ready to get out of the densely crowded dormitory and into one of
their own.

There was plenty to do now in the infirmary, where they had their own
toilets and sinks and could eat from the hospital kitchen rather than standing in the hours-long line at the mess. When Laura announced within a few
weeks of their arrival that she had commandeered a sizable shanty for them,
her eleven nurses agreed they were ready to move into their own space. The
shanty leaked when it rained and lizards, salamanders, and other critters
crawled inside, but they didn't mind. Or at least not too much.

Though their incarceration seemed to endlessly roll on, day after day
after day, the camp population nevertheless nourished the hope that the
American and Filipino troops would prevail. News from the outside came
from visitors to the fence and also from the *Manila Tribune*, copies of which
would find their way into the camp, but it was a newspaper no one could
trust. One headline, for example, had announced that California's shores

had been heavily shelled, and it caused no small amount of trepidation. Internees with hidden radios had to quell rising fears that the United States was fighting for control at home as well as in the Philippines.

When the *Manila Tribune* announced that Bataan had fallen, not one prisoner wanted to believe it. It wasn't until the camp public-address system announced that American troops on Bataan had indeed surrendered that the internees were finally convinced. The next day, the paper showed a photograph of two U.S. military generals on Bataan standing in submission before Japanese officers. For days afterward, as Eleanor worried for Penny's and Lita's safety, starving civilians—mostly women and children—flooded into Santo Tomas for shelter.

One of the women, a British veterinarian, had helped Army nurses in the two field hospitals. As Eleanor dressed the woman's many insect bites, she told Eleanor that she'd been at Hospital One the day General Wainwright ordered everyone to the island fortress of Corregidor and its warren of tunnels.

"Did you meet an Army nurse named Penny Franklin?" Eleanor asked her in a hurried tone. "Or a Filipina nurse named Lita Capel? They're my friends and I haven't heard from them since before Pearl. Did you see them? Are they alright?"

"I'm sorry," the woman said. "I never met anyone by those names. But that doesn't mean they weren't there. Hospital One was chaotic most of the time. We kept having to adapt. I might have worked near one of your friends and not known it."

Disappointment and renewed worry consumed Eleanor's thoughts long after the woman left.

Only a month later the *Manila Tribune*'s bold headline read "Corregidor Falls." The two-page spread included a photograph of General Wainwright, flanked by Japanese military, his head bowed in subjugation. The occupation was complete. The Philippines had fallen to the Japanese invaders. General MacArthur had left the islands, but thousands of his men were now prisoners of exultant Japanese occupiers.

There was no rescue coming for them. The war was not ending; it was just beginning.

Eleanor had been a prisoner for four months. Weeks upon weeks of deprivations and discomforts and disappointments had colored each day of their captivity. But it felt different now with the Philippines completely under Japanese control. Before, there had been American soldiers—brave warriors—battling on the islands for their release. Now there was no one.

"Who is fighting for us now?" Eleanor lamented quietly to Peg as she lay on her cot next to her friend and swatted mosquitos and tried to fall asleep.

But no answer emerged from her friend. Peg had drifted off.

Eleanor already knew the answer to that question.

They were fighting for each other now.

———◆———

Within days, as news came of a deadly prisoner march up the Bataan Peninsula, more and more sick and wounded internees were added to the STIC. One of the commandants had suggested the medical staff administer lethal injections for the chronically ill and permanently crippled. When the fleet surgeon replied that he and every other doctor there had pledged to do no harm and could not violate that oath, the commandant respected this.

Eleanor had nearly cried with relief. The thought that a Japanese commandant could so cavalierly encourage the deaths of dozens of sick people, as if they were little more than chattel, was chilling. What other terrible things would the enemy find easy to do?

Over the next few weeks, Eleanor waited to hear news of what had become of the Army nurses, and no one had a definitive answer. They were likely headed to the STIC, but Laura hadn't been advised as to when and she didn't know how many of them had survived that final battle on Corregidor.

Eleanor took to sending up little arrow prayers at night in her bed, pleading that God would watch over her two friends wherever they were. It was the only way she could stay connected to them—and she *had* to stay connected to them. Trusting she would see Penny and Lita again was one of the few hopes she had now.

She wanted to believe there was still a life waiting for her beyond that present moment, but it was difficult to imagine.

Eleanor endeavored to take each new day as an opportunity to see herself as having moved forward one more step toward the life that awaited her beyond this one. John Olson occasionally came to mind in weaker moments when she wished she could go back in time to when life—and her desires— were simpler.

On one May afternoon she was headed to the nurses' shanty to rest before her evening shift when a woman cried out in pain from within. Had one of her friends been bitten by a snake or stepped on a shard of glass? She hurried in to help, but even as Eleanor pulled the curtain aside, she could see that the female voice she'd heard did not belong to a fellow nurse, nor was she hurt.

The partially clothed woman on Eleanor's own bunk, lying underneath a partially clothed man, hadn't cried out in pain but in pleasure. Two internees had chosen the nurses' shanty for stolen moments of clandestine lovemaking. It was the only way spouses, lovers, and camp prostitutes could have sex. The Japanese had forbidden any kind of sexual intimacy between the internees, even between husbands and wives. People who wanted to have relations had to find clever ways of accomplishing it, including, it seemed, using shanties whose owners happened to be elsewhere for the moment.

The couple were so engaged in their lovemaking they did not see or hear Eleanor, and she backed out silently as she let the curtain fall. She was shocked by what she had seen—but also intrigued, curious, and mystified. Eleanor did not know the delights the couple were experiencing; she only knew what it was like to ponder them. She had only ever been kissed, and she had never seen anyone making love before. She had never seen the coupling, the synchronized movement, the obvious enthrallment.

It surprised her that what the man and woman were doing did not look entirely pleasurable, even though she could tell by their voices that it was. They both sounded as if on the verge of happy tears.

The thought came to her unbidden. This was the kind of intimacy John had with his bride. A second thought followed as quickly and as unplanned: John's lips on her own, his touch on her body instead of his wife's. The spontaneous imagining was so strong and so deep, Eleanor scrunched her eyes shut and spun away from the shanty.

And yet it was exquisite to imagine.

The first time Eleanor had felt John's touch—just his hand on hers—was the day she brought over to the parsonage a plate of *lefse*—a soft Norwegian flatbread made from a Lindstrom family recipe. She saw in her mind's eye John in front of the parsonage on that March morning, wearing not his vestments but jeans and a blue flannel shirt.

She had taken a leave of absence from her hospital in the Twin Cities to care for her sick mother so her father could tend to the daily needs of his dairy herd. Reverend John Olson was the new minister at the Lutheran church in her hometown of Silver Lake, and he was young, single, and handsome. He'd come over to the Lindstrom house several times already since Eleanor had arrived to visit and pray with her mother.

Eleanor had fancied John from the moment she'd met him. He was attractive, to be sure, but he was also kind and compassionate, told jokes in his sermons, cooed over babies, helped his elderly parishioners in and out of their cars, smiled and waved to everyone, and seemed to possess a heart of gold. He seemed to be the very embodiment of the kind of man she'd hoped to meet one day and marry.

A brave sun had melted much of the snow on the ground that day, and John was sanding the trim on the parsonage's window frames and siding. Beside him was a ladder and tarps.

"Going to do a little painting?" she said with a smile. He was clearly preparing to paint the whole outside of the house.

He laughed. The laugh was music. "Just a little. As soon as the weather turns for good."

"You know, I think the deacon board would be happy to take care of that for you."

"Yeah, they already offered," he said. "But I don't mind doing it. I kind of like painting houses. It's how I earned money when I was in seminary. I like covering up something tired and distressed with something beautiful and fresh. It's a nice way of reinventing things."

"I suppose you're right about that. What color will you go with?"

He glanced up at the house, squinted, and assessed, and then looked back at her. "I was thinking maybe a pale blue?"

"I'm kind of partial to yellow," she said. "It's such a happy color. And it looks nice with white trim. And those"—she pointed to the skeletal shrubs peeking out from the thawing ground—"are peonies, and the prettiest shade of pink when they bloom. They'll pair very nicely with yellow."

"Huh. Maybe you're right. Maybe yellow is the way to go."

"Are you sure you're not going to want some help with it?" she asked, feeling a boldness that had surprised her. "With the painting? I'd be happy to lend a hand."

"Oh, I couldn't possibly ask you. I know you're here from Minneapolis to help out with your mother."

Eleanor knew he was right. Although her mother was recovering, she was still abed most days. Still, Eleanor wanted very much to help him, wanted to be near him, wanted to paint his house. With him.

"Is that a plate of brownies by chance?" he said with a bit of a frown, pointing to the covered plate in her hands. "Not that I mind them of course, but"—he touched his waistline—"everyone in this town is such a good cook, and I'm starting to wonder if I'll continue to fit into my robe."

She smiled. "It's lefse, and my mother's recipe. She wanted to thank you for coming to visit and pray with her, so she asked me to make you some. You won't find any better lefse here in Silver Lake. That's what my dad would say. Actually, though, everybody makes lefse here. And it's all pretty much the same."

He moved toward her and reached out to take the plate. "I love lefse." His warm fingers brushed against hers. "I had a great-aunt who used to make it."

He was close enough to her that Eleanor could smell the soap he'd used that morning and see the sun glinting on flecks of gold in his hazel eyes. He seemed to stop and stare at her, too, in that moment. It felt like a very long time before he actually took the plate from her and stepped back, the touch broken.

She had seen John at church on the following Sundays when he stood outside and greeted everyone after the services. When he took her hand to shake it, she felt an electric connection between them. It happened each time. She hadn't been able to describe it to herself any other way.

How many times had she relived that day at the parsonage? Those moments on the steps of the church when they shook hands? Too many.

Those moments had been real, but they were not reality, and that was different. There truly was no purpose to her reliving old moments with John or imagining new ones with him. In fact, if anything, thinking of him was actually an unraveling, an erasing. Every forward step she had taken since that day he told her he was marrying someone else was snatched away when she allowed herself to relive that day outside the parsonage, the moments on the church steps, and the imagined time they'd never had.

She needed to stop.

The war was depriving her of so many things, but it wasn't depriving her of her thoughts, and if she did not take control of them, they would be her undoing.

"No more," she whispered to herself. Eleanor took several steps away from the shanty and positioned herself in the hapless shade of a derelict banaba tree. A few minutes later the lovers emerged, clothed. The man held the woman's hand as he looked this way and that to make sure their getaway went unnoticed. Eleanor could see the glint of their wedding rings as she peered from behind the tree. The couple smiled at each other, holding hands, and then hurried away.

When they were gone, she went inside the shanty to do what she had come there for. The couple had straightened to precision the coverlet on Eleanor's bed and fluffed her makeshift pillow.

It was as if they had never been there and Eleanor had imagined the whole thing.

ELEVEN

LITA

Malinta Tunnel, Corregidor Island
May 1942

L et go!"
      The voice wakened Lita with a jolt. Her head shot up and heart thumped. She quickly surveyed her surroundings, grounding herself. The darkened nurses' quarters, like all the laterals, were as stuffy as they'd been since her arrival a month ago, and seemed particularly so after the Japanese took control, making topside for the nurses off-limits.

"No, you . . . you can't . . ."

Given the tone and garbled murmurings, Lita didn't have to leave her spot on a lower bunk to know whose nightmare they belonged to—yet again. She flopped her head back onto her pillow. As if the Japanese soldiers weren't enough to keep her on edge, she had to endure Reyna in the very next bunk.

While of course Lita was relieved all eighty-some nurses had been safely evacuated here from Hospital Two well before Corregidor fell, the Army's grouping of the Filipinas in the same sleeping area wasn't a choice she relished.

Lita rolled onto her side and closed her eyes. The ragged rhythm of breaths rising and falling from the other nurses continued, though rustling suggested a few were now tossing in their beds.

"I—stop . . . no . . . get back . . ."

Oh, good gracious. Since the island shelling had ceased four days ago—among the very few benefits of Wainwright's surrender—the quiet amplified Reyna's verbalized dreams. Typically she would startle herself awake, or her mumblings would wane long enough for Lita to nod back off. Tonight the girl seemed destined to disturb the whole lateral.

With a groan Lita shoved off her blanket and in her khakis pushed herself to stand. She was still somewhat weary from her bouts with malaria. A second looting raid by the Japanese the night before hadn't helped. Add to that Reyna's nightmares—granted, worthy of sympathy if plaguing any other nurse—and Lita's final layer of patience dissolved.

Navigating by the room's nightlight, she stepped toward the incoherent mumblings. The nurse on the upper bunk had covered her head with a pillow rather than prod Reyna just below, surely not wanting to make her an enemy. For Lita it was too late for that.

She nudged Reyna's arm to no effect. Nudged again with more oomph.

Reyna's eyes shot open. She recoiled with panicked breaths as if under attack. "No, don't, *please* . . ." The utter terror on her face, a striking contrast to her standard unflappable composure, unexpectedly defused Lita's irritation.

"You're having a nightmare."

Reyna's attention skittered around the room, confirming. She relaxed her shoulders, her arms. Her panting slowing, she looked up at Lita.

"You're okay," she assured her.

Reyna appeared about to nod but her expression only firmed. "Of course I am." Then she flipped over to lie facing the other way.

The girl was something else.

Lita's fingers curled and temperature rose, in this instance not from illness. Now there was no chance of falling back to sleep.

Fuming, she headed out of the lateral and toward the latrines, not that she had a pressing need for a bathroom visit, but walking with purpose to cool off was a better option than belting out a scream. Besides, lying in bed wide awake would lead her to dwelling on Lon and her fears and her hunger. And whatever the Japanese had in store for them all.

She had just turned into another corridor when a noise caught her ear.

It was a snip of a voice. Clearly a grunt from Tojo. The monkey, mockingly nicknamed after Japan's prime minister, had recently made the compound his part-time home. Whereas the patients considered the animal amusing, the nurses ruled him a menace for good reason. His antics included stealing their soap, upending their belongings, and even smearing mud over their bedding.

Ready to shoo the monkey toward the tunnel entrance, Lita traced the sound to an apparent storage area curtained off. She pulled back the drape hung from a rope and discovered a small bedroom. Through the dimness she found not Tojo but a man, Japanese and wearing nothing but a towel around his waist. He was struggling to climb atop a woman in bed attempting to fight him off.

"Stop!" Lita burst out. "Leave her be!"

His face snapped toward her, and something slipped from his hand and clattered on the floor. The woman broke away and ran to Lita's side. Lita knew her only as Mary. A civilian nurse who'd been added to the group just before Corregidor fell. Why she was sleeping apart from the others, Lita didn't know. But Mary was still fully dressed in her khakis, thank heavens.

The man merely looked at them both, stunned by the disruption. After a moment, he scooped up the object he'd dropped—a knife—and held the towel in place with his other hand. Lita sensed an embarrassment about him, having been caught. A cowardliness, now that he was outnumbered.

Hoping she was right and not wanting to tempt him with a chase, she stood tall with chin lifted in lieu of a customary bow. She even raised a protective arm across Mary and felt her trembling.

Slowly he approached, and Lita's heart resumed its thumping. Once within several feet, he simply turned and slipped past the partially open curtain. Yet not until he disappeared around the corner and into the main lateral did Lita release a deep exhale. She glanced at Mary, who was expelling quick breaths.

"It's alright. He's gone."

Mary nodded. With a shudder she started to calm while gazing toward the bed. "This was our room, my husband's and mine. He's a colonel, but he's up above, a POW now." Her eyes moistened. "He said it would keep me safe, inserting me in the Nurse Corps here."

Lita rubbed the woman's shoulder. "Well, from now on, you're sleeping with the rest of us. Okay?"

Mary required no convincing.

———————◆———————

Within a few short days, the verdict came in. The Japanese commandant claimed to have completed a thorough investigation into Mary's reported assault and arrived at his conclusion:

The assailant was American.

Or Filipino.

But most certainly not one of his honorable men.

Maude Davison nearly blew a gasket. Had Tojo the monkey not just been killed by a Japanese soldier in a mishap, no doubt the commandant would have named the animal, too, as a suspect.

If there was the faintest question of whether the accusation was given any true weight, it was squashed by the Japanese guards who formed a new habit of snickering while strolling by the nurses' quarters in their so-called G-strings.

Lita might have been infuriated if not for another issue taking precedence: food. As in a lack of it. Rations were dwindling faster than ever. When weevil-infested cracked wheat became the standard cooked breakfast, the nurses turned to stealthy foraging. A path through a crawl space was thankfully discovered, leading to a lateral that Allied soldiers had stocked with canned goods. Josie Nesbit took charge as a regular courier.

Lita could see why the Filipinas who'd served under her at Hospital Two called her "Mama Josie." Especially in light of what she'd done for them. For Lita, too, as it turned out. Word had it the American commanders would just as soon have left the Filipina nurses back on Bataan had Josie not put her foot down.

Viewed as dispensable by one side, traitors by the other, they didn't seem to belong anywhere. A frustration with which Lita was all too familiar.

Still, she pushed away the thought, a task that came with genuine ease when, three weeks into June, Dr. Cooper announced a personal feat. He'd somehow convinced the Japanese commandant to allow the medical personnel and patients to relocate topside, to a bombed-out shell of what was once Fort Mills Hospital. Not only that, no Japanese soldiers were to enter without the commandant's explicit permission.

Compared to the cave the medical staff had been living in, the fresh sea air and view of the blue sky felt like utter paradise. It was precisely what Lita's body and mind needed to further heal. Same for all the others. Scouting parties sought out greens to eat. Freshly picked gardenias adorned washbasins. Netting offered protection from mosquitos. A salvaged radio delivered updates of the war.

Spirits were so high Lita didn't think they could raise much more—save over a total Allied victory—until the commandant paid a visit bearing gifts. Proudly he presented a large iced cake and beer. Why he did it Lita couldn't say, but she wasn't about to turn either one down. Even beer sounded heavenly after six months of drinking warm, chlorinated water.

Seated together under a star-filled sky that evening, refreshed by the light breeze, Lita and Penny alternated sips from a shared bottle of beer. Slowly they savored their pieces of cake until they each had one bite left, and Lita hesitated. It was her last sample of normalcy for who knew how long. Maybe ever.

Breaking into a grin, Penny picked up her final bite and held it up, knocking away the tension as she always could. "Seeing as we got cake and a bit of celebration, you know what that makes today?"

Lita had to think for only a second. "A partial HAM Day?"

"Indeed."

Brightening, Lita raised her own final bite. "To Eleanor."

"To Eleanor," Penny echoed. Then, smiles broadening, they tapped their pieces together like a daiquiri toast from another life and enjoyed every last crumb.

———◆———

One week later, the respite in paradise ended.

Lita rocked with the sway of the small boat, her pack shifting on her lap. The morning sun on the bay promoted a calm that was impossible to feel.

"We'll be okay," Penny whispered from the seat beside her. With the awaiting ship just a hundred feet off and a destination that could only be guessed at, Lita presumed her friend was referring purely to the trip ahead, until she added, "I'm not about to let either of us drown."

Lita became aware, then, of her own grip on the edge of the boat. She appreciated Penny's support and her evident memory regarding Lita's father, even now with so much else at stake.

At the freighter named the *Lima Maru*, one after the other, the nurses climbed up the long rope ladder. Lita pushed herself to tackle each wobbly rung, propelled by thoughts of sharks somewhere in the water below. She found relative relief in reaching the upper deck, where Penny rejoined her by settling on the floor. Surrounding them, a good number of nurses took to lying down, exhausted or nauseated or feverish from one illness or another.

As the anchor lifted, a Japanese officer greeted the group in English, offering rice cakes and tea.

"Where are we going?" someone asked. "What do you plan to do with us?"

"You are going to very nice school," he said with a bright smile. "To use like hospital. Many medicine there. Near Manila."

Lita bristled. She recalled their last days in the city. The bombs and death and destruction. All in a place she'd once viewed as a bustling, exciting metropolis compared to her island home.

"First, your patients will go," he continued. "You will be happy."

"Oh, we'll be happy," Penny muttered, "when you've all raised your white flags and we pitch your G-strings into a bonfire."

Lita suppressed a laugh. The Filipinas were fortunately being treated the same as the rest of the nurses, and she didn't want to jeopardize that. She couldn't help but smile, though, when Penny winked at her. It was a moment of needed levity as they pulled away from Corregidor.

An hour later, Penny helped Lita to her feet to view the destination that other nurses were gawking at. She soon discovered why. The once-pristine

Manila harbor had devolved into a graveyard of semi-submerged ships surrounded by garbage and debris. Her heart withered.

Once the patients were unloaded onto trucks, the male medical staff from Corregidor were lined up by rank and ordered to walk behind the slowly departing vehicles. The men would be paraded through the streets. A petty show of humiliation.

A vision of Japanese civilians coming out to cheer made Lita seethe, just as an enemy officer shouted orders at the nurses. He motioned toward a trio of idling flatbed trucks that would presumably follow to the converted hospital. So they queued up and helped each other board. After Penny stepped on and angled back, hand outstretched to Lita, a sudden grip on Lita's sleeve tugged her sideways.

"Acchida!" A soldier waved his rifle to indicate something behind her. And that's when she noticed: the Filipinas were being herded onto a bus.

Only the Filipinas.

The soldier ushered Lita with a shove. As she stumbled into a walk, she glanced back at Penny, who'd covered her mouth with one hand, her eyes reflective of the angst in the pit of Lita's stomach. Mama Josie stood on the neighboring truck, looking no less aghast.

Lita wanted to at least wave toward Penny, a sign not to worry, but a harder shove forced her up the bus steps. The armed guard followed her in. She took a seat in the first row beside a nurse whose cheeks glistened with tears. With all twenty-six Filipinas rounded up, the door squeaked shut and the driver pulled away. He steered them in the opposite direction the patients had gone.

The bus bumped and rattled down a series of streets. The city appeared as worn as expected, its sparkle further dulled by the Japanese soldiers on nearly every corner.

When at last the bus slowed, Lita glimpsed Reyna across the aisle. The rare sight of fear in her face was enough to launch dread through Lita. Other nurses whispered and pointed toward the destination ahead. Spanning a dozen square city blocks and encased by fencing and twelve-foot stone walls, the landmark in the heart of Manila was known for its pestilence and cruelty.

The notorious Bilibid Prison.

TWELVE

PENNY

Santo Tomas Internment Camp, Manila
July 1942

T he huge iron gates rattled open. On either side of them ran a masonry
wall—fifteen feet high—topped with loops of wicked-looking barbed
wire. The wall continued for another five city blocks in each direction, then
turned a corner, fencing in the entire sixty-acre campus of what had once
been Santo Tomas University, a Dominican academy founded over three
hundred years earlier. Penny could not take her gaze from those sharp, tri-
angular points of wire as the truck lumbered through the gates and passed
the armed guards standing in their little nipa huts.

It had been an hour since they'd gotten off the ship that took them from
Corregidor. After an hour in the blazing sun, her pale skin—hidden for so
long in the tunnels—now burned along the bridge of her nose and the back
of her neck. When the trucks carrying the Army nurses pulled away from
those holding Lita and the others, Penny's heart sank. They had been told
that the nurses would remain together. Instead the Japanese cordoned off the
Filipinas and sent them away with the doctors and wounded medics to some
unknown hell. For Penny the sight was worse than all the bombs and broken men she had tended. For all she knew, Lita had been sent to her death.

No, she thought, gnawing on the corner of one thumbnail, *that can't
happen. I won't believe it.*

The remaining Army nurses sat, thirsty and exhausted, waiting to see what would happen to them now. Many of them were ill and injured. They were prisoners of war, and even though they had known that fact in theory, it didn't sink in—perhaps not really—until those three flatbed trucks slid through the gates and they saw the barbed wire looming above them.

Once inside, two long lines of people formed along the plaza. Penny heard their shouts of welcome and of concern. These were not Japanese guards but civilian internees, raised on tiptoes to stare at them, waving their arms to catch the nurses' attention. Some stepped forward, offering pieces of fruit—mangos and coconuts and bananas—and when the nurses leaned forward to take the offerings, the onlookers begged them for information.

"Where have you come from?"

"Have our boys survived the death march?"

"Did they leave our soldiers alive on Corregidor?"

"Where are the doctors who were stationed there?"

"John Dunbar!" This was shouted by a pretty young woman who first appeared rather plump. It was only when she stepped forward that Penny realized she was pregnant. Alarmingly so. "Is my husband alive? Have you seen him?"

"*Urusai!* Silence!" Captain Akibo yelled as he jumped down from the cab of the lead truck. He lifted his rifle, bayonet glinting in the sun, and waved it at the crowd. "Move back!"

They eased away as he glared, first at the internees and then at the nurses, before he climbed back into the truck. Akibo had kept a wary eye on them the entire trip across Manila Bay and into the city. Penny felt that eye drift to her often, and more than once she saw him rub the gold chain he had taken from her between his thumb and forefinger, his dark gaze hidden beneath the brim of his cap.

The throng of curious onlookers stretched along the main entrance, and the women took in their desperate faces before the trucks veered away and drove toward a huge rectangular building in the center of the campus. It was a pale, weathered limestone, three stories tall, with a two-story tower on top and then, perched above that, a cupola. Almost two blocks long and sixty feet tall, Main Building dominated the campus and could be seen for miles in every direction.

"Out. Get your things," Akibo ordered, then waved a hand at Main Building. "Go inside."

Penny helped Maude down from the truck and frowned when she stifled a cry of pain. Every bump in the potholed road from the harbor had brought a wince, and Penny feared that the thin sheen of sweat on Maude's upper lip had less to do with the heat than it did with pain. But still, she insisted on carrying her pack, refusing Penny's help, and lifted her head in defiance as they were ordered to form a line.

The nurses were led up the concrete steps and through the entrance of Main Building. Here, too, crowds had gathered, men and women lining the hallways to get a look at the nurses and to ask about loved ones left behind on Bataan. Again the guards ordered silence but were ignored, a trail of whispers and questions following Penny down the marble hallway. She had no answers, no good news, and feared she would find none of her own in this place, so she kept her gaze on the tile floor and spoke to no one.

The nurses carried only the packs they had taken with them to Corregidor and wore—as they'd been ordered—their Army boots and khaki uniforms with the Red Cross armbands. Sweaty and disheveled, they were led into an empty room and ordered to sit on the floor. The walls were a faded yellow and paint peeled off in thin, brittle chips.

Penny scooted against the wall and occupied herself by picking off flakes with her thumbnail. She leaned her head back, following the lightning-bolt pattern of a crack in the plastered ceiling as she waited her turn for the guards to register her and check her pack for weapons.

Her eyelids grew heavier and she surrendered to the pull, closing them altogether, slumping against the wall. It was the first day since Christmas that she hadn't worked a shift in the hospital, hadn't assisted with surgery or kept to a strict schedule, and her body responded to this aberration by shutting down.

Penny didn't know how long she'd been asleep when Captain Akibo kicked her boot. She jerked awake to find him looming over her, a clipboard in hand with an armed soldier at his side.

Akibo pointed at her and demanded her name and rank.

He knew this already, but she humored him anyway. "Penny Franklin. Lieutenant, United States Army Nurse Corps."

Her name was scrawled onto the clipboard, and the second soldier lowered his rifle so the point of the bayonet made a small indent on the olive canvas of her rucksack.

"Empty it," Akibo ordered.

Groggy and annoyed, Penny shifted onto her knees, undid the clasp, and dumped the contents onto the floor in front of her. A change of clothes. Underwear. A bag of cosmetics. Sanitary pads. One novel. Lotion. He rifled through her belongings, poking at them with the tip of his bayonet, scattering her intimate things across the floor. Both he and Akibo seemed disinterested, and she thought they would move on, but Akibo bent and picked up a rectangular piece of silk. He raised it from the pile and turned it this way and that, staring at the insignia.

The quartermaster's flag.

Oh God.

Although not as recognizable as the American flag, it was still a sign of defiance. The Japanese had burned every U.S. military flag they found when they took control of Corregidor, with one exception.

Penny had stuffed it to the bottom of her rucksack the night Charley kissed her and hadn't thought about it since. Him? Yes. Often, in fact. But the flag? It wasn't a living, breathing, wounded man in need of care and had slipped from the forefront of her mind. She and Charley were at an impasse anyway. He would get it back, but only if he didn't die. It had never occurred to her that she might be the one to die trying to keep her promise.

But now she could see the wheels turn in Akibo's mind, could see comprehension gather in his eyes. The eagle. The arrows. Recognizable symbolism of the United States Army. He'd studied at Harvard, after all; he wasn't stupid.

Penny jumped to her feet and, without thinking about it, yanked the flag out of Akibo's hands. He was so startled by the impertinence that he stood there, mouth agape, before drawing back a hand to strike her.

"Wait! Look," she said and did the first thing that came to mind.

Penny swung the flag around her shoulders as though it were a shawl and tied the ends in a knot right at her collarbone. She preened a bit, this way and that, just to get her point across, then said, "See? *Clothing.*"

There were no grommets in the flag. Charley had thought through that at least and removed the small metal circles used to raise it up the flagpole. Instead there were only small slits in the fabric, and she'd taken care to place the knot so they couldn't be seen. Her little display had drawn an audience, however, and she didn't dare let up the charade. Penny undid the knot and reconfigured the silk into a scarf, first at her neck, then over her head like women in the movies.

All the while Akibo glanced at her with the sort of disdain he might reserve for a dumb animal. Then he shrugged and walked on to the next pack, leaving her things scattered across the floor. Penny didn't dare sigh in relief, so she took off the flag, picked up her things, and stuffed them back in her bag. The flag she folded carefully, however, matching the corners neatly as she'd seen men do so many times, then slid it back into its hiding place.

Only once everything was in its place did she dare glance around the room. Maude Davison was watching her—had clearly seen the whole spectacle—and by her knowing expression had figured out whose flag she was protecting and why. It wasn't so much a smile that Maude gave her as a nod of approval, and the heat built in Penny's cheeks.

After a moment, Josie Nesbit made her way across the room. "They've got you registered?"

"Yes."

"You can go to the bathroom now. They're letting us out in groups of five. Stay together. Come back quickly. Leave your pack with me."

Penny nodded and joined the other four nurses at the door. Together they slipped out in a tight group and found themselves once again the subjects of scrutiny. Both sides of the hallway were still lined with internees, eager to see the nurses and get news of their experiences. The lavatory was thirty feet down the hall, and the nurses answered as many questions as they could and asked some of their own as well.

Penny was about to ask an older, distinguished-looking man with a British accent about the war effort when she was nearly tackled.

"Penny!" a dear, familiar voice said, and there stood Eleanor, tired and thin but still radiating that soft light of hers.

"You're here!" Penny pulled her closer even as the guard at the end of the hall shouted for her to move forward.

"Since March." Eleanor's eyes brimmed with happy tears. "It is so good to see you! I've hated not knowing if you were okay."

"All we knew was that Cavite was bombed and its survivors evacuated. It's been awful wondering if you were alright. Tell me, please, what's going on with the war? We've heard nothing."

Eleanor looped an arm through Penny's and walked with her, whispering all the while. "We hear some details from time to time. There are some hidden radios here. The Allies have had victories at Midway and in the Coral Sea. Tokyo was apparently bombed in broad daylight. Everyone is hoping it won't be long now." She turned her head and looked back at the door where Penny had come from. "Wait. Please tell me Lita is with you."

"No." Penny swallowed hard. "We were together for three months on Corregidor. She's alive but has malaria. You know her, though, irrepressible as always. But we were separated this morning at the harbor."

"Why? You're in the same unit."

"The Japanese consider Lita and the other Filipina nurses traitors. They were sent off with the men. Someone mentioned a prison camp in Manila, but I don't know for sure if that's where they went." Penny's voice cracked and she cleared her throat.

"How can that be? A traitor? Because she was serving alongside the Americans? I don't get it. Wouldn't a traitor have to be Japanese?"

"I don't know. None of this makes sense to me."

"Bilibid Prison is here in Manila. Maybe that's where she is." Eleanor's eyes glazed over with a sheen of fresh tears, and she squeezed Penny's arm as they arrived at the lavatory door. "You go on. Use the restroom. I'll wait here for you." Eleanor darted away and joined the line of people at one wall.

Penny's first thought when she saw her reflection in the chipped mirror was that she looked like five miles of bad road. She ran her fingers across her face. Eyelids. Cheekbones. Dry, cracked lips. Lines marked the corners of her eyes that hadn't been there a year ago—little ruts that drifted out like chicken's feet toward her temples. She ran her tongue across the front of her teeth. When was the last time she had brushed them? She couldn't remember.

"I look like I've been run over," she muttered.

Her former self—the Penny before Corregidor and the Malinta Tunnel—would have made some wisecrack about her improved waist-to-hip ratio. But that Penny was gone now, and she knew that every tightened notch in her belt was something to fear, not celebrate.

Penny splashed some water on her face and waited for her turn in the stall. She was startled to find that nature hadn't just been calling, it had been screaming, and once she finished, her exhaustion and discomfort were replaced by a hunger so intense, it felt as though she was hollow.

Back out in the hallway, Eleanor resumed her spot as Penny and the others walked back to the registration room. "It really is so good to see you, El. I was worried sick," Penny said.

"So was I. But we're together now and I'm so glad."

Penny nodded toward the door. "I don't know how long it will be."

"Don't worry. It's relatively quiet in the infirmary today. Besides, I volunteered to come get information. I'll hang out here until you're done. Laura Cobb won't care how long I'm gone."

And quick as that, they had to part again. When Penny rejoined Maude and Josie, she noted that the room was buzzing. "What did I miss?"

Josie, wry as ever, asked, "What do you want? The good news or the bad news?"

"Good first, I suppose. Soften the blow."

"They're bringing us lunch."

"Dare I ask what?"

This made Josie laugh. "Better than we got in the tunnels. Noodle-and-vegetable stew. Pineapple. And hot chocolate. Or so I'm told."

A veritable feast as far as Penny was concerned. "And the bad news?"

"Once we finish eating, they're moving us again."

Penny thought of Eleanor out in the hall, waiting for her and eager to continue their conversation. "Where? Why?"

"Away from Santo Tomas. Across the street to some old convent. They don't want us telling these people any of what we saw them do on Corregidor or Bataan."

Santa Catalina Convent, Manila

The last six months Penny's life had been comprised of chaos and unrelenting noise. Bombings and bullet wounds and the rigid military life inside Malinta Tunnel. But once they arrived at the convent, her entire world went still and quiet, and, in many ways, she found this new reality harder to deal with. The rest gave her body a chance to recharge, and she no longer collapsed into sleep the moment she closed her eyes. But now, more often than not, she lay awake thinking of her past. Time and memory had caught up with her, bringing waves of latent remorse along with them.

She had a list of things that riddled her with guilt. It was short but grueling, and she flogged herself with it nightly as she lay awake listening to her fellow nurses sleep.

A daughter lost before she'd ever seen her face or given her a name. *Check.* This guilt was more nebulous, of course, because Penny couldn't pinpoint a single thing she had done wrong. The baby simply stopped moving one day near the middle of her pregnancy. She had failed to carry her daughter safely into this world. She didn't know how, but she felt it—all the way in her soul—that the loss was her fault. Otherwise, she would be in Houston now, rocking a toddler to sleep instead of nursing her friends back to health in the South Pacific.

And then, of course, there was her husband, Sam. Gone and in the grave. *Check.* A tragic accident, they'd said. It made no sense, they said. He was usually such a careful driver, they said. But Penny knew that his death was also her fault. He'd been up with her the night before he died, weeping over their lost daughter. He'd been exhausted when he left for work.

And he never came home.

And how did she respond? By running. And now she'd lost her parents too. They weren't speaking to her. Probably never would again, even if she did make it home alive. *Check*. She'd burned that bridge as well.

Yes, Penny Franklin had a lot to feel guilty about.

So the fact that she lay there, among her sleeping friends, and was neither ill nor injured took on an unreasonable weight in her mind. How could she have escaped Corregidor unscathed? Did it mean she hadn't pulled her weight in the tunnels? Had she gotten off easy? Or was it simply that her turn was coming, like some dark, malevolent cloud on the horizon that would consume her eventually? That theory made sense, in her current mood, so it was where she settled.

It was the middle of the night—near four o'clock, she guessed—and Sam's face drifted across her thoughts. She reached for it, tried to pull it closer so she could see his soft blond curls and the dimples that had stolen her heart in college. But the memory wavered like some distant mirage and was replaced with that of Charley Russell, he of the high cheekbones and somber gray eyes. His dark hair and brooding moods such a contrast to the man she'd known and loved.

"*Damn* those cards," Penny hissed and sat up.

Blanche Kimball, a nurse from Topeka, Kansas, had taken to telling fortunes for the nurses at night out of sheer boredom. Not that she actually could do such a thing, of course, but she had a full deck of cards, a good poker face, and could shuffle well, so everyone played along. It gave them something to do in the long evening hours since their arrival at the convent weeks earlier.

Blanche had been assigned to Hospital Two on Bataan, then in the medical dispensary on Corregidor, so Penny hadn't gotten to know her well before. The girl was small, charming, and well liked among the group but was weakened by malaria to the point of being a near invalid in the convent. The trouble was that every time she dealt Penny's cards, she came up with the eight of hearts—the sure sign of a love affair, if Blanche was to be believed. The others hooted and cheered and congratulated Penny—they'd all seen how she acted with the quartermaster's flag. But she boiled with anger. She'd had a love affair already. And look what it got her!

Was it a card trick, a sleight of hand meant to tease her? But no matter how closely she watched Blanche shuffle those cards, it always came up the same.

She kicked off her covers and, muttering, dressed for the day. It was still dark in the dormitory, but Penny managed to get her shirt buttoned and her shoes laced without waking anyone.

There was no hospital in the convent. No work. No schedule or rotations. The women did nothing but sleep, eat, and heal—physically and emotionally—from their ordeal. They had two rooms on the second floor but were not allowed to converse with the nuns who lived there. Meals were sent to them three times a day from the camp cooks across the street at Santo Tomas, and they ate in the sparse dining hall downstairs. They were guarded by a small—and similarly bored—group of Japanese soldiers whose only order, as far as she could tell, was to prevent them from leaving the convent grounds or speaking to the nuns. The guards were posted around the small property and kept the nurses from leaving. Other than that, they were left alone.

Having no wounds to stitch or instruments to sterilize, Penny took out her frustration on the convent steps. She swept them clean and then set upon them with a wire brush and a bucket of hot soapy water as four confused guards watched her from their nipa huts at the convent entrance.

It took an hour to work off the hard edge of her anger, and another to admit that she was being irrational. Cards couldn't tell the future and neither could Blanche. Penny was upset because she felt as though she'd betrayed her husband with that kiss. Okay, fine. *Kisses*. There were two. But she kissed Charley back after all. What's worse, she enjoyed it. And more than a little.

By the time she finished the broad bottom step, the sun was up and she was finally spent. Her fingers were puckered, and her hands blistered. Penny rocked back to her heels and dropped her shoulders. She rolled her neck.

"What are you doing?" Maude demanded.

Penny hadn't heard the front door open. She looked up. Shrugged. "I couldn't sleep."

Crisp and pristine as always, Maude pursed her lips and took in Penny's disheveled appearance. "You'll need to work on that."

"Sleep?"

"Lying. You're terrible at it. But no matter. There's someone I want you to meet."

"Who?" Penny asked.

"Her." Maude nodded to the front yard and the long drive beyond. A black limousine rolled toward the entrance, as strange and out of place as a zebra on the ice.

Several curls were plastered to Penny's forehead with sweat, and half of her uniform was damp with the water she'd used to clean the steps, but she stood anyway and tried to smooth the wrinkles from her uniform.

After some argument and gesticulation between the limousine driver and the guards, the car crept forward. No sooner had it stopped than out sprang the strangest woman Penny had ever seen. This must have been the inspiration for Popeye's Olive Oyl. A slender sprig of a woman, all elbows and knees with a dark, curly bob and eyes so perfectly round they must have been drawn onto her face.

"Maude!" she shouted from across the way.

Her walk was determined and—well, there was no way around it— *horsey.* How a woman could lift her knees so high or set her feet down so heavily when she walked, Penny didn't know. But this one clomped her way straight up the steps and pulled Maude into a hug so bone-crushingly tight that she gasped in pain.

"Stop that!" Penny ordered. "Maude is hurt. You are *hurting* her."

The strange woman flinched back in alarm. "You're not?" she said, eyes somehow wider as she stared at Maude.

"I'll be fine." Maude glared sideways at Penny.

"I didn't know."

"You couldn't have. It happened in December. Well after I saw you last."

After a moment of quiet appraisal, those strange, round eyes turned to Penny. "And who is this?"

"Penny Franklin." She extended a hand. She wasn't sure whether it was the long, sleepless night catching up with her or the utter strangeness of this encounter, but whatever natural caution she possessed was gone. "Who are *you*?"

Finally a topic this woman was clearly comfortable with. "I," she said with great flourish, "am Ida Hube. And I come bearing gifts."

———•———

"I don't understand," Penny said a short time later, staring at the piles of bags and boxes they had unloaded onto the convent steps. "Why are you doing this?"

"Because I'm a woman too. And no woman on this earth should be forced to live imprisoned like an animal." Ida flipped her bob with the tips of three fingers. "Besides, I have more money than God, and I'll be damned if I'm going to let the Japanese have it."

"But why did the guards let you in? They haven't let anyone in except the camp cooks, Laura Cobb, and one of the doctors."

Ida laughed. "Because, darling, they think I'm on their side."

"Ida is German," Maude explained. "Or at least German born. Her loyalties lie elsewhere, as you can see."

"When the Japanese took Manila in December, they tore a page from their friend Hitler's book and began to classify every person in the city by nationality. And wouldn't you know it? I'm considered an ally." Ida laughed long and loud at this. "So I have my run of the city. I also have a heavy pocketbook and open accounts at every store in Manila. So I thought I'd put them both to use. Go on, don't bother being polite. Look."

Penny didn't need to be told twice. Inside the two dozen bags and boxes was more bounty than either of them had seen since leaving the United States. There were sweet cakes and cans of condensed milk, Ovaltine and sugared nuts and squares of rich dark chocolate. Sewing kits. Three bags of sanitary pads. Undergarments. Camisoles. All different manner of fruits and cookies and tins of food. Fresh vegetables. Canned vegetables. Breads—both dessert and dinner. Mountains of yarn. Books. Needles and thread. Cash money. And flowers so fresh that sap leaked from their stems.

"Thank you," Maude told her. "Most of my girls are sick. This will help."

"It's the least I can do," Ida told them. "But I have to be off now. You'd best get those bags inside before the guards get too curious."

As quickly as she'd come, Ida Hube clomped back to her limousine and drove away.

Penny watched her go, still a little dazed and confused. "What just happened?"

"I believe that you have met our guardian angel," Maude said.

It had been a long night and a strange morning already, but Penny didn't want to admit that she still didn't understand. Maude could read her face well enough, however.

"We are at the mercy of the Japanese," she said. "Every nurse in this convent is effectively broke. We can't buy additional food or medicine, and we certainly can't barter for things like sanitary pads and sewing kits. Do you know what happens to desperate women caught in the ravages of war?"

Penny thought of the guards on Corregidor. The midnight raids had continued and had gotten so bad in the weeks before their transfer to Manila that someone had been assigned to stay awake every night so they had a few seconds' warning before the guards invaded their sleeping quarters. They had taken what they wanted, stopping short only at taking the women themselves—but their leers and comments had followed the nurses everywhere.

"I can imagine," Penny said.

"So can Ida. And these packages, if they keep coming, might be the difference between our girls warming a bed in exchange for a full belly"—Maude paused, leveling a meaningful look at Penny—"or not."

"This wasn't a coincidence, was it? You sent word to her. How?"

Maude grinned. "These nuns, and the priests they work with, are not as innocent as they seem."

Santo Tomas Internment Camp, Manila

Penny surveyed the small room that she would share with fifteen other Army nurses and considered the last twelve months of her life. She had arrived in Manila the previous August, eager to lick her wounds in paradise, away from the hovering gaze of her parents. But within months war descended upon the islands, and her idyllic respite turned into a mad dash for safety in the subterranean tunnels of Corregidor, then a forced transfer to the Santo Tomas Internment Camp—or STIC as it was called by the internees. Then the Santa Catalina Convent. But now they were back again.

STIC. Heh. Stuck is more like it.

Penny looked at the eight rows of cots placed head to toe throughout the room. There were only two feet of space between each row, and only enough room beneath each bed to store their packs and the various items they'd been gifted by Ida Hube.

Maude had delivered the news as soon as they'd gathered for breakfast that morning. "We're going back to work. Commandant Tsurumi has ordered us to be moved back into the main camp so the convent can be used as an extension of the hospital. Your vacation is over, girls. Get your things together. We'll be transferred within the hour."

The news was met with mixed emotions. Some of the nurses felt they were civilians now and shouldn't have to take orders. Others welcomed the chance to use their skills again but didn't like the idea of caring for civilians instead of soldiers—they were *Army* after all! But to Penny, this was the best news she'd had in six weeks. Eleanor was across the street, yet she'd not heard a word from her since their brief reunion in the hallway.

Penny hoped they would be quartered with the Navy nurses. Instead, the sixty-four women had been sent to an odd rectangular structure located behind Main Building that boasted four small rooms and a single shower, toilet, and sink. Each woman was given only enough space for a cot.

Corregidor felt confining at times and the convent oppressive, but this was a different kind of claustrophobia. She couldn't turn in a circle without touching someone else. Every breath of air, every inch of space was shared. Penny's cot was tucked into the farthest corner, and as she sat there, it was as though all of the walls were closing in upon her, pressing the other fifteen women ever closer. Her heart ticked a little faster and tiny beads of sweat formed along her brow, so when Maude appeared in the doorway, Penny sprang to her feet.

"You will report to the hospital first thing in the morning," Maude told the nurses. "I'll assign your schedules then. You have the evening to get situated and learn your way around."

Penny was out of the room and out of the barracks seconds later in search of Eleanor. She tried Main Building first, thinking it the obvious place, but after a bit of roaming around and questioning the inhabitants, she found the shanty where the Navy nurses lived. It was empty.

There were 3,800 people interned in the sixty-acre compound. Apart from Main Building dozens of structures were sprinkled across the campus, along with hundreds of little shanties in the shade of banyan and acacia trees, from one end of the compound to the other, built by the prisoners in an effort to find peace and privacy. Eleanor could be anywhere.

Penny decided she would try the hospital next, and if her friend wasn't there, she would start to wander through the palm tree–lined avenues and side streets, the parks, alleys, and athletic fields that crisscrossed the compound. If nothing else she would stretch her legs and get some fresh air. Thankfully it didn't come to that.

The camp hospital was located in a low, rambling building in the upper-left quadrant of the campus, three streets away from Main Building. She was given somewhat sketchy directions by a group of young boys playing stick ball on an open patch of grass near the main drive. It took nearly ten minutes to cross the campus, and as Penny pushed through the front doors, she saw Eleanor walking toward her at a fast clip. Both women stopped in their tracks, stunned—as they'd each been in search of the other—and then closed the distance between them with a hug.

"I just heard you'd arrived!" Eleanor said. "I can't tell you how glad I am that you're back. They wouldn't tell us where you'd been sent for the longest time. I was just now coming to find you."

"Same. Only I didn't know where to look."

Eleanor—ever a nurse—looked Penny over for signs of infirmity. She could see her friend note the dark circles beneath her eyes and her protruding collarbones. Penny wasn't gaunt the way some of the girls were after their bouts with malaria, but she wasn't the curvaceous woman who had arrived in Manila the year before either.

"Are you hungry?" Eleanor asked.

"A bit."

"Come on, then, let's get you something to eat and find a place to catch up."

Penny was grateful to be shown around by someone who knew what to do in this strange new place—so open and strangely normal. Eleanor led her down one of the four main thoroughfares that branched off from Main Building and browsed along a row of little nipa huts set up as shops. They were closing down for the day, but she bought two mangos, one banana, and a small bottle of carabao milk.

"We have to bring the bottle back tomorrow." Eleanor handed it to Penny for a sip. "That's the deal. They won't sell to me again unless I bring the bottle back. Everything works on the honor system here."

The milk was warm, but Penny didn't complain—even when the after-taste left her feeling as though she had licked a cow. It was rich and creamy and likely had more nutritional value than everything she'd eaten that day combined.

Eleanor led her up a grassy slope until they reached a small copse of acacia trees. They settled into the shade, leaned against the pale trunks, and sighed—then laughed—in unison. Compared to Corregidor, this campus with its palm tree–lined boulevards and open-air courtyards might have seemed like a reprieve if not for the barbed wire–topped walls and the hundreds of Japanese soldiers who patrolled the campus and surveyed them darkly beneath their caps.

"It's better than when I first got here, but a pretty prison is still a prison."

"Who *are* all these people?"

"Civilians. That's why the STIC isn't manned primarily by the Japanese army but the Department of External Affairs instead." She shrugged at the formal-sounding name. "I don't think the Japanese had a plan for foreign nationals, so they confiscated the university and dumped them all here. The campus walls make it easy to keep us in."

"And others out?"

Eleanor gave her a crooked smile. "Sometimes." When Penny raised an eyebrow she added, "You'll see."

"So who's in charge here?"

"His name is Commandant Tsurumi," Eleanor said. "But he's civilian, not military. An older fellow. He mostly lets us run the place how we want—within reason, of course. He told the original internees to set up a way to run the camp themselves, and they formed the executive committee. Tsurumi gives the committee thirty-five cents per day, per person in the camp. That includes food and supplies and maintenance for everything needed to keep almost four thousand people alive. It's not enough, obviously, so we have to supplement the rest ourselves."

"How can you possibly do that?"

"It's *we* now." Eleanor gave Penny a gentle jab in the ribs with her elbow. "We've had to get creative. It helps that pretty much everyone here—except us—is a civilian and came to the camp with all kinds of different professional experiences. We have dentists and doctors and dressmakers. Plumbers. Electricians. Cooks. Builders. There are teachers and musicians and welders, wrestlers and veterinarians. We've even got a golf pro. So everyone helps everyone else, and we also trade for our services. You can take classes in Spanish and French and auto repair in the Education Building. This used to be a university after all."

Eleanor pointed toward an indistinct spot. "There's even a chapel across campus. The priests run it and the guards pretty much leave them alone. Some men volunteered to start a garden in the north quadrant, so that helps supply the kitchens. Everyone gets a meal card. At the moment we have three decent meals a day. Some of the bankers brought in money—lots of it from what I'm told—and they've worked out their own little financial market. A lot of what happens here is bankrolled by them. Most of the Navy nurses have set up accounts. I guess they think we're a good bet, all that government pay accruing in our accounts."

"Why do you need money here?"

"Filipino vendors are allowed into camp every morning." Eleanor held up her mango. "That's how we get the extra food. Sometimes they bring in clothing. Or sugar. Flour and milk when we're lucky. You never know what they'll have. And you can't count on them having it again."

Penny shook her head.

"What?"

"I just . . . I haven't been around this many civilians since I left Houston. After all the rules and regiments, it feels very disorganized."

"Be grateful for that. If the Japanese ever figure out what we're really doing in here, they'll lock us down tighter than a jar lid."

Eleanor Lindstrom was one of those women who seemed one way on the outside—all soft spoken and gentle—but was really a rather complex creature. Probably more resilient than even she herself knew.

"What do you mean, 'what we're really doing in here'?" Penny asked.

"We've formed a package line."

"And what, pray tell, is that?"

"The guards aren't stupid. They know we want to communicate with the outside. They search everyone coming in. All the vendors and merchants and sellers who come to the gate each day. Mostly they're looking for weapons and messages. You know, contraband. Any liquor they keep for themselves, of course. But because Tsurumi had us organize our own community rules, we rely on those outside for a lot. Food and supplies and such. And there's also a steady laundry service that goes back and forth. Bundles of dirty clothes go out, bundles of clean clothes come back the next day. But the guards aren't so cautious with what goes out. That's how we communicate and find out what's happening outside the camp."

"So how do you get word back if all incoming packages are searched?"

"That's harder, of course. We have a radio that's kept hidden. We get some news that way. And the priests help as well. They can come and go as they please. The vendors are only allowed into the main square right inside the gates. Packages are left and distributed later after they've been searched. They don't really let us talk with the vendors. But occasionally one of them will slip a message or money into hollowed-out fruit or food packages. Sometimes they smuggle it in on their bodies. The guards don't make the vendors strip, so they can't catch everything. But mostly people speak in code."

"Code? On top of forming your own government, economy, and social system, you mean to tell me that you've also created your own language?"

Eleanor cocked her head and laughed. Penny had always thought the sound of it was like water rippling over rocks. "Not me personally, of course!

It's mostly pantomime and a made-up sign language. Sort of like, 'Scratch your left ear on Tuesday morning if my husband is still alive,' or 'Jump on one leg if you were able to get my letter posted.' Lots of thumbs-up and finger snapping and nose pinching. God knows what the Japanese think of it. We've never asked. And actually, we just do what we can for as long as we can. Nothing is permanent here. Things can change on a dime."

"Indeed they can." Penny squeezed her friend's hand. She tried to smile but couldn't quite manage it. "Last time we were all in Manila, we were about to celebrate HAM Day. Now we're all prisoners."

They sat quietly in the grass for a while longer until Penny found the words to express the fear that had been tugging at her mind since Wainwright surrendered to the Japanese at Corregidor. "What happens if we don't get out of here, El?"

"What do you mean?"

"I mean this place. The war. What if we don't win this one?"

Eleanor looked to the horizon, that flimsy line between land and sky. There was only the slightest waver in her voice when she answered, "We have to win."

THIRTEEN

LITA

Bilibid Prison, Manila
August 1942

A gunshot rang out. Seated on her bed, Lita jumped. The periodic blasts, even after six weeks, continued to unsettle her. Housed together in large prison barracks adept at trapping the afternoon humidity, further magnified by the rainy season, the Filipina nurses fell silent. As they'd received no indication of what awaited them, the usual question darted between gazes:

Will we be next?

Through the barred windows, vague chatter gradually resumed from inmates in the neighboring barracks. They were all Filipina resisters and smugglers, based on exchanges of furtive whispers between the buildings at night.

Slightly assured, Lita reclined back against the wall and batted away one of the room's many mosquitos. The inch-thin mattress beneath her did little to cushion the frame's metal rungs, but it was better than sitting on the filthy stone floor as she and the rest of the nurses toiled away their days in the confines of this room.

The prison, of course, was as squalid as she had anticipated, the food rations not much better. Their meals featured a cup of rice gruel twice daily with only a small piece of pork or chicken, a bit of mango if they were lucky. Bathing was limited to a washroom visit once a week, while a pair of chamber pots served as communal toilets, for which the nurses took turns holding up a sheet for a semblance of privacy.

Suddenly a guard appeared at the barred door, his ring of keys clanking. Lita straightened as the door swung open, and another guard marched in with a rifle in his grip. *"Tate! Tate!"*

At the order to stand, she climbed to her feet and assisted an ill nurse to rise from the next bed, same as others were doing for those requiring help. In a single long line, they all bowed deeply, as was expected, to prevent being struck across the face.

The armed soldier stood guard while an older Japanese man in a uniform bedecked in decorations strolled in. He had a neatly trimmed mustache on a portly face and clasped his hands behind him in a commanding fashion. Shuffling up to his side was a younger bespectacled soldier who addressed the group in heavily accented English. "This is Commandant Sato."

The decorated officer then spoke Japanese in a raspy bass, after which the younger man relayed, "He say your action to help Allies against Japanese Imperial Army is very bad. These are action of traitor."

The implied consequence, being death, sent a small ripple of gasps through the room. Or would they be sent to the prison's rumored torture cells? Faint screams heard at night supported their existence.

Lita held her breath as the officer resumed speaking in Japanese. Every passing syllable escalated the tension in her body as she waited for the interpreter to convey their fate.

"Commandant Sato," he said at last, "is very generous man. He say you may go free."

The nurses remained frozen at first. While the officer spoke again, thrilled glances of disbelief ricocheted among the women.

"To receive forgiveness, however," the interpreter soon added, and Lita braced for the stipulation, "you must sign paper."

Her attention swooped to the folder tucked under his arm before he turned to the closest nurse. He handed off a page from inside, along with a pen.

"To have freedom, you must sign. All of you. If not, no one leave. Tomorrow, I return for—"

"*Yoshi. Ike*," the officer cut in, a signal that he was done. When he pivoted to leave, the interpreter bowed to his superior, prompting the nurses to follow suit. The second the men departed the barracks, the door was swiftly locked.

Lita joined other nurses in gathering to learn what was on the paper. The weaker ones sank back down on their beds as an older nurse read aloud: "I hereby pledge my full and devoted allegiance to Emperor Hirohito and the Empire of Japan. I renounce any support to the Allied Forces—"

"Absolutely not!" Reyna exclaimed in Tagalog, face twisted in disgust. "We cannot possibly concede to this."

"Reyna, just wait—" someone said, continuing in their native tongue.

"Wait? For what? To pretend they're not the monsters they are? To say we actually support what they've done to our country, our families, our *patients*?"

Lita had to admit she agreed, despite the fact that the argument came from Reyna. The idea of signing an oath that sided with their enemies, the merciless killers who'd purposely targeted even a hospital marked with a red cross, sickened her. What would it say about her, about all of them, to be so easily bribed to gain personal freedom? As if all the deaths and starvation, the destruction of their homeland, meant nothing.

And yet as Reyna waited for the group to concur, Lita could see in many of the nurses' faces a sense of feeling torn. Plainly there were guilt and pride on one hand, fear on the other—not just for themselves, but surely also for the sickest among them. No doubt some yearned as well to help their families back home. Those stances deserved to be weighed.

All to say, the decision wasn't Lita's alone—nor did it belong to Reyna. "We should at least discuss this," Lita declared, turning heads toward her. "It's a decision for the whole group."

Reyna stayed quiet for a moment. "You're right," she said, eyes on Lita. "You should all talk about it—about the rightful reason I am never signing this despicable pledge. And anyone who considers doing otherwise should be ashamed." After a pointed glower, she walked away.

In essence she had decided for them all.

———◆———

Late that night, a sound roused Lita from sleep. It was another of Reyna's nightmares, she assumed. Lita's annoyance escalated until she registered a figure at her bedside. Dimly lit by the moon, a Japanese soldier towered over her and poked her arm with the muzzle of a rifle.

Her lungs sucked in a breath.

"Go," he whispered and jerked the weapon toward the partially open door.

Her mind in a foggy spin, she rose to stand in her khakis. Immediately he nudged her forward. The room's layered exhales attested to everyone still slumbering. She thought to scream, but would he pull the trigger on reflex? Would he panic and shoot others who shrieked in response?

Quick as a blink, she found herself outside, walking in her socks over dirt still damp from the rain. Fear flooded her veins.

She dared to demand over her shoulder, "Where are you taking me?"

"Go," he hissed, perhaps the only English he knew. Moonlight glinted on the barrel of his gun as it prodded her onward. Nearly stumbling on the muddy ground, she caught herself and continued past what resembled two more prison barracks. From what she'd gathered upon arrival, the rectangular structures were laid out in a circular pattern like the hands of a clock stopped at every hour.

The muzzle tapped the side of her shoulder, compelling a glance back.

"*Migi e*—go." He directed her toward an open door on the right. Her memory flashed on the lecherous guard at the Malinta Tunnel, setting her pulse to pounding. Did the soldier behind her have similar designs? Entering the building, she prayed she stood a chance of escaping unharmed as Mary had.

Then again, Mary wasn't alone; she had Lita. And at present, Lita had no one.

She could play along. She'd wait until he set down his rifle, an opportune moment to immobilize him with an upward swing of her knee, giving her an opening to break away. Though where would she go?

The muzzle again nudged her shoulder, directing her into a room. A small cell. She worked to control her breathing, just as she glimpsed a shadowed figure in the corner. Oh goodness—no! Now outnumbered, how could she possibly fight them both?

A *creak* swung her around to see the door close. The soldier, though out of the room, had shut her in.

"Lita."

She spun toward the voice, instinctively retracting as the man stepped toward her.

"It's okay," he whispered. "It's me."

Moonlight through the window's bars cast stripes over his face, confirming the eyes and nose and jawline she knew. "Lon?" Her voice quivered from relief, bewilderment. "How . . ."

"When I heard Filipina nurses were brought from Corregidor, I could scarcely believe it. It cost me a nice pendant"—he smiled, continuing in a hushed tone—"but to see you again, even for a minute, I'd have given up anything."

In a moment too surreal to be true, she touched his cheek. The feel of his skin brought tears to her eyes. "You're really here—with me."

His smile widened a split second before he leaned in close and kissed her. The warmth of his lips and sheer comfort from his presence made the cell around them, the prison, the whole world, fall away. When they paused for a breath, his arms enfolded her.

She held him tight and savored the thrumming of his heartbeat. Only then, with her temple pressed to his collarbone, did she notice how thin he'd become. His khaki undershirt hung loose on his frame. Coupled with the soft rattle of his dog tags, their plights of war and imprisonment slammed back.

She drew away to look at his face. "Have you been here all along?"

"Got sent here about a month after you left Little Baguio, along with the rest of the fellas on the hospital staff. At least the Filipinos were all set free.

Guess the Japs didn't know what to do with them. Staff from Corregidor arrived here last month."

"With the American nurses?" she asked tentatively, yearning to know where they were but also hoping they were someplace far better.

"Not that I've heard." As he answered, shadows accentuated a gauntness in his cheeks. The difference in his appearance, since last seeing him four months ago, was stark. His health would inevitably worsen the longer he stayed.

"You bribed the guard to see me," she said, an idea forming. "Could you do the same to escape?"

He shook his head, his smile now rueful. "Haven't got anything even close to valuable enough. I've pondered it, believe me. Over in our barracks, escaping's a well-covered topic."

She strained to think of any possessions she could supply, even from the other nurses, before recalling all that had been left behind.

"Besides," he added as if sensing her thoughts, "even past the wall there's barbed wire and electrified fences—four sets of 'em, they say—making it dang near impossible."

Then she remembered. "There's an oath, a loyalty pledge to Japan. They've offered it to the nurses in exchange for release." While she struggled with the notion of signing it herself, for Lon to save his own life, it suddenly seemed a small price. "Maybe you can get the prison officials to offer you the same." Even as the theory tumbled out, she knew how far-reaching it was, almost laughable, but she couldn't think of any other option.

"Wait a sec . . . ," he said. "You mean they're letting you go?" Not a trace of envy laced his voice, only hope, leaving her hesitant to answer.

"Actually . . . no. They're requiring all of us to sign, and at least one nurse is refusing." Now aware Lon would be nearby, she felt a hint of relief over the matter, albeit selfishly.

"So change their minds." The reply verged on an order.

She was about to rattle off arguments against the wretched oath, but there was no point; he'd discount them all as foolish, insisting it was only a stupid piece of paper. And yes, perhaps there was truth in that . . .

Then again, the issue was moot.

"The most adamant nurse is Reyna."

No need to explain more. He knew her from Hospital One, plus had gained an earful from Lita during their nighttime walks.

"I don't care who it is. You convince her to sign. You hear me?" His eyes made clear he couldn't rest without her agreement.

Given that a few nurses had already made futile attempts, the best she could muster was a murmured, "I can try." What was more, the notion of leaving Lon in Bilibid effectively reduced her incentive.

But then a realization seeped in, a reason that far outweighed pride or even her own well-being. "If they do release us, maybe I can find a way to get you out, and other prisoners with you."

"No."

Nothing else.

"'No'?"

"You get caught, and that'd be the end of you. No way you're risking your life for me."

"But, Lon, if I can find people to help—"

"I said *no*, and I mean it."

She stepped back from him, less in reaction to his firm tone than to his exasperating stubbornness.

His features softened. "Look, I'll be fine." Then he reached out and cupped her face with both hands, alleviating her frustration despite her will. "Knowing you're out there somewhere safe, that's all I need to help me push through. That's why you've got to do everything in your power to get yourself out of this place, then steer clear of trouble. Alright?"

She wanted to press her point, but if roles were reversed, she'd be demanding the same. With reluctance she nodded.

"I need to hear you promise." He knew her well enough to require as much.

Layering her hands over his, she met the intensity of his gaze. "I promise."

He let out a breath and smiled. "I love you, Lita." He kissed her again, this time cut short. For all at once the soldier reappeared and tugged her away, giving her no chance to even glance back before he ushered her outside.

No chance to tell Lon she felt the same.

Returned promptly to the quiet of her barracks, she perched on her bed. Closing her eyes, she attempted to keep hold of their brief encounter. With the feel of his lips and arms still lingering, she focused on the last precious words he'd spoken. And yet, what dominated the memory was the finality in his tone.

A sense of saying goodbye.

⸱

The next morning, drizzle sounded on the roof as the interpreter completed his silent count of signatures. His startle showed in the pursing of his lips. He looked up from the page in his grasp. "Sixteen name. Where are ten more?"

The nurses, all standing in line as instructed, said nothing. This undoubtedly took restraint from several, specifically those who'd resumed badgering Reyna since dawn. Lita, figuring they stood the best chance at swaying her, hadn't yet intervened on the issue that was anything but simple. Like her, most of the nurses, whether or not they'd signed the oath, were struggling with their choices.

"I need *all* signature," the man declared, "or everyone must stay." His growing fluster rang with worry. He, too, would face repercussions, it seemed, for failing the commandant's order. "You understand?"

"Oh, we understand just fine."

The room's attention swung to Reyna, whose smugness projected a challenge that reeled him directly over to her. The armed guard posted by the door clutched his rifle tighter. Never had Lita wanted Reyna to shut her trap more.

"What you say?" Under the brim of his cap, the interpreter's eyes narrowed behind his glasses.

"I said, we understand what you want. But that doesn't mean the rest of us will be signing that oath anytime soon." *Or ever,* she said beneath her words; her defiant look made this abundantly clear.

The man visibly seethed for a moment before he unleashed a slap across her face. It hit with such strength and speed it knocked her to her knees.

The nurse closest to Reyna reached for her.

"Dame da!" The interpreter forbade the assistance, instead glaring at Reyna, daring her to stand up and persist.

The tension in the room turned sharp as a dagger. Lita noted the balling of Reyna's hands as she pushed herself to rise—a sign she wasn't backing down. As maddening as Reyna could be, Lita dreaded where this was going and couldn't simply watch.

She stepped forward. "What she means, sir"—Lita raced to improvise, feeling every face angle in her direction—"is that it won't be signed *today.* Since this pertains to your emperor, it is obviously a very important document and should not be considered lightly. We are therefore extremely grateful for the additional time allowing us to discuss the oath in detail."

The interpreter studied Lita intently. As she aimed to uphold a mask of calm surety, out of the corner of her eye she glimpsed Reyna. Returned to her full height, the girl waited with a rigid look guaranteed to invite a harder slap, at minimum. The interpreter was rotating back to her when he happened to glance at his hand. Seeming to note the paper shaking, he dropped it onto the ground and peered downward awkwardly, as if embarrassed by the display of poor control.

"I return tomorrow," he stated gruffly, arms stiff at his sides. "For all name." Then he pivoted to exit and the armed guard departed in his wake.

The entire room exhaled from temporary relief, save for Reyna, who muttered a single word toward Lita before she tore away from the group.

"Coward."

———◆———

Lita sat on her bed for a full hour. It took that long for her aggravation to level off enough for a tempered approach. If not for Lon's encouragement hovering in her mind, she would have taken even longer to rise and plod toward Reyna.

At the far end of the barracks, Reyna sat on the floor near a corner with her back against the wall. Lita was a few yards away when Reyna spoke in Tagalog without turning her head. "You'll be wasting your breath like everyone else. I'm not changing my mind."

Lita had expected a remark to that effect and replied in their first language. "That isn't what I came to ask."

Dubious, Reyna looked up. "What, then?"

"Frankly, I was curious"—Lita took a seat against the adjacent wall—"why you've always disliked me so much."

This rattled Reyna a bit, catching her unprepared, which was Lita's intent. Aside from actually wanting to know. "I—haven't always disliked you."

"Yes, you have." Lita's reply was matter-of-fact. "Since our first week of nursing school. And as it seems we might die here, I'd appreciate finally hearing the reason. Did I offend you in some way? Or," she said, finding it slightly harder to voice the rest than it should, "is it because I'm a mestiza?"

Reyna scrunched her face. "No. It's nothing like that." She sounded sincere on this, though she refrained from elaborating.

"Okay. Then why?"

Reyna's lips moved wordlessly for a moment, struggling to reply. "Fine. I'll tell you, if you answer me first." She didn't wait for agreement. "Why did you become a nurse? Oh, wait, let me guess, as a way to immigrate to the States. Am I right? God's honest truth."

Lita balked briefly, not seeing what was wrong with that reason. "Sure. Same as half the nurses I know."

"Well, I'm not one of those. I never saw it as a mere ticket for escape. All I ever dreamed of becoming was a nurse, so I could help people *here*, in our own country. That's why for years I did nothing but work and save money to go to school for a job that, clearly, you didn't even want. And all through our schooling, while I stayed up countless nights studying, you breezed through exams, and with barely a care for what you were learning."

Incredulous, Lita interjected, "That is nonsense. I studied plenty and cared a great deal about—" She stopped, panged by a central truth in Reyna's claim.

The fact was, Lita had heavily contemplated skipping nursing school even after her mother died. But then locals in her village surprised her with a collection they'd taken up for her tuition, funds she was tempted at times to give back. But how could she? The gift was a tribute to her mother.

"I had my own pressures to fret about," she finished simply. "I was just good at hiding them. Something I've been fairly good at my whole life, actually. As for nursing, if you must know, it was my mother's final wish for me."

Reyna cocked her head a bit, a show of mild surprise, even intrigue. Yet for now Lita had divulged enough and needed to guide the conversation to what mattered. "If you're so passionate about being a nurse, then you have to see what's around you. Several of the girls, without better food and medical care, won't last but a month or two."

Reyna's eyes darkened and her jaw muscles shifted. She snapped her face away but kept her gaze low, plainly avoiding contact with the others. "I know that." At least her frustration on this point didn't seem directed at Lita. "But I'm not the only one who hasn't signed."

The justification, though delivered half-heartedly, wasn't untrue. Lita, too, had delayed penning her own signature. One could argue that in the large scheme of life, it meant nothing. And yet, in some ways it meant everything.

"They listen to you, Reyna," Lita said regardless. "We could convince them together, assuring them it's the right decision."

After a quiet beat, Reyna lay her head against the wall and stared at an indistinct spot. "We had seven thousand patients at Hospital Two. Hundreds were lined up for surgery when we were ordered to pack up. We didn't tell them we were going, but they knew. I could see it in their eyes as they lay there watching us leave, knowing they wouldn't be following. Those helpless, haunting eyes. I still see them, you know. Even when I sleep. Always when I sleep."

That's when Lita realized: "Your nightmares, that's what they're about."

"I'm alone in a boat," she said, clearly envisioning the scene. "I'm paddling across the bay, but patients start appearing in the water. Then they're everywhere and they're clawing, trying to get in. So I fight them off with the oar, afraid they'll flip the boat. Just like in Bataan, I know I can't save any of them." A sheen of tears moistened her eyes. It was a sight Lita never thought she'd witness, with an understanding she never imagined they'd share. Over a reason, above all perhaps, Reyna viewed the oath as a betrayal.

"Evacuating wasn't up to any of us," Lita reminded her. "Had we stayed, we likely would've ended up in Bilibid sooner. And who's to say they're not in Manila right now, maybe with the patients from Corregidor?"

Reyna kept her focus straight ahead. But she lifted her chin, a suggestion of a nod that seemed encouraging.

"Either way," Lita said, "you're not honoring anyone's sacrifice by choosing not to live." It was good advice, in fact, for Lita herself. "You could still be saving lives, even if they're not military."

Reyna huffed a breath, irritated. "I—maybe—I don't know."

Lita considered her own pride, the damaging effects learned from her mother, of not making amends when given the chance. She nearly offered up the lesson, but Reyna appeared to have reached her fill. Push too hard, and she'd dig her heels in for good.

Leaving it at that, Lita rose in silence and started away.

"Is there *anything* you've loved about it?"

The question wheeled Lita around. The reference to nursing sank in as Reyna's eyes pushed once more for the God's honest truth.

So Lita contemplated. Her first thoughts leaped to the horrors she'd endured, the surgical assembly lines and screaming, the direct hits and deaths. But then came lighter memories stowed in the corners of her mind.

She remembered the smiles of patients she'd saved, the bouts of laughter they shared. The satisfaction of removing bandages to find wounds healing and infections clearing. The simple gift of providing a comforting voice. She recalled the joy of waking to discover a soldier recovering who hadn't been expected to last the night, and of listening to touching stories of fellows' hometowns and sweethearts and families. And, of course, she thought of the soldiers whose hands she'd held when needed, at times through their final breaths.

"Yes," she answered at last. "I've loved quite a lot."

———◆———

That afternoon, Reyna once again addressed the room of nurses, this time with Lita at her side. By evening all twenty-six signatures appeared on the page awaiting the interpreter's next visit. Though the women were awarded their "freedom" as promised, that word—during war in a country occupied by the enemy—felt a relative term.

As they stood at Bilibid's main gate preparing to walk out, Lita could only hope that, in the end, whatever life lay beyond the prison barracks and barbed wire wouldn't prove to be worse.

1943

*Let me not pray to be sheltered from dangers
but to be fearless in facing them.
Let me not beg for the stilling of my pain
but for the heart to conquer it.*

—RABINDRANATH TAGORE, COLLECTED POEMS AND PLAYS

FOURTEEN

PENNY

Santo Tomas Internment Camp, Manila
May 1943

A lot could happen in nine months. Love. Loss. Life. Death. Penny had experienced that much and more during shorter spans of time. But when she thought of her first nine months in the STIC, Penny felt as content as possible given the bizarre circumstances of their confinement.

The Japanese, unable to comprehend the very idea of female military officers, had labeled them civilians and sent them to a civilian internment camp. It was the only mercy they were afforded but—considering how the Japanese army treated women in wartime—not a small one.

The nurses fell into a routine, each working a four-hour shift in the hospital and then filling the rest of their time with whatever diversion they could find. Penny's shift fell later, from two in the afternoon until six in the evening. Mostly she was grateful for this as it gave her a place to be and something to do during the longest, hottest hours of the day. The rest of her time was spent waiting in lines: for the shower, for the toilet, for rations, for news, and always, ever for liberation—that elusive hope shimmering on the horizon like a mirage.

There were a handful of radio operators throughout the camp, and every morsel of news that came across the airwaves was whispered about in hallways, then parsed for meaning until any benign phrase—*We expect a drop in barometric pressure Thursday*—could turn from weather report into rumor of pending rescue. The incessant toggling between hope and despair was nearly as exhausting as the unrelenting monotony of camp life.

Eleanor had the early shift in the hospital, working eight to noon. So most days she and Penny would meet beneath the shade of an acacia tree in the south quadrant of the campus after dinner and watch the sun set. It was here, one night in early May, that Penny told her friend about Charley Russell and the kiss they'd shared in those subterranean tunnels. She'd held the secret close, not telling anyone when it happened or, later, when they came to Manila. Speaking it aloud meant acknowledging that she had feelings for him.

"Do you remember that quartermaster I told you about at Sternberg?" Penny asked.

They were stretched out on the grass, eating a square of chocolate from the stash Ida Hube had gifted them.

"The awful one that made your life miserable? What was his name again?"

"Charley Russell."

"Right. What about him?"

Penny allowed a crooked smile as she watched Eleanor's face. "Turns out he's not a bad kisser."

It was fun, she had to admit, seeing the look of surprise on her friend's face. So she told Eleanor about their nightly chats at the tunnel entrance, and then the kiss, the flag, and the promise she'd made to keep it safe, how she'd dared him to stay alive and come retrieve it in person.

"Well, aren't you full of secrets?" Eleanor laughed and shook her head.

Penny shrugged. "I wasn't trying to keep anything from you. I just wanted to think about it for a while. And figure out how I feel."

"And have you?"

"No."

"You make it sound like you've done a bad thing," Eleanor said.

"What do you mean?"

"Judging by the expression on your face, it looks like you confessed to murder. It was just a kiss with a handsome guy, Pen. We should all be so lucky."

"It wasn't *luck*. It was a betrayal."

"Of who?"

"My husband."

Eleanor sat up and turned to her. "But you're not exactly married anymore. Sam is . . . gone. Don't you think he'd want you to be happy?"

Penny tapped her chest with two fingers. "He isn't gone in *here*."

"I mean, he's gone from this world. I don't think for you to be happy again he has to be gone from your heart."

"I'm not sure that I have room in my heart for more than one man."

Eleanor was thoughtful for a moment. "Maybe that's not something we get to choose. I certainly wish my heart hadn't made room for John Olson." She tipped her head to the side and peered at Penny curiously. "Do you love your quartermaster?"

The question stunned her, in no small part because she didn't know. She *should* know. She'd been in love before. She knew what it felt like. Yes or no. An easy answer. Except it wasn't. Not this time.

When she thought of Charley Russell, there were no butterflies, no thumping heart, no symptoms of infatuation. She hadn't seen him in almost a year, but there was a longing to see him again and to be quieted by the sense of stability he'd offered in those tunnels. And even that was something she'd only recently admitted to herself.

"I can't afford to love him," she finally answered.

"Why not?"

"Because I could die tomorrow. So could he. For all I know he might be dead already. And I think that's too much to ask of any woman."

"What's 'too much'?"

"To lose two men in one lifetime."

Oh, that look of pity Eleanor gave her. If Penny could pull the words out of the air and take them back, she would.

"So you *do* love him." Not a question, a statement. And, to her credit, Eleanor didn't grin.

But Penny couldn't admit to that. Not yet at any rate. "I don't *hate* him."

"You used to."

"I didn't know him then."

Eleanor laughed. And the sound of it made Penny wonder how John Olson could have ever chosen anyone else. Eleanor had the kind of sweet laugh that made men propose just so they could hear it for the rest of their lives.

"You hadn't kissed him yet, either."

"*He*"—Penny poked a finger at Eleanor's nose—"kissed *me*."

Soon their conversation turned to home and hope as they lay there on the grass. Of letters that never arrived. Of the men they'd loved and lost. But it took another hour on that hillside before Penny finally told Eleanor about the tiny daughter she'd buried beneath a pecan tree on her parents' property in Houston. It was a dot she had to connect. She needed Eleanor to understand why moving on from Sam felt like moving on from her daughter as well.

"She would have been four next month."

Eleanor didn't say she was sorry. She didn't have to. They just sat there in silence for a while, letting the memory of a little-girl-who-wasn't settle in the air around them. After a while Eleanor looked at Penny with those big blue eyes. "You're allowed to be happy again, you know?"

"So are you."

Eleanor smiled. "I'm working on it."

For several long moments they quietly watched as clouds chased each other across the sky.

"I'm glad you told me, Pen. About your little girl. It's like having another part of you to care for and love."

Penny reached for her friend's hand and gave it a squeeze. "I'm glad too."

———•———

The war orphans were a problem. Maude insisted that they be called "unattended children" since the technical definition of orphan did not apply in this instance. They had living parents. In Newt's case it was simply that knowing where they were did no good. The family of American expats had lived and owned a business in Manila for five years. Newt's mother had taken her older brother back to the United States to visit family in November 1941, just two weeks before the Japanese attacked the Philippines. Now stranded, her father had placed the girl in the care of grandparents, then left to join the Philippine guerrillas taking a stand against the Japanese out in the jungles. By January, Newt and her elderly grandparents were sent to Santo Tomas. But with the overcrowding and sketchy conditions, the oldest internees were released to fend for themselves in the spring. So there was Newt—a mere ten years old—left to run amok inside the prison walls.

In all fairness the little tomboy thought she'd won the lottery. No parents. No oversight. And whatever rules existed within camp seemed entirely optional to her. For the most part Newt did as she pleased. And what pleased her most was attaching herself to Penny like a shadow.

Penny only resisted for a month.

It took more effort to shoo the girl away and try to find her a reliable guardian than to accept that the child had already chosen her.

"What are we doing today?" Newt asked as they wrung out wet clothes from one wash bucket and dropped them into another.

The nurses learned early on that the only way to get their clothes reasonably clean was to soak them overnight and then wash them in the morning. But they had to assign someone to stand guard while the clothes dried so they wouldn't be stolen. Food, money, and clothing were the most sought-after items in camp, and anything not on one's person was bound to go missing.

"We're on laundry watch this morning," Penny said.

"I *hate* laundry watch. It's boring. I want to go shopping in the stalls."

"Doesn't matter if it's boring. It's our turn for the job."

"Yours. Not mine." Newt flung her arms wide. "I have no jobs!"

"Okay then. You can run along and play if you like." Penny held the door open and led Newt to the side of the building where six taut laundry lines ran between a group of trees. Four of them were already filled with dripping clothes, and Blanche Kimball sat on an overturned bucket shuffling cards in her lap.

"I don't want to play. I want to *shop*."

"Spoken like a true woman."

"I don't have any money, though."

Penny ruffled her short, dark curls. "Welcome to the club, kiddo. No one does."

"The guards do. I hear it jingling in their pockets when they walk."

Penny bent at the waist and stuck her finger in Newt's face. "You stay away from them, understand? They're mean to girls."

Blanche looked up from her perch at this pronouncement and gave a slight shake of her head. There was much debate among the nurses about what they should and should not tell Newt regarding the treatment of women by the Japanese.

"My turn." Penny motioned for Blanche to relinquish her seat. "You're off duty."

She nodded toward Newt. "Want me to take that one?"

"Ha. Good luck. Our little Newt has stuck herself to me like glue, I'm afraid."

"Doesn't surprise me. She looks like she could be your little sister." Blanche cocked her head to the side and inspected the girl a bit closer. "Or your daughter."

The comment was more paper cut than stab wound, and innocent at that—Blanche had no idea about Penny's past. No one did except Eleanor. But Penny winced at the words anyway. Then Blanche was off, walking toward the hospital. Soon Newt wandered away as well, bored of laundry duty.

"Don't break any bones!" Penny called after her. "Or burn anything down."

Penny did what she could for the girl, but Newt was slippery as a salamander and just as quick. She could climb trees and the sides of buildings, run faster than any of the boys in camp, and, after absconding with a magnifying glass from the hospital, had developed a penchant for burning leaves and scraps of paper.

She was an incorrigible delight, and every day Penny fought the urge to love her. This was someone else's child after all. She had no claim. Still, she was relieved three hours later when Newt stomped into the hospital.

"Here." She plunked a handful of change onto the metal table beside the bed where Penny's patient lay, slumbering through a bout of malaria. "Can we go shopping now?" Newt demanded.

Penny stared at the pile of coins. "Where did you get that?"

The girl grinned but didn't answer.

Penny grabbed the change, stuffed it in her pocket, took Newt's elbow, and directed her to the far corner. She bent low and whispered, "Did you steal that from someone? You can't steal, Newt. It's wrong."

Newt lifted her small, pointed chin in defiance. "It's not stealing if you take it from someone bad."

"Oh no. What did you do?"

"It wasn't hard," she said defensively. "I just bumped into him, then put my hand in his pocket. I didn't even take it all."

"*Who*, Newt?"

"That big ugly one who guards the food line."

"You stole this money from a *guard*?"

"He didn't see me. He didn't even know!" She held her hands up, fingers spread. "I have little hands."

And guts to spare, Penny thought. She set her hands on Newt's shoulders and squeezed, just a little. "Promise me you will not do that again. Promise."

Newt, ever the imp, grinned. "I promise I will not steal from that guard again." She wrapped her arms around Penny's waist in a firm hug, then skipped out of the hospital.

Two hours later Penny walked out of the hospital and back to Main Building, hands in her pockets, and realized that half the change was gone. It took another thirty minutes before she realized that Newt hadn't promised not to steal again—only that she wouldn't steal from that specific guard.

"That little cuss!" she growled under her breath. "She's a pickpocket."

———◆———

"Who told you?" Eleanor asked a few days later as they sat, once again, on the grass after dinner.

Penny turned to her but said nothing.

"You have a terrible poker face."

"That's what Maude says." Penny shook her head. Sighed.

"What else does Maude say?"

"That Laura Cobb volunteered all of the Navy nurses to go help set up the new internment camp. *Volunteered.*" Penny couldn't look her in the face, so she stared at the towering cupola above Main Building. The sinking sun caught the tip of the weather vane, and it looked like a sparkler on the Fourth of July.

Over one thousand additional prisoners had been sent to Santo Tomas since January, and the camp was bursting at the seams. The already-cramped quarters were becoming claustrophobic—people packed into rooms like crackers in a sleeve—and basic supplies were running low. Food and medicine were on strict rations. New clothing was nearly impossible to find. And even though the executive committee was promised thirty-five cents a day per prisoner, they were only getting thirty. To solve the problem the Japanese gave an order that another internment camp be built, and Commandant Tsurumi was instructed to send eight hundred male "volunteers" to get it operational. It was no coincidence that all of those volunteers were young, able-bodied men with construction skills, men who could build a camp out of whole cloth, complete with barracks, kitchen, and plumbing. And, of course, they needed a hospital and medical staff.

"You're going with them?" Penny asked.

"Of course. I'm Navy."

Something about the way Eleanor said those words stung a little. It was a clarification. Navy first. Friend second. Penny was being irrational. She knew that. But still, she didn't want Eleanor to leave. Being at the STIC with her friend for the last nine months had been one of the few comforts in this strange new reality she was living.

"Is it because Laura and Maude don't get along?"

They didn't, not since day one at Santo Tomas. The women had known each other before the Japanese invaded, but they'd never worked together.

But the bigger issue was Maude outranked Laura. The nursing staff at the STIC hospital only needed one officer in charge. It was as simple as that. So Laura Cobb stepped aside. But Army and Navy had different ways of doing things. Always had. Always would. Not better, just different. And those ways were so ingrained in the nurses that they couldn't be extracted, and there had been an undercurrent of tension in the hospital for months.

"No." There was a slight defensive note in Eleanor's voice. "We're going because there's going to be a hospital at this new camp. It must have nurses. Dr. Leach is going, too, and he needs us. We've been working with him since the rest of you left Manila."

"Ah. That's it."

"What?"

"We were evacuated, and you weren't."

Eleanor picked at a blade of grass. Spun it between her fingers. "Some of the girls—Laura, too, if I'm being honest—did feel abandoned to face the enemy on our own. I know there was this so-called War Plan Orange in place, and it didn't include us joining forces with the Army nurses in those jungle hospitals, but still. To be left here like that by the brass on both sides—Army and Navy—as though we had nothing of value to offer, stung."

"For what it's worth, we didn't know. We had no idea you'd been here all that time. Do you feel that way too?"

Eleanor paused and Penny knew she chose her words carefully. "I felt . . . I *feel* . . . like everyone is under orders. You. Me. All of us. That was the deal when we signed up, right? Laura volunteered us to serve in the new camp. If she lets the Japanese decide who goes and who stays, we'll get split up. Laura doesn't want that for us. And I trust her, Pen. I have to. And anyway, I'm beholden to follow her orders. You know that."

Penny leaned her head on Eleanor's shoulder and watched the last rim of golden sun sink below the far horizon. "How far away will you be?"

"A day's train ride, I think. The new camp is located on the grounds of another school of some kind. It's called Los Baños."

Penny couldn't help but laugh at that, and the thin layer of ice that had coated their conversation melted away. "You volunteered to go to a place called 'The Toilets'?"

Laughter was always good medicine, and Eleanor took a full dose as well. "Very funny. It's not an exact Spanish translation, I'll have you know. I think it's more like 'The Baths.'"

"And when do you leave for this outhouse assignment?"

"First thing in the morning," Eleanor said. "What's wrong?"

Penny closed her eyes. If she couldn't tell the truth to her friend, she couldn't tell it to anyone. "I'm just so tired of losing people."

———◆———

The entire camp awoke before dawn the next morning. Everyone knew someone who was leaving, and they all gathered on the broad, open plaza inside the massive iron gates to wish their friends and loved ones farewell. Hugs and tearful goodbyes were exchanged as women clung to husbands and lovers. Children cried for their fathers, while others shook hands with stoic faces. Then, when the Japanese had run out of patience, the men were separated into groups of fifty and loaded onto massive flatbed trucks.

They took what little clothing they had. Bedrolls. Pots and pans. Any tools or gadgets that might make the work ahead of them easier. The men leaned out of the trucks, waving or, in some cases, crying. Conscripted men being sent away.

Penny had said her goodbyes the night before and didn't expect to see Eleanor again, but there she was at the tail end of the line as the Navy nurses were brought into the yard, led by Laura Cobb, with packs slung over their shoulders, caps neatly pinned on, and heads held high. The camp citizens called them "Bluejackets" for the color of their uniforms and as a way to differentiate their branch of the military. They looked smart, marching in that straight line, with their crisp navy coats out of trunks at last and gold buttons glinting in the rising sun.

Penny didn't call out for her friend. Instead she watched her climb into the last truck with a sort of awe. Her self-pity from the night before was replaced with pride. It was one thing to respond in the midst of war—to be evacuated or transferred and adapt—but Eleanor had *chosen* to face hardship, to follow Laura's orders without question. They both knew she could be walking into the mouth of hell. But how much more noble to do that than to run away from it?

The engines rumbled to life, one after another, and only then did the camp loudspeakers attached to the roof of the Education Building begin to blast a recording of "Anchors Aweigh." Those who knew the lyrics belted them out and those who didn't hummed along as best they could.

For her part Penny stood silently, wishing she could cry. Wishing tears were a thing she could summon when sad instead of only when furious. Then Eleanor leaned out of the truck, scanning the crowd, and as it began to creep forward, she caught sight of Penny. She lifted her arm in farewell, and Penny answered with her own, waving madly. There was no fear on Eleanor's face, only peace and certainty, and if this was to be the last time Penny ever saw her friend, she was determined that would be the look she remembered.

Once the trucks drove through the gates, the crowd began to disperse. With a long, sleepless night behind her and a long, sad morning before her, Penny thought she'd return to the barracks and get some rest. She made the walk alone, Newt nowhere to be seen for once. Everywhere amid the camp there was chatter and conversation, but having lost a quarter of the population all at once, it felt sparse. She could feel the gaps where men should be, lounging against trees or playing checkers in the shade. She felt that hollowness inside her as well.

When Penny stepped into the nurses' quarters, she saw a man standing in the middle of the room. Like all the other Japanese soldiers, he wore a khaki uniform and stiff cap, but his bayonet was tossed casually across a bed, and his hands were on his hips as he studied the carefully made but empty cots.

She hadn't meant to gasp out loud, but he'd startled her, and the sound caught his attention. The guard looked up at her sharply. Then one corner of his mouth twisted into a sly grin.

Lieutenant Akibo.

He studied her quietly for a moment. "I wasn't sure which room was yours." He waved an arm around. "Or which bed."

"You can't be in here." Penny took a step backward. "What do you want?"

"To propose an exchange of services."

"Why?"

"Because you need something from me, and I want something from you."

"I don't need any—"

"Yes, you do," he interrupted. He sounded perfectly calm, almost bored. "Protection. Food. Resources. Supplies. And not just for you but for this entire little henhouse of yours. I can give that to you."

"And why would you do that?"

Akibo slipped his hand beneath the collar of his uniform and rubbed the chain of her necklace between the pads of two fingers. "Because I want a mistress."

The adrenaline hit Penny's system so quickly her muscles seized. She could get out of the building—she was certain of it—before he could reach her. She would scream for help. She would fight if she had to.

"Stop." He snorted in disgust. "I'm not interested in a conquest. I won't force you."

"How noble."

"I don't have to. You'll come to me before long."

"I won't." She had no explanation for the fact that her voice didn't waver.

"Things are changing at Santo Tomas. And they will continue to change. You will need me and what I can give you before long. But warming my bed will be the price."

She shook now, but with anger, not fear. "That will *never* happen."

"Then you will watch your friends suffer," he said, undeterred. "And that little girl who follows you around like a dog? She'll be among them. But when you tire of watching their pain, come to me. My offer stands."

"So much for not forcing me, then."

"My Western education taught me something my countrymen have not yet learned. Compliance and surrender are not the same thing," he said. "I want the latter."

The dam of tears she'd locked inside for so long burst open, carving a path down her cheeks. Penny clenched her teeth together in fury as Akibo finally lifted his bayonet, leaned it against his shoulder, and came to stand before her.

His eyes made a lazy trip up and down her body. "It's inevitable. You have no power here."

Her response, when it came, was filled with every drop of disdain she could muster. "I would rather have no power than no honor."

FIFTEEN

ELEANOR

Los Baños Prison Camp, Laguna Province
May 1943

The first thing Eleanor saw after stepping out of the filthy, stinking cattle car that brought her from Santo Tomas to Los Baños was a tangled jungle with glimpses of a higher peak in between the foliage: Mount Makiling. The sight, verdant and lush, was almost beautiful after seven hours crammed inside the sweltering boxcar. The servicemen traveling with them, so many they had to stand the entire trip, had insisted the nurses sit near the front where air circulated from the barred opening, but she still emerged from the train soaked to the skin with sweat.

Laura Cobb immediately asked the guard who ushered them off for water for the men. Despite rotating their positions throughout the trip, Eleanor had feared some would suffocate before they arrived. None had, but all of the men were parched and weakened by thirst.

"This heat. Too much," Laura said to the Japanese soldier, using an authoritative voice with her childish-sounding, few words. "Need water." She pantomimed taking a drink.

The guard shouted an angry reply in Japanese and shooed Laura away from the train car with his rifle. He yelled at Eleanor and the other nurses, too, as they followed Laura away from the tracks.

"They need water!" Laura shouted as she walked away. The guard matched her volume with a firm response.

"Dame da!"

No.

Another guard was shouting at them now, using his rifle to move them away from the tracks and closer to a waiting truck.

The difference between the train car and this tropical wonderland was acute. Everywhere Eleanor looked was a different shade of green. Parrots and monkeys chattered in the trees near the small depot, and insects buzzed. The sky was powder blue with tufts of cotton-white clouds rimming the vistas. She'd learned before leaving Santo Tomas that the former University of the Philippines College of Agriculture and Forestry sat two thousand feet above sea level in the middle of a rainforest. Isolated and a mile from the farming town of Los Baños, the college was now a prison camp only, and the beauty of the new surroundings was immediately tempered by the heavy mantle of their imminent reincarceration.

Behind the nurses the rest of the inmate passengers stumbled out of the oven that had been their transportation for endless hours. Eleanor longed to help them off the train. She made one attempt and was pushed back by a rifle-wielding guard. Laura again begged for water for them. None was given.

A spigot at the depot looked inviting, and as one inmate staggered toward it, he was shoved back to the line of detainees with the butt of a guard's rifle. One of the other guards, who spoke broken English, told the inmates—and the nurses—that anyone who broke formation to get a drink would be bayoneted.

Even before all the men were unloaded from the train cars, Eleanor and her colleagues were ordered to get into the truck's open bed.

"Go!" the English-speaking guard commanded. "In truck. Now."

They were apparently to be driven to the new prison camp. As the truck headed out of the depot and onto a narrow road, a much welcome breeze began to dry the clammy sweat under her filthy uniform, but she felt bad for the exhausted men they were leaving behind—Americans, British, Canadians, Dutch, and others from Allied nations—military and civilian—who she now understood would have to walk the three miles to the new camp.

It did not take long to reach the place. A gatehouse had been erected, and dozens of armed Japanese guards patrolled the as-yet-unfenced perimeter. The small college appeared at first glance to consist of several medium-size buildings and a collection of smaller huts and bungalows—some damaged by bombs dropped earlier in the war. The buildings didn't offer enough square footage for nearly eight hundred men, and they'd already been advised that the inmates would be constructing makeshift barracks to supplement the available space for sleeping quarters.

Eleanor could only hope there wouldn't be the same amount of over-crowding here as at Santo Tomas. Disease always flourished when too many weakened, undernourished people occupied the same space. The nurses were ordered out of the truck and made to sit on a patch of dirt outside an administration building just inside the campus-turned-prison. They waited in the soggy heat for the marchers, fanning themselves with banana leaves whenever the guards weren't looking and praying none of the men collapsed from heatstroke on the way.

When the men finally arrived with Dr. Leach, an American mission-ary doctor who'd been with the nurses since Santa Scholastica, the entire new prison population was escorted to the school's baseball diamond at the north end of the camp, and the men were finally allowed to sit. When drinking water finally did come, Eleanor and the nurses and a dozen corpsmen sprang into action to give it first to those who were the most dehydrated. Each of them only got a swallow or two of the tepid water. It wasn't near enough to slake anyone's thirst.

Eleanor couldn't help but wonder if this was a harbinger of things to come at this place. Los Baños was a prison camp, after all. Not an intern-ment camp. Things would be different here. Did Laura know just how different when she'd volunteered them?

Once the task of distributing water was completed, the nurses returned to their patch of grass and dirt by third base, and the company waited for their guards to assign them to their sleeping quarters. They waited and waited. Twilight fell and they were still waiting. As soon as the sun was down and the intense heat abated, the mosquitos came out to feed.

Everywhere was the sound of eight hundred men and the few Navy nurses slapping their arms and faces and necks. No guards came to lead them to sleeping quarters.

"I think they mean for us to sleep out here," Laura advised her nurses. "Stay together. Sleep back-to-back to stay warm if there's a chill, though I doubt there will be any chance of that."

Under the Geneva Convention it was against international law to make prisoners of war sleep exposed to the elements. All the nurses knew this, but none of them said anything. It would change nothing to mention it.

Sometime around midnight, well before anyone had truly drifted off, a man near Eleanor sang in a mock-cheerful tenor "Take Me Out to the Ball Game." Light laughter filled the oppressive air, and a dozen other men joined in for several choruses of the ballad.

As Eleanor lay on her back and swatted mosquitos and listened, she stared up into the brilliantly majestic evening sky. Unending infirmary duties and a nightly curfew had made stargazing at the STIC a rare occurrence. The canopy above her was so beautiful, far too beautiful to notice her—if stars could—huddled there on the dirt. Or maybe the quivering constellations were actually the shimmering voice of heaven assuring her the opposite was true. Perhaps the heavens were murmuring, *I see you. I see you. I see you. Do not give up.*

Eleanor turned over, moved closer to Peg's back, and swatted the mosquito feasting on her cheek. Thoughts of John only helped for a little while. Karin—he'd told Eleanor that was his fiancée's name—always crowded in. As she should, Eleanor scolded herself. Of course she should; John was Karin's husband. But a moment later she let his image drift in anyway so sleep might find her.

———◆———

When dawn finally chased away the night, Eleanor and the other nurses were led to a small structure in the middle of the camp where their bedrolls, duffels, and Navy-issued footlockers had already been delivered.

They were relieved to see their belongings had not been ransacked by the guards when they'd been searched, not that they had much left to interest a Japanese soldier. Still, it was all that they had.

They were also glad to learn they wouldn't have to share the structure and they would only have to sleep three to a room. But every piece of furniture had been taken from the rooms. There were no beds, no cabinets, no tables and chairs. They would have to improvise somehow in the days ahead. The second night at Los Baños they slept on the floor on their thin bedrolls from Santo Tomas, but it was still an improvement over the dirt and open air of the previous night, and with fewer insects to annoy them.

The following morning, they were shown to the school's former dispensary, which would now be the camp infirmary. As the nurses and Dr. Leach surveyed their new workspace, they saw very quickly a poorly stocked and even more poorly maintained dispensary—recent occupants had apparently utilized the sterilizing equipment for cooking rice, among other misuses. But the square footage was far better than their makeshift hospital at Santo Tomas. Here was space for actual wards to accommodate twenty-five patients at a time and even room for a surgical suite and a pharmacy. A simple kitchen was found in the basement. The downside was the place had been looted and most everything of value taken. What they needed to outfit the infirmary would have to be scavenged or fashioned out of other materials.

In those first few days, crude bedpans were made from corrugated roofing tin, and mosquito netting was woven from banana tree fibers. Eleanor and Peg made cough syrup concocted from onion juice and sugar. With no cups to offer drinks of water to their patients, the nurses foraged empty Coca-Cola bottles discarded by the university's former students and fashioned straws from reeds.

The beds had also been taken, so some inmates constructed bedsteads from pipes, while others plucked the flannel-soft material found inside the seed pods of *bulak* trees to stuff inside improvised mattresses and pillows. The nurses strung empty beer bottles at the bedsides so their patients could clatter them together to signal that they needed something. One of the nurses knew how to use the old sewing machine they found in the basement and fashioned new uniforms for the women from a bolt of denim that had also been left behind. Their old uniforms Eleanor and the others cut up and made into bandages.

There didn't seem to be any hope of a black market here. The college was in the middle of nowhere. If the nurses came up against a need, they had to figure out how to repurpose something already there into what could suffice.

Laura Cobb was back in a full leadership position again, and Eleanor felt the first faint glimmer of near normalcy in a year and a half. This was the way it had been before everything changed. Almost. But a dozen nurses and one doctor for nearly eight hundred prisoners who were often battling malaria, dysentery, beriberi—and worse—weren't enough hands on deck, as the saying went. Laura asked Eleanor and a couple other nurses to train a few of the men to assist them with dressing changes, bedpans, and bed baths.

A few actual medical supplies did find their way to the infirmary after the doctor and nurses started bartering with the Japanese sergeant in charge of the camp's many guards. If he came to them for medical advice, they gave it to him after getting him to agree to supply a resource they desperately needed.

Just as at Santo Tomas, the inmates were allowed by the Japanese garrison to elect representatives from among them to form an administration committee who would then deal with the camp commandant and his staff. The Japanese controlled all the details for tenko, lights-out, and curfews but left the day-to-day running of camp life to the committee, who doled out living arrangements and camp jobs like foraging, gardening, entertainment, and education. The one job the committee would not agree to take on was erecting the perimeter fence, which the Japanese had insisted the male inmates start building in the worst heat of the day after having just arrived, weakened and dehydrated, from Santo Tomas.

The head of the admin committee, Alex Calhoun, an American who had been a bank manager in Manila, refused on behalf of the rest of the men, and Eleanor knew why. The Geneva Convention stipulated that prisoners of war were not to be made to work in any capacity that was military in nature. The building of the fence to keep them prisoners was such a task.

After a day of heated discussions with the commandant's staff and an interpreter, the prisoners were allowed to rest while Japanese soldiers from a training camp were brought in to dig the postholes for the barbed-wire fencing.

Into this new life Eleanor and the others settled. Rice became the staple of their diet. Sacks were given to the internees who'd volunteered to run the camp's outdoor kitchen, and the rice pots were bubbling for every lunch and dinner hour. The internee cooks added vegetables from the school's wild-but-still-producing vegetable garden or bits of pork or carabao meat. Breakfast was usually a mush made of cornmeal and coconut milk with the occasional spoonful of raw sugar.

Twenty new barracks were constructed, each one a little longer than a football field and twenty-five feet wide and in which a hundred internees could sleep. Electrical wiring had been strung to the structures and bare bulbs hung from the thatched roofs. Cold-water showers were installed in between pairs of barracks, as well as pit toilets.

When these projects were completed, the prisoners learned there would be a second transfer from Santo Tomas before year's end. Many of the married civilian men had wives and children at Santo Tomas and were eager to be reunited.

Eleanor was ticking off the days, too, until more women arrived at camp, but what she wanted more than additional female companionship was for someone among the hundreds imprisoned here to have the skills, ingenuity, and moxie to build a shortwave radio. Hidden radios had been one of the main ways to get news from outside the Philippines when she'd been at the STIC. Whoever did such a thing risked execution if caught. But oh, how wonderful it had been to hear even the slightest bit of news from a station in San Francisco. It already seemed like a long time since she'd heard updates of what was happening in the rest of the world.

In those first few days at Los Baños, Eleanor had caught wind of rumors among the interned that they'd all been transferred to this remote location because the U.S. was gaining ground and the Japanese wanted bargaining chips hidden outside of Manila. She prayed that at least that much was true, that American troops were close. General MacArthur had promised he would be back for them. They just needed to hold out until he and his forces made good on that promise. It wasn't always easy to hold on to the hope that the Allies would be the ultimate victors.

Sometimes at night when Eleanor lay on her bedroll, thoughts of what life would be like if the Japanese won the war would crowd in and she'd have to fight to sweep away images of America flying the Japanese flag instead of the Stars and Stripes, and the White House—if it still stood—emptied of the president and his staff, the Capitol Hill buildings shuttered or bombed to ashes, of her father selling his milk for Japanese currency, bowing to any authority who told him how he was to manage his dairy herd, bearing the sting of a face slap if he didn't satisfactorily meet their demands.

She'd have to pinch herself until she nearly bled to force those visuals away, as well as the only slightly less terrifying mental pictures of the war continuing year after year and dying at Los Banõs before a rescue would come.

"That's not what's going to happen," she'd whisper. "General MacArthur said he'd be back. He'll be back."

This expectation that the general would make good on his vow—and when she focused on that and not the debilitating notion of the Japanese winning the war—sustained Eleanor as the days piled on, paired with the hope she'd see Penny and Lita again. Her very will to survive seemed to hinge on it. It was as if the need to have that HAM Day on the last Saturday of December 1941, which had been denied them in the cruelest of ways, was one of her primary reasons to keep going, keep waking up each morning, keep tending terrible wounds and fevered brows and the endless plague of mosquitos.

Most days she won the contest to stay focused on keeping that HAM Day date, wherever the three of them might have it. The ANC was probably a bombed ruin, but they'd find a place. A grass-hut bodega selling coconut water would be heaven after this.

She still had no idea if Lita was still in that prison or even if she was alive, and with Santo Tomas becoming so desperately overcrowded, Penny could easily succumb to a host of associated illnesses.

Sometimes when Eleanor lay awake, worrying over what she couldn't control and wasn't sure of, she'd medicate her concerns by picturing what she was confident of, of things normal and mundane even, which always led to thoughts of home in Silver Lake. She'd picture her parents and Lizzie and her old friends from her growing-up years safe from these horrors of war, and for brief moments she'd even allow herself to picture John Olson mowing the parsonage grass while rosy-pink peonies under the front windows nodded in approval against the house's lemon-yellow siding.

Perhaps it was foolish to allow herself those moments, but Eleanor knew she needed something magical to think about when the most terrible of worries assaulted her. These thoughts quieted her soul. She could ask forgiveness for her foolishness later. If she survived this.

When she'd pen a letter to her parents, she said nothing of these fears nor how she coped with them. Her letters would be read and censored anyway. She had no idea if her letters were transported to the Red Cross station in Manila to be sent home as they were supposed to be. Little else had been done for the prisoners as it was supposed to be. She had to trust that her family would believe the adage that no news was good news.

———◆———

Just as life at the new prison camp seemed almost routine, Dr. Leach was suddenly transferred out on a prisoner exchange and a civilian-POW American doctor was brought in from the Baguio prison camp to replace him.

Dr. Dana Nance had been raised as the son of American missionary parents in China. He was thirty-eight, married, and the father of three. He'd been working as a physician for a Philippine mining company in Manila, and fortunately his wife and children had been in the States when the war started. Likable Dr. Nance came to Los Baños with his own surgical instruments—a most welcome sight—plus an energetic can-do attitude. He was quickly elected to the admin committee.

Eleanor's relief that the new doctor seemed unruffled, even at ease, with being a prisoner was soon put to the test, however.

Within days of his arrival, the camp commandant brought a sick Japanese man to the internees' hospital, a civilian assistant under his employ. Through his interpreter Dr. Nance was asked if he would examine Mr. Hayasaki, who was writhing in pain, clutching his abdomen, and sweating heavily. The commandant's own medical sergeant from the garrison had not been able to help him. The feverish man was brought into one of the exam rooms. Dr. Nance signaled for Laura, Eleanor, and one of the other nurses to come with him.

It was obvious to Eleanor as soon as Dr. Nance pressed on Mr. Hayasaki's abdomen that he was probably suffering from acute appendicitis. The doctor turned to the interpreter and confirmed to him her suspicion. "If he is not operated on, the appendix will burst and the infection inside it will flood his bloodstream and kill him. He needs surgery. Now."

The interpreter spoke to the commandant and then turned back. "We will transport him to Manila for his operation."

"Mr. Hayasaki will die on the way," Dr. Nance said simply. "He must have the procedure now. You need to let me operate on him if you want him to live."

The commandant considered this, then turned and left the room.

"The commandant will decide," the interpreter said, and then he left as well.

As soon as they walked out of the hospital, Laura turned to Dr. Nance. "Are you sure you want to do this?"

"This man will die if I don't do it now. You know he will."

The patient moaned on the examining table for a long stretch of minutes before the commandant and his interpreter returned.

"You will do surgery," the interpreter said. "If Mr. Hayasaki dies, we will shoot one of your nurses."

Eleanor's mouth fell open in shock.

Next to her, she heard Laura whisper, "No!"

"The nurses aren't a part of this," Dr. Nance said quickly, his face awash in astonishment. "You can shoot me if he dies."

The interpreter relayed this to the commandant.

"No," the interpreter said. "Only one doctor here. We might need you. Do the surgery. If he dies, a nurse dies."

Laura turned to Dr. Nance. "I cannot put my nurses in harm's way like this!" she whispered to him in a raspy voice.

"He won't die," the doctor whispered back to her in a tone laced with both confidence and anger. "I've performed this surgery a hundred times. He will not die. Do not worry."

"How can you ask us not to worry?" Laura said, loud enough for the interpreter to hear.

The man took a step toward Laura. "The doctor will do surgery now."

Dr. Nance turned to Eleanor. "You and whoever else is on duty get the OR ready. Nurse Cobb and I will be there shortly with the patient." As Eleanor turned on shaking legs to leave, she heard Dr. Nance say to Laura, "I can do this. He won't die."

Eleanor threw on their makeshift scrubs, doused her hands in antiseptic, and readied the OR in a daze, laying out the doctor's instruments, the gauze, the bandages. The patient was soon brought in and prepped by the other nurses on duty. The ether can and the mask were prepared. A guard, the commandant, and the interpreter stood in the back of the room, unwilling to let Dr. Nance operate without them present. One nurse administered the anesthesia, another passed the instruments, Eleanor monitored the man's vital signs. Laura Cobb stood ready to help if needed, but Eleanor couldn't help but wonder if she stood ready to offer herself as recompense if the man were to die.

It seemed to Eleanor as though she was back in the Yard just after the raid on Pearl Harbor, crouched under a building, waiting for the bomb that would blow her to bits in a flash of bright pain. Then, as now, she felt detached from the moment. Strangely at peace, as if the danger she was facing couldn't possibly be real.

As the first cut was made, Eleanor could very nearly hear the whispered prayers of her colleagues, beseeching heaven that this man would survive. Dr. Nance widened the opening, and in mere minutes the inflamed and enlarged appendix was removed intact and placed in an emesis basin. Dr. Nance sutured the tissue and then the skin. The antiseptic was applied, the bandages were wrapped around the man's middle. But the tension in the room didn't begin to lessen until the ether mask was removed and the man too slowly regained consciousness. Again, as at the Yard, the killing bomb did not fall.

Later, as the commandant and the interpreter left, with the groggy patient being carried on a stretcher behind them, Laura turned to Dr. Nance. They were all standing at the door to the hospital watching the Japanese men return to the headquarters building across the road.

"That can't ever happen again," Laura said with quiet intensity.

"That man would've died, Nurse Cobb," Dr. Nance said, in a conciliatory tone that was nevertheless also heavy with intent. "I had to insist they not try to transport him."

Laura turned to head back into the hospital. "No, you didn't."

She went inside, leaving the doctor, Eleanor, and the other nurses who'd assisted alone on the top step with him.

"I didn't mean for that to happen the way it did," he said to the group. "I'd never do anything to endanger any of you. I never would've guessed they would involve you in this."

Eleanor could tell the doctor was sincere but that he didn't quite appreciate that Los Baños was no place to guess the enemy's next move. It was no place to assume anything would be as you'd expect it.

This was life in a time of war. You tried to make an ordinary routine out of bizarre and ever-changing details. Some days you could, some days you could not. Some days you were safe, some days you were not. Some days you rifled through your footlocker at the end of a long day at the hospital and you'd see a party dress you bought on a joy-filled day in Manila and you'd think, *I'll wear that again someday*. Some days you'd see that dress and think, *I should let it be cut up for bandages*.

Some days Eleanor was sure she would live to see tomorrow.

Some days she was not.

SIXTEEN

LITA

Manila
June 1943

W hile it was certainly possible Lita had misheard the man's ramblings, her gut told her otherwise, tempting her to probe.

Carrying a dinner tray to his hospital room, she bowed to the posted
guard. That morning she'd assisted in the patient's hernia surgery, one of
Dr. Garcia's specialties, but still the guard inspected the food by sight and
smell before approving her entry.

Last September, soon after her prison release, she'd been glad to find
work at Philippine General Hospital in Manila. Nursing might well be her
calling after all. Of course, she wasn't particularly fond of the overflow of
Japanese patients or special cases sent periodically from a local hospital the
Japanese had commandeered, nor that the surgeries required supervision
by one of their overseers. The job did, however, provide her with wages and
purpose; it busied her with helping others while distracting from constant
worries about the POWs at Bilibid—Lon, especially, who at least she knew
was still alive.

Because he had to be.

The alternative was unthinkable.

"Splendid. You're awake, I see." She forced a smile for the soldier lying
in bed, Kenji Yamada according to his chart. Roughly her age, he had

prominent cheekbones, a pointed chin, and watchful eyes, with which he afforded her but a glance. She closed the door behind her and delivered the tray to his night table.

"Would you like help sitting up?" She consciously chose to speak English and not to clarify with hand gestures, then waited for his answer.

He stayed silent. Only after looking at his food did he edge himself upright, stifling a grunt from discomfort.

When he was brought in that morning, per protocol Lita asked in Japanese—one of her few memorized phrases—if he spoke either English or Tagalog for swifter communication. He had shaken his head, a definitive no. Yet just after surgery, still high on ether and morphine, he'd rattled off some remarks to Lita. Generally nonsensical, but in English. Lacking even a trace of accent.

He'd lied, it appeared. Why? With his health at stake, what could have been the reason?

She transferred his tray to his lap now, figuring kindness might lure out the truth. "Would you care for anything else, Yamada-san?"

Blatantly ignoring her, he sipped his broth. Then he picked up his chopsticks and ate from a bowl of rice topped with generous pieces of fish. Sliced papaya and green tea waited to the side.

As she watched him, resentment swelled within her. Considering the paltry rations at Bilibid, or any of the POW camps, surely, she wondered just how malnourished the prisoners had become, how much longer they could go on that way. And here was yet another Japanese patient enjoying proper medical care complete with a real bed, pillow, and clean linens; a window with a second-floor view of the city; even the luxury of a private room.

She jumped to her point. "You speak English, don't you?"

He continued to chew, eyes on his food.

"I heard you speak it after surgery. Extremely well. So why claim that you can't?"

He waved his chopsticks toward her as if shooing a flea. *"Wakaran. Urusai."*

She comprehended the first word—saying he didn't understand. The tone of the second told her that she was irritating him. His implied condescension—after she'd helped to drastically improve if not save his life—heated her simmer toward a boil as he refocused on his meal.

The door swung open then, a well-timed intervention. Reyna leaned inside and stared. "What are you doing in here?"

Lita relaxed her clenched jaw. "Just delivering a meal."

"Yeah, the cook told me. Your shift is over. It's time to go." The contempt in her voice was a sound to which Lita had grown well accustomed. Since their time at Bilibid, the fact it was no longer directed at Lita had been a welcome change. In this case, that the target of her ire was the Japanese soldier went without saying.

Lita paused her line of inquiry, for now, and followed Reyna out.

———•———

Before the war—goodness, even a year ago—if anyone had told Lita she'd be voluntarily sharing an umbrella down a street in Manila with Reyna, never mind sharing a flat together, she'd have called them mad. Wartime hardships, however, had edged out Lita's pride for practicality. Never more so than when she found herself fresh out of the prison gates, with no belongings, no money, no way of returning by boat to her hometown even if she so desired.

"Got nowhere to go, do you?" Reyna had posed the question without warmth, but neither was it mocking. *"Well, what are you waiting for? Let's go."* The invite was so unexpected Lita lingered for a moment, wary of the girl's motives, before accompanying her through the city—what better choice did she have?

The small apartment they arrived at sat above a café owned by a friend of Reyna's cousin, who among her many relatives, including two brothers, was off in the jungles undermining the Japanese as a guerrilla fighter. Reyna's parents, meanwhile, resided on the island of Mindanao. Lita and Reyna soon landed jobs at the hospital within a mile's walk to pay their way. Still, only gradually over the next dry, then rainy season did their newfound sense of mutual respect evolve into something resembling friendship. Moreover, there was an unspoken bond from the experiences they'd endured and survived, as if their signatures on that oath had sealed them in an unexpected way.

"So maybe he's an interpreter." Continuing in Tagalog, Reyna tossed out the speculation through the pattering of warm drizzle, the umbrella handle in her grip.

"I doubt that."

"Yeah? Why?"

"Because as an interpreter he'd be proud of his skills. Or at least he wouldn't hide them."

Conceding that much, Reyna shrugged a shoulder of her sweater, donned over her white uniform in the same style as Lita's. "Either way, why do you care?"

"I just feel like he's being sneaky about something."

Reyna laughed. "Of course he is. Think of the source."

Lita continued to ponder once they crossed a street that teemed with bicycles, motorcars, and horse-drawn carts. "He could be some sort of spy, you know. Pretending not to understand." A related option dawned on her, stirring her hopes. "What if he's been planted by the Allies? Here to actually help?"

Reyna rolled her eyes. "Fat chance of that. Besides, I thought you made a promise not to get involved or take any big risks."

"I'm not taking any risks. I'm just . . ."

"Poking around," Reyna said, "and getting involved."

Lita looked away, as much as possible while remaining under the umbrella. Her frustration rose, less over the reminder than her feeling of uselessness—about Lon and the rest of the POWs; about Penny and Eleanor, wherever they'd been taken; about spending months not doing anything for the war, save for surgeries that actually *aided* the enemy.

"Answer me this," Reyna said. "Down at Little Baguio, did you ever work at the *Nippon* tent?"

The same as at each of the jungle hospitals, wounded Japanese soldiers had been treated in a ward kept separate from the rest. The nurses who worked there did so voluntarily, mainly out of curiosity. To Lita's surprise they would recount their pleasant exchanges with the patients, whose broken English and miming had conveyed stories of family and home. Nevertheless, after all she'd witnessed of the enemy's brutality, she couldn't bring herself to volunteer. "No. I didn't."

Arriving under the awning outside the café, where the smell of bitter coffee—a cheap, rationed substitute—seeped from the door, Reyna lowered the umbrella and rid it of droplets with a shake. "Me neither." She met Lita's eyes and lowered her tone. "Because I know which side of the war I'm on, and I know better than to trust anything out of their mouths. If you're smart, you'll remember that, too, and keep away if you can."

Lita gave a nod in understanding. Though as they passed through the half-filled café to reach the staircase to the upper floor, she couldn't say she necessarily agreed—about keeping away, that is. For at the sight of a woman blowing on her steaming drink, an idea bloomed.

One at least worth a try.

———— ◆ ————

By the end of morning rounds the next day, Lita's arms and back were slightly stiffened. But since the symptom left over from malaria, like her occasional headaches, had become her norm, she continued with her mission.

Again permitted entry, she entered Yamada's room and thankfully found him awake, this time already seated. He glanced up briefly from his newspaper—propaganda, more aptly—printed in Japanese. She closed the door with her foot, both hands carrying a ceramic cup.

Between the parted curtains, a downpour pummeled the window, streaking the glass.

"I thought you'd enjoy some green tea. I must warn you, though, it is *extremely* hot." She walked toward his night table. "I'll set it down so it can cool off before—" Deliberately stumbling, she spilled the lukewarm drink on his lap.

"*Kuso!*" He jolted and tore the blanket off in a panic, leaving a sheet over his gown and sending the newspaper scattering across the floor.

"I'm so sorry! Did it burn you?"

Registering the true temperature, he started to calm. "No—no, I'm fine."

Satisfied, she folded her arms, gripping the empty cup with a single hand. "Just like your English." She raised a brow. "As I suspected."

His eyes widened from the realization of his error, then promptly narrowed at her. He recognized he'd been tricked and summoned a seething tone. *"Wakaran."*

"Really? Because you appeared to understand everything just now."

When he struggled to respond, she hazarded to add, "Need I remind you that I, in fact, assisted in your surgery? Truthfulness would aptly convey gratitude."

He flapped his hand toward the door. *"Dete ike!"* he bellowed, ordering her to leave.

Lita was pushing the issue; she knew that. But it was too late to turn back, and frankly, it felt good to have the upper hand with even one Japanese soldier. "If you wish," she replied quickly. "Or you could explain to me why I shouldn't spread word that you're a spy—for one side or the other."

Right then the guard stormed in, drawn by the yelling. *"Daijobu desu ka?"* he asked Yamada, whose gaze cut back to Lita.

She did her best to portray unfaltering determination. She'd figured a permanent ban from the room was a likely outcome. Or would the punishment be worse?

Yamada deliberated in silence. Then he answered, *"Daijobu da."*

A look of confusion crossed the guard's face, but he obliged with a bow and exited, closing the door, leaving the two of them alone.

Relief fluttered through Lita, but then Yamada eyed her. "I'm not a spy." The denial—indeed in eerily flawless English—came in a quiet yet resolute tone.

Then again, if he were lying, would he really admit it?

"Okay," she said simply, and waited.

He reclined against his propped pillow and released a breath. "I'm *nisei.*"

The familiar term, meaning "second generation," startled her. "You were born in the States?"

"Canada."

She'd assumed he had only been educated overseas or possibly raised in part by an American, as was the case in her family, and now her thoughts spun with explanations. She asked in a near whisper, "Are you here to help the Allies?" Somehow, even when she'd mentioned the theory to Reyna, it hadn't struck her as quite so fanciful as it did in this instant.

He broke from her gaze, his discomfited manner affirming the answer.

"Then you actually *are* fighting for Japan." She couldn't keep the distaste from her voice.

"Listen," he muttered. "I didn't volunteer. Alright?"

She hastened to comprehend. "So . . . you were drafted?"

He looked toward the window, at the sea of gray clouds, as if longing to flee. At last he replied, "Several years ago my grandfather, over in Kyoto, got sick. With a heap of anti-Japanese sentiment growing in Canada, my family decided it was time to go back, so we did. Then the war broke out and the conscriptions began."

Reyna's warning suddenly returned, about mistrusting the enemy's words. "But you were born in Canada."

"That doesn't matter. Just my ancestral line. In the empire's view I'm still Japanese."

Lita took this in. She recognized the plausibility of his claim, supported by a tone absent of falsity. The scenario was a horrendous one she never would have imagined. Through her life she'd often felt stuck between worlds, but never to this extent.

"How are you supposed to do that? Fight your own people?" She meant to be sympathetic, not accusatory, but he jerked his face toward her and bit out a laugh.

"My own people? Do you know what they've done to the Japanese in Canada—all civilians, including kids and *nisei*, the elderly? Even ones who are only part Japanese? Same as in America, they've labeled them 'enemy aliens.' They rounded them up and stuck them in some filthy camp behind barbed wire. Not even like criminals—like animals in a pen." Bitterness oozed from his voice, and yet what shone in his eyes, Lita detected, was a deep sense of hurt. "In Japan I might not entirely belong, but I definitely don't belong there. That much I know."

Silence descended with a mix of emotions, for Lita as well. How was she to view him now?

A knock interrupted the thought. She turned as a nurse opened the door, the guard standing behind. "Pardon me, Lita, but there's a visitor looking for Dr. Alvarez. Do you know where he is by chance?"

The stoic doctor wasn't one to ever broadcast his whereabouts. Lita had heard, however, that a family member of his might have fallen ill, explaining his absence for the past few days. But she stopped herself from relating his personal business, particularly given their audience. "I'll speak to the visitor. Let me wrap up in here."

The nurse smiled and closed the door.

Lita rotated back to Yamada. But at a loss for a conclusion, she stated, "I'll have a new blanket sent in." The rain was the only sound between them before she headed toward the door.

"Don't," he blurted, angling her back, and finished softer, "tell anyone. About my English, or what I've shared. Being born in Canada, it's different than just being educated there. The military knows, of course—but if word spread in my unit, I wouldn't be trusted." He paused. "Please."

Her agreement, she realized, meant enabling him to rejoin the battle with ease. But the plea in his eyes, and the reality of the limited difference one enemy soldier would make in this massive war, led her to respond with a nod.

———◆———

In the hallway Lita recognized the visitor at a glance, having spotted him in the hospital on occasion. A slender Filipino priest in his eighties or thereabouts, he was distinct with a full head of hair gone white. His forehead and the corners of his eyes were creased with lines so deep, they resembled carvings in wood.

"Father . . . Domingo, is it?" she asked in Tagalog, and he answered in the same manner as she approached.

"That is correct." He smiled, though he bore a slightly quizzical look.

"I'm Lita. I was told you're looking for Dr. Alvarez. But I'm afraid he's out today."

"Still?"

"Yes, Father."

His expression dropped. "I see." He kneaded his aged hands and pondered.

A nurse rolled a patient past in a wheelchair, the wheels lightly squeaking, while an elderly patient shuffled by in the background.

"Is there anything I can help you with?" Lita asked. "Until he returns?"

The priest searched her eyes for a moment—for what, she didn't know. "How about a prayer?"

She fumbled for a reply, not because she was Protestant, but merely because the request was unexpected.

"Come, child. Come pray with me." He gestured toward the hospital chapel down the hall with an air of warmth but also a subtle urgency that compelled her.

"Certainly, Father."

Intrigued, if uncertain, she walked beside him and entered the small, vacant chapel—unadorned but for an altar and single stained glass window—and slid into a pew, where side by side they settled onto a kneeling cushion. Following his lead, she clasped her hands and bent her head, only for him to say quietly, "People are being interned at Santo Tomas, few with my ability to come and go. I assume you are aware of this."

She braced herself, curious where this was going. "Thousands of civilians, I've heard. A vendor mentioned bringing in food and clothes to sell."

"That is true. Covertly, many others deliver items that the Japanese would greatly frown upon. Is this something, I wonder, that you might be willing to do nonetheless?"

"Smuggling," she concluded, and caught him smiling a bit. He seemed pleased that she didn't balk—on the outside anyway. Inside, she recalled the women imprisoned in the neighboring barracks at Bilibid for committing just such a crime.

Lita sneaked a glance back toward the glass entry door to confirm they were still alone. "What kind of help are you looking for, Father?"

"Medical supplies," he said, still feigning prayer. "They do quite well concealing pesos and messages sent between various camps."

"So you need supplies to use?"

"Yes, and—well. A courier delivering donations of the like raises much less suspicion if one is a medical worker."

"A courier," she echoed, digesting the proposition.

"Rest assured, some Army nurses at Santo Tomas have recommended extremely shrewd tactics, such as folding the notes into pill bottles or rolling them into gauze—"

She looked at him then. "The Army nurses are there?" Before he could answer, she pressed, "My friend Penny Franklin—I'm desperate to know if she's alright."

He flicked his chin, a command to put her head back down, with which she immediately complied. "I cannot say that I do, but I will be glad to keep a lookout. Those I'm acquainted with appear to be faring well, all things considered."

A fresh dose of relief and hope buoyed Lita. It was dizzying, though equally maddening, to think her friend could be in the very same city yet completely out of reach. "And the Navy nurses? Are they also there?"

"None so far as I know. But I will certainly inform you if I hear more."

The mystery of Eleanor continued to weigh on Lita. "I would appreciate that." Then her mind seized on another person in great need. "And what of Bilibid? I have a fellow there, a medic named Lon McGibbons. Are you smuggling supplies into there too?"

"That is more difficult." He sighed. "As it is largely a military prison. But we are trying. In the meanwhile the money for food and bribing guards elsewhere is crucial, and the messages equally so. I would not trouble you if time weren't of—" He stopped.

Footfalls came from behind. Boot steps.

Lita's heartbeat picked up pace as the sounds traveled from the hall, moving closer.

She listened in silence, not moving, not breathing.

Finally the footsteps passed the chapel doors and faded down the hallway. One might view the daunting sounds as a warning. She had made a promise, after all, to stay safe and out of the fray. But as Reyna had pointedly reminded her, it was time Lita recalled which side of the war she was on.

"Father Domingo," she said, with hands still clasped in prayer, "what do I need to do?"

———◦———

On her walk home the following day, Lita didn't realize the depth of her thoughts until Reyna remarked, "You've been awfully quiet lately."

"Have I? A lot on my mind, I suppose."

"Such as?"

Lita had been debating whether to share about the priest and her agreement to serve as a courier soon, even if Dr. Alvarez returned shortly. She had no doubt Reyna would support the scheme and likely insist on participating herself. But Father Domingo had warned that the more people who knew, the greater the risk of discovery. It was the reason medical supplies would have to be siphoned off secretly at the hospital, so as not to compromise others. Then if ever questioned, they could honestly say they knew nothing.

Still, this was Reyna who was asking, clearly worthy of trust . . .

"What's going on over there?" She motioned toward the city square a few blocks down, where a large number of folks were amassing.

Crowds these days were rarely a good thing, yet Reyna was already heading over. Lita grumbled, knowing there was no halting the girl. She'd hurry to at least stay at her side.

They were partway to the front when a suited man on a platform came into view. His white armband bore the red insignia of the Kempeitai, the wretched Japanese military police. Flanked by two rifle-wielding soldiers, he spoke over the murmuring crowd in English, thick with a Japanese accent. "We have law here. And you will all learn to honor, respect, and obey."

Reyna stopped abruptly and gasped.

Lita frantically sought the source of her friend's reaction. Past the heads of onlookers she spotted another figure on the platform.

Dr. Alvarez.

He was kneeling with hands bound behind him, eyes filled with terror.

A third soldier, posted behind the doctor, was unsheathing a sword. The blade glinted in the evening sunlight as he raised it high.

"This," the speaker declared, "is what happens to collaborators."

Lita had no inkling what the doctor had done, but she needed to intervene, to plead for mercy. In a panic she charged toward the front. Before she could reach it, Reyna pulled her back.

And the blade fell.

SEVENTEEN

PENNY

Santo Tomas Internment Camp, Manila
July 1943

T he nurses were wearing thin. It took only three days for the Japanese to replace the eight hundred "volunteers" who went to Los Baños. No sooner had they left than the soldiers went through Manila and rounded up foreign civilians, mostly old and infirm, and brought them to Santo Tomas. Three hundred and twenty-five elderly men. Seventy-seven mothers, along with their children, the vast majority of them toddlers. These were the new arrivals to the internment camp. Scared, helpless men, women, and children, too many in need of specialized care.

They were heaped into the care of the executive committee with no instructions. House them. Feed them. Keep them alive. But if they died? That, too, was the responsibility—indeed the *fault*, the Japanese said—of the committee. There was no reprieve for the nurses, only overcrowding and constant shortages. Penny was not glad that so many had gone to Los Baños, but she was grateful that the camp numbers weren't above five thousand now.

To make matters worse, they were deep into the rainy season. Unlike previous years June had been tolerable—only one or two storms a week—but as they moved into July, she could feel a change in the air. It was like Houston in August, heavy and oppressive. And with that humidity came an unrelenting dampness—of clothing and bedding—along with swarms of mosquitos and a surge in malaria cases. Now half the hospital beds were filled with patients wracked by fever or diarrhea and vomiting.

The storms drove the internees indoors more frequently. The rain washed out gardens. The wind blew down the shanties. Penny once had a friend in college who often complained about "mud season" in Vermont. But she was convinced it had nothing on monsoon season in the Philippines. By the first week in July, she wasn't sure what they cursed more: the mud or the Japanese army.

After the new influx of internees, it took weeks to find a sense of normalcy, to find space for everyone, to teach the new arrivals how to live in this strange walled-in community. But there were changes for the nurses as well. Soon after Eleanor and the Navy nurses had been transferred to Los Baños, the executive committee informed Maude Davison that they were moving the Army nurses into Main Building and converting their existing quarters into a children's hospital. They told her she would need to reconfigure her schedule and assign a dedicated pediatric team to care for them.

Many of Penny's colleagues were furious at the news—they didn't want to move again—but she was relieved. The current quarters were separated from everyone else in camp, easy to enter, and unguarded. Captain Akibo had rattled her and—even though she refused to show it—she was scared.

A part of his argument made a hideous kind of sense. Everything was falling apart. Santo Tomas was in an untenable situation, barely keeping up the appearance of organization. It was only a matter of time before it devolved into chaos. And who would protect them then?

But he'd been clear about his terms. He wanted a mistress. Not just an hour or a night. Akibo wanted ongoing payment.

No. Never. Penny slammed that mental door shut, disgusted, anytime it creaked open.

These were the thoughts that kept her up at night. But at least now she was safely ensconced on the second floor of Main Building, with a few more inches of personal space and surrounded by hundreds of other internees—restless and fetid though they might be at times. Akibo would have to be bold indeed if he were to seek her out here.

"I can hear you thinking," came a little voice from the cot beside her.

Penny turned her head to the left and found Newt staring at her in the dark, the scant moonlight glinting off her pale eyes.

"Why aren't you asleep?" Penny asked.

"You think loud," Newt said.

Before their move to Main Building, the child had taken to sleeping on a pallet in the nurses' quarters. But when they moved, she was given a cot beside Penny. It was all the room she needed, and she was so small she barely used half of it. The girl had little save the clothes on her back and she mostly ran barefoot. Newt rejected even the basic principles of grooming and personal hygiene. She refused all braids and bows and found the very concept of a hairbrush to be a personal offense. So Penny kept her unruly curls snipped to chin length and turned her one skirt into a pair of cropped pants. The overall effect made her look like a pixie. Sometimes the nurses debated the possibilities of her real name, but nothing seemed to fit. So Newt she remained.

Penny rolled onto her side and smiled. "Sorry for keeping you up."

"You can't help it."

"What do you mean?"

"You're always trying to figure stuff out."

"Well, how about you let me do that part and you get some shut-eye?"

"Can't."

"Why?"

"I've been waiting to tell you something."

Penny reached out and patted the girl's hand. "You've been with me all day, Newt. Why wait until now?"

"Because no one is listening now."

Penny wasn't a mother. Not anymore. Or maybe never. She wasn't sure how her situation worked. But she knew when she needed to pay attention.

"Newt." She slid out of bed and onto her knees beside the girl. "What's going on?"

"I heard some of the guards talking today when I—" She broke off and pressed her lips together.

"When you what?" Penny asked. "Were you stealing again?"

"Just a little."

"A little is too much. But never mind that for now. What did you hear?"

"They said the camp com . . . comman . . ."

". . . dant. Commandant. Tsurumi. What about him?"

"They said he's being replaced by someone else. And they were really happy about it." Newt squeezed Penny's hand. "If they like him, he can't be good."

———◆———

Whereas Commandant Tsurumi oversaw Santo Tomas with a method-ology best described as benign neglect, it was immediately clear that the new camp commander, Kodaki, would have a more hands-on approach. Like Tsurumi, he was a civilian. However, he seemed to feel the weight of a watchful Japanese government in ways that his predecessor had not.

By the time Penny and her colleagues were up and about the next morn-ing, it was obvious the number of guards had increased overnight. Previously they had been stationed at the camp gates and building entrances, but now they were on street corners and in hallways as well, keeping a watchful eye on the comings and goings of the internees.

"I told you," Newt whispered as she and Penny walked toward the front gates to see what the package line had produced that morning.

"You're a terrifying little creature. You know that, right?"

Newt flashed her a bright, toothy smile, then laced her grubby fingers through Penny's as they walked along the main avenue. "Do you think there will be anything for us?"

As it turned out, there was something for most everyone. Packages were delivered to the camp at dawn each morning—mostly by Filipino civil-ians outside the camp, those doing laundry or delivering food—and were searched by the guards before they were distributed. That morning, brown paper packages wrapped in string were stacked twenty high and fifteen deep within the gates. Each was stamped with the words *South African Red Cross* and *Prisoner Parcel*.

"What's this?" Penny asked, stopping a few members of the executive committee, each carrying one of the packages, while they were still a block from the gates.

Jim Hobbs, head of the committee, shrugged and she could see the bony points rise through his threadbare shirt. "Humanitarian aid," he said, then seemed to blush. "The kind of thing you're happy to send but embarrassed to need."

"I'm surprised the Japanese allowed it," one of the other men said, weighing the package in his hands.

"International law," Hobbs answered. "They don't have a choice."

It wasn't quite enough packages. The South African Red Cross had only sent three thousand packages—the last official number they'd gotten. So many of the internees had to share. But—considering what was inside—they were happy to do so. Each package contained three cans of bacon, one of meat spread—the infamous Spam—margarine, and several tins of condensed milk. Canned tomatoes. Marmalade in a little glass jar. Cheese pudding—this, Penny thought, was a South African delicacy, and she happily traded hers for a sleeve of crackers. There was also tea and sugar, a wrapped slice of stale chocolate cake, cold cream, and a bar of soap.

Penny gave her cake to Newt and laughed as she shoveled it into her face in three large bites.

As the packages were being distributed, Penny watched and waited for word from Ida Hube. At least once a week the strange German woman sent parcels for the nurses—to be collected by either Penny or Maude. Sometimes they contained cash but mostly were filled with food and personal items the women couldn't get anywhere else. Sanitary napkins. Socks. Underwear. Toothpaste. But that day, there was nothing. Penny waited until the crowds had thinned, just to make sure, but as she and Newt were turning to go, a man called out Penny's name.

"Franklin!" he shouted. His accent was heavy, turning his *f*s into *p*s, and she almost didn't understand him in time. "Franklin!"

Penny spun on her heel. The man who caught her eye looked over her uniform and cap, then studied her face, searching for something. Finally, he gave her a sharp nod of recognition, then approached her, careful of the guards still watching.

"Your order." He extended a fabric bag that had already been rifled through by the guards.

"I—"

"From a friend on Corregidor," he added in a whisper.

"Oh. Yes. Thank you . . ."

He winked and then he was gone, back through the gates.

Newt watched the exchange with her usual sharp perception. But she said nothing as they walked away. It took a bit of doing, but Penny finally got Newt situated in the hospital helping some of the nurses wash sheets. She didn't open the bag until she was back in the nurses' quarters. She sat on her bed and found three coconuts inside the bag.

Strange, she thought.

Penny dumped them onto the bed and heard an empty *thump*. Two were fresh and filled with milk, but the third was hollow. She turned it over and found that the end had been cut out and the plug stuffed back in. It came out with a bit of wiggling, and she saw the envelope inside. It was much thicker than a letter would indicate. When she pulled it out and ripped open the seam, she found a thick wad of cash and a short note scribbled in unfamiliar handwriting. There was no date, so she had no idea how long ago it had been written.

> Franklin,
>
> I'm still on the Rock along with all of the engineers. The Japs kept us here to help repair Malinta Tunnel. It's nasty work. Lots of hauling rock and moving debris. But we found some cash stuffed in nooks and crannies along the walls. I guess some of the guys put it there for safekeeping before the invasion. We've been shoving it in pockets and in our boots for weeks now. But it doesn't do us any good here. So I thought I'd send it along to you. There's a chap here who comes and goes every few weeks, bringing supplies across the bay. Says awful things about the Japs when they're not listening—they've locked his brother in Bilibid Prison—so I'm going to see if he's willing to

smuggle it through to Santo Tomas. I'm coming for that kiss, Franklin. That's a promise.

C. R.

She thumbed through the bills and found nearly one hundred pesos, in various denominations. It was enough to keep the wolf from their door for several months. More if they were careful.

"God, forgive me for every terrible thing I've ever said or thought about that man," she said, then stuffed the money into her pocket to go show Maude.

Blanche Kimball first fell ill with malaria while working at Hospital Two on Bataan. Most of the nurses stationed in the jungle had, but she was among the few who couldn't seem to shake the disease. After being evacuated to Corregidor, many of her rounds in the hospital were spent sitting down—either doing administrative work behind a desk or resting in a chair bedside. She'd rallied for a while at the convent, but since the move to Santo Tomas, she had spent as much time as a patient as she had a nurse. Her weight plummeted and her skin turned sallow. Blanche needed more help than the meager camp hospital could provide.

"She's in bad shape," Penny whispered to Maude, after once again sponging Blanche's forehead down with a cool cloth. She lay on her back, sound asleep, the deck of cards held loosely in her hand. "Her liver can't take much more of this."

Maude studied Blanche's still form. The windows were open, and it was raining again, so the lazy circle of the overhead fans pushed the cooler air around the room. Still, it did little to blunt Blanche's fever.

"There's nothing else we can do for her here," Maude said.

"What about in the city? Can we ask for a transfer?"

It was done, but rarely. Occasionally the camp doctors were allowed to send their sickest patients—the ones who needed emergency surgery or treatment not available at the camp—to a hospital in the city.

Maude shook her head. "None of the doctors can escort her. They're too busy."

"I'll do it," Penny said.

"No. You—"

"Someone has to. Why not me? I take her to the hospital, or I sit here and mop her forehead. Either way I'm watching her."

"You can't just walk out the gates with her. There's a system. You have to be escorted by a guard. And one of the priests."

"Why a priest?"

Maude shrugged. "They get to come and go from the camp as they please. The hospital as well. The campus was confiscated but the priests aren't internees themselves. Sort of like the nuns at Santa Catalina."

"I don't care if the pope himself has to accompany us. I just want to take her somewhere she can get help."

Maude looked at Blanche and pursed her lips. "I'll see what I can do," she said, then walked away.

Penny bent over her friend again and ran a cool cloth over her forehead. She pushed the damp hair away from Blanche's forehead, straightened the covers, and pulled the cards from her hand so they wouldn't fall and scatter across the floor. On a whim she cut the deck in half.

"I'll be damned." Penny looked right at the eight of hearts.

She tapped the card with the nail of her right index finger, considered shuffling again, but put the card in the front pocket of her coveralls instead.

It took three days and no small amount of convincing on the part of the head doctor, but eventually the new commandant signed orders releasing Blanche Kimball into the care of Philippine General Hospital.

"Are they letting me go with her?" Penny asked.

Maude squinted at her suspiciously. "I'd imagine so as you were requested to be part of the transfer."

"I was? By who?"

"Oh, don't feign innocence. You know well enough. Father Domingo was here this morning asking for you."

Penny wanted to argue, to say that she'd never met a Father Domingo and certainly hadn't wormed her way into the transfer. But she feared Maude would change her mind, so she kept silent. Getting Blanche to safety was too important.

"You have to stay with her until she's released," Maude added.

"I have to babysit her?"

Maude, in her typical acerbic way, asked, "Do you really want a woman and fellow United States Army officer to be left in a foreign hospital unconscious and unattended for an undetermined amount of time?"

"No."

"Neither do I. So I suggest you find a way to make yourself useful while you're there." She said all of this without looking up from her chart. "And, Penny?"

"Yes?"

"Look out for yourself as well."

Within an hour they had Blanche loaded onto a stretcher. It was carried toward the gates by two hospital volunteers. Penny and the priest assigned to accompany them walked behind.

"I am Father Domingo," he said with a small bow.

She shook his hand. "Penny Franklin."

He was slight—almost fragile looking—but she suspected that beneath the billowing robes he was built less like a toothpick and more like a steel cable. Old, yes, but not infirm. And this was confirmed when he helped hoist the stretcher into the back of the truck. Then he pulled Penny up, and the grip of his hand around her wrist was a vise.

She had not been outside the gates in a year, and as they rolled back with a rattle and a *clang*, she felt the strangest kind of sensation. Not *freedom*—the two armed guards in the cab of the truck were proof of that—but a *release* of sorts. Like coming up for air after sinking to the bottom of a swimming pool.

"Where are you from?" Father Domingo asked.

"Texas," she said. "Houston."

"And what kind of woman are you, Penny from Houston in Texas?"

Like the other Filipino men she'd met, his accent was strong and his gaze intense. He sat in the bed of the truck and leaned forward, elbows on his knees, and didn't break eye contact.

"What do you mean?"

"You are American," he said. "Therefore you are bold. And you are a nurse, so you are kind. But the thing I need to know is whether or not you are brave."

"Why do you care whether or not I am brave?"

"Cautious too. That's good."

"What are you getting at, Father?"

"I have been told that you are a person to be trusted."

Penny scooted away slightly, her sense of unease beginning to grow. "Oh? With what exactly?"

"Moving messages and money in and out of Santo Tomas. You would be willing to do this, would you not?"

Penny didn't react immediately, but after several seconds she did turn her head this way and that—as though stretching—so she could look through the back window of the truck cab. The second guard was twisted in his seat, watching them, but she felt certain he couldn't hear what they said over the rumble of the engine and the bustle on the street.

The priest was so forthright she couldn't determine whether it was a trap or an offer. "You're rather blunt."

"War is not the time to be polite. And we only have five minutes before we reach the hospital. Once your friend is admitted, I will be returned to camp." He smiled so wide she could see every tooth on top, all the way to the back of his mouth, but not a single one on the bottom.

"You want me to help conspire against the Japanese?"

He gave her a solemn bow. "It is God's work. You will help, yes?"

It was ridiculous. Rash, even. But sometimes the decision to trust had to be made in seconds, not days or weeks. At the very least they shared a common enemy. So she took a leap of faith. "Yes."

"Good. Then I am glad I requested you."

"Why? How did you even know my name?"

"We share a friend."

"Which friend?"

Penny's mind raced, ticking off all the possibilities. Most of the nurses and many of the internees were involved in various activities that attempted to thwart the Japanese. It could be anyone.

Father Domingo laid his head back and closed his eyes. "You will find out soon enough."

EIGHTEEN

LITA

Philippine General Hospital
July 1943

The *whisk* of a blade came from behind, sending a twist of tension through Lita.

But the sound, she realized, wasn't that of a sword, only of scissors. A nurse was slicing away gauze from a patient's chest, changing the dressing. Ten days had passed since the execution of Dr. Alvarez, and now Reyna wasn't the only one suffering from nightmares, nor despising the Imperial forces more than ever.

Lita commanded her muscles to relax and proceeded out of the ward to continue her rounds. Passing Yamada's room, she was grateful the guard was gone, for the time being, along with the patient. Reyna was right; it was wise to steer clear of him, which was precisely what Lita did his last few days of recovery. Regardless of his quandary, they stood on opposite sides of the war. When he'd passed her in the corridor on his way out of the hospital, his aloof silence indicated he felt the same.

"Ah! Lita, I've found you."

At the familiar voice she cringed. But she quickly tempered the reflex before turning to the caller. Her discomfort certainly didn't lie with Father Domingo, not personally. If anything, she was utterly awed by the bravery of his underground work—even more so as she teetered on relinquishing her own role as a courier.

"Father, what a surprise. I didn't expect to see you today."

"I had not expected to be here." He offered a tender smile, unknowingly upping her guilt.

A day prior, as planned, an unseen contact left an envelope of pesos and messages—some personal, others military in nature—tucked under a corner of the chapel altar. She was to hide them in medical supplies for her second delivery run, a task she now had doubts of seeing through. Not because she wasn't wholly eager to help, but because her heightened nerves while being thoroughly searched during her first delivery, at Fort Santiago a mere day after Dr. Alvarez's murder, had verged on giving her away.

The priest gestured down the hall. "Come along with me, will you?"

"Uh—yes. Certainly." For privacy, no doubt they were headed for the chapel. There, perhaps she'd suggest Reyna as a replacement, though still she dreaded the disappointment bound to show on the man's face.

After rounding a hallway corner, he slowed near the entry to a sick ward, where the head nurse, an older Filipina with short hair and a thick chin, stood holding a clipboard.

Father Domingo said to Lita, "You two are acquainted, are you not?"

She found the question odd, thinking he meant her colleague. But then, just past the nurse, she glimpsed a woman in khakis with fair skin and light brown hair, and she could scarcely believe the sight. "Penny?"

When her attention connected with Lita, morphing into shock, Penny's mouth dropped open and her blue eyes lit up.

Giddiness launched Lita forward to share a hug that, much like their last reunion, couldn't have been better timed. "I only recently learned you were at Santo Tomas," she said over Penny's shoulder.

"And I feared you were at Bilibid."

"I was. For a time. Thankfully they let us go." Lita pulled back to view the face she hadn't seen in a year, hollower in the cheeks but still freckle-dusted and lovely. "Have you been released too?"

"Briefly. To escort a patient," Penny said. "Apparently, I was requested to tag along."

The conduit becoming clear, they both looked at Father Domingo, who sent them a wink. "You ladies catch up while I pay some visits. I shall soon circle back for a little chat of our own."

Lita could easily predict what that discussion would entail, but her worries for the moment dropped away. As the priest treaded off, Lita beamed at Penny. "How on earth have you been? Tell me everything!"

"Shhh." The Filipina nurse flicked them a mildly chiding look and said in Tagalog, "Patients are resting. Go on. Take your talking elsewhere."

Lita thought of the chapel and whispered to Penny, "Here, come with me."

But Penny's movements stopped short. "Wait. The woman I brought in, Blanche—I need to make sure she's fully settled."

The Filipina nurse, understanding, tsked while flicking her hand, a message that the matter was handled and to *please-oh-please* go away.

———◦———

Sharing a pew, Lita and Penny waited for the sole other person in the chapel, an elderly man with head bent and hands clasped in prayer, to depart before they dove in.

"I still can't believe it," Lita said. "I told Father Domingo that if he ever needed someone to trust, he should call on you. But I never imagined it would land you here."

Penny grinned. "He didn't clue me in either. Just referenced you as 'a friend.'"

A wise move, of course, given the nature of his dealings.

"Speaking of friends . . . ," Lita began tentatively. "Have you heard anything about Eleanor?"

"As a matter of fact," Penny replied, "I've heard plenty." At the dangled bait Lita leaned forward. "We wound up at Santo Tomas together."

"What? You're joking."

"Since last July. Till two months ago, when she was sent to Los Baños. She was doing well, though."

"Oh, Penny, I'm so glad to hear it." A vision of Eleanor, healthy and strong, arose in Lita's mind. It loosened the knot of fear carried deep inside her since the outbreak of the war. "And Charley? Any word from him?"

Penny's smile weakened. "Just a note. Smuggled in a coconut with a bit of cash. He's still on Corregidor helping repair the tunnels for the Japanese. That's all I know," she said. "And Lon?"

Lita gave a heavy shrug. "I saw him once in Bilibid. He's still there, I would guess. But the conditions of the prison were terrible. After all these months, I hate to think . . ." When she couldn't finish, her friend squeezed her hand.

"That fella of yours is strong. And he'll push through knowing he's got you to come back to."

Lita remembered his expressing that very sentiment. What she refrained from personally expressing now, however, was her simmering regret that she ever let him into her heart. No stranger to loss, she should have known better. What result had she expected in the middle of a war? But even to Penny she couldn't voice such a dark thought.

"I could say the same about Charley," she offered instead.

Emotion welled in Penny's eyes. She just as soon shook it off. "Enough with anything blue. This is a happy day." Her lips curved up as she straightened in her seat. "So what have you got for meals here? It will be a kick to eat *anything* outside of camp."

"That I understand, for sure," Lita said. "It was good to hear that at least vendors bring in food for you all."

"They do. Assuming you have cash to pay for it. The nurses are doing alright for the moment thanks to Charley."

Lita recalled the duty that had been asked of her, to help those interned, like Penny. Before saying more, she peeked back at the doors to confirm they were closed and resumed in a whisper. "A doctor here was smuggling money and messages into camps. He was caught by the Kempeitai—not for that but for having a radio, it turns out. He was even printing pesos to help. They killed him on the street, Penny. They made a show of it. As an example."

"Oh God, that's horrible."

"Father Domingo—he'd asked me to help with smuggling when Dr. Alvarez was gone for a while. Now that he's never coming back, it's up to me to deliver the packages he would have handled. One for Santo Tomas next, in fact. And I want to, believe me, I do. But after seeing Dr. Alvarez," she confessed, her voice tinged with shame, "I'm scared."

Penny responded without hesitation. "You have every right to be."

Lita nearly laughed at that. "No, I don't. Other people are risking just as much. More even."

"Listen." Penny squared her shoulders to Lita. "At Santo Tomas I'll gladly be on the other side of that package line, ready with bells on to personally pick up your deliveries if that would help. But if the pressure is too much, I wouldn't blame you one bit for backing out."

Lita deliberated, soaking in the support, finding strength in it. Already she dreaded her friend's absence. "How long are you here?"

"Until Blanche's malaria symptoms improve. Several days, I'd guess. All to be spent inside the hospital. There are guards seeing to that."

A stay of days was better than mere hours, but still. "Too bad you can't at least leave at night for a decent sleep. I'd have you stay with Reyna and me."

Penny gaped. "Now hold on a second. Weren't you . . . Isn't she . . ."

"My nemesis?" Lita smiled, recalling how much she and Penny had been unable to share. "Things have"—how to put it?—"changed."

"I would say so." Penny laughed. "Good thing I've got some time. We obviously have loads more to talk about."

———— • ————

Father Domingo, as Lita expected, was tickled by the news, for he'd had every intention of recruiting Penny next. She not only volunteered the second he went to ask, but also suggested a promising donor named Ida Hube for when Lita needed additional funds.

"She's eccentric," Penny said. "But exactly the kind of person you want on your side."

With Penny included as, literally, a partner in crime, Lita chose to be firmly on board.

Five short days later, Blanche recovered enough to return to camp. Thus once again Lita and Penny had to say goodbye. Thankfully the parting was cushioned by plans to see each other at Santo Tomas, which they did. Twice a week at the package line, from that point on. They were forbidden from speaking or even coming within ten feet of each other. But just a regular trade of smiles did wonders for Lita's soul. And with each visit, her nervousness lessened and confidence grew.

Meanwhile, she continued to lament that, even as the months passed and rain gave way to the dry season, deliveries to Los Baños weren't an option. Aside from the long train ride required, word had it that packages rarely if ever made it past the guards.

Unlike at Bilibid. There, whether through skillful negotiation or bribe money or both, the camp commandant finally agreed to the receipt of medical supplies once a week. While no package line was permitted, only drop-offs subject to thorough searches, and no messages came out—to Lita's knowledge anyhow—she relished the idea that her notes of both encouragement and endearment were finding their way to Lon. Because she at least had to send him those. Regardless of her muddled emotions, she cared for him deeply and worried over his safety.

Hence, when Father Domingo arrived at the hospital one morning in early October with an update from Bilibid, having at last been allowed to pray with the prisoners, she dared to ask, "The fellow I've told you about, Lon—'Gibs,' he's called—did you hear anything about him?"

The priest kept his volume low despite their being at the end of a vacant corridor. "Indeed he is there, and our paths had the good fortune of crossing."

Relief swept through Lita. "You spoke with him. Did he receive my messages? Is he alright?" At Domingo's solemn hesitation, she bristled. "What is it? Tell me."

"There was an incident," he said, his words measured, "with the guards and an older gentleman—a Dr. Thomason?"

Thomson. Her stomach clenched. "I know him as well."

"As the doctor was recovering from an illness, he was slow to bow to the camp commandant. When a guard began striking him, your friend stepped in to protect him. The doctor is doing fine, but Lon suffered a terrible beating as punishment."

Her throat tightened as memories flooded back, of broken and battered GIs she'd treated, ones who'd barely survived hand-to-hand combat with Japanese soldiers. She forced herself to voice the words: "Will he make it?"

The priest looked at her thoughtfully. With a gentle smile, he said, "It will take time, but I do believe he will mend well."

She envisioned Lon lying on a cot, his body struggling to recover, much the way hers did from malaria as he sat at her bedside, offering her comfort without her even knowing.

"I need to see him," she said, fear turning to resolve, and an idea dawned. "What if I pretended to be a nun? I could go in and offer prayers with you."

He shook his head so quickly Lita worried he deemed the suggestion blasphemous, before he explained, "The commandant will not allow this. He feels it is not necessary. It has taken a concerted effort to get permission just for myself."

"But, Father, what if—"

He raised his hand to stop her, a signal he wasn't finished. "I did, however, witness prisoners who are in dire need of surgery. As the commandant will not permit any transfers here for hospital care, after a great deal of beseeching—and other valuable offerings—he has agreed to permit a doctor on the premises for a single day. I cannot promise, but I will try my best to insist a nurse is needed for proper care and efficiency."

Lita took this all in and arrived at her final question. "When are we going?"

Father Domingo chuckled. Then he patted her arm. "Soon, I hope. Lord willing, very soon."

———◆———

The date for the surgeries was set three days in advance. This would qualify as "soon" by most standards, but not for Lita as she awaited final approval for her entry, which didn't come through until the morning of the slated day.

She was so eager to accompany Father Domingo and Dr. Garcia, she didn't consider the daunting wave that would roll through her as she arrived at Bilibid, a place she'd hoped never to step foot in again.

When the guard motioned for them to enter, she girded herself with thoughts of seeing Lon. And she walked through the gates.

Laden with bags of surgical supplies and linens, they passed the first of the prison barracks. Faces crowded the barred windows for a look. How grateful Lita was to be on the outside of those buildings, though her heart ached for those inside.

Guided by a guard to a room with a large table, water, buckets, and electrical lights, they got to work. The patients were fetched by fellow prisoners as the surgeries progressed. For ten hours straight, Lita assisted with infection control and shrapnel removals, a punctured lung, an appendix removal, and more.

Periodically Father Domingo peeked in, and Lita would present a question in her eyes: *When?*

Each time he waved his hand a little, urging patience. Though she genuinely took pride in helping each patient who came through, the time on her watch told her the day was nearly over, her window of opportunity closing.

A Japanese man appeared and announced, "No more surgery." He was the same bespectacled interpreter from her time there. "You all go now."

She worried how he'd react if he recognized her, that he might view her obstinance as cause to put her back behind bars. "But, sir," she said regardless, "we need a bit more time."

His brow sharply creased, reminding Lita of the hard slap he'd given Reyna. Just then, Father Domingo returned and bowed respectfully, then spoke in English with a heavy Filipino accent. "If you would kindly permit," he said, "we have one more patient to call on, merely to confirm his healing."

The interpreter debated in silence while Lita mentally pleaded for him to agree.

Dr. Garcia chimed in, "I will gather our supplies while they go see to the healing patient, so we may depart promptly after."

After a moment the interpreter declared, "Five minute."

Lita held back a smile, not wanting to seem overeager. "Yes, sir." The second he exited, she yanked off her gloves and blood-tainted apron, then thanked the doctor and rushed out with Father Domingo.

Through daylight fading to dark, he led her around the circular compound and to the entry of prison barracks. Upon seeing the priest, the guard unlocked the door, showing familiarity with the visitor.

Father Domingo motioned for her to enter. As she stepped inside, a sea of gazes found her, followed by a handful of smiles. They were American soldiers, some of them standing, others lying on their cots. From their bedraggled states, it took her a moment to recognize several of them as staff she used to know.

"Lita?" It was Dr. Thomson, his typical warmth emphasized by the crinkling at the corners of his eyes. He walked toward her and tenderly held her shoulders. "I believe you're looking for someone just over there." He motioned his chin behind her.

She turned to find Lon, resting with eyes closed. A glorious sight if not for his appearance that caused a cinching in her chest.

Bruises discolored his face, and half-healed cuts marked his forehead and cheek. Khaki fabric bound his arm in a makeshift sling, and spots of blood dotted his undershirt and trousers. Lita could easily imagine the beating the rest of his body had suffered.

Not wanting to wake him but recalling her limited time, she knelt beside his cot. The surrounding fellows appeared to be busying themselves, providing semi privacy.

She stroked Lon's temple, careful around his wounds, and his eyelids dragged open.

"Hey," he breathed, and the edges of his mouth slowly rose.

She offered a smile in return. "Hi," she said.

"Heard you might be coming by, but thought for sure I must've been dreamin'." With effort he reached out and touched her cheek. "Oh yeah. This has definitely got to be a dream."

She laughed a little, even as tears pricked her eyes.

"Now, see. I thought you agreed to get out of this place and steer clear of trouble. Huh?"

"That all depends," she said. "Are you calling yourself trouble?"

He started a laugh that he sucked right back in from the pain of his injuries. How many ribs were bruised or fractured? She desperately wanted to free him from this godforsaken place. The mere notion of leaving him here while she had an apartment to return to, with a comfortable bed and decent rations—it was almost too much to bear.

She ran her fingers over his umber hair, her gaze not leaving his. "You know what I think?" she said. "It's your turn to make *me* a promise."

He smiled. "Name it."

"You get yourself well, Lon McGibbons, then when the war is over, you're going to come and find me. Understood?"

A glimmer shone in his eyes as he gave a nod.

"I need to hear you promise."

She expected him to smile, recognizing his own words flung back at him. Instead he gazed at her for a long moment and answered in a tone steeped in sincerity. "I promise."

She released a breath, striving to keep her emotions from pouring over.

How absurd she'd been to ever regret letting him into her heart; as if it had been a choice. As if he weren't part of her forever. No matter the outcome, she wouldn't give up a single tender moment they'd shared.

"Lita." Father Domingo's voice reached her ears, and she despised what it meant. "Lita, I am sorry, but it's time."

No doubt the interpreter was keeping a close countdown. Defy his order by even seconds, and any future access for Father Domingo, or others, could be denied.

She leaned down and placed a lingering kiss on Lon's mouth, then forehead. By his ear she finally spoke the words she'd yearned to reciprocate. "I love you too," she whispered, then she forced herself to stand and walked out without looking back, her only sure way to keep from crumbling.

NINETEEN

ELEANOR

Los Baños Prison Camp, Laguna Province
October 1943

L aura Cobb had told Eleanor and the other nurses to expect it.
Until the next transfer from Santo Tomas arrived, there were a
dozen of them and nearly eight hundred men. Many of those men had
wives and fiancées and girlfriends waiting for them back home, but a great
many did not.

"You will be of interest," she had cautioned them. "I'm not going to tell
you what to do or not do. I'm just telling you what will certainly happen.
You should decide ahead how you're going to handle that interest."

Peg, who was engaged, was the only one of their number with whom
Eleanor had shared anything of her personal life, and even then it wasn't
much. She had told Peg only that there was a man back home she had fallen
for who hadn't felt the same way and that he'd been the reason she joined
the Navy Nurse Corps.

So when the inevitable happened, Peg was quick to tell Eleanor to let
herself have some fun and enjoy the attention. A lot of their fellow nurses
were.

But try as she might, Eleanor couldn't muster the matching interest needed to respond to the invitations to take a starlit stroll or to play a game of checkers or to share a rare bar of chocolate. Not when those invitations appeared to be prompted by romantic intentions.

"You need to forget that fella back home," Peg told her one evening. "Let him go, El."

"It's not . . . That's not why . . ." Eleanor fumbled for the right words. "He's married now. It's not like I think I still might have a chance with him."

"Then why not have some fun?"

Eleanor smiled as she shrugged. "I'll think about it."

But Peg shook her head as if she knew Eleanor wasn't going to think about it, nor would she let John go, even though she didn't even have hold of him. The sweet memory of having fallen in love with him was still a tonic, and memories of their lives outside were all they had in here. Some of the other nurses were lessening the sadness of not being able to return to those lives with prison-camp romances. She was lessening it by occasionally reliving the few short months she'd last been home, before she knew John was in love with someone else.

Besides, the news they were hearing out of Santo Tomas forty miles away was sobering, leaving Eleanor with no wish to enjoy a lighthearted date. Even with everyone at Los Baños having been transferred out, word was the population there had swelled to nearly four thousand internees. The already-meager food rations had been cut in half not just because supplies were running low but no doubt also to increase suffering and subservience. Relief supplies sent by the International Red Cross were being opened and tins of meat being left to rot in the sun.

Eleanor wanted to believe the rumors couldn't be true, but there was no reason to believe they weren't. She could only hope Penny was getting enough to eat and wouldn't end up in the infirmary herself. And where was Lita? Eleanor still had no way of knowing.

As the rainy season neared its end and the hot, dry season began, the next two hundred prisoners from Santo Tomas arrived—two hundred women, single or married without children—at Los Baños. The men with families—wives *and* children—would have to wait until after the new year. After so many months of seeing no other females at Los Baños, it was strange to see fellow women again, to hear their voices, tend to their illnesses, hear one of them laugh or sing a Bing Crosby tune as she hung up laundry.

Eleanor asked one of them, an Australian gal about her age who'd worked for an international travel company in Manila, how the conditions were in Santo Tomas and if she ever had occasion to visit the camp hospital there and meet an Army nurse named Penny.

The woman had been mending a torn seam when Eleanor approached her. She hesitated only a moment. "It was terrible there, but I'm not altogether sure it's that much better here. Maybe a little. Maybe. And no. I didn't meet a nurse named Penny. But I tried to steer clear of the hospital. Anyone who wasn't sick didn't want to go anywhere near it. Sorry."

It seemed as though the year would come to a close with no indication that the situation at Santo Tomas had improved and with no communication from Penny or Lita. The former radio operator at the Yard, Jerry Sams, had indeed been able to fashion a radio he hid in a sewing box—kept in plain sight—that his guards never checked, and there was the occasional bit of news of the war that circulated in covert whispers and messages in the camp.

Italy had surrendered to Allied forces. Russians had recaptured the city of Kiev in the Ukraine. B-24 Liberators had bombed Japanese positions on Wake Island, three thousand miles away. There was always distressing news, too, though. The Japanese had executed one hundred American POWs on Wake Island in retaliation.

As they prayed for the Allies to claim ultimate victory, the Los Baños inmates had continued to improvise nearly everything they needed out of repurposed items. There was still no running water or indoor plumbing for the men to use. The mud had been a constant aggravation in the wet season, and now the relentless heat without much rain was the camp's secondary tormentor.

Eleanor wanted the war to end, to be sure, but she often found herself longing more ardently for simple things like an emery board and soft toilet paper and Post Toasties for breakfast. She wanted a sleigh ride and home-made ice cream and to hear her sister giggle over a silly joke. She wanted to pat her favorite Holsteins in the milking parlor and cuddle the barn cat's kittens and watch the moon rise over the prairies.

She wanted more than anything the tangible reality of those simple things, but she knew she'd be happy with mere glimpses of what now felt like a faraway life. And even those Eleanor was being deprived of.

There had been no word from home in a year.

1944

Courage isn't having the strength to go on; it is going on when you don't have the strength.
—THEODORE ROOSEVELT

TWENTY

LITA

Manila
January 1944

Two years had come and gone since the Japanese first attacked the Philippines, and Lita struggled to imagine when, if ever, the war would end.

Medical supplies were growing scarcer by the day. After six months of her smuggling, the hospital had barely enough to get by, leaving her even less to siphon off for the camps. Plus, the new head nurse had become suspicious of missing inventory, making Lita's task even more challenging. And with fewer supplies to rig, the pesos and notes were harder to conceal, which forced her to repeatedly choose between increasing her odds of being discovered and reducing her insertion of funds and messages.

All to say, she was bringing less to Penny today than she wanted. Not that her friend would fault her.

In the early morning sunlight Lita disembarked from the bus. Over her shoulder she gripped the strap of her day satchel, her delivery tucked inside, and turned for Santo Tomas. She proffered a cordial look to a Japanese guard posted at the corner.

"Nurse!" a woman called in Tagalog. "Please!" A middle-aged Filipina nun hustled from across the street toward Lita, who stopped for her approach.

"Yes, Sister?"

"Oh, I am so glad to see you. I need your help. It's urgent."

Had Father Domingo sent her to Lita? Why would she seek assistance out here in the open? And with a Japanese soldier just yards away.

"Come, please."

Lita dropped her volume. "What is this for?"

"A child. At the convent. He is very sick. I was just heading out to find a doctor."

She'd targeted Lita for her uniform, not her identity. A relief. Although Penny was waiting. And a detour would mean not having time to complete her delivery, allowing for the standard security search, before her bus ride to work. Miss that, and her tardiness could be just the excuse needed for the head nurse to start eyeing Lita closely, further hampering her ability to smuggle.

"His fever," the nun said, a plea in her eyes. "It has been three days, and it's only gotten worse."

Lita dreaded the worry her absence would cause Penny, but her friend would understand.

"Take me to see him."

———◆———

What Lita discovered at Santa Catalina Convent, just down the road, left her speechless.

Sister Cecelia, the nun who'd recruited her, was guiding her through a communal room, where roughly twenty sets of eyes stared from small Filipino faces. Cross-legged on the ground, the children bore legs as skinny as their arms, and small patches of scalp shone through the thin hair of many.

"Now, now, children," an older nun said, her Tagalog raspy. Planted on a chair before the group, she was holding a splayed book. "Pay attention or you will miss the story."

Lita touched Sister Cecelia's elbow to pause her steps. "Is this a school?" she whispered as the older nun resumed her reading.

"Of sorts. They are all orphans. Our resources are sparse, but we teach them what we can."

"So this is an orphanage?"

"It was not intended to be. But with their parents and local relatives all killed in the war, they have nowhere else to go."

Several of the children continued to sneak glances at Lita. When she sent them a smile, they hunched or turned away bashfully. A few merely studied her.

"This way, please," Sister Cecilia said anxiously.

Lita followed her into a hall and up a set of stairs to reach a windowless room lit by candles. Blankets lay in rows on the wooden floor, numbering enough to suggest each served as a bed for the children.

A soft, rhythmic *creak* sounded from a rocking chair in the corner, where another nun hummed a soothing tune while rocking a boy in his underclothes. Lying limply with a washcloth over his forehead, he couldn't have been more than four.

Lita walked straight over and touched the child's cheek with the back of her hand, registering his flaming temperature.

"Any other symptoms?" she asked Sister Cecilia, who kneaded her hands while replying.

"He's barely eaten for a week. Not that we have much to give him. But even getting Jun-Jun to drink has been difficult."

A splotchiness colored his sweet, small face from the heat of his fever. Of all the loss of life she'd witnessed, nothing pained her more than the death of a child.

Lita set down her bag and fished out the glass bottle of aspirin that camouflaged tightly folded notes. She shook out several pills and passed them to Sister Cecelia's hands that held a slight tremble.

"These are aspirin. If you could fetch me some water, I'll help him to swallow one. You also need him to keep drinking. And he should have a lukewarm bath to help bring his temperature down. You'll need to give him another aspirin every six hours until the fever breaks."

Sister Cecilia nodded along, though she looked flustered trying to retain the instructions through her fog of worry. From the despair in her eyes, Lita sensed there had been others: that already she had tried and failed to save the lives of children under her care; that one more loss, on this day, might break her.

Lita placed a calming hand on the nun's arm, stilling her. In so many ways the burden of war extended far beyond the front lines, forging battles few would ever see.

These nuns, it appeared, were on their own. Unlike Lita, an orphan herself—though being older she rarely identified as such—the children here didn't have a village to aid them with a collection of funds, not even for such basics as food.

Perhaps she could change that. All she'd require was Ida Hube's support and trips to the black market. Just another set of illegal acts to add to her list . . .

Discarding thoughts of the consequences from her coming actions, the first of which was missing a day of work, she said, "Try not to fret, Sister. Until his fever breaks, I won't leave his side."

TWENTY-ONE

ELEANOR

Los Baños Prison Camp, Laguna Province
January 1944

T he new year arrived but nothing about it seemed new. The holiday
season had come and gone with an improvised celebration as festive
as the inmates could make it. Carols on Christmas Eve, larger rice portions
on Christmas Day with the tiniest flecks of fresh mangoes and pork stirred
into the pot, and hugs and good wishes at midnight on New Year's Day.

The first part of January, however, the camp commandant had what
Eleanor could only describe as a change of heart and allowed the Red
Cross to at last send in a load of letters and packages that had been sitting
undelivered for months. Eleanor was overjoyed to finally get a letter from
her mother, even though correspondence from home had to contain little
more than sanitized local news of the most useless nature. Her mother's
note, written in script she would recognize anywhere, was still a connection to home. In the package with the letter were three new toothbrushes
and toothpaste, freesia-scented talcum powder, five new pair of underwear,
writing paper, peppermints—these had been in transit so long they were
stuck together in one globular fist—and a pair of soft-soled slippers. There
were also photographs of Lizzie dressed up for her first winter dance and

of newborn calves and her mother's blue ribbon for her needlepoint at last year's state fair.

There was no mention of the new reverend and his wife, and for that Eleanor was grateful. Before she read it, she'd been half afraid her mother would announce that the new couple were expecting their first baby. Nor was there any mention of having received word from Eleanor. If mail from Los Baños had indeed been sent, it had not yet made its way to Minnesota when her mother had written this letter.

Too soon the contents of the note had been read and reread and the peppermints pounded apart and eaten. It was too much to consider that it might be another year before she heard from home again. Eleanor went to bed that night hugging the items her mother had sent her—even the new underwear and slippers—to her chest.

The following morning, feeling a bit blue, she went about her shift in the hospital with little enthusiasm. But as she was finishing a lunch of rice and mung beans mixed with bits of papaya, Peg came looking for her.

"There's going to be a baseball game. Us versus them. Come out to the diamond with me."

"Us versus *who*?" Eleanor was sitting outside the hospital in the shade of a banyan tree, and she squinted up at Peg.

"The Japs of course. Come on." Peg started to yank Eleanor to her feet.

"But my shift!" Eleanor struggled to keep the last bites from her bowl from spilling as she let Peg hoist her up.

"I already asked Laura if you could come with me. She said yes. She doesn't want to watch it. Come on!"

Peg allowed Eleanor to swing by the camp kitchen to deposit her bowl and then led her past the main gate, which was open but guarded heavily so the internees who would be allowed to watch the game could head to the athletic fields beyond the barbed-wire perimeter. Several hundred internees and Japanese soldiers were already there, and the first inning appeared to have just started.

The American internees had already been allowed to form teams and had been playing baseball for many weeks for exercise and diversion. Bats and balls had been confiscated from the former school's athletic building, and surprisingly the commandant permitted the inmates to use them, while heavily guarded of course. Eleanor had never seen the Japanese soldiers or guards playing.

"Do the Japanese even know how to play baseball?" she asked Peg.

"Who cares? And anyway, it was the commandant's idea to have this game. He shouldn't have suggested it if he wasn't prepared for a little competition."

"Yes, but what if they get clobbered? You know how they are about honor and shame. It . . . it could go badly for us." As Eleanor said this, a Japanese soldier at bat popped a fly into the air. The ball was easily caught by an American infielder. It was the third out in less than five minutes.

"Yeah, I already heard that the admin committee suggested to our team that they throw the game. I don't think they will though." Peg nodded toward the diamond and the two teams switching positions after the quick inning.

Peg settled onto a patch of grass near home plate. Eleanor sat next to her. The rest of the spectators were spread out past the foul lines and some on a set of wooden bleachers that had seen better days.

The internees—a collection of mostly Americans and a few Canadians and Britons—quickly racked up runs in the bottom of the first, as the Japanese players were unable to field the hits and the prisoners connected with every ball lobbed to them. One of the American players rounded third base for home and then looked at Eleanor as he ran past, barefoot, at an easy clip, the ball still being chased with much comical effort. He smiled and waved as he passed.

Eleanor recognized that face. But from where?

Peg leaned into her. "Do you know that guy?"

As soon as the question was out of Peg's mouth, Eleanor remembered who he was. She hadn't seen him since the day she arrived in Manila two and a half years ago.

"I do," Eleanor said, as echoes of his name returned to her. Ensign Mathis or Matthews or something like that. "He was from a Navy HQ detachment that met the ship that brought me to the Philippines. He helped me get where I was supposed to be. I haven't seen him since."

He had joked that he hoped he wouldn't see her again, unless it was somewhere pleasant and outside the hospital at the Yard. A smile crossed her face. They were definitely outside the Yard's hospital.

"He's a dish." Peg grinned and elbowed her in the ribs.

Eleanor watched the ensign touch home plate with his foot and then turn to look at her again before making his way to the makeshift dugout. "I guess he is."

"You *guess*? He's adorable. I insist you go over there and say hello when the game is over."

"Yeah. Okay. Maybe," Eleanor said numbly, her mind still on that long-ago day when she got off the ship and Manila was a garden paradise.

"'Maybe' nothing. I'll take you over there myself."

After only one more inning—the Japanese had hit nothing and the Americans had a double-digit score—the commandant, who'd been playing for his team, stood up and abruptly called the game to a halt. There would be no more games. He ordered the bats be rounded up and marched his players back to the compound. A dozen guards spread out over the athletic field shooed the internees to follow them. The ensign walked over to where Peg and Eleanor were standing up and brushing dirt and grass off their denim uniforms.

He looked a bit different from the last time she'd seen him. The ensign had been in his whites that day, twenty pounds heavier for sure, and with a regulation haircut. The man who stood before her now was wearing dungarees and a chambray shirt. His hair was relatively short but still touching his ears and collar, and he hadn't had a close shave in a few days. But his eyes were bright, and he seemed genuinely glad to see her. He carried his boots slung over his shoulder.

"Hey," he said when he reached them. "Nurse Lindstrom, right?" He stuck out his hand. "David Mathis."

She shook it. "Nice to see you, Ensign Mathis. We meet again. Outside the hospital at the Yard, just like you asked."

He laughed. "How about that! It's technically Lieutenant JG by now. But who's paying attention to anything like making rank these days? Please just call me David."

"And I'm just Eleanor. And this is my friend, cohort, and roommate, Peg."

"Nice to meet you, David." Peg shook his hand. "Shortest baseball game in history, eh?"

David laughed. "No doubt. My guess is that's the first and last time our captors will challenge us to a game."

A frowning guard motioned with his rifle for them to get moving and the three of them started walking back toward the main gate.

Peg turned to them. "I actually have patients I need to get back to, so I'm going to run along." She gave Eleanor a barely perceptible wink and then jogged ahead, leaving Eleanor and David to walk at a regular pace.

Eleanor looked down at David's dirty feet as they walked. "You always play baseball barefoot?" Then her face flushed. Of all the ways to begin a conversation, she had to say that?

But he laughed. "No. Just trying to ward off jungle rot. Had a bad case of it last year at Baguio. I take my boots off for several hours a day now. I'll put them back on when we get back inside the perimeter, I promise."

"Sorry. I shouldn't have asked. It's none of my business."

"I would guess jungle rot is unfortunately too much your business right now," he said with a smile.

She smiled back. "You're right about that. That's actually really smart, what you're doing. I wish more of the inmates would think about their feet. We barely have anything here to treat jungle rot. It gets really bad in the wet season."

Eleanor sighed inwardly again. Could she really say nothing more interesting than comment about feet and jungle rot?

He didn't seem to care. "You been at Los Baños long?"

"Seems like a long time, but I guess it's not," Eleanor replied. "We were transferred here from Santo Tomas last May. Only nine months ago. Seems longer."

"I hear you. I was at the prison camp in Baguio before. I was transferred here in December."

They reached the perimeter and David was allowed by the guards to stop walking and put his boots back on. The hospital was one building in on the left, and Eleanor was torn. She wanted to keep talking to this man who knew her before, and yet she knew Laura fully expected her to come back inside and finish her shift.

They reached her destination minutes after stepping back inside the barbed wire.

"I'm afraid I am expected back inside the infirmary." She nodded toward the pink stucco building.

He seemed a bit sad too. Perhaps he also liked talking with someone who had known him before. "Perhaps we can get together later and get caught up?"

It was a funny way to say what he meant, and they both laughed. She again felt her face flush a little. "I get off at seven."

"That's still time before curfew for a cocktail."

She grinned. "A cocktail?"

"I have a nice bottle of coconut water. Has a lovely bouquet and smooth finish. A very good year. Well, actually, it's not a very good year. But it was a good coconut."

"That sounds nice."

"My barracks are way down by the chapel, and there's nowhere to sit down there, of course, so how about I bring the fine wine here and we can sit on the steps of the hospital and have it?"

"Okay."

He left and Eleanor stepped back inside the infirmary. Peg was all smiles when Eleanor told her she'd be seeing David after her shift.

"It's about time you had some fun, El," Peg said. "When was the last time you were on a date?"

"It's not a date. We're just getting together to talk."

"Hey, in this place, that's a date."

Eleanor laughed. "Okay, okay. Just don't make more of this than it is."

"Don't you make less of it."

The rest of her shift passed slowly. Eleanor found herself puzzled by the subtle fascination she was feeling toward David Mathis. It wasn't quite attraction, although Peg was right. With his sandy-brown hair, gray eyes, and five o'clock shadow, David was certainly easy on the eyes. It was perplexing to think maybe, possibly, with David, she could begin to wean herself off her persistent emotional addiction to John Olson.

Finally, her shift ended, and Eleanor headed for the front door. She wished she had thought of asking to meet at seven thirty so she could've had time to pop over to her nearby quarters to change into a simple cotton dress and run a comb through her hair. *But this isn't a date*, she told herself as she crossed the threshold and saw David sitting on the steps waiting for her.

He looked like he might've shaved. The razors the internees were allowed were so dull, it was difficult for any of the men to appear properly shaved, but she caught the whiff of the medicinal-smelling shaving powder the men used as she took a seat next to him.

"Gosh, you smell nice." He handed her a tin cup of coconut water.

"I do?" Eleanor couldn't imagine why. She'd been cleaning out a pus-filled wound before her shift ended. Then she remembered. She'd sprinkled on some talcum powder when she dressed that morning.

"Yes."

"I think it's freesia you're smelling. My mother sent some powder to me. First package from home I've had in almost a year."

"Well, it smells great. My mother sent me comic books and socks and toffee peanuts, so I smell like the jungle." He took a swig from the bottle, which had perhaps held vinegar or cooking oil in an earlier life.

"I love toffee peanuts," she said.

"So did everybody in my barracks. They were gone in ten minutes."

"That was nice of you to share."

"Seemed like the right thing to do. Some of the guys didn't get anything this last Red Cross delivery."

"I should have shared my mints, I suppose. They were stuck together like someone had already licked them, though."

"Maybe somebody had."

They laughed. And then they began to talk. It was an easy conversation and lacked the awkwardness she'd felt before with getting to know a man she knew nothing about and who didn't know her. Eleanor shared about where she had grown up, what it was like being the daughter of a dairy farmer, and how she'd spent her winters ice skating on the pond, her

autumns going on hayrides, and her summers catching fireflies and showing calves at the state fair.

He told her he had been born and raised in San Diego and that he spent
his summers on a surfboard—and his winters too—and that he liked aba-
lone and lobster and sports and his dog Pablo, whom his mother and father
were now caring for.

"I've two older brothers who are also in the Navy," he said. "I'm not sure
where either one is. Tim was still in flight school when the war started, and
Russell was assigned to a battleship based out of Norfolk. This last letter
from Mom made it seem like they are okay. She couldn't say where they
are, of course. The censors would have cut it out."

"No sisters?" Eleanor asked.

"Nope. Just us three."

"It must be hard for your parents for all of their children to be in the
military right now."

"I suppose it is. So why did you join the Navy?" David asked. "I haven't
met very many Minnesotans in this line of work, if you get my meaning."

Eleanor was enjoying his company and the conversation and the little
bit of space she was sensing between herself and her old obsession.

"I needed a change. A big one."

"You certainly got it. I'm curious as to what made you want a change
this big."

She decided to be honest with him. "I got my heart broken," she said as
casually as she could.

"Ouch. That has happened to me a time or two," he said, although she
thought he probably wasn't still dreaming of the people who had crushed
him like she was. He took another swig. "So here's where you wanted to
come to mend?"

"Seemed like a really good idea at the time," she said, and they both
smiled.

They were quiet for a moment.

"What are you going to do when this is over?" he asked. "Are you going
to stay in?"

"Aren't you the optimistic one."

"Oh, absolutely. I have full confidence in the U.S. Armed Forces. We won't be here forever. We will win this war and we'll get out of here."

"Well then, in that case," she said, "I guess I should say I really haven't thought about it."

"You should ask to get assigned to San Diego. I think you'd like it. We have the sun without the humidity or bugs, and we have the ocean and palm trees and there are no geckos or monkeys trying to get into your bedroom."

"Sounds nice."

"It is."

They talked for a while longer, until the coconut water was gone and the nine o'clock curfew sounded.

David stood and then helped Eleanor to her feet.

"I'm sure I'll be seeing you around," he said.

"Just not in the building behind me, right?"

He grinned. "Roger that. Good night, Eleanor."

She watched him head down the camp's main dirt road toward the men's barracks in the southeast corner of the campus. She hadn't asked David if he was married or engaged or had a girlfriend back home. She probably should have. But tonight had been fun. Why risk spoiling it?

There was always tomorrow to ask, wasn't there? Or the next day. Or the one after that.

Or the one after that.

TWENTY-TWO

PENNY

Santo Tomas Internment Camp, Manila
February 1944

In January 1944 control of Santo Tomas Internment Camp—along with every other civilian prison camp in the Philippines—had transferred from the Japanese Bureau of External Affairs to the War Prisoners Department of the Imperial Japanese Army. A new camp commandant—a senior military officer named Colonel Onozaki—rumbled through the gates early one morning during the second week of February. It was not yet dawn, but the sound of revving engines and shouts woke the camp.

Many of the internees, Penny among them, wandered outside to watch the caravan of military vehicles thunder through the streets and drive directly to the low, squat structure the Japanese used as headquarters. Every light was on in the building, and four dozen soldiers stood outside in formation. From a distance she could see Onozaki alight from his vehicle and receive the salutes with a nod.

Penny went back inside and woke Newt. "Get up. It's Tuesday."

Eleven now, and precocious as ever, the little girl sprang out of bed, her hair poking out in every direction. "The package line!"

Penny brushed Newt's hair—with no small amount of difficulty—and made her dress for the day. They wandered down to the front gates together. Father Domingo was expecting a response from a contact, and Ida Hube had promised another cart of supplies for the nurses. On Tuesday mornings she would often pull up to the gates in her shiny black limousine, and members of her staff would pop out like bedsprings and load a cart with food and supplies for the nurses. The guards never let Ida inside, and they always insisted on pawing through the cart—sometimes taking a bar of chocolate or tins of cookies as payment—before letting it through.

Until that morning.

"Why is she yelling at that guard?" Newt asked.

Penny could see Ida on the other side, arms flinging about in fury—pointing first at the guard, then at the gates—but she couldn't understand much of what Ida said. No doubt because half of the diatribe was German profanity, but she did spit out the occasional "Ridiculous!" "Outrage!" "Crime!" in English.

Others were starting to gather at the gates as well—on both sides—and a buzz of conversation filled the air. Lita stood in the crowd raised up on tiptoes. She had a laundry parcel in one arm and was shielding her face from the rising sun with her other hand. Penny shifted closer to her usual position and they made eye contact, a smile passing between them. This ritual was a comfort to Penny, a way of being certain that Lita was alive and unharmed. The gates remained locked, however, and countless packages and bags and boxes were stacked outside, waiting to be delivered. Before long, people on both sides of the gates were shouting and arguing with the guards.

That was when the uniform cadence of marching feet could be heard coming from the Japanese headquarters. The crowd hushed and, almost in unison, turned to watch the two lines of soldiers approach the gates. Fifty in all. Uniforms crisp and eyes like flint, their rifles leaned against their shoulders, deadly points of the bayonets on display. The crowd stepped back, and the guards marched directly toward the gates, turned, and, in formation, lowered their rifles so they pointed at the internees.

Penny grabbed the collar of Newt's shirt and eased backward between two older men who, given the state of their confusion, seemed both hard of hearing and nearly blind. Then the camp loudspeakers crackled to life above the Education Building.

She recognized Akibo's voice immediately.

"Under direct orders of Colonel Onozaki, the package line is being disbanded immediately. Residents of Santo Tomas are to have no contact with anyone outside camp."

The speakers crackled again, then fell silent. Penny didn't wait to see how the crowd of internees would respond to the news or how the soldiers might retaliate. She simply took Newt's hand and retreated, as fast as she could without breaking into a run, back to Main Building.

Like his predecessor, Onozaki could not speak English. It was a weakness that Captain Akibo exploited the moment he arrived at Santo Tomas, and by the time Onozaki got his bearings in camp, Akibo wasn't simply an interpreter. He was a trusted advisor to the commandant. So it made sense that when Onozaki summoned the executive committee, lead doctor, and head nurses to a meeting, Penny saw him standing at Onozaki's right side, behind the desk.

Akibo's hands were folded casually behind his back, and his face was tranquil, but his eyes latched onto Penny the moment she entered the room and followed her until she took her place between Maude and Josie. She could feel the weight of his gaze and chose to watch Onozaki instead.

Penny thought it was easier to hate an evil man if he was ugly. Onozaki, however, stood six feet tall and had the sort of distinguished look that men so often benefit from in middle age. His face was all sharp angles: high cheekbones, square jaw, and straight nose. His mouth was pressed into a tight line, however, and his eyes seemed fathomless and cold. He radiated a sort of anger that put the room on edge. As Onozaki surveyed the small group assembled in his office, it occurred to Penny that a handsome villain was a far more terrifying thing.

He neither greeted those assembled nor addressed them beyond that initial look, and when he spoke, his gaze seemed to drift through them to the wall beyond.

"This camp has been mismanaged." Akibo took a small step forward. "Colonel Onozaki is going to change that."

Back and forth they went, first the commandant, then Akibo.

"You have had unnecessary contact with the outside world. You have been told harmful lies about the kind and gracious Imperial Japanese Army. All of that ends today."

Onozaki spoke again. Akibo turned to him. And Penny watched Akibo.

"Strict regulations will be put in place. You no longer have need of the package line."

"That's where most of our extra food comes from!" Jim Hobbs argued.

Onozaki's eyes zeroed in on the man who stepped forward. An older American who had lived in Sacramento before the war, Jim had the great misfortune to have been traveling through Manila on a retirement trip when the Japanese attacked Pearl Harbor.

"Thirty-five cents a day per person isn't enough to feed everyone," Jim added. "Even if we got that much, which we haven't in over a year, we *need* the package line."

Akibo gave a rapid-fire interpretation of Hobbs's complaint, then just as quickly delivered Onozaki's reply.

"You no longer need the package line or the daily allowance because the Japanese army will provide the camp with food and medical supplies going forward."

"What food?" Hobbs demanded.

Onozaki's eyes tightened at the corners. "Whatever is necessary. Fish. Rice. Vegetables. Milk. Cassava bread."

"What about salt, sugar, cooking oil, and tea? What about fruit and flour?"

The reply, once interpreted, was terse. "If it is available."

"What about mail?" Jim asked. "According to Articles 71 and 72 of the Geneva Convention—which your prime minister has signed—all prisoners of war are entitled to send and receive letters and parcels while in captivity. And, as stated in those articles, food and clothing are considered valid contents of such parcels. Can we be assured that the leadership of this camp will honor the commitment your country has made?"

It was a clever argument and Jim had been shrewd to make it. The Japanese prime minister had signed the convention, but the Japanese never ratified it and couldn't technically be held to it. But rejecting the convention outright was not just dishonorable but a statement of their intent to commit war crimes.

It took several moments for Akibo to translate, then relay the response. Onozaki said simply, "All mail will be searched."

It was neither a promise nor a refusal, but it was the only answer they were to have that day.

Maude wanted to know the new rules on medical supplies. They were low on bandages and anesthetics. Aspirin and laxatives remained in short supply, as did bed linens and surgical tools. One of the two sanitizing machines was broken, forcing them to boil their tools in cooking pots. Rust was becoming a problem. She said all of this as quickly and respectfully as she could, gaze centered on the first button of Onozaki's shirt. The problem was Maude had not been asked to speak. Nor did she bow when finished.

Neither Akibo nor Onozaki addressed her questions or even acknowledged that she had spoken. The group was promptly dismissed.

Once outside, Maude grabbed Penny's hand and squeezed as though her hand were wrapped around the commandant's neck. "I am a first lieutenant in the United States Army," she whispered. "And he ignored me as though I don't exist."

"You are a *woman*. To him you don't," Penny said.

"As if he doesn't exist in this world because a *woman* carried him into it!"

It wasn't often that Penny saw Maude lose her temper. She could clamp a severed artery or thrust her hand into an open wound without so much as a flinch. But to be dismissed and ignored brought her right up to the ragged edge of her composure.

"Do you realize what he was saying about the food?"

"That they are taking control of what we eat."

"And *how much*. We are on a subsistence diet already. That's with the allowance, the vendors, and the package line. And we're still seeing symptoms of malnutrition throughout the camp." Maude stopped in the middle of the road and turned to Penny. Her fists were clenched and nostrils flared. "We can treat malaria and dysentery and arthritis. We can operate and dispense medicine and set broken bones. But there is absolutely nothing we can do to save the people in this camp from starvation."

———◆———

The first food shipment promised by Colonel Onozaki fell short of both the promised items and amounts. It contained only fish, rice, yams, squash, and one thousand loaves of cassava bread instead of the fourteen hundred that were needed. There was no milk for the children. No salt to flavor the food. They were informed sugar and flour would be in the next shipment.

"What are we going to do?" Penny asked Maude as they stood outside the mess hall, dinner tickets in hand.

Only three weeks into Onozaki's command and the lines were twice as long as they'd been since his arrival. She saw many of the bankers and businessmen who had kept the camp economy functional since its creation. These men typically bought their meals from the vendors and food stalls and ordered supplies directly through the package line. Now, having money meant nothing if there was nowhere to spend it.

"Jim Hobbs and several other administration staff went to Onozaki this morning to complain," Maude said. "They insisted that we'd been promised adequate food for all internees but were given only two-thirds of what we need. They demanded the package line be restored and the vendors be reinstated."

"What happened?"

"Onozaki abolished the executive committee. All administration of the camp will be handled directly by the Japanese now."

Penny didn't have to imagine how such an administration would negatively affect those inside the camp walls. Already their movements were being restricted, and the guards questioned anyone who ventured too far from Main Building or the shanty complexes. A curfew had been put in place upon Onozaki's arrival. All internees were to be inside their quarters between seven at night and six in the morning. Anyone caught outside during those hours was to be shot on sight. She rattled this off to Maude as they took their place in line outside the mess hall.

"It makes it easier on them," Maude said. "They only have to bother with us for thirteen hours a day."

"What about the roll call? What does that accomplish? Twice a day now! We have to line up like children on a playground. We have to *bow* to them when we pass."

"Control, mostly. But also intimidation." Maude leaned heavily on the cane gifted to her by Father Domingo and winced as they moved forward in line.

Three years now Penny had worked with Maude, first in peacetime, then in combat conditions, and now in this strange hybrid world in which they were both captive and caregiver. She had aged considerably. Grayer. Older. Withered, as though her formidable height had been shaved away— Penny could look her in the eyes now instead of having to tilt her chin upward when they spoke.

Maude's limp was pronounced and the skin across her neck, hands, and collarbones had taken on the consistency of tissue paper thanks to her significant weight loss. If she had to wager, Penny would say Maude was nearing one hundred pounds—an excessively low weight on her almost-six-foot frame.

Even as Penny noted these changes in her mentor, she'd begun to avoid mirrors herself. Only a handful were sprinkled around camp—mostly in common restrooms—but she tried not to look. Vanity was a double-edged sword: it brought either pride or self-loathing. But ever since that glimpse in the mirror upon her arrival, Penny refused to hate herself for the great privilege of growing old. The passing years and accumulating signs of age meant that she was surviving this place, and even though she didn't have to celebrate the physical manifestations of that victory, she wouldn't punish herself either.

Newt found them as they neared the mess-hall doors and cut in line so she could stand beside Penny, her own meal ticket clenched in her grubby hand.

"I'm hungry," she announced, rising onto the tiptoes of her bare feet to see how many people were in line ahead of them.

Penny ruffled her messy hair. "That's because you're growing."

Except she wasn't. That's what the look that passed between Penny and Maude communicated. The child hadn't grown in months. Newt should be near Penny's shoulders, if not taller. But she barely passed the top of her ribs. Her hair wasn't growing, rendering the contentious haircuts unnecessary, and that limitless energy she'd once had was gone now, replaced by daily naps that could last up to three hours.

When their turn in line came and they held out their tin plates, each of them received one scoop of watery rice, a portion of canned fish, and a bit of overcooked succotash from the cooks. Penny might have requested more for Newt, but guards had been assigned to the mess hall the week before, and two of them stood at the front of the line, bayonets ready, in case any prisoner tried to negotiate more than their allotted serving.

Maude led them to a table near an open window, and when Penny sent Newt off to fetch them cups of water, both she and Maude scooted several forkfuls of their dinner onto the child's plate.

"I hate them," Penny hissed. "I *hate* them for this. She's only a child."

"There are a thousand children in this camp. They don't care about her. Or any of us for that matter." Maude waved around the crowded room. "They *want* us hungry."

"So they can starve us to death?"

"So they can control us."

———◆———

Penny thought of Maude's words as she and Newt rushed back to Main Building a short time later. It was nearing seven o'clock, and though the sun was still well above the horizon, the camp was shutting down on schedule. Three men had been caught out after seven since the curfew was put in place. And three men had been shot, then buried in a trench dug along the inside of the camp walls. The Japanese said it was because they were caught trying to go over the wall, but no one believed them.

"Hurry," Penny said, cursing herself for not making Newt wear shoes.

"I'm trying! Your legs are longer than mine."

They rounded a corner onto the main boulevard but came to a complete stop when Captain Akibo stepped into their path. He looked surprised to see Penny—at least he hadn't been stalking her this time—but not displeased. He gave them a satisfied smile and took a large bite out of the chocolate bar in his hand.

Newt's eyes went large with envy, and she didn't move her gaze as he took a second, then a third bite and chewed slowly, savoring it in front of them.

As Penny moved to step around him, he asked, "Are you ready yet?"

For Newt's sake, she swallowed the string of profanity that rose in her throat, and the single word she managed to spit out sounded pathetic to her. "Never."

"Pity." Akibo knelt on the concrete before Newt. He took another deliberate bite. "She looks hungry."

"Let's go." Penny gripped Newt's hand as tight as she could without hurting her.

Akibo peeled off the last of the foil wrapping and held out the chocolate piece to Newt. "Go on," he said.

Penny wanted to rip it from her hands, but it would be cruel. The child had licked her plate clean at dinner but was still hungry.

Newt shoved the chocolate in her mouth before he could change his mind, and when Akibo rose to his feet again, he looked at Penny. "See. I can be a *very* nice man."

TWENTY-THREE

ELEANOR

Los Baños Prison Camp, Laguna Province
March 1944

It didn't feel like the beginning of a romance, though the other nurses lovingly teased that Eleanor's friendship with David Mathis sure looked like it was. She liked how easy it was to talk with him—this had been true with John Olson as well—but she didn't sense the magnetic pull that she'd had with John. There was something calm and ordinary about their relationship. David didn't make her heart flutter.

On their third "date" she'd asked him if there was someone special waiting back home in San Diego for him, and he answered by asking her if it would bother her if there was.

"That means there is, right?" she asked. They were eating lunch together on the grass near the camp cemetery, one of the remaining open spaces still within the perimeter.

"In a way. Barbara and I had just started seeing each other when I got my orders to Cavite. It seemed like we were headed somewhere. She wrote to me when I first got here like we were. I didn't hear from her much during the first year as a POW. And I haven't heard from her at all this second year. I'm not sure what she's thinking."

"Mail has been slow in coming. Especially here," Eleanor said. "She might have written you many times this past year and her letters are sitting in a Red Cross cargo container that the Japanese won't allow to be delivered."

"Maybe. I don't know. Sometimes I think she's moved on."

"I'm sorry." She was.

"Yeah. I'm not sure how I feel about it myself. Sad. Relieved. Mad. Confused. All of them, I guess."

"I can understand that. All except the 'relieved' part."

David gave her a kind, knowing look. "Want to tell me what happened? You don't have to, of course."

Eleanor sensed an immediate willingness to share with David exactly how she'd ended up in the Navy Nurse Corps. She'd not really told anyone about the day she'd decided to tell John Olson how she felt. Even Penny and Lita only knew that one minute Eleanor was telling the handsome reverend she was falling for him, and the next he was telling her he was engaged and apologizing profusely for somehow leading her on.

"You really want to hear it?" she asked.

"If you want to share it."

She inhaled deeply and let the breath out. "I was working at a hospital in Minneapolis and I took a leave of absence to help out back home. My mom had come down with a terrible case of pneumonia, my dad has a dairy herd, and I knew they needed me. I'd been given the okay to stay three months, or until Mom was back on her feet. A new minister had just been installed at the Lutheran church in my hometown. John Olson was the first young pastor I had ever met. Fresh out of seminary and full of smiles and good humor. And he was so caring, David. He'd come over to see my mother to visit with her and pray with her, and then he'd stay and chat with my dad. And then he'd stay even longer and talk with me. He was so . . . nice to me."

"And good looking? Like me?" David grinned.

Eleanor smiled back. "He was that too."

"So what do you mean by he was 'nice' to you?" The smile on David's face was still there, but he'd crinkled his brow slightly in puzzlement. "It had to have been a special kind of nice. Nice to the mailman and nice to the old lady who lives across the street and nice to you had to be different if you believed he felt the same, right?"

Her face warmed a bit. "He was engaged. I was mistaken."

"But how do you know you were mistaken? Maybe he was actually having second thoughts about his engagement and that's why you felt a connection with him. It happens, you know."

"He would have told me if he was when I told him how I felt about him. He's a man of his word, near as I can tell. I really do think that when he told me he never meant to lead me on, he meant it. He really is a kind man, very good to people, and he'll be an excellent minister."

"And so how was it you didn't know beforehand that he was engaged? I'm curious."

She flinched a tiny bit, the pain still fresh as always. "I'm pretty sure everybody in the church knew he was engaged, including my parents. No doubt it was one of the reasons the church leaders had been so excited about him coming on board. He was going to be bringing in a new wife. But I didn't know this, and why would anybody tell me? It shouldn't have mattered that I be told. And it doesn't matter now."

Eleanor thought back to the humiliating moment when she'd gone to the parsonage and told John she was in love with him, the bravest thing she had ever done. She recalled the look in his eyes when he took her hands and told her how desperately sorry he was to have assumed that she knew he was engaged. "He said he deeply regretted causing me to misinterpret our friendship. He took all the blame for my poor discernment. All of it. And then he said the wedding would be in Brainerd in a few months, where his fiancée was from."

"Wow. That's . . . that's tough."

"It's why I really joined the Navy Nurse Corps and why I was so relieved that they took me right away. My heart was shattered, and I didn't know how to fix it. I wanted to get as far away from the broken pieces as I could."

David bumped his shoulder gently into hers. "I would say eight thousand miles about does it, don't you think?"

She laughed and it felt good.

He looked at her thoughtfully. "Is it okay with you if we continue to get together like this? I really like talking with you, Eleanor. I feel . . . comfortable around you. And I like that you're not expecting too much from me."

"I like talking with you too. And I feel the same way."

A few minutes of silence passed between them. "But I think it would be smart of us to let each other know if we're starting to feel differently." David looked into her eyes with greater depth. "It could happen. I almost wouldn't mind if it did."

She held his gaze. "I know exactly what you mean. I almost wouldn't mind either."

"So we have a deal?" He held out his hand.

She smiled and shook it. "We do."

———◆———

In April the nurses learned another round of inmates were coming to Los Baños from Santo Tomas. They were told by the admin committee that they'd be losing their dormitory and would now be bunking in the infirmary's basement, a tiny space compared to what they'd grown used to.

"Will there be any Army nurses coming with them?" Eleanor asked Laura Cobb as they prepared to move their few belongings, hoping Penny might be among the new arrivals and yet knowing the chances were slim.

"No. They're needing to relieve some overcrowding. It's still going to be only us running the hospital. And we're likely going to be busier than ever."

Laura's words proved true. The hospital instantly filled when the one hundred–plus new transfers from Santo Tomas arrived, as many of them arrived sick and weak. And this time, women and children were among the inmates. Eleanor hadn't seen a child in so long she found herself sometimes staring in awe when she saw a mother sitting in the dirt braiding a daughter's hair, or a pair of nuns walking across the camp in their long black habits with little children following them like ducklings.

It made no sense to her that civilians were made to live in the camp like this, especially the young mothers and their children.

"What possible threat could they be to the Japanese Empire?" Eleanor asked Peg one night as they lay in their cots in the dank basement. "The wife and young children of a British banker having the rotten luck of working in Manila when the war came? What danger are they to Japanese forces? Why can't they just be sent home?"

"I'm quite sure it's not safe to cross the Pacific. It's a war zone. And I'd wager the Japanese wouldn't use any of their ships to transport the families of civilians back to the U.S. or Europe. Not now. And they certainly wouldn't allow a ship from an enemy nation to land and take them out of here."

"Not even a Red Cross ship? Our military would never use a Red Cross ship as a front for a warship."

"They won't do it, El." Peg turned over and curled up into a ball on her bedroll.

Eleanor knew Peg was right. Those women and children were the family of the enemy.

The Japanese forces would never do what the enemy wanted.

TWENTY-FOUR

LITA

Santa Catalina Convent, Manila
May 1944

L ita became aware her mind had drifted when the room went silent. At the back of the convent's communal space, she was parked with all three nuns at the long table typically used for the orphans' schooling. As it was evening now, the children sat cross-legged on the floor, listening.

"And *that*," Reyna announced in Tagalog, seated on a chair at the front, "is theee end!" She shut the book with equally dramatic flair.

All at once the kids, ranging in ages from three to seven, called out stories they longed to hear next. It was a massive eruption of titles thanks to their expanding library, and thus to Ida Hube.

Over the past four months the gregarious woman had come through in more ways than Lita ever expected. It was no wonder Penny had called Ida a guardian angel. Aside from gifts of food and funds for Lita's purchases from the black market, Ida insisted on supplying the children regularly with learning tools. Books naturally were among them, and each connected differently with malleable minds hungry for experiences beyond this building and city, far past these islands. Most of all, in a place they had barely or never known: a world without war.

Recently Ida had become especially generous with the kids, but for a lamentable reason. The new commander of Santo Tomas had shut down the camp's interactions with the public, eliminating Ida's usual support of the nurses. As of three months ago the package line, like the vendor sales, had become a thing of the past. At this very moment Penny was a stone's throw from the convent, where Lita remained a frequent visitor, and yet any chance of communicating, even seeing each other from ten feet apart, was no longer an option. Same for Father Domingo, thereby ruling out any visits to Bilibid. And while Lita persisted with her drop-offs there as medical supplies allowed—which was to say, not very often—she could only hope her messages were getting through.

In her free moments she liked to envision Lon seated on his cot, healed and well while reading those notes, perhaps imagining scenes similar to her own recurrent daydreams: of the two of them in the States, married and happy; he in a dapper banker suit and she in a uniform from the local hospital, where she'd work alongside her sisters until she and Lon started a family of their own. How they'd be treated, being a mixed couple, did enter her mind. Her sister, who'd married an American, had voiced some early challenges in her letters, though being only half Filipina had helped. One benefit of being a mestiza. Either way, for Lita it was a worry for another day, and one she had full confidence she and Lon could conquer together, should the future guide them there.

These were among the thoughts that had distracted her from the reading, an activity at which Reyna had grown more and more animated as the months went on. A point evident by the group's overt love of her storytelling.

"Read another, Auntie!"

"Pick mine, pick mine!"

"Just one more, Auntie Reyna, please!"

Lita might have been envious, even in the slightest, but glimpsing a softer side of her roommate was entirely worthwhile.

"Sorry, little ones," Sister Cecilia interjected through the din while rising from her seat. "That's enough for tonight. Off now to bed."

The children groaned in ragged unison.

Lita offered an assurance. "We'll be back to see you soon. Before then, we all need a good night's rest!"

And she meant that, herself included.

True, when she'd fallen under the head nurse's scrutiny, Reyna made pointedly clear to the woman that Lita deserved to be trusted and valued for her experience and skills—and even the head nurse knew better than to battle Reyna. Yet being tardy or sluggish wouldn't exactly support that claim.

"Up, up," the nun ordered. "Grousing will only make Nurse Delos Santos and Nurse Capel choose not to return. Is that what we want?"

The room quieted instantly, and Lita fought off a smile that would undermine the warning.

"Everyone, say good night," another nun added.

The children scrambled to their feet and called out their good nights. The sight of them shuffling toward their bedroom with fuller cheeks and thicker hair, more fat and muscle to their limbs, never ceased to warm Lita's heart. They still weren't the ideal image of prewar health, but they were significantly better, and for that she felt great pride.

About one boy, admittedly, more than the rest.

As always he ended the visit by scuttling over to hug Lita.

When she twisted to face him, he threw his arms around her neck. "Aww, thank you, Jun-Jun," she said. Then noting his height, she drew her head back and mussed his hair. "Goodness, did you get even taller this week?"

Grinning, he nodded with vigor, eyes twinkling, his little round nose cute as ever.

"You'd better stop growing so fast," she said, feigning a lecture, "or I'll have to put a brick on your head and slow you down. Got that?"

He let out a giggle, a sound so pure and sweet she wished she could store it in a jar. Then he bounded off with the others to ready for sleep and, hopefully, to dream of good things to come.

———◆———

"Thanks again for joining me tonight," Lita said, once back in their apartment as she hung up her coat on a peg by the door.

"Yeah. Sure." Reyna's nonchalant tone made Lita secretly smile. Because when it came to the convent, she saw right through her friend's indifference.

Reyna clicked on the lamp between their narrow beds. "So, are you hungry?"

Always was the understood answer for anyone these days. Still, the city's available rations were invariably better than any meals provided in the camps or prisons, so there was no room to complain. "What did you have in mind?"

"Supplier delivered goods to the café this morning. I figured we could poke around and borrow a little."

Lita rolled her eyes. "Last I checked, 'borrowing' means you plan to give it back."

"Okay." She shrugged. "So we'll eat half and return the rest."

"That's not exactly what I meant."

"Hey, you're the one being a stickler about the whole borrowing thing."

Lita couldn't help but laugh.

Reyna boasted a smirk that, upon a noise, abruptly fell. From the floor below came a pounding on glass and a man's unintelligible shouts.

It was a caller at the café entrance. But the place was shuttered for the night, the manager already gone before she and Lita passed through.

"Lock the door," Reyna ordered. As Lita did so, her friend hustled to the window and peeked past the curtain. The intensity in her face when she twisted back stiffened Lita's spine.

"It's the Kempeitai," Reyna said.

A hard lump formed in Lita's throat.

The pounding grew louder. It took Lita minimal effort to decipher the reason for their presence. She opened her mouth to tell Reyna, but sounds of shattered glass cut through the air.

The café door had been broken down.

Could she escape out the window?

Lita rushed to Reyna's side at the curtain. On the street just below were silhouettes of two armed guards with white armbands that shone in the moonlight. Memories of the military police in the square, and in countless nightmares since, flared through her mind. In a flash she saw herself kneeling on that platform. A sword raised above her. A crowd watching the swing of the blade.

Footfalls ascended the stairs.

Boot steps. Several pairs.

Lita faced her friend and strained to push the words past her throat. "I'm sorry, Reyna. I didn't want to put you in danger. But I should have told you—about my smuggling things into camps."

"Through medical supplies."

"You *knew*?"

A wistful smile touched her lips. "I knew."

Lita nearly laughed despite the terrifying unknown. Or likely because of it. She squeezed Reyna's hand. "Don't worry. Okay? I'll make sure they know you haven't done anything. I swear it."

The footsteps halted. "Open!" With the man's shout came a hammering on the door. Wood striking wood. The butt of a rifle.

Lita's heart thrashed so fiercely it seemed it might burst from her chest. Reyna gripped her hand tighter just as the door flew open, kicked in by a soldier who then stepped aside. A suited Japanese man with a thin mustache and brimmed hat strode in, a Kempeitai officer no doubt.

Lita and Reyna bowed deeply, as expected. When they rose, he opened a palm-size notepad and glanced at a photograph. Then he regarded Lita's face with his beady eyes. A second armed guard now stood on the landing.

Lita was gathering the courage to confirm her identity when the officer shifted his focus.

"Delos Santos, Reyna?" His English carried a thick accent.

Stiffly she stepped forward, and Lita's defenses rose. This was all her own doing. "Sir," she asserted, and his gaze jumped back to Lita. "She's my roommate. But she hasn't done anything wrong. I assure you."

He turned back to Reyna as though Lita hadn't spoken. "I am Inspector Matsumoto. You are under arrest for crimes against Empire of Japan." At his signal a guard marched in and gruffly rotated Reyna to place her in handcuffs.

Lita's thoughts collided in confusion as the men prepared to take Reyna away. "Inspector, please—there must be a mistake."

"No mistake."

"Can you just tell me what she's accused of?"

He slapped his notepad shut and replied as if incensed by every syllable. "Selling false coupon for fuel ration. And giving money to guerrilla."

Guerrilla fighters. Like Reyna's cousins and brothers living in the jungles.

The inspector pivoted and departed for the stairs, and a guard jerked Reyna by the arm to follow.

"Reyna, wait . . ." Lita scrambled for what to say yet came up short.

Her friend looked back over her shoulder and jutted her chin. In her eyes was a sense of strength and assurance, her own message not to worry. Then she disappeared down the stairwell, leaving Lita dazed and staring at their open, broken door.

TWENTY-FIVE

ELEANOR

Los Baños Prison Camp, Laguna Province
August 1944

Summer arrived at Los Baños and with it a new quartermaster. Lieutenant Sadakki Konishi's duties as second-in-command included oversight of finances and all supplies. He arrived on the heels of a new commandant, the previous one having been relieved of his duties on account of being too soft, so the rumor went, on his prisoners.

To Eleanor, Quartermaster Konishi looked more like a boy than a man. She was taller than he was, and she was only five feet six. Nearly every adult male prisoner towered over him. Konishi was also only a couple years older than her at twenty-eight. His age and his stature and the instant rumors that he was excessively cruel made Eleanor think he was a small man out to prove he was big and bold and fearsome.

Even though Konishi was second-in-command, it was quickly clear to all in the camp that he was now calling all the shots. The new commandant, Major Yasuaka Iwanaka, had no obvious aspirations to prove himself. He preferred to stroll around his personal vegetable garden in a kimono and paint watercolors and dabble in haiku.

One of Konishi's first decrees was that the guards' bayonets be again fixed; the previous commandant had let them be removed. He also charged the members of the garrison with random searches of the prisoners' belongings. The Japanese custom of bowing, which the internees had grown lax about, was now of utmost importance. Under Konishi's new rules, any internee—no matter how young or old or what gender—who did not bow deep enough when approached or when approaching a member of the Japanese military would be struck across the face. The *binta* was seen as the ultimate physical display of contempt. Even children were not spared.

The worst of his initial declarations was to decrease the food allotment per prisoner by 20 percent. He also forbade any Filipinos from coming to the fences to sell food to the inmates. Children's rations were cut 50 percent.

Dr. Nance complained. He warned Konishi that he was seeing signs of malnutrition and that malnourished people were weak people who could not fend off illness or infection. Konishi claimed the reductions were because of financial constraints, but that made no sense. The lush foliage around the camp included banana and coconut trees full of fruit that fell to the ground and rotted, all within view of any hungry internee standing at the perimeter fence. A truckload of fruit brought to the camp by Filipinos living nearby had been ordered dumped on the ground. Only after hours in the hot sun and after swarms of insects had rendered the food a slimy mass of rotting fruit did he allow internees to poke through it.

The internees scavenged extra food wherever they could, including sifting through the garrison's trash cans. They consumed any plant or leaf or blade of grass that was edible, as well as worms and snails and even stray cats. Soon the infirmary was dealing with skyrocketing cases of beriberi.

For Eleanor it was hardest to try to relieve the pain and suffering of children dealing with the swollen limbs, aches, vomiting, difficulty in walking, and confusion that were the hallmarks of the preventable condition. The cure was an easy one if only they had access to basics like nuts, pork, beans, and lentils. She would walk past the guards at mealtimes and see their heaping plates of food, and she'd want to either weep or scream.

"Those men are eating the cure!" she lamented to David one evening during a break in her shift. "How can they do what they are doing to innocent children and babies! Have they no heart?" She heard the desperation in her voice and the pulsating throb of her own hunger as she cried out to him.

David, looking hollow cheeked and pale, shook his head. "I don't know what beats inside their chests, Eleanor. But I know what beats inside of mine. We have to survive so we can tell the world about the inhumanities we have suffered here. The world must be told. We have to survive. Don't give up. Don't let your patients give up."

"But, David! People are dying! The children can't live like this."

He pulled her close and she thought he was forgetting who she was and where they were. She thought he was about to kiss her. "Jerry Sams has heard on his radio that MacArthur has returned," David whispered in her ear. "He's back. He's landed at Leyte. He brought troops and ships and tanks and planes. We have to hold on."

For a moment she could only stare into the humid night. Had she heard him correctly?

"What?" She needed him to say it again. Say it all again.

"MacArthur is back in the Philippines," he whispered. "The end is in sight. We have to hold on."

She wanted to believe he was right. She was desperate to.

But as the days progressed there was no indication rescue was coming or even that U.S. troops were back in the Philippines. A load of Red Cross packages for the Los Baños internees that contained much-needed food was blocked from delivery by Konishi for no other reason than he wished to deny them the food.

Patients at the hospital began to die from starvation-related causes. First a sixty-nine-year-old American businessman, followed within days by several other older civilian inmates.

All of the nurses dropped weight and found themselves close to fainting whenever they had to work on their feet in the hospital for long stretches. All of them stopped menstruating—the only good thing to result from the widespread malnutrition. There were no sanitary pads in the camp, had never been, and women and teen girls had been using torn bits of fabric, rinsed and used over and over again, for their monthly cycles.

Dr. Nance came back to the hospital one afternoon after a visit to camp headquarters to make an appeal. He slumped into a chair in the staff break room, a tiny closet-size space.

Dr. Nance rubbed a hand across his forehead. "He won't do it. He won't restore the rations and he won't release the Red Cross packages."

"Not even for the children?" Eleanor said, feeling tears prick.

"He said before he was done with us, we'd be eating dirt."

The doctor rose and brushed past her, unwilling to hear more questions with terrible answers.

Konishi meant to starve them—not just subjugate them; he'd already done that.

He meant to kill them.

To kill them all.

TWENTY-SIX

PENNY

Santo Tomas Internment Camp, Manila
September 1944

For months the Japanese Zeros swarmed the skies above Manila. They buzzed the city, like belligerent bees, doing mock dogfights and elaborate air drills while those below in Santo Tomas watched in irritation and wished the racket would go away.

But on the last day of summer, the planes droning above them were not Japanese. There, brazenly painted on their sleek wings, were the white stars and blue circles of the United States military. The internees stood, shocked, as two planes circled the camp, tipped their wings, then flew off into the distance. The roar of engines was replaced by cheering, but it only lasted a few minutes before Akibo's voice rattled through the loudspeakers and the guards hustled everyone indoors.

Penny heard the shouts ringing from one end of campus to another. "They've come for us! We're free!"

But they hadn't. And they weren't.

Word spread quickly from those huddled around the last remaining radio in camp. Onozaki had confiscated most of the remaining electronics when he took control of the STIC but had no knowledge that one escaped his search. There hadn't been many radios to start with, and this one was

270

guarded ferociously. It was operated by a civilian electrician from Wales who, like so many others, had been passing through Manila that fateful December four years earlier. He understood their need to stay connected with the outside world, however, and believed nothing the Japanese told them. That one radio was now their only source of real information. So he had bolted it inside a five-gallon metal bucket and moved it around camp every day. Mostly it stayed inside Main Building, but sometimes it went to the hospital, camp kitchens, or shanties.

Within an hour he was reporting that American pilots had performed a stealth raid on Manila, dropping bombs on targets along the waterfront and receiving fire from antiaircraft guns throughout the city, but the planes were gone as quickly as they'd come and so was the news.

Still, the whispers and hope spread throughout Santo Tomas, encouraged when later that afternoon, the bombers returned, more brazen than before, and fired on a second round of targets. Smoke rose along the horizon, and as the prisoners crowded at the windows, they saw the warm glow of fire throughout the city.

Surely it wouldn't be long now. The nurses whispered this to each other as they lay in their cots that night, listening, longing for the sound of deliverance. *Surely?*

———◆———

The shrieking whine of air-raid sirens became a daily part of life in Manila over those next few weeks, but the internees of Santo Tomas rarely heard them. Monsoon season still raged upon the islands and brought with it the clamor of wind and rain many days. What they did notice, however, was the increase in troops stationed throughout the camp. Two hundred additional soldiers were sent to guard the internees, and they took to performing public marching drills several times a day.

"We're starting to look less like an internment camp and more like a military base," Penny groused one evening as she and Maude walked from the mess hall to Main Building. Her hands were tucked in the front pocket of her khaki coveralls, and she absentmindedly ran her thumbnail along

271

the edge of the playing card she'd swiped from Blanche's deck. The eight of hearts was beginning to look a little worse for wear.

The rain had finally let up an hour earlier, and dozens of Japanese soldiers were mustered in the plaza before the main gates practicing hand-to-hand combat. Others were doing target practice on the confiscated baseball field, and the relentless *pop-pop-pop* of gunfire echoed through the air.

After the first sighting of U.S. planes, Onozaki ordered that the roof of the cupola atop Main Building be removed so it could be turned into a watchtower. It was the highest point in the city, and it gave the Japanese the perfect vantage point to radio in the location of any approaching bombers. Now guards were stationed there around the clock, scanning the horizon with binoculars.

"Don't you think that's the point?" Maude said. Hope deferred made the heart sick, and every day, with those incessant sirens, they *hoped* it would be their day for liberation. But it never was. "If we look like a military base, we look like a target."

"You don't think—"

"Of *course* I do. The Japanese will never have to answer for their actions here if our own planes bomb us into oblivion first."

"No." Penny shook her head. "Internment camps have protected status. International law forbids any attack on them."

Pity pooled in Maude's eyes. "Do you really think the Japanese registered this camp? Or any other on the Luzon peninsula?"

"But those packages from the South Africa Red Cross? Someone knows we're here."

Maude shrugged. "All I'm saying is don't get your hopes up, Penny."

The words hadn't fully passed her lips when the sound of air-raid sirens filled the sky. It had been three weeks since the American bombers blazed a path across Manila, but here they were again thundering out of the clouds.

Maude could no longer run, and Penny wasn't about to leave her, so together they hobbled along the boulevard, arms above their heads, and made their way to Main Building. Across the city came the retaliating *boom* of antiaircraft fire, but no planes fell from the sky that night.

In reprisal for the perceived offense, however, the next morning Onozaki cut food rations in the camp to less than one thousand calories per person per day. The internees watched as excess food was carted out of the camp kitchens and burned in a great bonfire on the plaza. They listened to the voice of Captain Akibo, speaking on Onozaki's behalf; it crackled through the camp speakers.

"You will pay for the hubris of the American military," he said.

———◆———

The tiny chapel at Santo Tomas was the one place relatively untouched by Japanese presence. For nearly four years Father Domingo and the other priests ministered to the internees in large and small ways. They performed mass. They prayed for the sick. They offered last rites, officiated at funerals, and, as Penny learned when Blanche Kimball fell ill the year before, they worked with the Philippine underground to smuggle resources and intelligence throughout the prison and civilian camps.

It was from Father Domingo that Penny learned how poorly the Japanese were faring in the war. The Allies were gaining ground, winning vital battles across the South Pacific. They had invaded France as well, and were pushing the Germans back across the continent. It was only a matter of time. The war could not last much longer.

But now their Japanese captors were behaving like wounded dogs, lashing out at the prisoners and tightening control in any way they could. Penny felt they'd gone from being pawns in an elaborate chess game to an unwelcome drain on the war chest. Every mouth fed in Santo Tomas was a bullet that couldn't be manufactured and fired at Allied soldiers.

The world was watching, however, and the Japanese could neither eliminate the internees outright nor release them to fend for themselves in a war zone. To the enemy the solution was simple. Four thousand people lived cheek-to-jowl within the sixty-acre campus. A third of them were elderly. A third helpless children and their desperate mothers. A problem starved was a problem solved.

Cut the sugar rations in half.

Cut the bread rations in half.

Institute a nightly blackout across the city so the campus could not be seen by enemy planes.

Eliminate the milk and fruit altogether.

Stop all hospital transfers for mortally ill prisoners.

Deliver only rotten fish and vegetables. And—just to be sure the shipments were unusable—let the crates sit outside the gates, in the blazing sun, for days before sending them to the kitchens.

Conduct unannounced inspections of living quarters.

Cancel all social activities.

Refuse all shipments of eggs delivered to camp.

Open and search all incoming mail.

Every day it was something new, a fresh deprivation. Perhaps the Japanese hoped the captives would turn on one another and eliminate the problem for them. Or maybe it was simply an emasculated adversary looking to exercise power anywhere they could.

"Father, forgive me for I have sinned," Penny said, kneeling inside the confessional one morning as a torrential rain fell outside. "I have hatred in my heart."

Father Domingo slid the screen back. Penny wasn't Catholic, but he didn't seem to mind. To him she was simply a friend and he treated her as such. He patted her hand. "So do I."

"A patient died on my shift yesterday. An old man. It was just whooping cough. I've been begging for his hospital transfer all week, but the commandant refused. No one in. No one out. Not for any reason."

Once Onozaki eliminated all hospital transfers, the number of deaths in camp rose from one or two each month to over a dozen as the fall progressed.

"He didn't have to die," she said.

"This will not last much longer."

"How do you *know*?"

"I have faith," he said.

"You haven't been outside these walls since July. But you continue to receive intelligence about the war." She peered at him, the dim light casting his face in shadow. "How?"

His eyes were old and watery, their former brown diluted to a muddled sort of gray. He smiled at her, his lined face twisting into a devious grin. "Child. Santo Tomas is not as secure as our enemies believe."

Penny could get nothing else out of him, so she ventured back out into the storm, letting the rain pelt her face and the wind tear at her clothing. It felt cleansing in a way, to be so battered by nature. Her shift didn't start for another three hours, and she didn't want to go back to the oppressive crowding of Main Building, so she made her way through the maelstrom to the hospital.

"What is this?" she asked when Jim Hobbs shoved a blank piece of paper in her face.

"Onozaki will not listen to reason! He refuses to reinstate the executive committee. So perhaps he will accept formal written complaints. I'm hoping to gather one thousand."

Where he had found the reams of paper, much less the pens and envelopes to conduct such an endeavor, she could not guess. The task provided a welcome distraction, however, and she deposited herself behind Maude's desk. After drying her hands and forearms on a stack of bedsheets, Penny set her fury to paper.

The exercise was cathartic. Penny assumed many others felt the same because, a few days later, the camp loudspeakers crackled to life once more. Captain Akibo's voice penetrated the air, translating Onozaki's response.

"The commandant will no longer receive written complaints," he said. "His time is far too valuable to be troubled by such trivial matters. It has been determined that prolonged internment, separation from family, and lack of regular communication is the cause of all normal and expected weight loss within Santo Tomas. The Imperial Japanese Army cannot be required to meet the strange and unhealthy dietary requirements of the Western palate. Nor shall it try. Many of our guests come from the United States—operators of their own war camps—who do not attempt to accommodate the palates of their Japanese countrymen. To even make such a request is offensive.

There is no malnutrition among the citizens of Santo Tomas. There is no lack of food. But if your gluttony requires such an excess, then perhaps you might consider raising fish in the old campus swimming pool."

———◆———

A few resourceful women fried weeds and clumps of grass—okra, when they could get it from the meager camp gardens—in the cold cream that once came in the Red Cross prisoner parcels. After months of excessive deprivation, face lotion was the only emollient left in camp. The smell filled the hallways and open spaces of Santo Tomas. To Penny it was the scent of rancid grass clippings, and she would neither eat it herself nor feed it to Newt.

What to feed the child and *where* to find it became some of the most pressing thoughts in Penny's mind. To her immense gratitude, Father Domingo always seemed to have something extra to give Newt in the evenings after their unfulfilling meal in the mess hall. A slice of bread. A banana. Boiled eggs or coconut milk or random pieces of fruit that were overripe but still edible.

Penny didn't know where he got it and she didn't ask, but it was a tiny miracle she did not take for granted. As she walked toward the chapel in search of what he might have for Newt one evening, she smelled the smoke. Then heard the commotion.

A crowd had gathered outside the chapel. Flames billowed from the windows and smoke belched out the doors. Two guards stood in front, dousing the little church with gasoline.

"What are they doing?" Penny demanded, pushing her way to the front.

"Burning it," Jim Hobbs answered. He stood to her left, eyes large and filled with tears.

"I can see that! *Why?*"

"They caught the priests doing something."

"Oh God, are they in there? Please tell me Father Domingo isn't in there!"

She moved to take a step forward, but Jim clamped his hand around her wrist and pulled her back. From behind them came the sound of marching feet and then the honking horn of a military truck. The crowd pressed back to make room, and Penny saw Father Domingo in the bed, covered in mud, barefoot, with his hands tied behind his back. His eyes were closed and his face placid, but she could see where tears had cut tracks down his dirt-stained cheeks.

The guards pulled him from the truck, then dragged him to stand before the burning church. Penny willed him to open his eyes, to look at her, but he did not. Instead he mouthed a silent prayer, the words of which she couldn't hear.

Without waiting, without explanation, one of the soldiers lifted his rifle, pointed the barrel at Father Domingo's head, and pulled the trigger. The old man collapsed to the ground, limp as a rag doll, as the report echoed through the camp.

The shot reverberated through her entire being, and she did not realize that she was screaming until Jim pulled her away from the scene.

She glanced back, over her shoulder, and saw the guards pitch Father Domingo's body into the burning building. The horrified crowd scattered in all directions.

"Stop," Jim growled in her ear as she struggled to get free. "The guards are looking at you."

Penny couldn't see his face through her tears. And while she understood every word he said individually, together they made no sense. "*Why?* Why did they do that? He's a priest! He's a *good* man!"

"Because Father Domingo and the other priests dug a tunnel out of camp. And they'd gotten through, apparently. Some months ago. They were smuggling food into the chapel."

"How could they kill him over *food*?" she sobbed.

"The Japs consider it treason. Direct defiance of camp orders. And they're desperate anyway because of what happened in the Leyte Gulf this morning."

Penny stopped struggling then. She stood straight and pushed the tears off her cheeks. "What happened?"

"The Americans have landed with an entire battalion of troops. They've come to liberate us!"

"How do you know that?"

He grabbed her by the shoulders. Shook her gently. "It came through on the radio a couple of hours ago. Everyone has been talking about it. The Leyte Gulf is about four hundred miles south of us. But still. They're here!"

Four hundred miles seemed an eternity away to Penny when a man was dead, his corpse burning even now, and a child was starving in her cot in Main Building. Penny shook out of his grip and stumbled away. The Americans might as well be on Mars for all the good it did her tonight.

It could take weeks, months even, for the American forces to reach them. And what would become of Maude in the meantime? Of Newt? Neither of them had an ounce left to lose. Every meal—or lack thereof—mattered. Penny had to find a way to get them more food. She had to . . .

The thought came unbidden, unwelcome.

Should I consider Akibo's offer?

For the first time since he had cornered her in the nurses' quarters, Penny let the thought take root. She'd been married, had given her body to a man. How different could it really be?

All the difference in the world, she thought, and wept her way back to Main Building.

———◦———

Newt went to sleep complaining that her stomach hurt, and Penny, try as she might, could not drift off at all. She stared at Newt's profile: her button nose and lips slightly parted. The curls falling across her brow. She listened to the faint whistle of a child's snore and cursed herself for caring at all, for loving the girl, for putting herself in this position. She never should have taken Newt under her wing. Who was she to keep a child alive? Hadn't she failed at that all-important job once already?

Penny tried to close her eyes but saw the burning chapel. She tried to cover her ears but heard the report of that single gunshot. The smell of smoke burned in her nose. The taste of tears on her tongue. One worry after another chased itself through her mind, so, desperate for distraction, she reached under her cot and pulled the quartermaster's flag from her pack. If

Charley were here, he would know what to do. He would be calm and collected. Penny draped the flag around her shoulders and curled into a ball.

At some point, hours later, sleep finally found her. It dragged Penny beneath the surface of consciousness, tormented her with dreams of loss and lurking menace. She was floating there, in a restless, unhappy slumber, when the door to the nurses' quarters was kicked open and the lights thrown on.

Some of her colleagues awoke immediately, screamed, and flung covers from their beds. But others roused slowly, blinking at the light, confused by the shouts and orders of the Japanese guards who forced everyone to their feet.

Newt, wearing an old blouse for a nightshirt, leaped from her cot and clung to Penny. She picked the girl up and held her against her chest. Newt looked flushed and her skin was clammy, so Penny pressed Newt's face into the crook of her neck and cradled those dark curls in the palm of her hand.

"Radio!" the soldiers yelled in broken English. "Where is radio?"

Penny knew, of course, where it was that particular evening. So did several other women in the room, but not a single one of them said a word as the guards flipped over beds and cut into mattresses with their bayonets. Packs were emptied, clothing was strewn about, but the women simply shook their heads and feigned ignorance.

If she wanted to, Penny could stretch out her right leg and touch the bucket with her toes. Whether by luck or great misfortune, the radio was stored in the far corner of the nurses' quarters that night. All it would take was a single soldier tapping the bucket to know it was empty. Knock it over and they'd find the radio. And God knows what would happen to the women in this room. They would all be seen as collaborators.

Newt couldn't weigh more than seventy pounds, but still, she felt heavy. Penny guessed she was barely one-twenty herself at this point, and every day without a full meal drained her strength even more. Her arms ached, but she didn't dare let Newt down. The girl was clearly terrified, and her body tensed in waves against Penny.

Across the room Blanche Kimball cried out when a guard yanked a pillow from her hands.

"Where is it?" he demanded, then ripped it in half and shook out the stuffing all over the floor. "Where is radio?"

Penny eased backward into the corner and juggled Newt's weight as she lowered herself onto the bucket. She could feel Newt's tears drip onto her neck, and she rearranged the girl in her lap.

They ransacked the room, moving ever closer to Penny's corner. No bed was left unturned, no box or basket or pack unsearched. Finally a guard approached Penny and lowered the tip of his bayonet until it sat level with her eyes.

"Up!" he demanded.

Newt moaned and trembled in Penny's lap. "Shhh," she whispered. "It's okay. I won't let anything happen to you."

"Up!" He eased the bayonet closer to her rib cage.

She tried to think of a lie—any lie—that might explain why the radio was in this room, but her mind was a blank sheet, frayed at the edges by terror. Her only choice was to comply, then to beg for mercy.

Penny scooted forward and gathered Newt into her arms so she could try to stand. But the child stiffened, her eyes opening in horror, and then she vomited—cold cream and weeds—all over Penny. The guard. The floor. The wall. The stench of stomach acid and rancid grass made Penny gag. The warmth of it dripping from her chin and her arms made her shudder.

The world is filled with strange mercies. Little miracles that save us when we least expect them. And while Penny Franklin had never thanked God for the physiological reality of vomit before, she did thank Him for providence that night, because the guard was every bit as sickened by the sight and smell as she was. He looked at them, disgusted, and backed away.

Newt cried again, hard, gut-wrenching sobs, and Penny rocked her in that corner as the guards finished searching the quarters. As her friends and colleagues began to put their room back together, Penny carried Newt to the shower and they stood beneath the feeble, lukewarm spray, fully clothed.

"I'm so sorry," Newt sobbed.

Penny used a sliver of soap to wash the girl's hair. "Why?"

"For being sick."

"That's not your fault. I'm not mad. I'm *happy*."

Newt lifted her little impish face. "You are?"

"Of course! You scared that guard away. You saved us." Penny lathered soap in her fingers and washed Newt's cheeks. "Do you feel better now?"

She nodded.

"I do have one question though," Penny said.

"What?"

"Where did you get that awful grass?"

Even in the dim light of the shower Penny could see Newt blush. "I was hungry and they were cooking some downstairs. I stole a handful."

TWENTY-SEVEN

LITA

Santa Catalina Convent, Manila
December 1944

While Lita didn't normally subscribe to superstition, this particular year she would rule out nothing that could help protect the residents of her new home: all twenty-two of them. Twenty-five if she included the nuns. Thus, throughout the convent every window and door was left wide open. Among the many Filipino New Year's Eve traditions, the practice drew good fortune inside. Or so people said.

"Auntie Lita, watch this!" Calling out in Tagalog, the little boy wove around the other children playing in the communal room, his wooden toy plane held high. "It's flying!"

"I see that!" She smiled from her seat at the back table with Ida Hube. A visitor only on occasion, the woman had arrived tonight with presents to surprise the children, a bit of a belated Christmas in time to ring in the new year.

In a hop between languages, Lita switched to English while touching the sleeve of Ida's dress. "It's truly remarkable what you've done here, Ida. Not just the gifts, but everything."

"Oh, darling, as I've told you before, it was nothing." Her black bob swayed as she leaned in with a conspiratorial voice. "I can't very well take my money with me to the grave, now, can I?"

How she'd managed to scrounge up the toys, let alone ingredients for the festive family meal, called *media noche*, was a true wonder. They even had pigs' feet for kare-kare stew and large plates of pansit, the long noodles on the holiday meant to grant long life. Lita was more grateful than ever given the growing scarcity of food throughout the city.

It seemed the worse the Imperial forces fared, the more resources they withheld. And while the increased frequency of Allied military-target strafing and bombings was encouraging, the damage reduced perishable resources. On the upside, according to reports on Sister Cecilia's radio—an illegal possession God would forgive, she'd claimed—the Allies had won a series of major air and sea battles around and over the Philippines, most recently ten days ago in the Camotes Sea. Lita could only pray they'd retake the islands before many more Filipinos, and those imprisoned in the vicinity, starved or otherwise perished—her loved ones among them.

"Ida," she said, spurred by the thought. "By any chance, through your contacts, have you heard any updates—"

"About Reyna?"

Lita smiled at her own predictability. Since her roommate's arrest eight months ago, it was far from a new question—voiced by the children as well, who frequently asked when *Tita* Reyna would return from her "travels." The partial fib from Lita prevented frightening the kids. Or, more vitally, endangering them. She needed to protect them, as Reyna—with her own secrets—had clearly protected her.

"I am afraid not," Ida replied. "Only that she is still being held by the Kempeitai. The fact she is alive but not being tried is a good sign, suggesting they have no damning proof. It is maddening, I know. But if she is as strong as you say . . ."

"She is," Lita insisted, a reminder to herself.

"Then I have faith you will see her free and safe one day soon." Ida laid her hand on Lita's, a welcome reassurance. "Presuming, that is, you stay out of trouble yourself." She winked.

Did she know?

Was she guessing?

Either way, the issue now was largely moot. It had taken Lita several months after Reyna's arrest to gather the courage to dare another delivery. Since then, between a crackdown on messengers and a scarcity of supplies, opportunities for smuggling were rare.

"Auntie, Auntie!" came a little girl's voice. "Look at us!"

Latching onto the diversion, Lita turned to find a trio of girls giggling while bouncing around like jumping beans, two of them holding brand-new little rag dolls as they boasted, "Look how high we're getting!"

"We're going to be sooo big!"

They were practicing for midnight, when a huge jump at the stroke of the new year would—again based on superstition—cause the person to grow tall.

Lita laughed softly. Having given up on trying more than a decade ago, she chose not to break the news.

Then a rattling noise drew her ear. At the doorway near the kitchen, the cook, a gruff yet kind Filipina, was setting down a box. "Before I leave for the night," she said in her naturally booming voice, "who here wants a noisemaker?"

The question equated to the *pop* of a starting pistol. In a burst of squeals the children charged for the box and pulled out pots, pans, spoons, and tin cans.

"Wait, children—wait!" Sister Cecilia urged from across the room. "We have three more hours until we scare those evil spirits away!" Through the chaos of tapping and drumming, she seemed to recognize her cause as lost. She caught Lita's eye and shrugged, and they shared a little laugh. Besides, few among the children, for all their determination, would still be awake by twelve.

"Well, goodness," Ida said suddenly, "is it nine already? I do believe I should get some rest." Beneath her smile appeared a hint of fluster.

Lita couldn't blame her, though personally she found the mayhem comforting. And not just tonight. Reminded of her household as a child, she simply adored all the laughter and singing, stories and bickering, lively group meals and kisses good night. Without planning to, she'd become a tita, or auntie, not only to Jun-Jun but to every child here. Each of whom she'd come to cherish beyond measure.

"Shall I walk you out?" Lita offered, rising from her seat with Ida.

"No need for that, my dear. But I do thank you for a grand evening. Oh!" She glanced past Lita's shoulder. "It looks as if my chauffeur has come to fetch me. How do you like that for timing?"

Lita turned to see a shadowed man approaching from the long hall linked to the entry. Yet she also detected two men in his wake. As the first man neared the illuminated communal room, his face, slightly shaded by his brimmed hat, gained clarity.

And Lita ceased breathing, even as she reflexively bowed.

Leaving the convent's front door open had brought the opposite of good fortune, evident in the arrival of the Kempeitai officer. Inspector Matsumoto.

"Capel, Angelita?" he demanded through the torrent of giggling and rattling.

Slowly she unfolded to her full height and connected with his glower.

"You are under arrest."

1945

Hope is the thing with feathers
That perches in the soul
And sings the tune without the words
And never stops at all.

—EMILY DICKINSON

TWENTY-EIGHT

ELEANOR

Los Baños Prison Camp, Laguna Province
January 1945

Eleanor was eating her mother's lefse, warm and soft and sprinkled with sugar. She was sitting on the porch with Lizzie, and the breeze swirling about them was lilac scented. From within the house she could hear strains of Glenn Miller on the radio and her mother humming along. Across the lawn laundry flapped in the sun; three pair of her father's overalls and his checked shirts— blue and yellow, white and red, orange and brown.

It was so wonderful. All of it.

Something tugged on her arm, and a part of her instantly knew she was asleep and on the verge of being awakened.

"I want to stay here," she said, and her very words began to tear at the fabric of her dreaming thoughts.

"Roll call is in twenty minutes," Lizzie said.

But it wasn't Lizzie. It was Peg. The lefse disappeared, as did the porch and the lilacs and the music and the laundry on the line.

Eleanor opened her eyes.

Peg was leaning over her. "Come on. You don't want to be late. Who knows what they will do if you are, even if you are a nurse."

Eleanor sat up groggily and was instantly aware of her hunger. She dressed and ran a brush through her hair, hardly noticing the clumps the bristles were gathering. Everyone's hair at the camp was falling out in little handfuls as malnutrition did its worst.

"Where was it you wanted to stay when I woke you?" Peg said as they made their way to the assembly for the morning count.

Eleanor sighed. She could almost taste the lefse on her tongue. "I was just dreaming of home. That's all."

"Ah," Peg said and nothing else.

After tenko, they went to the outdoor kitchen to see what the internee cooks had been allotted to make for breakfast. Both women received a half cup of rice mush, tasteless and gritty. There was no milk or honey or sugar or salt to flavor it with. The guards had plenty of those items in their garrison kitchen, but these were not shared with the prisoners.

Then Eleanor and Peg walked to the hospital, where they would care as best they could for patients sick with malaria, dengue fever, beriberi, dysentery, intestinal parasites, scurvy, tropical ulcers, and other ailments— all with little or no medicine. The Red Cross had sent boxes of medical supplies to the camp, but again Konishi refused to let them be delivered.

Their twelve-hour shifts made the days long, and the little they were given to eat made them weak. Eleanor often felt light-headed as the day wore on. When she did, Laura would insist she lay down for a few minutes.

The rest of the camp was also feeling the mind-numbing effects of malnutrition. Classes for the children taught by internee teachers were soon canceled as the little ones could not concentrate on any of the lessons. They were too hungry and their young minds too distressed by lack of nutrition.

Breakfast and dinner were the only meals served now, both consisting of rice mush and whatever bits of protein or vegetables the cooks could forage. The internees were no longer allowed to work the camp garden—Konishi's orders—or scavenge among what was left of it. Since the spring, with husbands and wives reunited at Santo Tomas, the birthing of babies soon followed. But the nursing mothers could produce little milk. Some could produce none at all. The nurses had been stockpiling tins of dehydrated milk powder since the first of the year, and Eleanor was immensely glad they had. Every infant born at Los Baños would have died without it.

The few stores left in the hospital's pharmacy included morphine and local anesthetics, but Dr. Nance could not say how long these would last, and he informed the nurses that both had to be saved for surgeries and emergencies. Those with cuts requiring stitches would have to receive them without painkillers.

In the early days of the camp, the hospital was set up for twenty-five beds, but now the nurses were caring for up to two hundred patients a day. The hardest moments for Eleanor were when one of her patients died from a condition that would have been easily prevented or treated on the outside. It happened nearly every day, sometimes several times a day, and to all the nurses—not just Eleanor.

The bodies had to be buried immediately as the heat of the day set about decomposition with alarming speed. Camp carpenters begged the Japanese guards for enough wood to build coffins. The names of the deceased were burned into the wooden crosses that marked their final resting place in the camp cemetery. David Mathis had volunteered to be part of the digging team for this sad task. It was arduous work for men weakened by near starvation.

One afternoon after David had spent the morning at this chore, he came by the infirmary to see if Eleanor had anything to soothe the blisters on his hands caused by the handle of the shovel.

She had an aloe plant that she kept in a windowsill, and she cut off a bit of one of the spears. "Do you still believe General MacArthur is in the Philippines, waging war against the Japanese occupiers?"

"Of course he's here." David held out his palms.

"But how do you know he hasn't been pulled back out? Like last time?" She dabbed the aloe's healing salve onto the blisters despite the ache.

"Haven't you seen the fighter planes in the sky, Eleanor? I know you have."

"How do you know they're our fighters?"

"Because I do. They're ours. Our liberation is on the way. It's only a matter of time. We have to keep looking for it. It's coming."

"But it's been two months since we heard that MacArthur is back. Two months, David. And look at us. Look what they're doing to us. You buried a child today. That child was in my care. And I could do nothing for him."

He took her hand, smearing aloe on her wrist as he did so. "It's happening, Eleanor. We are going to be liberated. We just have to be patient."

"Why is it taking so long?" She kept her hand in his.

"The Japanese have tens of thousands of troops in place. They are dug in. Heavily armed. We will win. But first we have to fight. Alright?"

Tears trickled down her face and she could not stop them. "But we are losing the fight here. Every day we are losing it. That little boy you buried today was only five years old . . ."

He stood and pulled her into his arms. "I know this is hard. It might get harder. But we have to keep getting up every day and hoping every day and waiting. Every day. We have to. This is how we will survive."

"Some of us."

"Yes. Some of us. But just because not all of us will make it doesn't mean we should stop hoping. Okay? Promise me you won't give up."

She hadn't been hugged in a long time. She couldn't remember when last she had, and she did not answer him at first.

"Eleanor?"

"I promise."

"Good. Because you need to see San Diego. And I want to be the one to show it to you. I really do think you'd love it there."

They stayed that way for several long minutes, neither one moving.

When David broke away, he was looking at her in a different way. Eleanor was thinking he was going to kiss her—and that she was going to let him—when the door to the exam room opened and Dr. Nance stepped in.

He stared at both of them for a second and then spoke as if he didn't know he had interrupted a private moment. "I need you in exam three, Eleanor," he said, and then he turned and departed, leaving the door open.

David stepped back.

"Let me cover those blisters," Eleanor said, wiping away the tears that streaked down her cheeks.

"You go. I can find something to cover them."

She reached behind her to a shelving unit made of bamboo and a basket of rolled muslin strips. She handed him one.

"I'm going to hold you to that promise." He took the rolled muslin.

Eleanor smiled at him and left the room, with the memory of his embrace still lingering about her.

The next day as the camp ate their meager breakfast, a formation of American war planes flew over the camp, low enough that the internees jumped up and down and shouted just in case the pilots might see them. Their Japanese guards ran into ditches and dove under tables, assuming the planes were bombers on a mission.

Eleanor, eating with Peg, heard an internee shout that the aircraft were P-38s, which meant the American Army Air Corps had to have an airstrip on Luzon or another nearby island.

Eleanor watched in fascination as the planes flew on into the horizon, past their field of vision. The guards who had fled for cover climbed out, and those who spoke English yelled at the internees to be silent or there would be no supper allotment.

The sight of the aircraft was the talk of the camp that day. David found time to come to the infirmary to ask Eleanor if she'd heard the news and seen them. "I told you. It's happening."

A few days later two dozen American four-engine bombers flew over the camp high above the prisoners, headed toward Manila.

Again David made his way to the hospital later that day to make sure Eleanor had heard the latest. "San Diego, here we come, eh?" he said, smiling. He still had his good looks even though his cheeks were sunken and he'd lost any fat on his frame.

"Looks like it," Eleanor replied, and for the first time she started to believe he might actually be right. Their liberation was at hand. And with it, the end of the war.

And yes, she was warming up to the idea of staying in the Navy Nurse Corps and asking for San Diego as her next duty station. She was beginning to imagine her life beyond her imprisonment and an existence without John Olson as even a faint part of it. It was appearing to be more and more possible.

She wanted to tell Penny and Lita about her new friend David, wanted to see them break into wide smiles when they realized that she was at last moving on from a life that now seemed to belong to another person, a life where a lost love had kept her bound.

Three days later, minutes before dawn, a commotion broke out in camp, rousing Eleanor from sleep. She sprang up to a sitting position. Peg was sitting up in her bed, too, as were the other nurses not working the night shift.

"Something's happened," Eldene said from inside their sleeping quarters.

"Good or bad?" Peg asked.

"I don't know."

Eleanor and the others got out of their beds, hastily dressed, and then ascended the basement stairs. Two of the nurses on duty were standing at the hospital's entrance, looking out into the half-light of the dimly lit camp. To their left where the majority of the camp lay, internees were pouring out of their barracks. Some were shouting, some were hugging each other, some were crying. At the commandant's quarters a stone's throw from the camp kitchen, not a light was on, despite the ruckus happening right outside it. In front of the building was a smoldering fire where a fire had never been before.

"What's going on?" Eleanor asked one of the nurses standing at the door.

"I think the Japanese have left," her colleague said, her voice laced with disbelief. "I think they burned all their papers during the night."

"What?"

"Look! I think they're leaving." To their right and past one other building was the main gate and the perimeter fence, both usually heavily guarded. There were no guards on the perimeter, and at the main gate there was only a small contingent of soldiers packing up a truck.

Daylight was starting to turn the gray world of night golden.

Could it possibly be true? Eleanor wondered. Were they free? It was too spectacular a thing to believe.

Then a voice squawked over the loudspeaker. One of the admin committee members was calling for the internees' attention for an important announcement.

The nurses waited, hardly daring to breathe.

Eleanor recognized the voice of Martin Heichert, the current chairman, a Los Angeles man who had been an administrator of a General Motors operation in Manila when the war broke out. Eleanor could scarcely comprehend his next words:

"Los Baños Prison Camp has been officially released to the administration committee. The garrison is gone, and as of this moment, we declare ourselves free!"

From every corner of the camp came the sound of jubilant shouting and cheering. Eleanor turned to Peg and hugged her, and soon all the nurses were weeping and embracing each other.

Seconds later, Heichert continued. "Ladies and gentlemen, it is important for you to know that there is no news of an American invasion yet. We know only that the Japanese commandant and his garrison have abandoned the camp. The area all around is still a war zone, still very dangerous. The committee requests that everyone remain in the camp. We will keep it secure and patrolled until American forces come in and transport us out. Until then I hereby rename the Los Baños Prison Camp, Camp Freedom!"

Again there was shouting and clapping and whistling. And there was still more good news. Heichert went on to say that the committee had gone into the Japanese garrison's warehouse and found enough food for two months. There would again be three meals a day.

Eleanor closed her eyes in gratitude. Finally. Finally the little ones would stop dying because of malnutrition. Finally her hair would stop falling out, and she wouldn't have to eat worms and bugs to get protein in her diet. Finally they could all start thinking clearly again.

The Japanese flag had already been taken down, and now an American flag that someone had kept hidden all the many months of their imprisonment was raised. Over the loudspeaker came a recording of "The Star-Spangled Banner." Every nurse standing there and watching the flag being raised had tears running down her face. Someone among the British captives produced a small Union Jack, which also went up the flagpole to the strains of "God Save the King."

Martin next asked that the camp remain calm and disciplined and to continue with their usual daily chores and assignments. The request made sense, but the prisoners had gone without for too long. As soon as the announcement concluded, dozens upon dozens of internees stormed the former Japanese-held buildings and then emerged from them with mattresses and linens and anything else the Japanese troops had been in too much of a hurry to take. Within an hour "No Looting" signs were posted by the committee, but the worst of the ransacking had already happened.

David found Eleanor at the line for breakfast where the mood was festive and joyful. "Let's go into town," he said. "It's only a mile and I've got things I can trade for food and maybe get some new shoes and a knife or something. We have no weapons here."

Wide-eyed, Eleanor gaped. "But the committee wants us to stay in the camp. They don't think it's safe out there," she said, both excited and fearful about stepping outside.

"I really don't think between here and town are the trenches of war. We're in the middle of nowhere. Besides, we're free. If we want to go into town, we can go."

The prospect of walking into town unshackled was a heady thought too grand to ignore.

"Let me go make sure it's okay with Laura if I come," Eleanor replied.

As it turned out Laura did not mind if Eleanor went into town, especially if she could find aspirin and antibiotic ointment and Vaseline. Anything, really, for the dispensary. She even gave Eleanor a pair of her earrings to barter if she needed something to trade.

David and Eleanor weren't the only members of Camp Freedom wanting to head into town for a shopping trip. Several dozen made the trip with them. The villagers were only too happy to hear the Japanese had left Los Baños and were eager to trade such delicacies as eggs, sugar, chicken, and rum for the internees' personal items from home. For Laura's earrings, Eleanor was able to procure aspirin and real cough syrup. David was unable to find a villager willing to trade for a knife, but he did get some used sandals, some sweet buns, and a bag of dried mango slices. These Eleanor and he ate on the walk back.

Word of the Japanese leaving had reached more of the locals, and as

David and Eleanor reentered the camp, they saw carts and trucks from farmers and grocers filled with fresh fruit and vegetables. A steer that a local farmer donated to the camp was butchered that afternoon and served in a stew hours later. It was the finest meal anyone could remember having in many months.

The next few days were more of the same. Despite some getting sick from eating to excess after months of deprivation, the majority of the camp looked nearly healthy again. On one of the first few evenings after the Japanese departed, the former prisoners heard over the now-unhidden radio that two hundred thousand troops from the U.S. Sixth Army had landed at Lingayen Gulf in northern Luzon and were now marching south toward Manila.

David was with Eleanor when the news came over the loudspeaker that surely their days at Camp Freedom were numbered and they would all soon be on their way home. Once Manila was retaken, the troops would come for them. David took Eleanor's hand and squeezed it. "Told you so," he said teasingly.

She squeezed it back. Then she leaned in and kissed him on the cheek. He grinned in wide-eyed surprise. "So you did."

Three days later Eleanor was awakened in the middle of the night by a loud commotion in the camp.

She bolted upright and so did Peg.

"The Americans are here!" Peg exclaimed, and the two of them flew up the stairs in their pajamas, too eager to greet their liberators to even think of changing into their uniforms.

But the uproar outside was not the sound of liberating forces.

Konishi and the garrison were back.

TWENTY-NINE

LITA

Kempeitai Headquarters, Manila
January 1945

T he piercing glare was blinding. Lita squinted against the overhead light as a guard's grip led her farther into a room. Her eyes fought to adjust after two days—or was it more?—confined to pitch blackness in a square space so small that, seated against an unseen wall, her sandaled feet could touch the other side. Her only food had been an occasional scoop of rice gruel and a cup of water that tasted of old pipes.

The guard released her to stand beside a chair. Vision settling, she identified her surroundings as a sizable, windowless office. Behind a conference table sat Inspector Matsumoto.

She lowered into a bow. Her back ached from sleeping curled up on a concrete floor, the air filled with the stench of her chamber pot and the agonizing screams from unseen rooms.

"Capel, Angelita," he said, and she righted herself.

"Yes, sir."

"Take seat."

She lowered onto the chair as he flipped through paperwork in a file, a pen in hand. The guard stood to her side, facing the inspector.

"What are you?" Matsumoto asked.

She struggled to understand the question. "I'm . . . a nurse."

He flicked a nod to the guard, who turned and slapped her face. The sting left from his hand prickled like tiny needles.

"What are you?" he repeated.

She lifted her head. "I . . ." At her stunned, befuddled hesitation, another slap struck the same cheek.

"Are you American?"

She shook her head and quickly thought to voice, "No."

The next hit seemed to burst through her head, and she found herself sprawled on the floor. The sight of the guard's fist made clear he'd punched her in the jaw.

"Sit," Matsumoto ordered.

Her eyes watered as the throbbing pain spread over her face. She climbed back onto the seat with trembling arms.

"Are you American?"

She elaborated quickly. "My father was an American missionary, but my mother was Filipino. I was born here, on Leyte."

He absorbed this, then flipped a page, surveying the information. "You serve with the Allies. As nurse. Yes?"

She measured her answer. "I previously worked alongside a U.S. Army unit through Sternberg General Hospital, yes."

"At Bilibid Prison, you sign oath to Empire of Japan?"

She swallowed hard, avoiding his gaze. "Yes."

He looked up from his paper. "But you work with Resistance and bring contraband to camps. Is this not true?"

Already Lita had recognized she was stuck. If she admitted to the crime, she'd likely end up like Dr. Alvarez. At the root of her arrest, she'd presumed prison guards had discovered money or messages in her medical supplies and traced the contraband back to her. But if the inspector already had proof, why bother asking? Clearly they were pursuing either a rumor or suspicions given her ties to Reyna.

"No." She clenched her jaw in preparation to be struck. She hadn't planned on the guard's fist walloping her in the stomach. The impact doubled her over, stealing her breath.

"You bring contraband to prisoner. Yes?"

She wrapped her arms around her middle as she gasped for air, her internal organs feeling shoved into her spine. When she at last raised her head, Matsumoto's beady eyes bored into her. The edge of his mouth curled up.

"Maybe after rest, you remember more. Today is easy. Tomorrow much harder." He glanced at the guard. *"Owarida."*

The soldier pulled her by the arm to stand.

The interrogation was over.

For now.

———◆———

From the dimly lit corridor with a series of closed doors, Lita was tossed back into her box. A lightless, concrete tomb.

Was it day or night? She didn't know. To calm herself and pass the immeasurable time, with jaw throbbing, she murmured songs she'd learned from her family: folk songs, hymns, and lullabies. Through them all she thought of Lon and Penny and Eleanor. Of the children and her sisters. And she thought of her mother—not about her death or links to shame, but about her smile that lit up a room. Her sweet shuffle of a walk. The love and pride she put into every dish, from her crispy lumpia to her creamy leche flan.

Lita's hunger suddenly grew, amplifying the ache in the bruised muscles of her stomach.

At last a Filipina revisited with a pushcart, letting in a slant of pale light. The woman emptied the chamber pot into a metal drum. She added gruel to Lita's bowl and water to her cup. Then she shut and locked the door, leaving Lita to the darkness and to the sound of harrowing screams.

———◆———

Matsumoto proved a man of his word. The next session was harder.

For her denials the guard struck not with his hands but with a bamboo stick. On her arms. Her hands. Her shins.

The pain coursing through her body originated from spots too numerous to register. With tears wetting her face, she yearned to tell the truth, to say whatever was required to end this.

She could claim it was just one package. A slip in judgment. A simple desire to help.

But already she knew he wouldn't believe that. And the meager confession wouldn't be enough. Any admission of guilt would be followed by demands for details: how, when, where.

Who.

He'd want names of who recruited her, who received the packages, who provided the pesos. And to whom were the messages sent? Through her mind's eye she saw Father Domingo and Penny, Ida and Lon.

"You bring contraband to camp?" Matsumoto asked with growing impatience.

Her answer came easier then, despite her fears. "No. Only medical supplies."

In what seemed an instantaneous moment, Lita opened her closed eyes and discovered herself somehow back in her box, lying on the floor. Pain emanated from the back of her skull. A lump verified she'd been knocked unconscious.

Another session had ended, thankfully.

But another was coming.

———◆———

The dreaded sound of boot steps drew closer and, once more, halted nearby. Then her lock was released and the door was opened. A sense of panic scaled her chest.

She climbed to her feet, limbs battered and bruised, and aimed to walk steadily with the guard. Silently she ordered herself to be brave, stay strong like Reyna.

Oh, Lord in heaven, was Reyna enduring all of this still?

Along the corridor, coming from the other direction, was a Kempeitai officer and a soldier, conversing in Japanese. They were about to pass by when the soldier glanced her way. His speech stalled and his eyes went wide.

It was Yamada. The *nisei* soldier.

Lita had an urge to call to him for help, as any drowning person would to someone on the shore. But immediately he looked away, resumed his conversation, and continued past her.

Abruptly the guard turned her toward the open door and delivered her to the interrogation room she'd grown to know well. This time, in addition to Matsumoto, another suited man awaited.

After Lita's usual bow, she was guided to her chair next to the seated stranger. On the conference table before him was a square contraption with switches and dials. She watched in a terrified daze as he stretched a long wire from the machine. He wrapped it around her right index finger, then secured it in place with tape. He did the same to her left pointer finger and declared to Matsumoto, "*Hai.*"

He was ready.

One of his hands settled on a dial, the other on a switch, and a depraved eagerness etched his features.

Every inch of Lita's body braced for the terror that was coming. Her time with the stick and fists was over. Her continued denial would now be met with surges of electric shock. How long could she hold out? How many volts until they broke her?

Matsumoto reclined in his chair across the table, his file folder splayed. "Let our question begin—once again."

Lita sought to send her mind elsewhere, to detach from the reality of this nightmare. As she did so, a whistling came to her, a song from her past, her father's.

In the background the men spoke to each other in Japanese. She tried to block them out, aware the inspector's questions would follow.

But a sharp tugging on her index fingers snatched her focus. The stranger was removing the wires. Matsumoto was standing, gathering his paperwork.

It wasn't a whistling she'd imagined. It was a distant siren. An air-raid alert.

The wailing grew louder.

"We continue tomorrow." Matsumoto signaled the guard to escort her back.

———•———

Explosions reverberated for hours through the concrete floor, the walls. Allies were dropping payloads on enemy targets. Lita feared the Kempeitai headquarters could well be among those, until it occurred to her that it just might be a merciful blessing.

This was her last thought before drifting off, only to wake at some untold hour from the sound of footsteps stopping outside her door. Again she was pulled to her feet by a guard. But their typical corridor walk didn't ensue. Rather, he stretched a long strip of fabric before rotating her away from him. As he raised the blindfold, she glimpsed a figure down the corridor.

Yamada. He was standing there, watching.

Her view went black, and an explanation formed: perhaps he resented her for figuring out what he didn't want others to know and convinced the Kempeitai not to waste their time, eliminating two problems at once.

Her pulse raced as she stumbled beside the guard escorting her—to where? A courtyard execution?

She was wrong before; she wasn't ready to die.

"I don't know what he told the inspector," she pleaded to the guard, "but please, don't listen to him. I'm begging you, please."

She detected walking through a doorway and felt the brush of an outdoor breeze over her face. By the arm she was guided to step upward, then to sit on what seemed to be a bench. She envisioned a truck bed, based on the sound of an idling engine and the scent of gasoline fumes. With the rev of a motor, the vehicle swayed and rumbled toward a destination unknown.

THIRTY

PENNY

Santo Tomas Internment Camp, Manila
February 1945

Open-mouthed, Penny stared at the letter. The envelope was stained and torn, the seal partially broken. The sender's name was smudged though still readable, and the postmark was November 1941, St. Paul, Minnesota. Mere weeks before Japan forced America into the war. It was addressed to Eleanor Lindstrom.

"I'll be damned." Penny dropped to her cot. "He wrote to her."

Penny rubbed her thumb across the sender's name: John Olson.

The letter had been delivered by the Red Cross that morning in a moldering bag of undistributed, pre–Pearl Harbor mail found in the rubble of the demolished post office at the Cavite Naval Yard. It had been forwarded on to Santo Tomas under the assumption that Eleanor was still interned there and then given to Penny when she heard those distributing the mail call out Eleanor's name.

"I'll give it to her," she'd said, and now wondered if she could keep that promise. Penny hadn't seen or heard from Eleanor in eighteen months.

Three weeks earlier the radio had told them that several platoons of American soldiers had finally landed on the Luzon peninsula and were working their way south and east to Manila. Half the guards at Santo Tomas had been pulled out of camp and sent to reinforce other areas of the city.

The remaining soldiers were scared. The internees could see how they flinched every time the air-raid sirens went off, how the sound of distant gunfire and cannons made them nervous. And not two days ago, the internees heard the Marine Corps bombers north of the city raining gunfire onto the Japanese forces.

The tide was turning, but she still knew that a boat could be capsized in such waters. What hope Penny Franklin had for deliverance was held loosely. The 942 days in this place had taught her that longing for salvation would only lead to despair.

She ran her finger across the script on the envelope. Reverend John Olson's handwriting. Why on earth had he written Eleanor after rejecting her? Hadn't he done enough? Penny wanted to tear the envelope open, to see him justify his actions. But reading this letter was wrong. It wasn't hers. She should tell the Red Cross to forward it on to Los Banõs and mind her own business. But what if something happened to it on the way? How would Eleanor ever know what it said? If she read it first, that wouldn't be a problem. She could relay it, word for word, later . . .

Penny slid her thumb under the torn flap.

Paused.

"No," she told herself, then looked at the neat, square letters of Eleanor's first and last names. "It's not yours to open. Not yours to read."

Penny pressed the letter flat against her chest and leaned back against the wall. She closed her eyes, listening to the distant booms of battle. She would give this letter to Eleanor herself, in person, when they were reunited. Because they would be. They *had* to be. She would make sure of that. And she would stand right there while Eleanor read it—as a good friend would— just in case the words inside had the power to wound.

———◆———

Penny nearly ran into Akibo when she pushed through the front doors to Main Building, and it took a moment to realize that the terrified, bleeding child with him was Newt.

Penny had stuffed the letter in her pack, then wandered out of the nurses' quarters and down to the first floor, without paying much attention to her surroundings. She was lost in thought, wondering—and worrying—about Eleanor. If she was still at Los Banōs. If she was healthy. If she was—God have mercy—alive.

So when she'd stepped out into the bright afternoon sunshine, she hadn't looked where she was going. Penny pulled up short the moment her mind registered the Japanese uniform, and she reflexively started to bow. It took a heartbeat longer to recognize Akibo.

Then Newt.

Tears streaked Newt's dirty little face and blood trickled from the left corner of her mouth where it was split. Already a bruise was blooming across her jaw.

"What—" Penny asked, agape, as Akibo shoved the child toward her.

"She is a thief," he interrupted.

Penny pulled Newt behind her back and held on to the quaking child with one hand. "You hit her!"

Akibo stepped close, his breath hot on Penny's face. "She was caught with her hand in the pocket of a guard. You are lucky I only slap her when they bring her to me. I could have punished her in other ways."

She sucked in a breath, aghast. If Newt weren't there, her little face pressed into Penny's back, she would have told Akibo exactly what she thought of his threat. Instead she hissed, "She is a child!"

"She is enemy. And you," he said, finger pointing right at her face, "should remember how much you owe me." He stepped away then, but slid his eyes up and down her body once for good measure, then nodded. "You owe me."

THIRTY-ONE

LITA

Imperial Japanese Military Tribunal, Manila
February 1945

From the Kempeitai headquarters Lita had been transferred to a local prison, not a courtyard execution as she had feared. But after three weeks in a cell with other Filipinas awaiting trial, that possibility verged on reality.

The door opened and five Imperial officers entered the courtroom.

Lita's throat tightened and her mouth went dry. In unison she and her assigned Japanese lawyer rose from their chairs planted behind a small desk and bowed. She'd met him just minutes ago and knew only that he was fluent in English and a Yale graduate. What a pair they made—he with his self-assured smile and tropical suit, and she with her fading bruises and inmate clothing of pajamas, ironically stamped *U.S. Army Medical Corps*. She was grateful at least for the prison washroom where she'd been allowed to bathe once a week, making her appear less dispensable. She hoped.

The five judges comprising the military tribunal took their seats behind a long stretch of table set on a platform. Once the center man rapped his gavel and spoke briefly in Japanese, Lita followed her lawyer's lead and sat back down.

A young male clerk stepped forward and read from a paper.

"He's presenting your summary of charges," the lawyer whispered. "He says you've been accused of providing illegal contraband to American prisoners at several camps."

Her stomach teetered on nausea. No doubt hunger was contributing, as she'd been too nervous to consume even her breakfast of gruel and seaweed.

Standing off to the side, the guard who'd escorted her here gazed around with a look of boredom she desperately envied.

Then a name amid the clerk's speech caught her ear.

In a rush she whispered to her lawyer, "Did he say Yamada, Kenji?"

The lawyer gave a nod while still listening to the clerk.

"What about him?" she said. "Tell me."

The man replied quietly, "Apparently he went to the Kempeitai to add a report to your file."

A sinking feeling rolled through her. "But—why? Why does he have any say at all?"

"His uncle is a Kempeitai officer."

She stared, taken aback. "Inspector Matsumoto?"

"No. Some other officer but highly respected. Shh, one second."

The clerk had finished, and the middle judge took over in an authoritative voice. When he ended a phrase emphatically, the lawyer related, "He says you've been found guilty."

Her defender's tone was so matter-of-fact she thought she might have misheard.

Warding off panic, she demanded, "Is this because of Yamada? Because of what he told them?"

"Yeah." He turned with a smile of relief and added to her surprise, "Because of him, you get to live."

———•———

Transferred by truck the following morning, along with other female prisoners, to the Women's Correctional Institution, Lita continued to digest all that had happened.

Yamada's being the nephew of a Kempeitai officer certainly helped explain his special treatment at the hospital. Still, his vouching for her character and medical skills wasn't a factor she had foreseen.

Of course her final sentence remained daunting—at least in her own view versus that of her lawyer's.

"Only four years' hard labor," he'd told her, seeming pleased with himself, though he hadn't uttered a single word during her three-minute trial.

Only was an absurd descriptor to pair with "hard labor," but indeed it was better than death.

Inside the walled compound located in a rural area east of Manila, the new arrivals were each given a rice sack made of burlap for a dress, a blanket, and a soup spoon. To reach their cells, a female official led them through a courtyard, where prisoners were busy with various chores in the sun-soaked humidity.

Lita trailed the group, hampered by her sore right thigh not fully recovered from her beatings. She was about to file into the one-story wooden building when she noticed two inmates chatting in the garden, specifically the woman weakly hammering the earth with a shovel. An attempt at tilling the stony ground. The gal paused to brush her hair back from her thin face streaked with sweat.

Lita stopped, and gaped. "Reyna?"

Sure enough, her roommate turned, and for the first time since being arrested, Lita smiled from sheer, unexpected joy.

But Reyna only stared. And without responding, she angled her body away and resumed her shoveling.

"Capel," the official prodded.

Confused, Lita gathered herself and rejoined the others.

———◆———

Four women were assigned to each cell, where wooden benches topped with grass-stuffed pads served as beds. Assigned to floor duty, Lita was given a mop and bucket and instructed to begin straightaway.

While cleaning a community area, she pondered her friend's reaction. Perhaps Reyna hadn't recognized her. Lita, too, had lost weight, and the past month of hardships and sleepless nights had no doubt worn on her appearance. She'd wrestled with fears over the trial, a spike in air raids from Allied bombings, and dangers threatening the convent.

At the start of lunch break, Lita eagerly trekked into the mess hall to find Reyna. Provided with a half cup of rice gruel mixed with boiled weeds, she approached her friend eating at a table.

"Reyna."

Again she halted but this time didn't bother to turn.

"It's me—Lita."

Reyna stared down at her gruel for a moment before she downed her last spoonful. Then she up and left the table, deposited her bowl in a bin, and departed the room without a word.

Lita struggled to understand. The shunning was obviously deliberate. But why?

Reyna was such a prideful person. Was she embarrassed to be seen laboring like a slave? Or had she felt abandoned, despite Lita's having no means to contact her?

Perhaps, unjustly, Reyna blamed her for pressure over that ridiculous loyalty oath that, in the end, couldn't prevent either of them from winding up right back behind bars.

Whatever the reason, Lita was determined to find out.

———•———

Later that evening, as everyone prepared for sleep, Lita stood patiently, waiting to pounce. When Reyna emerged from the lavatory—which was to say, a small room for the chamber pots—Lita pulled her aside by the arm, spurring her friend to retract with a quick look of fright.

Lita suddenly recalled the brutality Reyna had likely endured at the hands of the Kempeitai and stepped back, providing her space. It would be logical to surmise that such cruelty had left her reclusive and distant. Yet Lita had witnessed her chatting freely in the garden.

"Reyna, what is it? Why aren't you speaking to me?"

"I—just—" She continued to avert her eyes. "It's almost lights-out."

Lita fumed. "I know. And I don't care."

Reyna tried to charge past, but Lita blocked her.

"You're going to get us punished," Reyna snapped.

"So be it." Surely the consequences wouldn't be worse than anything they'd recently suffered. "And I'll do this again tomorrow night, and the night after that, until you tell me what's wrong."

Reyna looked off to the side, as if wanting to run but having nowhere to go.

Lita softened her tone. "Reyna, what's wrong? Have I done something?"

Stiffly she shook her head.

A small consolation.

"Then what? You can tell me."

Reyna's lips went taut, a clear attempt to suppress her emotions.

"Was it the Kempeitai?" Lita asked quietly. "Did they break your spirit?"

The question drew a mirthless laugh. She looked at Lita then. "They did more than that. They broke *me*." The admission was one Lita never fathomed she'd hear from the toughest person she knew.

"Oh, Reyna . . . I'm so sorry."

Tears brimmed in Reyna's eyes. She angled away again and wiped at her face, and that's when Lita noticed her friend's index finger. Both of them. Blackened, as if charred through. The cause was horrifically evident. How many sessions with that machine had the poor girl survived?

Lita couldn't stop her own eyes from misting. She touched Reyna's arm, gingerly this time, but again her friend pulled away. "Don't," she breathed, and now her tears were falling. "I don't deserve it."

Lita gazed at her, trying to comprehend.

Slowly Reyna turned back, chin and voice trembling. "It was me. I gave them your name. For so long I tried to be strong. But I needed them to stop. They promised they'd let me live if I just gave a name . . . and I couldn't . . . I couldn't take any more." A sob edged into her words. "I'm so sorry, Lita. I'm so, so sorry." The plea in her eyes, the shame, wrenched Lita's heart.

Lita herself had been tortured for days. Reyna presumably had endured it for months. How could Lita truly blame her? She couldn't say with even a speck of confidence that she wouldn't have done the very same had she known of Reyna's activities—likely cracking sooner.

Besides, Lita knew firsthand the burden of carrying guilt for an act that couldn't be changed, the uselessness of it all. She realized then how easily her mother would have forgiven her if given the chance.

Through a blur of tears, she peered at Reyna and insisted, "Now, you listen to me. You have nothing to be sorry for. Nothing." She held her friend's other arm. "What you did kept you alive. And I could not be more grateful for that. Do you hear me?"

Reyna took this in, lips tight yet quivering. After a long moment, she tendered a nod. Then Lita enfolded her in a hug, and together they wept until lights-out.

THIRTY-TWO

ELEANOR

Los Baños Prison Camp, Laguna Province
February 1945

I t had been a stretch of seven blissful days.

A week of eating enough food at each meal, of dispensing proper medicine to the patients in the infirmary, of seeing the camp children laughing and playing again, and mothers nursing their newborns.

Seven blissful days of freedom.

Not a one of them had ever expected to see Konishi and his troops again. Not with the news that American troops—tens of thousands of them—were marching toward Manila. Not with the sight of American war planes continuing to soar in formation high above their heads.

Had the internees known Konishi would be back in just a week's time, they might have fled the camp and taken their chances hiding in the jungle, dangerous though that might have been—especially if they had known he'd been ordered back in shame to Los Baños by an angry command post. His men came back to the camp in humiliation, some with injuries and bandaged heads from skirmishes with guerrilla armies of Filipino resisters. And when Konishi saw that his buildings had been raided and his food stores pillaged, he was livid.

That afternoon—their first as, again, prisoners of the Empire of

Japan—Konishi had ordered every internee to line up outside their barracks for a midday tenko and for an announcement. Over the loudspeaker, an interpreter told the assembled prisoners that they were to bring back all they had stolen. Every article of clothing, every dish, every grain of rice. If the looted items were not returned, the punishment to the entire camp would be severe. Additionally, anyone who had been outside the camp in the last week was to be questioned as to what they did, what they saw, who they talked to, what they brought back with them.

The announcement concluded with a declaration that anyone attempting to leave the camp or who was seen even talking to someone outside the fence would be executed.

The food that had been taken from the Japanese stores was brought back, though a small percentage had already been consumed. For this offense Konishi ordered that daily rations be cut in half and reduced to two servings a day, with each meal now the equivalent of about two hundred calories—or two tablespoons of peanut butter. No food from outside was allowed in the camp, even if it was donated by the villagers. Anyone accepting food through the fence would be shot.

Already devastated by Konishi's return, Eleanor's blood now ran cold at this announcement. The average two-year-old was supposed to eat at least a thousand calories a day according to the dietary guidelines she'd learned in nursing school. Konishi was again sentencing all of them to a slow and painful death. They would all start dying of starvation-related illnesses—the sickest and weakest first—if the Americans did not come for them, and soon.

She said as much to David as they sat under a tree and surreptitiously ate the last two dried mango slices he'd managed to hide. The guards had searched all the barracks after the afternoon announcement and removed everything the internees had bought in town, as well as their American money and much of their personal belongings to compensate for the food stores that had been eaten. They'd also found and confiscated the radio.

"We won't survive, David. Not like this."

"I know we won't," he replied.

This surprised Eleanor. David was usually so positive about their imminent rescue. It worried her that he did not try to correct her now, that he didn't counter her concern with a confident proclamation that they would ultimately be victorious.

"Some of us are coming up with a plan," he murmured, as he chewed the last of the mango slice.

Alarm instantly zipped through her veins. Prisoners with a plan always meant danger. "What do you mean?"

David looked at her and then clearly decided he'd said too much. "It's nothing you need to worry about."

"What plan?" she asked again.

He shook his head and shoved the empty mango-slice bag into his pants pocket. "It's nothing, Eleanor. I shouldn't have said anything. And hey, when they bring you before Konishi tomorrow to ask where you went in town, don't mention that you were with me. Just say that you went to see about getting some aspirin and cough syrup. It's true that's what you did. They don't need to know the rest."

The alarm morphed into something closer to dread. "You're scaring me, David."

"You don't need to be scared."

"But I am scared. Why don't you want me mentioning that I went into town with you?"

"Because they don't need to know," he said easily, dismissing her concern. "It's not a good idea for any of us to let Konishi know who our friends are. That is information he could use against us. So don't tell him."

She could tell there was more to his request, but she also knew that if she asked him to explain himself, he would not tell her. He was protecting her from something, and she didn't know what it was.

"Please, please be careful," she said.

"I will. I promise."

When she was taken to Konishi's office to account for her time in town, she did as David asked. She did not mention that she had walked to town with a friend. She told the interpreter that she'd taken a pair of her supervisor's earrings to trade for medicine for the dispensary. This was noted and Eleanor was dismissed.

As she stood to leave, a group of twenty or so female internees pushed past a sentry and made their way into Konishi's office. Eleanor recognized a few of them as women she had treated at the infirmary for one ailment or another, as well as mothers whose children she'd cared for. The women looked indignant, and Eleanor stepped aside to make room for them at the front of the desk.

Konishi looked up from his note-taking at the assembly in front of him. Eleanor quickly realized he had not summoned these women to his office. One of them stepped forward.

"We demand that you restore our full rations and that you give the camp kitchen enough food for three meals a day." Another woman spoke up before Konishi could have his interpreter fire back a response. "We want to be able to buy food from villagers who come to the fence." Another one quickly stepped forward. "If you do not give us more food, we will tell the guerrilla armies what you have done, and they'll invade this place." And another said, "When the Americans get here and see how you have starved us, they will make you pay."

Konishi, finding his voice, yelled at them to be quiet and to get out, but they did neither. The women continued to shout their demands.

Eleanor wanted to applaud. She wanted to cheer. But she was also afraid. The ruckus the women were creating had drawn the attention of guards standing outside. They were rushing in now with their rifles and bayonets and started to prod the shouting women out of Konishi's office.

"The Americans will see what you have done!"

"You will pay!"

"They are coming and you will pay!"

Eleanor watched in rapt fascination until one of the guards poked her, too, and Konishi yelled at her to get out.

She walked back to the hospital amazed at the women's courage and told the other nurses on duty what they had done.

"I wish I was braver," she told David that evening.

"You are brave. Every day you walk into that hospital to do what you do with practically nothing, you show how brave you are. Those women were brave for ten minutes. You are brave every minute of every day. Only someone with courage could go into that hospital and care for people the way you do under the circumstances we are in."

"I don't feel brave," she said.

"I don't think bravery is something you feel, Eleanor. I think it's something you possess. I see courage in you all the time. Everyone at the camp does. You nurses are like angels from heaven to all of us."

She chuckled at this. "Angels? Us? With wings and everything?"

"I'm serious. Everywhere we go in this camp, we are made to feel like we are worthless—except at the hospital. That's the only place where we feel like we matter. You make us feel like we are worth saving. You make us feel human again."

She felt tears coming; from where she didn't know. Were they tears of gratitude? Distress? Affection? Weariness? Fear?

Eleanor swiped them away, hoping David wouldn't notice. But he did. He bent over her and kissed her forehead. It was tender. Sweet. The best and most beautiful first kiss she'd ever received from a man. He stood. Abruptly, perhaps. As if the sweetness of his gesture surprised him as well.

"I've got to go." He turned and walked away before she could say anything else.

It was as David was walking away, with the petal-soft feel of his kiss still on her skin, that she realized it had been weeks since she had thought of John. The kiss from David had brought John to mind but only for a fleeting moment. As David disappeared from view, she realized that moving on from John would mean letting go completely and that letting go would feel like this. Good and bad at the same time.

But mostly good.

THIRTY-THREE

PENNY

Santo Tomas Internment Camp, Manila
February 1945

I t was obvious the Americans were on the outskirts of Manila. The sounds of shelling and explosions could be heard across the city, along with scattered gunshots. At times the groups of internees gathered outside Main Building swore they could hear shouts toward the north of the city. All morning they waited, encouraged when the sounds of battle flared up and discouraged when they died down.

By afternoon things grew quiet, and they feared the Japanese had pushed the Americans back. They looked to the guards for clues about how the battle went, but they were just as mercurial as the internees, singing one moment and sulking the next.

Everyone in camp could feel it in the air, however. Their imprisonment would end today, one way or another.

———◆———

By five o'clock that evening the Japanese ordered all the internees to go indoors. They retreated in droves to Main Building along with the hospital and the Education Building. Penny, Maude, and Newt watched from the second-floor window in the nurses' quarters as the guards rolled a dozen barrels through the doors.

"They're putting gasoline in the stairwells!" Jim Hobbs warned the internees as he went from room to room in the building. "The bastards are going to blow us up rather than let us be rescued!"

A thrum of anxious conversation passed through the internees at this news.

Fires burned throughout the city, and the report of machine guns grew closer. Some of the internees said it was on the other side of the gates now. So they threw open the windows to listen. Soon the sun fell below the horizon, but the sky still glowed a bright orange, and then they heard the *rat-tat-tat-tat-tat* echo, if not on the other side of the gates, at least a few blocks away.

But it wasn't until the Japanese cut the power to the camp at nine o'clock that they really began to fear. It seemed as though the scent of gasoline wafted up the stairs, so thick and oily in the air they could taste it. When flares went up on the other side of the camp wall, several of the women screamed and dove for their cots, certain they were about to be burned alive.

A low rumbling built in the earth. It emanated from deep within the ground and rattled up through the floor and into their bodies. The roar of engines and the crunch of tank tread followed.

The internees ignored the orders they'd been given, along with the countless barrels of gasoline in the stairwell and the hallways of Main Building. By the hundreds and then the thousands, they drifted out into the night air to see what was about to descend upon them. In the cupola-turned-guard-tower, men were shouting. Waving their arms. The Japanese soldiers had given up on their choreographed marches through the camp, and now they scurried from one shelter to another, looking over their shoulders in fear. It was as though the internees no longer existed. All attempts to frighten and manipulate them were abandoned. They had bigger problems now.

And two of those problems—in the form of fifty-thousand-pound Sherman tanks—broke down the gates of Santo Tomas with a *boom* and a *clang* loud enough to wake the dead.

The men, women, and children now gathered outside Main Building froze. It hadn't occurred to them that it could be anyone but the Americans. Yet now, seeing the great metal behemoths roll toward them, they hesitated. Shrank back.

The first tank rattled right up to the front steps of Main Building, and in the momentary lull that followed, Penny could hear the scrape of a latch and then the metal whine of hatches being lifted on each tank. Two dark figures, rifles in hand, rose from the bellies of those beasts.

In all the years that followed, she would never forget what happened next.

The soldier in the first tank took off his cap and said, in a perfectly distinct American accent, "Hello, folks!"

As the crowd around her erupted in cheers, Penny Franklin sank to her knees and sobbed. She wasn't the only one, of course. Weeping filled the night air. But then—strangely—it was replaced by the sound of wavering voices, one turning to ten turning to a thousand, all of them choked by emotion, singing a familiar refrain.

"God bless A-*mer*-i-*caaaa* . . ."

Penny didn't sing. Even then, in that moment of euphoria. But she did remain exactly where she was, on her knees, face turned to the night sky, tears streaming down her cheeks, and whispered every word of that song as though it were a prayer.

———◆———

As more tanks and trucks rolled through the gates, the American troops threw on a series of floodlights, illuminating the center of camp in a strange, unnatural light. Onozaki had no intention of making it easy on them, however. He and seventy of his officers had fled to the Education Building shortly before the tanks broke down the front gates and barricaded themselves inside, along with the two hundred internees who had taken shelter there. Before long, the windows were thrown open and men hung out, waving their arms.

"Help!" they shouted. "They're holding us hostage!"

The whine of the camp speakers filled the night air, followed by crackling, then the sound of Akibo's voice. "In exchange for the lives of the prisoners in this building, Commandant Onozaki requires the safe passage of all Imperial Japanese troops out of Santo Tomas and through enemy lines so we can join our forces. A team of negotiators will be sent out in ten minutes."

A team, Penny thought, no doubt led by Akibo himself and justified in the belief that they were not surrendering—an act of great dishonor—but performing a tactical maneuver.

The internees were furious at the demand, and they shouted, "Kill the monsters!"

But the American soldiers, sensing the rage building in the crowd, moved through the internees, reassuring them that the time of Japanese control over Santo Tomas was finished. They had no more power here.

As she'd guessed, ten minutes later, Lieutenant Akibo led a small group of officers out the front doors of the Education Building and across the plaza. The crowd stepped back, glaring. Most cursed them. Some spit. Akibo pretended not to care, but Penny saw his jaw clench as he approached the steps of Main Building. To be so insulted by prisoners! She could almost see the waves of fury radiate from him.

Penny watched as a group of American officers surrounded them. A tall, burly sergeant stepped forward. He unsnapped the chin strap under his helmet, then pulled it off. Like many of the red-blooded American men she knew, he was chewing a plug of tobacco. He spit a wad of brown juice right at Akibo's feet, then smiled.

"Hand over your weapons," he ordered. "Raise your hands."

Each of the Japanese officers carried a pistol and a sword. Some of them had bayonets as well. But none of them moved. After years of absolute control, the realization had come late that they'd lost it in the span of one evening.

"That wasn't a request," the sergeant said, and his men drew weapons of their own. Metallic *clicks* filled the air as hammers drew back.

Penny raised up on tiptoe to see Akibo's face. He caught the movement out of the corner of his eye and met her gaze. Hatred. Domination. Power.

They were at the root of his prolonged torment of her. Even as his eyes tightened into a glare, Penny their sole focus, the other officers reluctantly obeyed.

Guns, swords, knives all dropped to the ground with muffled thuds. Four sets of hands rose into the air, accepting defeat.

But not Akibo's.

Still fully armed and defiant, he ground his teeth together.

"For an English-speaking man, you ain't very smart," the sergeant told him.

This, to Akibo, must have been the final insult. Finally he lifted his hands, but not in the air. They went toward the small pouch affixed to the shoulder of his uniform. Too defiant for even the possibility of defeat, every soldier in the Imperial Japanese Army was issued a suicide grenade. Better death than surrender.

As Lieutenant Akibo reached for his grenade, the sergeant pulled the trigger. The shot went clean through Akibo's right hand—blowing a plum-size hole in his palm—then into his chest. He toppled backward onto the steps with a howl of fury. Blood spread across the steps.

"Penny!" A tiny body crashed into hers and there was Newt, tears in her eyes, hair wild. "Is it true? Are we free?"

The little girl had lived half her life in Manila. She could no more differentiate a U.S. military uniform from a Japanese uniform than she could speak Latin or rebuild a carburetor.

"Yes, honey." Penny scooped the child into her arms. "It's true."

"Is that why they shot him?"

"No, honey. They shot him because he was going to hurt us." She knelt and caught Newt's face in her hands. "I don't want you to look, okay?"

The only thing preventing the internees from stomping Akibo to death were the soldiers. But they spit on him and hurled insults regardless.

"Stay here," Penny said.

She pushed through the crowd until she found the sergeant. "I need to speak with that man." She pointed at Akibo. "I'm a nurse."

He lifted an eyebrow. "You want to treat him?"

"All I said was I need to speak with him."

Just in case, the sergeant leaned over Akibo and removed the grenade as Penny knelt beside him.

"What do you want?" he hissed.

As Akibo had done so long ago, Penny reached out and undid the first button on his shirt. "I want what's mine," she said, then bent closer. "And I'd like the record to show that I owe you *nothing*."

She carefully undid the clasp, then slid the necklace into her pocket. The American sergeant watched, stone-faced, as she continued.

"I am a nurse and an officer in the United States Army. I have taken an oath to care for those who are ill and injured. And I can tell, by the pink foam bubbling from the corner of your mouth, that the bullet has nicked your lung. Do you want me to treat your injury?"

Few things reveal the true nature of a person like success and defeat. And in Akibo's case, the civil, urbane nature he had tried to project—with all of his American education—dissolved at Penny's offer.

He was wrong about one very important thing he'd said when she first arrived at Santo Tomas: She wasn't powerless. Not in the ways that really mattered. Mercy was always power.

He, however, remained without honor. Akibo's teeth were pink with blood when his lips curled around them. "I would rather die."

"I will leave you to it, then."

THIRTY-FOUR

LITA

Women's Correctional Institution, Mandaluyong
February 1945

S tay strong, darling.

Since the note from Ida Hube arrived four days ago, tucked in a basket of food—enabled by her bribery of a senior guard—Lita had clung to the supportive words. Particularly now, as the smoky air, even inside the cell house, stung her eyes from aerial bombings that had recently become a daily occurrence.

Aircraft engines droned, as usual, layered by the thudding of anti-aircraft guns. From a distance came the whistling of falling bombs and roars of explosions. The notion of the Allies gaining ground was a wondrous thing yet was accompanied by fear. It was a strange thing to cheer for the side whose efforts in fighting for your homeland were also destroying it.

Mopping the floor of a cell, Lita attempted to push away visions of the convent burning from incendiaries, the children encircled by fire. Calling out for her, knowing only that she'd left them and had never come back.

Which could very well be the case.

An errant payload could just as easily end her own life, if not the equally formidable threat of starvation. A day after Lita's arrival, rice rations were cut to two spoonfuls per meal. The spinach and *kamotes*, which her father called sweet potatoes, that Reyna struggled to grow in the stony garden were too paltry to sustain any number of inmates. And although Lita had been rationing Ida's foodstuffs when sharing with others, those, too, would be gone shortly.

With every passing day of laboring from sunrise to sunset, she could feel herself tiring faster. Even more so than from her usual lingering effects from malaria. Reyna, too, had weakened noticeably since her arrest. And while she would sometimes darkly jest about winding up in the "dead house," the outbuilding for the deceased near the prison's front gate, they all knew it was a fate that hovered over them all.

"Soldiers!" A frantic scream traveled through the cell house. "Soldiers are here!"

Lita froze at the warning. She listened for the *crack* of rifle shots. Just days ago they'd rung out from the adjacent hospital when Japanese troops, according to a prison guard, executed all the American and British patients.

It had only further proven what Lita long suspected: even if the Imperial forces lost the war, it scarcely meant the soldiers would simply lay down their guns and walk away.

"Lita! Lita!" Reyna rushed inside and into view. "They're here."

Lita's thoughts spiraled with places to hide, spots she'd considered for just this event, but then Reyna's mouth curved up. A smile.

"Who?" The word barely formed against Lita's fear that good news couldn't be real.

"Americans." Tears shimmered in Reyna's eyes. "The American Army. Come see!"

Lita hurried after Reyna to reach the courtyard. The sight of GIs beaming proudly while carrying their rifles nearly caused Lita's legs to give out.

Several inmates, including Reyna, planted kisses on the soldiers' cheeks. Some even went straight for their mouths. None of the fellas complained.

Instinctively Lita searched their faces. Upon asking, she confirmed no soldiers were from Bilibid. But then watching the scene, she soaked in the exuberance of the moment and cried tears of joy.

"This has definitely got to be a dream." She heard Lon's words in her mind and wished desperately that he were here—aware that in a way he was.

———◆———

Led by a colonel's jeep, the liberated inmates rode open trucks toward what the driver called a "safe zone." They moved slowly over roads jammed with convoys. Allied tanks, trucks, and soldiers were everywhere.

Lita's thrill from the liberation gradually dampened, however, upon entering the city. She was unprepared for the actual scope of Manila's devastation. As if struck by a colossal typhoon, entire blocks had become piles of rubble. Of the buildings that remained, many bore shattered windows and pockmarks from bullets. Roofs were half torn away. Once-vibrant trees were burned to charred stumps. Bloated corpses—some Japanese; the majority Filipino women, kids, and the elderly—lay strewn across sidewalks, their stench strangling the air.

It was the aftermath at Little Baguio on a massive scale. Except here there was a convent that might no longer be standing, with children whose lives might not have been spared.

THIRTY-FIVE

ELEANOR

Los Baños Prison Camp, Laguna Province
February 1945

The women's demands at the quartermaster's office had changed nothing.

Only a few days later, while Eleanor was working at the hospital, a gunshot rang out. And then another one. And another. A minute or two later a Japanese officer strode into the infirmary and told Dr. Nance a prisoner had been shot. He needed to come.

Nance reached for his medical bag and told Eleanor to grab material for tourniquets and follow him. "Someone probably tried to escape."

At the northern perimeter of the camp, near an incline and a grouping of trees, lay a man. Blood was puddled about him. Dr. Nance and Eleanor ran to render assistance, but it was obvious when they reached him that the internee was already dead from bullet wounds to his head, chest, and abdomen. There were no bullet wounds to his back where one would expect a prisoner trying to escape would be shot. Tucked under the man's arm was a chicken, its neck already wrung. Near the body was a burlap sack of spilled coconuts and bananas.

The man had snuck out of camp to get food.

"He was shot when he came *back* to the camp?" Nance exclaimed in utter bewilderment to the officer.

"Take the body away," the officer said.

"But look! He had just snuck out to get food," Eleanor found herself saying, equally bewildered. "And he came back. He came back!"

One of the guards turned to her and told her in broken English to be silent.

"I'll need one of my orderlies to help me carry his body," Nance said.

The officer pointed to Eleanor. "She will help you."

Dr. Nance and Eleanor stood. "Take his legs, Eleanor," the doctor said.

As she lifted the dead man's legs and Nance grabbed him under his arms, a bag of rice and some candy fell out of the man's pants pocket. One of the guards bent down, grabbed the items, and shoved them in his own pocket.

Word of the killing spread through the camp. Eleanor learned the man, whose name was Pat Hell, had a sick friend in his barracks. He had gone in search of food so his friend would have the strength to fight off whatever was making him ill.

And then it happened again. An internee named George Louis, who'd been a mechanic for Pan Am before the occupation, was shot trying to sneak back under the perimeter fence. He'd gone out to bring back food too. Again Nance went out to the fence, and again Eleanor went with him. As they neared him they could see that George, lying on the ground with blood at his shoulder, was still alive.

Nance started to rush toward him.

One of the guards raised his rifle to stop him. "No."

"He's not dead! Let me go to him!" Nance pleaded.

"No."

"Please! Let me help him."

"No."

Nance turned to Eleanor and one of the committee members, a man named Gray, who had joined them at the fence.

"Go to the commandant's office," he said to Eleanor. "Ask to speak to Konishi. With Gray along you should have no trouble gaining an audience with him. Tell him the medical director of this camp respectfully requests that this wounded man be delivered to the camp hospital for medical care."

Eleanor and the other man sped over to Konishi's office. When the interpreter had been called for, Eleanor bowed low and repeated Nance's entreaty, word for word.

The interpreter listened to Konishi's response and then turned to Eleanor.

"The inmates at this camp are aware that anyone caught escaping or on the outside getting food will be shot. This is known to you. The man shall be executed."

"*What?*" Eleanor gasped.

"You can't do that!" Gray exclaimed. "International law is very clear on this. A prisoner cannot be executed if returning to the camp, only if caught trying to escape."

The interpreter delivered this message to Konishi. But the quartermaster replied, "It is the commandant's order that this man be executed."

Konishi was done discussing the matter. He told them to leave.

By the time Eleanor and Gray met up with Nance again, George Louis had been dragged a bit farther into the compound. Another internee gave him a cigarette to smoke to distract him from the pain of the gunshot wound in his shoulder. Dr. Nance was standing many feet away, a rifle trained on him should he attempt to render aid.

"He's going to be executed," Gray said to Nance in a somber whisper. "Konishi won't be persuaded. He said the commandant demands it."

"This is madness," Nance whispered back, shaking his head.

While they watched, Japanese soldiers approached George Louis, rolled him onto a wooden stretcher, and bore him to the guard post near the main gate.

Seconds later, another shot rang out.

George Louis's body was delivered to the hospital a short while later, with a fatal gunshot to the forehead.

Dr. Nance was instructed to write on the death certificate that George died from a single bullet wound received while attempting to reenter the camp from outside it. He refused, and no one from the commandant's office demanded he comply.

An hour later, the cemetery crew came to collect the body for burial. David was among them.

"See if you can come with me," he said to Eleanor when he was sure no one else was listening. "I want to tell you something."

He walked away before she could respond to help lift the body into the plain wooden coffin that fellow internees had made.

Eleanor turned to Dr. Nance and Laura, who were overseeing the transfer.

"I'd like to go to the burial if that's alright," she said to them.

Nance and the head nurse both nodded, thinking perhaps Eleanor needed to see this man—whose only crime was sneaking food into the camp—safely resting in peace.

She stood at the grave site with a handful of other internees who'd come to pay their final respects to George Louis. The camp priest spoke of George's last selfless act on this earth, his courage and concern for his fellow inmates, and then he commended George's soul to God. The priest prayed over the coffin and made the sign of the cross, then the short service concluded. The few gathered walked away as the cemetery team lowered the coffin into the ground and then shoveled dirt on top of it. Eleanor lingered.

She waited until the task was done and the two other members of the team started to walk away to return the shovels to the Japanese; they were not allowed to keep them in between burials. She and David stood for a moment over the freshly packed earth.

Then he turned to her. "The man who gave George his last cigarette?" David said. "He was able to speak to George for a few minutes. George told him he spoke to a man in town who had been traveling through this area on his way to Manila to get medicine for his wife and was now traveling back home to Mindanao. He had noticed our camp out here in the jungle on his way to Manila. It seemed such an out-of-the-way place for a POW camp so he thought perhaps he should make the Americans aware of it. He found out our 148th Regiment had retaken the Pandacan district. Eleanor, he asked to see someone in charge, and he told them he guessed there were maybe two thousand of us here. The Army didn't even know we are here, but they know now. They know! It won't be long now."

Eleanor looked at him, incredulous. "How could they not know we are here? How could they not know that?"

"That's . . . not the point," David said. "The point is they do now."

"Then where are they? Why haven't they come? Did he tell them we are starving? Every day we have less to eat. Every day someone in this camp dies because of it. Every day!"

"I know. I just . . . I thought you'd find this little bit of news encouraging. It's actually really good news."

They walked in silence for a few minutes. And then he seemed to suddenly remember how small the camp was, how many guards were on patrol, how easy it was to notice who the inmates conversed with. How easy it might be to eavesdrop on them.

"I've got to go." He was gone in a second, and Eleanor wished she had thanked him for trying to cheer her up.

It was good news, what he had told her. She was grateful that the Filipino man had taken the trouble to let the American military in Manila know there was a prison camp in the middle of a jungle near Los Baños.

But they could only wait so long for their rescue.

THIRTY-SIX

PENNY

Santo Tomas Internment Camp, Manila
February 1945

P enny went in search of the burly sergeant who shot Akibo. The Japanese
were gone, having marched out of camp within hours of its liberation.
Onozaki had led his men through the gates, their dead and wounded on
stretchers, as the newly freed internees heckled their departure. Onozaki
had arranged the release of the prisoners himself, after a short firefight
in which a number of Japanese and American soldiers were killed. To
Onozaki it was a negotiation, not surrender, and they left Santo Tomas
to the Americans. Still, a week later, it felt strange to be standing here, no
longer subjugated by their captors.

"Ma'am." The sergeant tapped his helmet as though saluting. "How can
I help?"

"Corregidor? The Japanese kept some of our men there when the island
fell. Engineers mostly. But a quartermaster, too, by the name of Charley
Russell. They were tasked with rebuilding the tunnels."

He nodded.

"Can you tell me . . ." Penny cleared her throat. Tried again. "Are they
alive? Have you gotten any word?"

The corners of his eyes pinched together in sympathy. "All I know is we're fighting to retake the island. But anyone left behind was sent to the Cabanatuan Prison Camp over a year ago."

"Where is that?"

"A hundred miles north of here. We liberated it ten days ago."

Penny grabbed his sleeve. "Charley Russell. Was he there?"

"I don't have the names, ma'am. There were only five hundred men left by the time we got there. The rest had already been moved through Bilibid Prison, then put on hell ships and sent away."

"Bilibid? You've been there too?"

He nodded. "There were over a thousand men left when we got there— all of them sick or wounded. But I don't know about your fella."

"It's okay," she whispered, finally, and hated the way her eyes stung. "Thank you."

"Don't worry. We'll get them all back. One way or another." He gave her an apologetic pat on the shoulder before returning to his post.

Penny looked to the north, to the far horizon and billowing towers of smoke. Manila burned, and beyond the wreckage lay the peninsula. Somewhere out there, Charley Russell was waiting for her, and she had to believe that he was still alive and would keep his promise. That he would come for her. For the flag. For that kiss. Because the alternative was beyond comprehension.

———◆———

Santo Tomas was chaotic that afternoon. People coming and going. Military trucks roaring through the streets. And all across the city they could hear the constant barrage of gunfire. Shouts. Screams. The STIC might have been secured by the U.S. Army, but the rest of Manila had devolved into a kind of hell that Penny could not allow herself to think about. So she paid no mind as a convoy of trucks rumbled through the front gate. More soldiers, she assumed. More food and supplies to ward off four years' worth of neglect and malnutrition. It wasn't until someone called her name that she paid the new arrivals any mind.

"Penny!"

She searched the crowd but saw no one she recognized.

Again her name rang out. "Penny!"

Three times it rose above the noisy courtyard. And then she saw a figure, small and thin, waving at her frantically as she eased down from the bed of a truck. Dark hair. Broad smile.

"Lita!"

Another young Filipina woman climbed from the truck and they exchanged a few words before Lita moved toward her with a limp. Penny met her halfway and pulled Lita tight. She was alarmed at the way Lita's ribs pressed through the thin burlap dress, at her dull hair, and at her hiss of pain at their embrace. "Are you okay?" She set her hands gingerly on Lita's shoulders.

"Yes. Mostly. Long story."

"Is that Reyna?" Penny nodded at the other girl who still stood beside the truck.

"It is."

"She okay?"

"About the same as me."

They hadn't seen each other in a year. But one glance was all it took to know that a lifetime's worth of sorrow had passed for each of them in those long months.

"Eleanor?" Lita asked.

Penny shook her head. "I don't know."

"Is she still at Los Banōs?"

"Last I heard. But it's been a year and a half. No word on whether they've been liberated yet."

"And you?" Lita asked. "How are *you*?"

Penny looked at the fading bruises on Lita's jaw and collarbones. The tattered clothes. And that look in her eyes—a well of loss that was fathoms deep. "I could ask the same."

Lita smiled faintly. "But I asked first."

"I'm better this week than last."

"I've been so worried about you. And Father Domingo. I haven't heard anything from him since before I was arrested."

Penny caught her breath. "Lita—"

"It's okay. I'm fine, really—"

"He's dead. Father Domingo. He was executed five months ago when they discovered the priests had tunneled out of the camp."

"Oh, heavens . . . no." Lita, tired and overwhelmed, battered by experiences Penny had yet to learn about, looked at a loss from the wave of emotions.

Penny wrapped her arms around her friend, and they stood in the courtyard, letting the late-afternoon sun warm them.

After a moment Lita pulled away and squared her shoulders as though ready to take this next bit of news on the chin. "What about Bilibid?"

"Liberated on the fourth. The day after Santo Tomas."

"And the men that were held there?"

"I was told that just over a thousand of them were still there when our troops arrived. The healthy ones were sent on the hell ships, but the sick and wounded were left behind. The Army has it secured, same as here, and is using it as a staging point." Penny watched the fear gather in Lita's eyes. "You're worried about Lon?"

She nodded. "I saw him a second time at the prison, and he *was* wounded. But it's been over a year."

"Well, then, I'll keep asking around. I'm sure we'll know more soon."

Lita nodded again with a trace of wistfulness, and asked, "Have you heard anything about Santa Catalina? I'd been living there, helping care for the kids the nuns had taken in. After all the bombings, though, and the way the city looks . . ."

"Not to worry. We'll find out about them too. In the meantime I'm sure the sisters have kept them all safe." Penny looped her arm gently through Lita's. "Come with me. Let's get you some clothes and something to eat."

Lita glanced back over her shoulder and motioned for Reyna to join them. But she followed at a distance, giving them space to talk.

As they walked toward the mess hall, they were intercepted by Newt. She had an Army K-ration in each hand and one between her teeth. As usual the girl threw herself at Penny, crashing into her with a force that nearly knocked her over. She mumbled something unintelligible around the foil packet in her mouth. Her entire body quivered with excitement, and the stream of words never stopped even though the only one Penny could decipher was "food."

"And who is this?" Lita asked.

Penny ruffled Newt's tangled curls and shrugged. "I suppose you could say that she's mine."

THIRTY-SEVEN

LITA

Santo Tomas Internment Camp, Manila
February 1945

No one Lita asked at Santo Tomas knew anything about the condition of the convent. Since it was just a ways down the road, however, folks were confident that if any major explosions had occurred, the internees would have heard them.

This put Lita's mind at ease just enough to dine with Penny—with cautious food portions, of course. Especially for Reyna, overindulging could be a dangerous shock to the system. After bathing, Lita borrowed an actual blouse, skirt, and fresh sandals. Reyna did the same. They almost looked and felt like real people again.

By late afternoon Lita had full intention of venturing to Santa Catalina. But hit by a sudden wave of exhaustion, assuredly from the lowering of her constant guard, she couldn't resist a nap on a cot Penny had scrounged up for her. When Lita opened her eyes, she was covered in a blanket. And it was almost evening. The next day. She learned this from a woman departing the room, leaving Lita all alone.

The surrounding cots were vacant but for mussed blankets for those who must have slept and woken and were now roaming the camp. Rumblings from distant explosions continued. Goodness, those hadn't roused her either.

Sitting up, Lita had to chuckle at her clothes, all wrinkled from top to bottom. So much for appearing freshened up.

"Well, look who's alive." Penny smiled, entering the room.

"Apparently I was tired."

"I'll say. I confess, a few times I did check to make sure you were breathing." She said this lightly, though surely there was valid truth in it.

"Did Reyna get some rest?"

"She did. A good deal, I think. She's been catching up with some nurses from Hospital Two."

"Oh good. That's wonderful." Reconnecting with them would hopefully help get Reyna back to her old self—the nicer version, though.

"How about some food? You must be hungry by now."

"I'm still waking up, but I'm sure I'll be famished soon." Moreover, another task took precedence. "Before then, I thought I'd go check in on the kids at the convent."

"The sun's already setting, and it seems a bit dicey out there. You don't want to wait until morning?"

"No, but thanks. I've already waited long enough."

Penny pursed her lips, hesitant. "Alright. I'll come with you. No chance I'm letting you out of my sight that soon." She winked, and Lita agreed with a smile.

———◆———

"Sorry, girls," said the American guard, young and dark haired, posted at the gate. He projected over the fading buzz of aircraft engines. "Wandering out there isn't a wise idea."

"We're not wandering," Lita clarified. Again.

"Would it be better if we go in the morning?" Penny asked him.

"Honestly? I still advise against it."

The pale orange sky was swiftly losing light, and Lita was losing patience. She could have been halfway there already. "Then how about you send a GI with us?"

"I would if I could, but there ain't a single one to spare."

Lita huffed, not hiding her exasperation.

With an air of reluctance the guard leaned in and lowered his volume. "Look. The reports we're getting are ugly. The Japs—they know they're losin', so they seem hell bent on taking as many Filipinos down with them as they can. Old folks, kids, babies even. They're hunting them down. A real blood-bath. I can only imagine what they'd do to a couple of pretty gals like you."

The recollection of casualties on the sidewalks wrung Lita's stomach. She had taken them for people caught inadvertently in the cross fire, not the targets.

Penny stared at her, equally shaken.

"Lita!" Reyna called over in greeting. Strolling with a pair of nurses from Hospital Two, she said something to them, then broke away as they continued on. "What are you two doing over here? Are you heading out?"

"No, miss," the guard answered for them. "I was just making clear that you're all staying put." He was about to add more, but a soldier at the far end of the gate hollered to summon him. "Be back in a jiff."

The instant he walked away, Reyna whispered, "What's going on?"

"It's the children at the convent," Penny said.

Terrified she'd waited too long, Lita decided, "I'm going there now. By morning it could be too late."

Reyna's expression turned grave. She didn't probe for details. Furtively she peered over her shoulder toward the gate guards. "I'll give the cue when we can slip out."

"I'm ready when you are," Penny said.

"Reyna," Lita interjected, though touched, "Penny and I can go. You should stay and rest."

Reyna furrowed her brow. "I'm as much their tita as you are." Then she softened and smiled wryly. "Plus, I don't need any fellow telling me what to do."

Indeed, there was a glimpse of the old Reyna.

———◆———

Shadows from the surrounding buildings grew as Lita led her friends at a steady clip. Their gazes constantly darted to the front, the back, the sides. Searching for any signs of movement in the shops and apartments flanking them.

A short burst of machine-gun fire rang out, halting them all at once.

"That sounded awfully close," Penny whispered, voicing what Lita was thinking.

"Let's hurry this up," Reyna said.

Lita nodded, and they hastened their steps to a plodding jog.

What was her plan now? Initially it had been to confirm the children were okay. But was anywhere outside Santo Tomas safe?

Then came a scream. Prolonged and curdling from somewhere to the left. At the jungle hospitals, they'd all learned the sound of agony. More recently, Lita recognized it from the torture rooms of the Kempeitai. Clearly so did Reyna, who winced.

"We're nearly there," Lita reminded them both, an assurance even as her pulse accelerated. Her leg ached from so much movement, but she shoved the thought down.

From the bend in the road, Santa Catalina appeared up on the right. As they hustled onward, Reyna's gait gained a tired rhythm, and Lita's own energy was draining. Penny, too, seemed to be pulling strength from a depleted well.

Still, there was no time to rest.

Upon reaching the front door, Lita let out a small sigh of relief. So far, the building appeared intact and showed no sign of intrusion.

She tried the handle. Locked. A good thing, potentially. The group could be holed up inside. Then again, there were side doors and windows. Plenty of ways to break in. She needed to get them out, bring them to the only "safe zone" she knew.

She knocked lightly. Dull, ineffective sounds. The door wasn't markedly thick, but still, it was solid wood. Lacking a choice, she pounded twice with her fist. Penny inhaled a sharp, nervous breath. The pounding felt amplified with the sounds of munitions waning.

"Come on, come on," Lita murmured toward the door. Penny faced the other way, keeping lookout.

"I don't see any lights." Reyna was peeking into a large window over to the side, tilting her head to see between the curtains of the nuns' office.

"Might be good news," Penny whispered. "Maybe they went somewhere else to be safe."

"Where, though?" Lita said. "With eighteen kids, who'd have space for them?" An obvious spot dawned on her. "The storm cellar. Around the back."

More gunshots blasted. These ones from a rifle.

They all faced the road and listened. Another shot fired from somewhere unseen. Too close.

Now muffled screams followed. Far too close.

"Let's go," Reyna ordered. Quietly they sprinted around the corner of the building, slipping past the line of shrubbery.

The slanted cellar doors lay shut, with the padlock missing from the latch. The children and nuns could be in there—or had been.

Lita leaned down low and first tapped on the heavily weathered planks—a gentle alert—then whisper-shouted in Tagalog where the doors met at the middle: "Sisters, it's Lita. I'm coming in."

She grabbed a ring pull and tugged. The door rattled yet only budged a little. Secured from within.

"They're inside," she said to her friends, hopeful. Suddenly she wondered if the children might be safest right where they were. But then she noted the condition of the cellar doors. Likely from years of typhoons, the hinges were rusted and bolts a bit crooked; one door was slightly cockeyed, leaving a thin crack. She doubted it would take much work for dogged Japanese soldiers to break through.

A tiny slice of light shone through the crack. Further encouraged, she tapped on the planks again and directed her words through the opening. "Sister Cecilia, open up. Reyna and Penny are here too. We're here to take you to Santo Tomas."

Penny's face flickered with a surprise that then dropped away as she nodded, because it was the best solution.

"Lita," Reyna rasped, holding up a rusted padlock. "It's been broken off."

A hand-size rock lay on the ground by Reyna's feet. Either the nuns had removed the busted lock at some point, or the people taking shelter down below were strangers. If the latter, could they possibly be armed themselves?

Men's voices drifted vaguely from the direction of the road. Faint boot steps.

Lita had to take the risk.

"Please, open up. It's Lita. We don't have time."

The planks rattled.

A sliding noise suggested a wooden bar being removed.

Then the left door pushed up a few inches, revealing Sister Cecilia— thank goodness.

Lita spoke to her in Tagalog. "Are all the children in there?"

"Yes," she replied, fear riding her features. "Two other families also."

This news jarred Lita if but a second. "Of course. We'll take you all." From the corner she caught a movement in the shrubbery and stifled a gasp. Penny had snuck over and was surveying the road. Twisting back halfway, she waved for them to hurry.

Reyna was already helping open the cellar doors fully and with caution. The creaks from the hinges raised the tiny hairs on Lita's arms.

"Sister," Lita said, "we have to go *now*."

But the woman was heading back down, causing Lita a jolt of panic until she glimpsed the nun holding a finger to her lips, reiterating silence to everyone below. Then she sent the children up the stairs.

Lita's relief from the mere sight of their sweet, beloved faces helped tamp the anxiousness gripping her.

As swiftly as possible, the cellar was vacated and the whole group funneled past the shrubbery. Several pairs of children clutched each other's hands. Sister Cecilia carried one of the littlest ones. The two sets of parents, offering grateful looks, took care of their own children while helping others along. At the rear, Reyna and the other nuns assisted in keeping the kids moving.

Along the side of the building, Penny and Lita peered around and found the area clear. They were about to head out when the men's voices returned, louder. Speaking Japanese. The sounds of boot steps affirmed their approach.

Lita spotted them at last, coming down the road from the right. She pulled her head back to stay out of view with Penny and glanced over at Reyna, who stared with intensity; she'd heard the men too. Lita raised a hand, a group command to wait and be still.

But these were children. And they were fidgety.

Lita's heart pounded harder with every rustling movement that could give them away.

A metallic hammering sound came from the front of the convent. Lita stealthily peeked and discovered the pair of Japanese soldiers now at the door. One was slamming the butt of his rifle at the door handle; the other began striking a window with his own rifle. They had crazed eyes and their uniforms and bayonets were covered in blood.

They were so close Lita feared they could hear her breathing.

The front door handle clattered on the ground. Over and over the soldiers kicked the door until it flew open, and then they stormed inside. The rest of the road was clear, for the moment.

Lita looked at Penny, a wordless message traded between them. This was their only chance.

Penny took the helm with a child clinging to each of her hands. She kept tight to the buildings on the left, traveling as quick as their small legs allowed.

A hazy gray-blue was now dimming the sky, the orange nearly vanished.

Lita stayed behind to usher the others past while keeping an eye on the front door, prepared to hold back any remnants of the group and attempt to hide them should the soldiers reemerge. It was just a matter of time before they discovered the place empty.

When Reyna brought the last of the children around the corner, Lita joined her while continuing to peek back at the convent.

The children at the front were now rounding the bend. From there it was a straight path to the camp.

Almost there, almost there, Lita told herself, until interrupted by a high-pitched wail.

A little girl near the back was shrieking, having fallen. A nun picked her up and tried frantically to calm her. But the girl, holding up the hand she seemed to have scuffed, only screamed louder.

A collective panic seized hold.

"Run!" Lita ordered in a quiet yell, and she motioned for those in her view to charge forward. She glanced back at the convent and caught sight of what resembled a figure before it dropped away as she followed the bend herself.

The gates of Santo Tomas appeared up on the right, but a stretch still remained.

Penny was sprinting with the children while checking behind her, making sure all the others were keeping up. Soon the ones in front were veering toward the camp gate.

Battling exhaustion, Lita focused on her own feet—*right, left, right, left*—as her legs begged to stop, wanting to collapse like a marionette's.

Reyna's breaths sounded shallow as she pushed herself with evident effort, yet Lita didn't realize how far they'd fallen behind until Jun-Jun broke away and barreled toward them.

"Tita," he called out. The fear in his voice told her he didn't want to lose her again.

"Jun-Jun, no," she urged in Tagalog. "Go the other way."

But he embraced her waist, slowing her. "Jun-Jun, you have to go. Run to my friend Penny. *Please.*"

Reyna swiftly pried him off and rushed with him toward Santo Tomas.

A shot blasted from behind, and Lita stumbled to the ground. A searing pain from landing on her kneecap shot through her leg like lightning. Through her instant tears, she strained to look back and found one of the soldiers standing at the bend with rifle raised.

Her thoughts jumped back to the kids. She was relieved to see the last of the group turning into the camp.

Another shot rang out, and she reflexively flattened herself as her limbs shook. Back outside the gate, Penny swooped up Jun-Jun in her arms and was yelling for someone to help.

Lita's body protested moving, yet her mind countered with logic: remaining here was suicide.

She was scrambling to rise when Reyna arrived at her side, hunched low, and grabbed hold. Together they were halfway to standing when Lita's knee buckled from the weight.

"Just go," Lita urged.

Ignoring her, Reyna continued to guide her up.

But then more bullets flew. A peppering of them.

Lita ducked low on the ground with Reyna, hands over their heads, until the shooting stopped.

At last when Lita dared raise her eyes, she discovered the gate guards holding their rifles, and behind her a Japanese soldier on the ground, sprawled and lifeless.

THIRTY-EIGHT

PENNY

Santo Tomas Internment Camp, Manila
February 1945

"S he can't come with us," Maude said.

"But we can't leave her here," Penny whispered. A mere day after rescuing the children from the convent, she felt more protective of Newt than ever, her nerves still frayed by their close call with the Japanese soldiers. "She's just a child."

Newt sat on her cot, arranging the contents of a K-ration in order of most to least desirable. Every day since their liberation the child had weaseled an extra ration out of the hands of Army soldiers and taken them back to the nurses' quarters where she cherry-picked her favorite items—usually the cake, candy, gum, and dried fruit bars—and gave the canned meat and cheese to other children around the camp. The cigarettes were confiscated by the nurses and passed around in the evenings.

"I think you've forgotten whose child she is, Penny."

"That's not fair."

"You have been really good to that girl. But she has a mother. And it's not you."

"Her *mother* is in the U.S. Thousands of miles away."

"And her father is here."

"Maybe. If he's even alive. Somewhere out in the jungle fighting hand-to-hand with the guerrillas. We can't leave her alone to wait for him."

"No. He's *here*."

"What?"

Maude set her hand on Penny's shoulder. "She cannot come with us because her father is at the hospital. He's asking for her."

"But—"

"I wanted to give you the chance to say goodbye."

"No." Penny shook her head. "That doesn't make any sense. It doesn't . . . I can't . . . I need more time."

And the thought almost made her laugh. Time was all she'd had for the last four years. Endless piles of time. The never-ending stream of days had nearly made her insane, and now she'd give anything for just a few more. But suddenly all the sand had slipped through the hourglass.

"You have thirty minutes," Maude said. "I'll go tell him she's on the way."

--------◆--------

Penny took Newt to the acacia tree.

"I have something for you," she said as they settled onto the grass and leaned against the tree.

Newt wiped crumbs from her mouth. "What?" she asked around a mouthful of dry biscuit.

Penny reached into her pocket and pulled out the necklace. It lay in her palm, a twisted vine of gold chain with that oblong nugget at the end.

"For me? *Really?*"

Penny undid the clasp and hung it around the child's neck. "In a few hours a plane is coming to take me away from here."

"Take me with you!"

"I wish I could, baby. But your father is here. And your mother is waiting for you both in America. They miss you. And it's time to go home."

Newt stilled beside her, and when Penny looked at her face, she saw fat tears dripping off the end of her little button nose.

"What's wrong?"

"My father . . ."

"Yes?"

The fear in those big blue eyes made Penny's stomach hurt.

"I don't remember what he looks like."

"That's okay." Penny pulled the little girl against her chest. "He'll remember you."

After a while Penny tipped Newt's chin upward. "I do hope you will remember me, though."

For an answer, Newt threw her arms around Penny, smearing crumbs all over her shirt.

———◆———

The child's father had grown a beard during his years in the jungle, and Newt's fears proved accurate. She didn't recognize him, and when he reached for her, she shrank back.

"Don't be afraid. It's me," he said. "It's Daddy."

Penny held her at a distance, unwilling to force the child into the arms of a stranger. But then Newt saw his eyes—the same bright blue—and heard his voice. She leaped from Penny's arms to his. It took every ounce of willpower she had not to reach for the girl—*her girl*—and drag her back.

"How did you find her?" Penny folded her hands behind her back.

"We got to Manila yesterday," he said. "The guerrillas, I mean, and we all went in search of our families. I'd left her with my parents. We lived on the outskirts of the city, and I thought she'd be safe there. Safer than the jungle, at least. But the neighbors told me that the Japanese had taken all the foreign nationals to Santo Tomas earlier in the war. When I got here the guards said that all of the older people were sent somewhere else when the camp got crowded. The kids stayed but no one recognized her name—do you really call her Newt? It took me ages before I found anyone who'd seen her. I . . ." He shook his head, and Penny thought he might burst into tears. "I didn't want to leave her. But I couldn't take her with me either. Do you understand?"

Newt's father looked at her, pleading, desperate that she not think him unfit.

"I do." Penny reached out her hand and wiped a fat, happy tear off Newt's cheek with her thumb. "We've all had to make impossible choices."

Penny shrugged, not sure what else to say, then sat on the nearest cot while he asked her questions about the camp and how Newt had fared. They talked for nearly an hour, trading stories until, slowly, the knot in Penny's stomach untangled. The grief would remain. She was certain of that. But she was no longer afraid of releasing Newt into his care.

Finally, at a sign from Maude, Penny stood to leave. Her time was up.

Newt's father grabbed Penny's hands so hard the knuckles ground together. "Thank you," he said, eyes flooded. "I can never repay you for what you've done for my daughter."

"You don't have to." And she meant every word. "It was an honor."

He stood and gathered Newt tight against his chest. "Come on, then. Let's go home. Your mother is waiting."

Penny didn't flinch or suck in her breath, but the words landed like a punch anyway. *"Your mother is waiting."* A blow, straight to the heart.

It's not me, she thought. *It was never me.*

Father and daughter walked down the hallway, hand in hand. Penny waved and smiled madly every time Newt turned around. But as they approached the doors, the little girl pulled her hand free and ran back. She threw herself in Penny's arms and held on for dear life.

Then she turned that impish face upward and grinned so wide, Penny thought the girl's face might crack in half. "My name is Ellen."

"Well," Penny said, stifling a sob, "to me you'll always be Newt."

She watched them go. Watched until they'd gone through the doors and disappeared around a corner. But it wasn't until Maude draped an arm around her shoulders that Penny let the tears fall unhindered.

"Sometimes love can break your heart," Maude said.

Penny looked at her friend. Tried to smile but couldn't. "In my experience it's the only thing that does."

———◆———

Penny found Lita beside the burned-out husk of Father Domingo's chapel and settled onto the grass beside her. She pulled her knees tight against her chest and wrapped her arms around them.

"How'd it go?" Lita asked.

"Awful." Penny shook her head. "It's not like I didn't know it would happen eventually. That I couldn't keep her. I guess I just liked pretending."

"And now you've come to say goodbye to me." A wry smile curved one corner of Lita's mouth.

"I hate today."

"It was coming eventually."

"Seems to be what we do, right? We find each other. Then we say goodbye. Then we find each other again."

"And say goodbye. Again."

"It's not a bad pattern, if you think about it." Penny bumped her shoulder. "Means another reunion is on the horizon."

"Doesn't mean we have to like the wait in between."

"Nope." Penny lay back on the grass and stared at the bottle-blue sky. No planes, no clouds. "General MacArthur is planning to meet with us. He's taken too much heat for letting us get captured. Maude says he's on his way to thank us in person for our 'brave and noble service' before he sends us home and trots us out in front of the cameras."

"*Us*, meaning all of *you*." Lita winced. "Sorry. I'm happy for you all. Truly."

"No, you're right. It isn't fair. You and Reyna and the others were there too. You did everything we did in the hospitals, and after that even more with the Resistance to keep our soldiers alive. You sacrificed so much. They should acknowledge that."

Lita shrugged. "At least you'll get credit on our behalf."

"I wouldn't call it that exactly."

"But I thought you said—"

"They'll use us as a bit of spit polish to make better headlines back home. They'll present us to the world as vulnerable girls instead of capable women. They'll say we've been *rescued* instead of acknowledging that we've been doing a damn fine job of rescuing ourselves over the last four years." Penny frowned. "Maybe we didn't knock down those gates with a couple of Sherman tanks, but we sure as hell helped save a lot of people. That's not the story they're going to tell, though."

"I'm glad you're angry," Lita whispered.

"Why?"

"Because I couldn't bear it if you were *happy* to leave." Lita smiled sadly.

A gentle breeze ruffled the ends of Penny's hair as she pushed up onto her elbow. "I told you I would talk to Maude. There has to be a way that you can come with us. If not now, then later. I'm going to write to my senator. Tell him everything you've done. I can find a way for you to come to the States. To be with your sisters. I know it's what you've always wanted."

Lita looked at her, something unreadable clouding those brown eyes, then turned to the chapel. They sat quietly for a long moment before she said, "It's odd, isn't it? All through the war, we spent so much time apart, worrying about each other . . . Somehow this feels worse. Knowing for certain we'll be so far away."

"It really is goodbye, then?" Penny picked at a blade of grass.

Lita gave her hand a tender squeeze. "Just for now. Like you said."

For a girl who used to cry only when she was angry, Penny found that any and all emotions could open the floodgates now. If she was happy, she cried. If she was tired, she cried. But sadness? That burst the dam wide open.

———— • ————

It didn't take long to pack. Less than ten minutes. Eleanor's letter was wrapped carefully inside the quartermaster's flag and placed at the bottom of Penny's rucksack. She checked three times to make sure it was still there before buckling it closed.

Maude Davison—champion of patients and nurses—turned to survey the nurses' quarters one last time. A tall woman who didn't have much on her frame to begin with, she'd dropped to less than one hundred pounds. Penny thought she looked like a willow switch wrapped in khaki as she stood there, assessing the room one last time. Every cot had been stripped, every bag packed. Floors swept and windows closed.

The nurses were lined up wearing new Class A olive-green uniforms that had been flown in from Australia and delivered to the STIC that morning. The girls were going home, and top brass couldn't have them looking ragged. But no amount of new clothing could hide their battle scars, their limps, illnesses, and thin bodies. Though cinched tight at the waist, every uniform was too large.

"Why send these now?" Penny tugged at her new collar. "Why not wait until we're evacuated to Leyte?"

When Maude turned to her, a glimmer of mischief shimmered in her eyes. "Because, Lieutenant Franklin, we're about to meet General MacArthur."

"On behalf of the United States Army, and in honor of your outstanding service, I hereby present each of you the Bronze Star for valor and a field promotion of one full rank."

The man standing with General MacArthur was Brigadier General Guy Denit, chief surgeon in the Southwest Pacific, and at this pronouncement he began to move down the line of nurses. Fifty-four women in all. To every uniform he pinned the Bronze Star and a battle ribbon for serving in the Pacific theater. Maude was first, of course, and Penny's eyes smarted with tears at the proud salute she offered in return. By the time Denit got to her, Penny had collected herself enough to make eye contact. But she received her medal with a solemness that surprised her. She could feel the weight of this moment settling into her bones.

Douglas MacArthur, general of the Army, had acknowledged the magnitude of their service. But Lita wasn't standing in this line. Neither was Eleanor. And . . .

Well. That's it. It's all over.

Still, Penny lifted her chin when MacArthur stepped forward and addressed them. "You have served your country under extraordinary circumstances," MacArthur said. "As the first American female prisoners of war, you have a special place in the history books. But to have served four years as prisoners, in combat conditions, you have my respect as well. Those back home have followed your story closely. They call you the 'Angels of Bataan and Corregidor,' and now you may return to the United States in honor. I thank you for your brave and dedicated service."

With a salute he dismissed them, and the nurses fell out of rank, some in tears, others in amazement as they gazed around Santo Tomas one last time.

Earlier in the day, when the nurses changed into their new uniforms, Penny transferred the eight of hearts from her coveralls to this new right-front pocket. She patted it now. It was a habit, a touchstone. For two years she'd been walking around the STIC with the card in her pocket. It was bent, worn, and frayed at the edges from all the times she'd pulled it out and held it as though staring at a photo. It was irreplaceable. And it reminded her that she was allowed to hope.

Penny glanced up as Maude slipped a hand into the crook of her elbow. "C'mon, *First* Lieutenant Franklin," she said with a wink. "Let's go home."

Penny helped Maude into the back of an Army truck that waited for them beside the main gates. Then she threw in her pack and climbed inside. The engines rumbled to life and sputters of diesel exhaust rose around them in a flimsy black cloud that soon dissipated in the cool evening air.

Penny looked up as they rolled through the gates, but the barbed wire was gone now. They were free.

THIRTY-NINE

ELEANOR

Los Baños Prison Camp, Laguna Province
February 1945

War planes continued to dot the sky from far above, but for Eleanor and the others at Los Baños, it was what was happening right there on the ground that held their attention. Only days after George Louis's execution, Konishi directed a handful of his garrison to start digging a long and wide ditch in the southeast corner of the camp.

The inmates could only imagine what it was to be for.

For the Japanese to jump in when the bombs started to fall?

That didn't seem likely. The Americans wouldn't drop bombs on a camp full of POWs.

What other purpose, then, could a ditch that size serve?

Eleanor could think of only one. Wanting to be wrong, but not knowing if she was, troubled her every spare moment.

She wanted to ask David what he thought about the ditch, but it seemed like he was avoiding her. She wondered if it was because she had snubbed the bit of news he'd brought to her on the day of George's death. That had been insensitive of her, and the more she thought about it, the worse she felt. She owed him an apology.

She looked for him at breakfast the next day and did not see him.

Disappointed, she went to the hospital after eating her three dollops of mush and hoped to have better luck at dinnertime.

The morning wore on, slow and tedious. Sometime before noon, shots were heard near the northern perimeter.

Just like the ones they'd heard before on the day George Louis died and the man before him.

"Not again," Dr. Nance said as a Japanese guard strode up to the hospital and asked that he come get a body. Another internee had been caught trying to bring in food from the outside and he'd been summarily shot.

Dr. Nance signaled for Eleanor to bring the tourniquets and come with him.

"Whoever it is, they won't let us help him," Eleanor said.

"But first we try anyway. On the off chance he's still alive, we have to at least try."

She quickened her pace, and they followed the guard to the fence. From a distance they could see a man lying not far from where that first man had been killed.

As they neared him, the man moved ever so slightly. He was indeed still alive. The two guards standing near him were talking to each other casually as if it was just another day at work. A dirty pillowcase lay near the fallen man with mangos and bananas spilling out of it.

As they drew closer, Eleanor could see blood puddling underneath the man's middle. His back was to them and there were no wounds there. He'd been shot like the others, in the front as he stole back into camp.

It was a travesty, an injustice of the most—

And then she recognized the tousle of sandy-brown hair, the lean frame, the bare feet.

David.

Eleanor ran to him, surprising the guard who was leading them, and fell to her knees beside David. She turned him over before the two talking guards had time to react.

"David! David!" Eleanor wailed.

His eyes fluttered open.

One of the guards reached down and pulled her back violently. He yelled something in Japanese. The other talking guard raised his rifle to shoot David in the head, and Eleanor wrenched free and flung herself protectively over him.

Everyone except David was shouting.

"Wait! Wait! Wait!" The doctor threw himself down over Eleanor, and the guard pointing the rifle at David lowered it a few inches.

It would not do to shoot the camp doctor. He treated the Japanese garrison on occasion too.

"Please just let me talk to her! Please! Wait!" Dr. Nance begged.

The guard said nothing. He didn't lower his rifle completely, but neither did he raise it again.

Eleanor was weeping over David's frame. He felt so cold. The blood pouring out of his abdomen and chest was pooling now in her lap and at her knees.

"Don't go, don't go," she cried.

"Eleanor, please move back from him," Dr. Nance pleaded. "You've got to move back."

But she stayed where she was. The guard took a step forward to get a better angle to shoot David a third time—and without harming the doctor—and Nance quickly positioned his body to shield them both.

"He won't survive this," Eleanor heard the doctor saying to the guard. "This man won't survive. Do you understand? He will die. Let her say goodbye, please? They are friends. Let her say goodbye."

From the corner of her eye Eleanor saw the guard with the raised rifle take a step away.

Eleanor sat back only as far as needed to look into David's eyes.

"David," she said.

"Remember . . . your . . . promise . . . to me . . . ," he whispered, his teeth scarlet from the blood filling his mouth.

"Don't go! Please! I am so sorry. I should have been a better friend to you. I am so sorry. Please don't go."

"You . . . were . . . the best friend to me." David gasped as he reached one shaking hand toward her. He touched her face. "Live . . ."

David's hand on her face fell and his body shuddered.

And then he went still.

Eleanor pulled him toward her as a cry of grief tore through and out of her, from the deepest part of her soul.

———◆———

David Mathis was laid to rest that afternoon. A downpour kept his grave from being dug until several hours after he had expired, but this allowed time for Eleanor to sit with the body in the hospital while everyone waited for the rain to stop. She had asked to be the one to care for his body: to stitch the wounds closed, sponge away the mud and blood, wash his hair and his hands and his feet. Dr. Nance told Eleanor that one of the other nurses could do that, but he seemed to understand when she insisted that it be her.

The task was now complete and David lay on a cot in one of the exam rooms. He looked as though he were merely sleeping. Only the ghostly paleness of his skin suggested it was not sleep that kept his eyes closed.

When the cemetery team—all of them David's barrack mates—arrived following the digging of the grave, Dr. Nance came into the exam room. "They're ready for him."

Eleanor nodded once but did not rise from her chair or turn to look at the doctor.

"I'm very sorry this happened, Eleanor," he said. "David was a good man."

"The best," she said. "He didn't deserve this."

"No. He didn't."

She sighed, felt tears threaten, and blinked them back, hard. "I don't know why he took such a terrible risk today to go get that food. He knew what had happened to George Louis and that other fellow. I wish he had told me that's what he was going to do today. I would have told him not to do it."

Dr. Nance took a step forward to stand next to her. "Today wasn't his first time to sneak out of the camp for food. I was just told by his friends outside that he had done it many times. He did it for the children in this camp. Every time he snuck out and found anything at all to buy or trade for, he brought it back and gave it to the mothers with little children. Every time."

More tears burned at Eleanor's eyes, and this time she let the drops fall. They landed in her lap, two by two, sounding like soft rain on a leaf.

"Did you love him?" Dr. Nance asked. "Did he love you?"

Under normal circumstances she might have found the doctor's questions intrusive, but Eleanor was instantly glad he asked. She'd been asking herself the same questions for days. She realized as he waited for her to reply that she'd known the answers for a long time.

"I was beginning to," she said. "And I think maybe he was beginning to love me too."

"Good. I'm glad you were. You will be able to tell his family what he did and about the lives he saved. There are children who will leave this place to grow up in a better world because of what he did."

"You also are sure we're getting out of here?" she asked wearily. "David had been too."

The doctor bent down so he was at eye level with Eleanor. "There are men inside this camp who are communicating with Filipino Resistance on the outside," he whispered. "Plans are in the works. It's going to happen."

"But that ditch."

"Don't think about that ditch. Don't look at that ditch."

"There's a machine gun posted at it now," she said numbly, because in the last few days one had indeed been installed. "Didn't you see it?"

"I can't think about that. And you shouldn't either. I heard what David said to you before he died. He doesn't want you to lose hope." The doctor stood. "I think he knew people look to us for it and we can't let them down. They're looking to us."

Dr. Nance waited until she rose from her chair, then he opened the exam room door and let the cemetery team inside.

She watched as the men carefully lifted David's body and placed it in the plain wooden coffin. As they nailed it shut, she closed her eyes but opened them again as the men lifted the coffin to carry it outside where a cart was waiting.

A crowd had gathered around. Many of them were families with young children. These had to be the little ones David's bravery had saved. The mothers were crying; some of the fathers too. There were barrack mates of David's, members of the baseball team, and Peg, all waiting to walk with Eleanor to the camp graveyard.

The procession was slow and dignified. Some of the guards who watched sneered at the parade of mourners; others seemed nearly transfixed by it.

At the grave site the same words of comfort were spoken by the camp priest as had been spoken too many times before. The sign of the cross was given. The blessing offered. One of David's barrack mates began to sing "Amazing Grace," and the rest of the gathering joined in. All too soon the service to honor David was done. The coffin was lowered, and the wet earth was shoveled over the top of it.

The team left to return the shovels and Eleanor turned to Peg, standing next to her.

"I'd like a few minutes here alone if you don't mind."

Peg squeezed her hand. "Sure."

Once Peg walked away, Eleanor knelt on the muddy soil covering David's grave. She touched the wooden cross that had been burned with his name and the rank he would have worn if there had been no war:

Lieutenant JG David William Mathis, USN
March 4, 1921–February 17, 1945

Eleanor had not answered David as he lay dying that she did remember her promise, and so she spoke it now as she ran her finger across his name.

"I won't give up, David," she said. "I promise you. I won't give up."

She stayed there until she could feel the mud seeping through her uniform onto her skin.

Eleanor walked back to the hospital in her muddy clothes with the ditch on her right. She shielded her eyes from it as if a bitter-cold wind was blowing in her face, as if she was resolutely moving forward despite it.

———•———

Dr. Nance and Laura Cobb offered Eleanor a day off to mourn David's death, and while she appreciated the gesture, the last thing she wanted to do was lay on her cot in the muggy basement and contemplate the sorrow of losing him.

"I'd like to keep working if that's alright," she said, and both seemed relieved.

The hospital was full; it always was now, and there were even patients lying in cots in the hallways. Dr. Nance often had to perform lifesaving surgeries by kerosene lamp as the electricity to the hospital was routinely shut off. The surgical instruments he used were being sterilized with water boiled at the camp kitchen—not the most sanitary of places.

Nearly everyone in camp was suffering from beriberi now; some had the condition so horribly their swollen legs prevented them from being able to walk. Older internees were expiring with bloated faces and limbs that had doubled in size from swelling. The cemetery team added to their number, not just to make up for David's absence but because more people were dying every day.

The morning after David's death, Konishi stopped giving the camp kitchen white rice—the only food the internees had been allowed—and provided instead sacks of unhusked rice the locals called *palay*, even though the kitchen crew had no milling equipment to separate the rice from the indigestible hulls. The work to separate each individual rice kernel from its hull was so arduous that the forty internees working in the kitchen were unable to husk enough in one day for just one meal.

They decided to give the internees their two cups of palay a day and instructed them to find whatever way they could to hand mill the rice kernels, even though most did not have the energy required to attempt this feat. Those that boiled the palay unhusked ended up in the hospital with bleeding intestinal tracts, and because of this Eleanor went with one of the members of the admin committee one morning to implore Konishi to reconsider.

"Please, sir," the committee member said, bowing low before the quartermaster. "Please restore the white rice until we can devise a way to husk the palay."

The interpreter relayed the request and Eleanor heard the answer. She was familiar by this time with the Japanese word for "no."

"May we send the palay out to be threshed in town?" the committee member asked.

"No."

"The unhusked hulls are making the prisoners very sick, sir," Eleanor said, also bowing low.

"That is not the quartermaster's problem," the interpreter said.

"I must remind the quartermaster that it is his responsibility to keep his prisoners fed. He must give us food. It is the rule of war."

"The quartermaster has given you food," the interpreter said. "Palay."

"But we cannot eat it!" The committee member raised his voice, and Konishi ordered them both out of his office.

As Eleanor and Peg spent that afternoon trying different instruments and tools at the infirmary to break open the husks, Peg looked up at Eleanor with sunken eyes. "Performing surgery with unsanitized instruments? Giving us indigestible food? Konishi is just finding new ways to kill us," Peg said.

Eleanor knew Peg was right. These were two new and highly effective ways to kill everyone at the camp. But Peg's words made her wonder what David would have said to this, and the second she considered it, she knew.

"Then we have to find new ways to survive," Eleanor said.

It felt good to find words of hope from within her, and it felt good to see Peg's face brighten just the tiniest bit. This was their task: Find a new way to survive. For as long as they could.

She could see so clearly now that this was what David had been trying to tell her all along. Hope was what kept you putting one foot in front of the other. Hope was what kept you laying down your head at night and rising from your cot the next morning. Hope was what kept you mopping fevered brows and changing dressings and administering aspirin, when you could get it. Hope was what made you pick at husks of rice until your fingers bled.

Hope was what sent you out into a forbidden village to get food for starving children.

Hope hadn't killed David; evil men had. Hope had been his companion until the very end. And even then, hope had escorted him from this life to the next. Hope had done that. Not fear. Not defeat. Not gunshot wounds.

David had been right to hold on to hope. He'd been right to tell her to do the same.

Hope would see her through, too, even if tomorrow was to be her last day on earth.

She thought of John then, but in a way she hadn't to that point. In another life she and John might have found each other before each of them made different choices. It would have been a wonderful life. They would have been very happy, she was sure of that.

But it was this life she was living right now that had been charted for her. This life. Perhaps it would be a short one. Perhaps she would be called from it that very day or the next or the one after that.

It had also been a wonderful life. Not a life entirely full of wonderful events. No, not by a long shot. But a wonderful life in its own way. She'd seen in this war the very worst one human could do to another. But she'd also seen the very best. Perhaps only the people who see the very worst get to see the very best.

Or maybe it was just that because she'd seen the worst, she'd been able to recognize the best.

That was its own kind of wonderful.

And the knowledge of this was as beautiful in her mind as the first day of spring.

Hope, she was discovering, could do that. It could let a person see the glorious light of the sun from even the darkest corner of a dungeon—even if within the dungeon there was no way out. Even if the dungeon was the last place you'd see this side of heaven.

Eleanor smiled and reached for Peg's cup of palay. "Go rest. I'll do yours."

———◆———

Friday, February 23, began the same as any other morning at Los Baños Prison Camp. Most of the Japanese guards were outside their barracks, performing the usual morning stretches, attired in little more than their underwear. The hospital staff was preparing to transition from the night shift to day, and the morning's meager ration of husked palay was being tossed into a pot on the camp kitchen's outdoor stove to turn it into a barely palatable mush.

Eleanor had just washed a handful of threadbare diapers needed for the hospital's two newborns and was laying them across a wire strung on an exterior wall so the morning sun could dry them. She felt weak from hunger. Did she have the strength to also wash out the baby bottles from last night, or did she need to rest for a few minutes first? The two new mothers inside the hospital were producing no milk due to their severe malnutrition. Eleanor had prepared watery powdered milk for the hungry infants earlier that morning, and they would soon need to be fed again.

As she considered whether she needed to sit for a moment, Eleanor heard a rumble above her head. She shifted her gaze to the sky and froze with one diaper in her hand as she saw a parachute drift down quietly on the other side of the camp fence, perhaps the length of a football field away. Then she saw another one and another. Before she realized that the parachutists were paratroopers, she heard rapid gunfire and the *bang! bang! bang!* of small explosions.

"Take cover!" someone shouted, and Eleanor dropped to the dirt and scooted as close to the outside wall of the hospital building as she could.

All around was the sound of shouting as the Japanese guards started scattering in all directions to fetch the weapons they'd locked in a storage unit while they exercised.

From the corner of her eye, she saw something large and heavy mowing down the front gate as if it were made of paper. A tracked vehicle of some kind. She couldn't see the entirety of it.

A rush of adrenaline coursed through Eleanor as she cowered in the dirt. That vehicle had taken down the gate, not been escorted through it. They were being rescued!

A band of Filipino guerrillas was suddenly running past her, shouting and raising guns and machetes. Shots rang out and several Japanese soldiers fell as bullets tore through them. Eleanor kept her head down but peeked out to see if she, too, needed to run. She saw a Filipino guerrilla bring his machete down again and again on the Japanese guard attempting to open the lock on the arms storage unit. The guard's blood spurted in all directions.

Now Laura Cobb was running up from the outdoor eating area with the other nurses who had moments earlier been readying to begin the day shift. Eleanor sprang to her feet when she saw her.

"We're being evacuated!" Laura yelled as she approached the hospital. "We have to hurry. The Japanese will no doubt be sending in reinforcements." Eleanor fell in step with her as they ran into the hospital.

Laura turned to her. "Eleanor, you get those two newborns, swaddle them safe in their blankets, and get their mothers. AmTracs have stormed the gates to evacuate us. You and they need to be on the first one out of here. Hurry!"

Eleanor sped down the hall into their makeshift maternity ward. The two mothers who had given birth only the day before were on the floor on their hands and knees, trying to crawl out of their room.

"What is happening?" one of them said. "Are we being attacked? Where's my baby?"

"We're being evacuated!" Eleanor said quickly. "You need to put on your shoes. I will get the babies. You stay right here and wait for me."

She left before the two women could ask her anything else, shouldered her way past other people fleeing the hospital, and ran into the nursery next door. The two infants were sleeping soundly in their little cots.

Eleanor grabbed the unwashed baby bottles and tin of powdered milk and tossed them into a canvas bag used to move supplies around the hospital, along with the only clean diapers left. She slung the bag over her shoulder and then lifted the two swaddled babies out of their beds.

The two mothers were at the door of their ward when she returned to them, one hanging on to the other. Both were weak from hunger and childbirth. They could not run.

"I need two corpsmen!" Eleanor shouted into the chaotic halls of rushing people. "I need two corpsmen right now!"

One appeared almost immediately, a young man perhaps her own age, but only one. Another man at least two decades older, a civilian who had been admitted the previous day for an eye infection, stopped in his flight out of the hospital. "What do you need?"

"Can you carry someone?" she asked him. He was emaciated, as they all were, and half his face was covered in a bandage.

The man looked at the new mothers, at their slim frames. "I can," he said.

Within seconds the mothers were swept up into the arms of the two men, and the little party was running past American GIs and Filipino guerrilla fighters routing out any Japanese guards still alive. They sped to the front of the camp just past the hospital where the first two amphibious tractors—the AmTracs—were waiting.

Laura directed the hospital evacuees to the first two transports while able-bodied internees queued up for the next arrival of AmTracs, only minutes behind. Forty-eight more of the tracked vehicles were inbound. Eleanor helped the two mothers aboard the open-air vehicle. She handed them each their child, settled the man who had helped her, and then went back to get her final instructions from Laura. Two other nurses were on the AmTracs with Eleanor, including Peg, and they also jumped off to hear their final orders.

"Look," Laura said to them. "You're not out of danger yet. The AmTracs have to get to the beach at Laguna Lake, and right now we're still in occupied territory. It's two miles to the water and the jungle is full of enemy positions. Snipers in the trees. You keep your head down and you tell your patients to do the same. Go now."

The other nurses returned to the vehicles, but Eleanor reached out to grasp Laura Cobb's hand. "What about you and the other nurses? What about Dr. Nance? Are there enough AmTracs for everyone?"

"We're all getting out of here. Don't you worry. The able-bodied will walk and we'll get there. I'll see you on the other side."

There was so much Eleanor wanted to say in that moment, but there was no time to say it.

"God be with you," she said to Laura.

Her supervisor and mentor squeezed her hand in return. "God be with all of us." And then she spun away.

Eleanor climbed back aboard the AmTrac and made sure the patients, including the new mothers, had been made as comfortable as they could be on an armored flatbed meant for carrying cargo. As the two AmTracs lumbered away, Eleanor saw smoke rising from the camp. Buildings were on fire.

Aboard their vehicle were several armed GIs ready to defend them if need be. Eleanor took a chance that the one nearest her would not mind if she asked him some questions. "What's happening with the war?" she said. "We haven't heard anything. Do you know what has happened at Santo Tomas?"

"It's already been liberated. A couple weeks ago," the man said easily, as if it were old news.

"Everyone there was safe?"

"Well. I suppose to an extent. Was everyone here safe?"

David came to her mind in a blinding instant. Good, kind David. Eleanor shook her head. "No."

"The Japs are losing. I can tell you that. Hitler is too. It's just a matter of time now."

"Thank you for coming for us," she said a moment later.

"Of course, ma'am," the soldier said, and then he stood to gain a better vantage point of their surroundings.

The ten-minute drive to the beach seemed the longest ten minutes of Eleanor's life, especially as small-arms fire could be heard off in the distance. Twice they were told to duck and cover. And even when they got to the beach, there was still the task of crossing a section of the immense lake, at the AmTrac's agonizingly slow speed of only ten miles per hour in water, and out in the open. But with each inch they moved forward, and as the jungle fell behind them, Eleanor finally began to believe their captivity had ended.

They had been rescued.

Liberated.

She was a prisoner of war no longer.

When the vehicle finally pulled itself onto the sand on the other side, several of the patients cried tears of gratitude and thanked their liberators.

"Are we safe?" one of the new mothers asked her. "Is it over?"

"I think it might be," Eleanor said. "Yes, I think we're finally safe."

Waiting Army ambulances at the second staging area took the freed Los Baños prisoners to the former Bilibid Prison, now under the control of Allied forces. Having been awake for more than twenty-four hours, all Eleanor wanted to do was sleep when they arrived, but she stood in line in the former prison's massive plaza to be logged in as was required, then stood in another line for a bowl of creamy pea soup and fresh bread, which she was careful to eat only a few spoonfuls of while cautioning others around her to do the same. Their shrunken stomachs and tortured intestinal tracts would need time to adjust to normal amounts of food again.

She knew this time the liberation was real. She was free. But she didn't feel liberated. She didn't feel free. She didn't know what she felt. Relief wasn't quite right, nor was gratitude, though she was aware of both. Perhaps there wasn't an accurate word yet for the new emotion swirling around inside her heart and mind. Maybe there never would be.

And then Eleanor saw another line of liberated prisoners lining up at an American Red Cross table, inquiring if there was mail waiting for them. She summoned strength and waited her turn to do the same. The worker looked for Eleanor's name among the boxes of waiting correspondence and produced seven letters from her family in Silver Lake, which had been written over the last three years. She took the envelopes over to a bench on the plaza perimeter and read the letters, over and over, relishing the news of life at home and loving her mother for keeping her tone light and positive, knowing that her daughter—if she was reading the letters at all—was reading them in a prison camp.

The American Red Cross had also set up a station to write letters that would be posted for the freed prisoners on the next available transport. She had been assured that all of the families of the liberated prisoners were receiving telegrams notifying them of their release, so letters home were not absolutely necessary, but Eleanor jotted a note to her parents to thank them for the letters and cards and to let them know she loved them and would see them soon.

When Eleanor could keep her eyes open no longer, she returned to the bench and stretched out to catch a few moments of sleep as she waited for sleeping quarters to be assigned. She held the letters to her chest and let sleep claim her.

When she awoke an hour later, stiff and sore but somewhat rested, she heard two Army privates talking on another bench close to hers. She raised herself up to look at them and recognized the men as having been at the prison camp with her.

When they saw Eleanor, one of them nodded to her in recognition. "Did you hear?" the soldier said.

"What? Did I hear what?" Eleanor asked.

"Intel at headquarters has learned that we were to be executed this afternoon at Los Baños. They were going to kill us all."

———— ◆ ————

The first two days at Bilibid were ones of rest, both restorative and fitful. The news that they had all narrowly escaped Konishi's executioners at the ditch filled Eleanor's nights with troubling dreams and her daytime hours with alternating spans of relief and then unease. The nurses were billeted in the same cellblock, but the doors were open and the cots were comfortable. At least there was that.

The Army's plans were to transport the nurses to Hawaii on a flight set to leave the first week of March, and in the meantime Eleanor and her colleagues were to rest, gain strength, be refitted for new uniforms, and help out in the former prison's hospital.

"They really expect us to work right now?" Eleanor had asked Laura, after she informed the nurses of what she'd been told in an afternoon briefing on the second day. It didn't seem like a smart idea, given how weak and malnourished they all were. Most of them were still dealing with starvation-related dry beriberi, which greatly affected their manual dexterity, Eleanor included. In that respect they needed a hospital bed as much as anyone else did.

"Apparently that's what the Army expects, but that is not what is going to happen," Laura said calmly. "Not a one of you is to step into that hospital to work. Am I clear? You need to rest. That's an order. We're leaving here in three days if I have my way. And I intend to."

Eleanor wanted to hug Laura in relief. All she wanted was what Laura said she needed. Rest. Not just for her body but for her mind and her soul.

Laura dismissed her nurses, then called for Eleanor to hold up a minute.

"I have news about the nurses who were at Santo Tomas. I know you had a friend or two there. I know why they aren't here with us."

"Are they billeted at some other camp?" Eleanor asked, wondering if she could arrange for an Army jeep to take her there if it wasn't far away.

"All of the Army nurses were airlifted out of Manila before we were even liberated, Eleanor. They've been gone for days."

A profound sadness immediately enveloped her. "*All* of them?"

"As far as I know. Sorry about that. I know you were hoping to meet up with friends."

"And the Filipina nurses? Any word of where they are?"

"Just that they were imprisoned for a time after Corregidor, then released. Got themselves home to their families, I would imagine."

Eleanor's relief that they had been freed from the Japanese was tremendous. She yearned to rush out and find Lita, but how? Her friend didn't have family here, not in the traditional sense, which meant she could have gone anywhere in the country.

For the rest of the day, Eleanor could not shake her disappointment that both Penny and Lita were gone. She would, no doubt, eventually find them through military information channels, but it wouldn't be easy, and it wouldn't be quick. Especially not with a war still raging. And when she did find them, all she would be able to do was write letters. She wouldn't be able to hug them or laugh with them or cry with them. They would surely be miles, even a country, apart.

Eleanor had lost much, gained some back, but this was a deprivation that seemed the most unfair to her. They had been liberated, the three of them, but the war—even in its victories—was still keeping them apart.

FORTY

LITA

Bilibid Prison
March 1945

The scene felt strikingly surreal. More clearly than ever, Lita recognized that people created the atmosphere of a place. Even a prison. Where until recently Japanese guards had wielded their treacherous authority throughout Bilibid, Allied soldiers and officers now roamed freely. Many were smiling, some even laughing, as if back in the carefree Manila that Lita used to know, the city it could become again.

No, not could—*would*—for the sake of the children under her care.

Every evening since rescuing them two weeks ago, Reyna had read them bedtime stories in their snug yet safe room at Santo Tomas. How easily they giggled at Reyna's character voices or leaned forward, elbows pressed into their crossed legs, entranced by a tale's suspense. Lita had been simply watching, delighting in the children, when she realized: while their profound resilience and continued ability to love unconditionally were more inspiring than anything she had ever encountered, their potential futures hinged largely on the support of those they trusted.

That revelation was only further reinforced as she'd tucked them in for sleep. One by one she had given them hugs and kisses and, as usual, asked what they were most grateful for on that passing day. The answers ranged from silly to sweet, as was their norm. But more than a few had formed a habit of replying: *"Ikaw, Tita."*

You, Auntie.

Each consequential squeeze of her heart had guided her closer to a decision, an altered course for the path of her life. One of which, despite a world of uncertainty, she couldn't have felt surer. And yet, part of her would remain forever unmoored unless she learned what became of Lon.

Though dreading the answer that most likely awaited, she now scanned the teeming prison grounds for the barracks being utilized for records. As much as she'd prefer never to step foot in one of those buildings for the remainder of her life, it was her best bet, she'd been told, to track down the truth.

"Nurse Capel. Aren't you a sight for sore eyes."

Lita spun toward the voice, and her smile stretched wide. "Dr. Thomson."

Since she'd last seen him here, he looked even more fragile. He'd gained a visible hunch and his fringe of gray hair was nearly gone, but the twinkle in his eye was more pronounced than ever.

"It's so marvelous to see you." She welcomed his handshake, his aged, callused palm once more providing comfort. "I've been terribly worried, not knowing what happened to you all. Especially when I heard about the ships to Japan."

"Well, I suppose getting old and rickety finally had its benefits. Prison commandant didn't think I'd be of much use for their emperor's labor force." The twinkle appeared to inadvertently dim at that. Obviously he'd known far too many younger soldiers and pals who hadn't been so fortunate.

Lita steeled herself. "And Lon? Do you know where he could be?"

She'd been checking in regularly with a sergeant at Santo Tomas who verified Lon's absence from Bilibid, and thankfully he wasn't believed to have died there nor, incredibly, to have been shipped out either. But information was still being sorted in a frenzy. If not for the escalation through the month of what was being called the "Manila Massacre"—with a hundred thousand civilian Filipinos slain, by grim estimations—she would have come here regardless long before now. As it was, this time she'd listened to the gate guards' warnings and stayed until the area had been largely cleared of the Japanese offenders and the streets deemed relatively safe. She now had the children to think of, after all.

"The only thing I've been told," she said to the doctor, "is that the records of his being here ended six months ago."

Dr. Thomson pondered for a moment. "I suppose that'd be about right," he said as if to himself.

Tentatively, she prodded, "Right for . . ."

"For when he got out."

She narrowed her eyes. "Out—as in, he was transferred?"

"As in, he escaped, my dear. Along with another GI. The third fella with them got caught sneaking under an electrified fence. Guards finished off the poor bastard—pardon my language."

Lita swiftly shook her head that she didn't mind, eager to hear the rest. "Where were they headed, do you know?"

"Can't say exactly. The goal was to make contact with U.S. military any way they could. Figured they'd try connecting through the Resistance. They were aiming to send an alert about our POWs being put on board those ships you heard about. Word had it they included oil tankers, making them a prime target for our subs."

Lita hastened to process it all: the dark irony of soldiers surviving Bataan and the prison camps—through starvation, disease, and beatings—only to be killed by their own side; the great risks Lon had taken to escape the seemingly inescapable for a chance to save others; the presumption that he never returned.

"And you haven't heard from him since?"

Dr. Thomson smiled gently. "Not yet," he said, but with an air of optimism she preferred to believe was real.

Upon their heartfelt parting Lita assured the doctor that, along with the nuns at Santo Tomas, she'd be praying for his safe travels, as his homeward-bound ship would set sail in three days. Then she headed for the prison gate to exit, barely registering anymore the ache in her knee. Given all

Dr. Thomson had shared, her mind continued to swim. So much so, from her first glance up ahead at the blonde Navy nurse intersecting Lita's path, she questioned if she was imagining things.

"Eleanor?" she ventured.

Amid a crisscrossing of service members, the woman stopped and angled back with a searching gaze.

A stirring of joy in Lita quickly expanded into a full-blown bubbling at the confirmation it was her friend. She looked older and more worn, as they all did. But she was alive and well and just a few yards away.

When Eleanor connected with Lita's eyes, a pleasant shock swept over her face. Lita burst into a grin, and they both rushed forward and reunited in a hug. Four years of separation dissolved in an instant.

"I can't believe you're here." Eleanor stepped back, beaming, and held on to Lita's hand. "I've thought of you so often, hoping you were safe. I can't tell you how relieved I was to hear you'd been released from the Japanese prison."

"Hearing you were alright made me just as happy," Lita said. "Penny told me you were even at Santo Tomas with her." In a playful mutter Lita added, "I was a little envious, I admit, not to be there with you two. But *mostly* happy."

Eleanor laughed, a familiar, treasured sound.

"Oh no," Lita said, remembering, "you missed Penny. She shipped out the week before last."

Eleanor nodded with a touch of solemness. "I heard."

"How long have you been here?"

"About five days now at Bilibid. How about you? Where have you been staying?"

If not for the element of war, the staggered overlapping of their paths, always missing each other until now, might have been comical. "At Santo Tomas, actually."

"No—that close? Oh, I wish I had known." Eleanor shook her head with regret but then abruptly revived her smile, as if tossing aside issues that couldn't be changed. "So what have you been doing? Tell me. I want to hear everything."

Lita's mind raced. Where on earth to begin? With the Philippine General

Hospital, her smuggling, the convent? Or with the Kempeitai and the trial or the rescues during the massacre? She wanted to share all about Reyna and Ida Hube, Yamada and Father Domingo. And, of course, about the children. "How much time have you got?" she asked in jest.

In an instant Eleanor's mien deflated as if pricked by the question.

"What is it? What's wrong?"

"We're leaving, Lita. The Navy nurses. Today."

Lita gawked. "To where? How soon?"

"Hawaii. They're transferring us to the airstrip at Clark Field. We're heading to the truck now."

At a glance past the gate, where nurses were boarding an Army truck, Lita's spirits plummeted. She looked at her friend. "But you just got here."

"I can't believe this is happening after all we've been through." Sorrow dipped Eleanor's tone and her eyes lowered.

Lita felt an urge to simultaneously laugh and cry at the absurdity of their finally being together, only to be swiftly split apart.

After a quiet, maddening moment, Eleanor shook her head. "I need to believe this is only for a little while, that before long the war will be over and you'll be immigrating to New York." She raised her gaze to Lita's. "Then the three of us will find a place to meet. We won't ever be more than a long train ride apart. Right? How can I get on that plane otherwise?" She understandably awaited easy agreement.

Though Lita's reply was slow to leave her mouth, being the first time she'd voiced her decision aloud, she had no reservations over whether it was the right one.

"I'm not going, Eleanor. To the States, I mean. Not anymore."

Eleanor's brows knitted in confusion. "But—I thought—your sisters have been working so hard with your application—"

"It's true. They have."

Explaining to her sisters in a letter would be a daunting task, but she had faith they would appreciate her reasons. While she would always be their bunso, she was also a grown woman who'd seen and endured things they could never fully comprehend, including saving the lives of cherished youngsters who had become her family.

"It just wouldn't be right for me to leave. There are children I've helped who are depending on me now. And my country and its people have an enormous amount of repairing and healing to do." The very notion of her prancing around Brooklyn while the kids—*her* kids now in her heart—were here wading through the aftermath of war was incomprehensible. She could only imagine how many more children would be orphaned before it was all over. Pridefully it was her turn, together with the nuns and Reyna, to be like the village that had once aided her when she was in need.

Eleanor nodded slowly and offered a weak smile in support. "I think I understand," she said, her eyes rimmed with tears, spurring Lita's to well up too. "But gosh, Lita, we'll miss you. So much."

"I'll miss both of you too. Terribly." She held Eleanor's hand tighter, and Eleanor wiped a droplet sliding down her cheek.

"Penny knows, then, that you're staying?"

Ironically, Penny's offer to help her immigrate had sparked the realization that, at long last, she knew what she wanted for herself, which no longer included leaving. If not for the unlikelihood that Penny was still in Hawaii, Lita would ask Eleanor to share the news.

Rather, she shook her head. "She will when I write to her." Then Lita shifted to the positives. "I'll also tell her that one day, you two will have to come back here, when it's the paradise you both remember. And we'll reminisce about how we all first met and giggle over the gay times we had, and the ugliness of war will feel like a lifetime ago. Promise me you'll both come? I'll make sure there's cake. And even daiquiris."

Eleanor laughed softly and nodded. "I promise. For both Penny and me."

Lita smiled. "What a day that will be," she said, managing but a whisper.

Only a moment passed before a shout pulled Lita back to their surroundings.

"Lindstrom!"

Eleanor turned at her name, toward a Navy nurse who stood just outside the front gate. "Come on, we're supposed to be on the truck! I've got your duffel!"

"I'll be right there," she called over with a hitch in her voice. When she swiveled back, her eyes glistened with fresh tears.

"No sad goodbye," Lita insisted, even as her own tears fell. She embraced Eleanor and said over her friend's shoulder, "We'll see each other again."

Eleanor drew back and smiled. "Till next time, then."

Lita nodded with conviction, the sealing of a new pact, and watched her friend hurry away and onto the waiting truck.

———•———

Two days later, the message arrived in their sleeping quarters just before breakfast.

Amid the room's usual morning bustle and chatter at Santo Tomas, Lita was helping the children fold the blankets on their cots when Reyna stopped to read the note delivered by a runner.

Yet again Lita was struck by the difference of life without the occupation, in this case the ease of sending a message into the camp. No sneaking them through medical supplies or hollowed-out fruit or the hems of clothing. No threat of imprisonment or death for the simple act of communicating.

It was remarkable, really, how easily things could be taken for granted, until they were gone.

Lita broke from the thought at the sight of Reyna holding a hand over her mouth, stunned by whatever she had read.

Bracing herself, Lita left the children to their folding and approached. "Reyna? Is everything okay?"

"It's my brothers," she murmured, still looking off in a daze.

Lita had feared this day would come. Over time they'd traded countless stories of their families, about their siblings most of all. And although Reyna wasn't one to dabble in the sentimental nor to voice her angst, Lita sensed in her a deep-rooted care for her brothers and worries over their safety.

Since the month-long massacre had ended, word continued to pour in about Resistance members who'd emerged from the jungles and eliminated the stragglers terrorizing the city, but also about the many guerrilla fighters who'd died protecting their homeland.

"Reyna. I'm so sorry." Lita lightly grasped her friend's arm, and gradually Reyna turned to her with a tearful shimmer in her eyes.

"They're back," she rasped.

Lita stared. She wasn't clear exactly what that meant.

"It says they're staying with my cousins, at the café." Reyna's lips slid upward. "And they're all okay. Lita, they made it through."

With the release of a breath, Lita matched Reyna's smile as the good news fully sank in.

But then Reyna jolted. "I have to go. Right now. I've got to see them."

"Of course you do."

"Come on, then. Let's go." Reyna rushed to tuck her blouse into her skirt.

Lita loved the idea of joining but also wanted to allow space for what was certain to be an emotional reunion. "You go on. This should be a private time for your family."

"Well, yeah." Reyna shrugged as if this was obvious. "That's why you should be there. So hurry it up."

Lita warmed at the gesture. Reyna was right: after all they'd been through together, they, too, were family. But she also noted the impracticality of their both running off without planning.

"Reyna, I do want to go, truly. But Sister Cecilia still needs an extra hand with breakfast." The other nuns were away from camp for the day, and herding eighteen children was no solitary task. "Next visit, though. We'll plan for it."

Hopefully in the next week or two, they'd be settled back at the convent, making any outing that much easier.

Reyna groaned yet gamely conceded, as the children, too, were her priority. "Deal."

———◆———

In the plaza late that afternoon, Lita flopped down on a low stone wall to catch her breath. Shaded by a tree, she smiled as the children and other youth in the camp squealed and giggled while continuing to play tag. She questioned if she'd ever had their level of energy, even before the occupation. The joy of their friendships, of course, she related to firsthand.

At the thought, she envisioned Penny and Eleanor riding trains to reunite somewhere in the States, and a pulse of envy struck her, though briefly. Neither time nor distance could diminish the bond they shared, as their separations during the war had already proven.

"This seat taken?"

At the man's voice she looked up to tell him it wasn't saved, as Sister Cecilia was busy chatting with parents who were helping supervise, when Lita caught sight of his face.

And she froze.

Before her in a fresh khaki uniform, face clean shaven and brown hair trimmed beneath his garrison cap, stood Corporal Lon McGibbons. His amber eyes gleamed in the sun. An edge of his mouth quirked upward, a half smile, as he waited for her to respond. Yet not until he uttered her name did shock release her from its clutches.

Springing to her feet, she enwrapped him with her arms. He held her just as close, and her heart set to hammering. She detected a trembling that seemed to stem from them both.

Though never wanting to let go, she at last eased back to view his face. "Is it really you?" Preparing for his answer, she feared she was dreaming.

His smile widened. By way of an answer, he placed a tender kiss on her lips. It was a kiss that soon deepened, sending a shiver over her skin. If not for his arms around her waist, she might have collapsed from the sudden weakening of her legs.

Gradually he broke away and gazed at her face, as if he, too, was reconciling reality. "My God, you're beautiful." He caressed her cheek with his thumb, as he always did.

She was tempted to cling to this moment, but her mind was spinning with questions: of where he had been, and how long he'd been back, and so much more.

"Dr. Thomson told me you escaped from Bilibid. You said it would be impossible."

"Yeah, well. Pretty sure I said *nearly* impossible."

She laughed a bit and went to continue, the words in her mind tumbling over themselves. "I have so much to ask you."

He regarded the stone wall with his chin. "How about we sit? 'Cause, believe me, I wanna hear everything from you too."

So they did sit. And they did exchange stories from their time apart, including he and his buddy fighting with the guerrillas until the area was liberated, then just yesterday reporting to Bilibid, where Dr. Thomson kindly sent him this way. What they didn't do was speak of *everything* they'd survived, namely the worst of it.

She sensed him stopping short on some accounts, just as she did with details of her own. Some stories weren't ready to be voiced.

They also laughed at times, and more than once Lita found herself listening absently as she simply watched him speak. It was difficult to shake loose the encapsulating awe that he was here at her side, that somehow they had not only managed to survive but found their way back to each other.

Though, she wondered suddenly, how long would it last?

"Pardon the intrusion." The phrase in Tagalog pulled Lita's attention to Sister Cecilia. "But, Lita, we ought to head toward the mess hall for supper now."

Only then did she notice the sun's progression toward the horizon, and the children lining up in their assigned pairings for any journeys through the camp.

"Of course, Sister." She rose, as did Lon. "Please, though, first let me introduce you. This is Lon, the gentleman I—"

Breaking into a grin, the nun rejoiced with a single clap. Then she made the sign of the cross and grasped Lon's hands, exclaiming in Tagalog, "What a blessing, dear boy. We have prayed for you often."

He nodded warmly, clear on her intent though not her words.

The nun turned to Lita with a hint of regret. "I do hate to trouble you at such a time, but I will need help with the little ones." There was no need to explain. The parents who had assisted with supervising the games would be occupied with their own families.

Lita arched a brow at Lon. "Any interest in seeing our circus of a mealtime?"

He smiled at her. "I wouldn't miss it."

———◆———

At their usual table in the mess hall, a circus was precisely what the children delivered. As always it was a juggling act for Lita—mopping up spilled drinks, replacing dropped forks, managing a picky eater, praising those who finished their plates. When she reached between two boys to quell a squabble over papaya on a spoon, the chunk flew through the air and smacked her on the cheek.

She gasped from the startle, and the piece plopped onto the table. The culprits cowered in their seats.

"*Patawad po,* Tita," they said in near unison.

Sorry, Auntie.

The group plunged into silence as she placed her fists on her hips. She went to admonish the pair, but feeling the sticky trail on her face, she couldn't contain her grin. The table burst into laughter, joined by her own. And when she glanced at Lon, parked at the end of the table, she delighted in his smile.

Back in the sleeping quarters, after the children had washed up and readied themselves for bed—another lively circus act in and of itself—Lita took up the slack in bedtime-reading duty. Her character voices couldn't compete with Reyna's, nor would she want them to, but the children gasped and giggled all the same.

When she glimpsed Lon watching from the back of the room, he smiled again, but in a wavering manner that gave her pause. And in that instant she recalled the question she dreaded to ask, and the news she had yet to share.

———◆———

With all the children in the room settled in for sleep, and Sister Cecilia at the camp's church for nightly prayer, Lita set a kerosene lamp on a table. By its flickering glow she lowered to sit beside Lon on a blanket in the corner.

Silence hovered between them, laced with the unspoken.

"How long will you be in Manila?" she finally pushed herself to ask, and his tone dropped with his answer.

"We're shipping out tomorrow."

A pang pierced her chest and she remembered. "With Dr. Thomson and the rest."

He nodded.

Although she and Lon had never explicitly discussed sharing their lives together after the war, it was a scenario that had seemed natural for them both, which made her admission now all the more difficult.

"Lon, I need you to hear . . . about my plan of going to the States . . ."

"I know." There was an understanding in his voice, though with an underlying sadness.

She tilted her head, unsure.

"You already found your home."

She was surprised, though she shouldn't have been, and contemplated his words. While the Philippines did finally feel like her true home, it was more than that; she at last had found her place. In every way.

But that didn't mean they couldn't be together.

"You could come back after the war," she said, "and be with me, here in Manila."

A glimmer entered his eyes. "The thought actually occurred to me tonight." He brushed a lock of hair from her temple. "'Cause just the idea of being without you . . ."

Her hopes spiked, and an image flashed through her mind, the possibility of it all.

Then he swallowed and looked away, and despite his evident struggle, his decision was plain before he continued. "But this place—I just couldn't come back, Lita. Not after all I've seen." He added under his breath, "And done." Following a quiet stretch, he faced her again but with an apology gripping his features. "I wish that wasn't the case. I swear to God, I do."

She saw it in his eyes; he needed to heal, and the setting tied to his battles, literal and internal, would only keep his wounds raw.

She loved him—so much that she would have to let him go.

"I understand," she whispered, her emotions brimming. "And . . . it's okay." She worked to keep her voice level. "You promised me you'd live and that you'd come back to find me, and you did."

Moisture welling in his eyes, he offered a smile. After a moment, he said, "Here, let me show you something." From his trouser pocket he produced a handful of small papers and set them on the blanket. They were heavily wrinkled and smudged, each with a handwritten message.

The notes she had sent.

She gaped at the pile. "You got them all."

"Sure seemed like."

As she leafed through them, he added, "Trust me, I did try to take care of 'em, but they've been through a lot."

She smiled. "I'm just happy they reached you."

"Me too. They kept me going through some pretty rough days," he said, then clarified, "You, I mean. You did that."

He had done the same for her. The mere thought of seeing Lon again had helped carry her through the bleakest of times.

She looked up at him, and a tear slipped from her eye. "I guess we helped keep each other alive, didn't we?"

He cradled her cheek, and she let herself sink into his palm. "Yeah," he said. This time when he kissed her it was long and bittersweet. And when he gazed at her face afterward, it seemed he was etching her features into his mind.

"C'mere." He guided her to curl up beside him. With his arm wrapped around her like a shawl, she leaned her head into the curve of his neck and felt his cheek settle upon her hair.

Together they sat in the dimness, listening to the rise and fall of the children's breaths. She strove to memorize every detail of this moment— the weight of his arm, the warmth of his body—to keep them locked in a compartment deep inside.

She couldn't say when she had drifted off, but she awoke on the cusp of dawn, lying alone on the blanket with another one draping her. The first streams of sunlight were filtering through the window. She didn't have to look around to know he was gone.

An ache filled her heart and her tears returned.

On the edge of the blanket lay a single note, one of the messages she'd written for Lon. Had he left it behind by accident? Or with purpose? Sensing it was the latter, she picked up the paper and read in silence:

Don't ever forget the courage and goodness I see in you.
Through the hardest of times, even when we're apart,
no matter how far away, know that I'm with you, forever.

Sinking back against the wall, she held the words close to her chest. And through the last of the morning quiet, she watched the sun continue to rise, delivering the promise of a fresh day.

FORTY-ONE

PENNY

San Francisco, California
March 1945

S he was afraid to go home. That was the simple truth of it. Home was
Houston and an empty house she'd once shared with her husband.
Home was her parents—five miles down the road—and the painful reality
that they had never once written to her, not even after learning she'd been
taken captive by the Japanese or in the weeks since being telegrammed
about her release.

Home was a concept she no longer understood. But work made sense.
So when the nurses were flown first to Hawaii and then to California,
Penny threw herself into the task assigned them by the United States
government: get dolled up and smile for the cameras. She surrendered to
the required manicures and hair permanents. To the new clothes and copi-
ous amounts of makeup. And she didn't cry—or at least not much—when
they stepped off that plane and into the bright San Francisco sun and saw
the crowd of families that awaited them. Everyone had someone to run to.
Except for her.

No one noticed. Or so she thought. But she covered well and milled
through the crowd. Hugged her fellow nurses and shook the hands of those
they loved. And when the military speeches were over and it came time

to meet the press corps, Penny was right out front. The yammering and questions made her head hurt, and the flashbulbs made her eyes water. She hated every moment of it. But it was a good distraction.

"I'm sorry they didn't come," Maude whispered in Penny's ear. "They should have come."

Penny shrugged. She couldn't explain it either.

Maude pulled her into a tight hug and Penny could hear her breath hitch as she stifled tears. "I am proud of you. You did your job. You never faltered. And I wish I could have told them that myself."

About the time the nurses were showing signs of exhaustion, they were all hustled off to Letterman Army Hospital and given rooms of their own. Rooms with starched sheets and vases full of fresh flowers. A full dinner and a new nightgown. It smelled so clean and sterile Penny couldn't sleep. She could smell the bleach, could hear the *squeak* of shoes as orderlies padded up and down the tile halls. So she lay on top of the blankets, counting her ribs beneath the thin cotton fabric. She ran her fingers up and down, up and down, as though playing a piano. For hours she did this, until she fell into that weird sort of slumber she experienced only while traveling: a nervous kind of sleep that hovered right beneath the surface.

The next few days ran together. Tests and physicals. Interviews and photo shoots. The Army hired beauticians and tailors to paint and prune them, so they didn't look emaciated and unhealthy to their new, adoring public. There was a press conference in which they each received a letter from President Roosevelt and a strange visit from a movie star who waxed eloquent about their bravery but never looked them directly in the eye.

Penicillin. Now that was a shock. While they'd been wasting away in the Philippines, the world had invented a brand-new medicine that—had it been available in the camps—would have saved many of the lives they'd lost. The nurses were given a full round of the stuff to rid them of any unknown illness. It made Penny's skin itch and her throat tighten and— miracle drug or not—she decided not to finish her course.

They had to endure nearly two weeks of this nonsense before being released on a mandatory sixty-day leave. The rucksacks had been replaced with shiny new leather suitcases in Hawaii, and Penny was folding her new clothes and placing them carefully inside when Maude knocked on the door.

"Headed home?" she asked.

Penny shook her head, ran her hand over the quartermaster's flag. "Not just yet. There's something I need to do first."

She knew that Maude was curious, but she didn't ask, and Penny didn't offer.

"Okay, then. I'll see you in two months when your leave is over." She turned toward the door.

"Maude?"

"Yes?"

"I enlisted for three years."

"You've already reupped?"

"No. My required term of service ended two years ago."

Maude's mouth dropped open in surprise. "Why didn't you say anything?"

"Because it didn't matter." She laughed. "It's not like the Japanese would have sent me home."

"You're not coming back, are you?"

Penny shook her head. And then Maude crossed the room and pulled Penny tight against her shoulder so she could unleash every last tear she'd locked inside since arriving back on U.S. soil.

———— ♦ ————

Like the other nurses, Penny hailed a cab. But instead of going to the airport, she checked herself into a hotel near Hamilton Field and waited. She ordered room service and watched television for two days—baffled by the commercials but entertained by Dick Tracy. Were they really turning comic strips into television shows now? When had that started?

Finally, on the tenth of March, Penny donned one of her new dresses, packed her bags, and went to the airfield. The crowd was much smaller this time and the reporters nonexistent. They'd feasted on the Army nurses' arrival, but by the time the Navy nurses landed, their rescue was old news. No families had been flown in for this reunion. No speeches were given.

The dozen women walked down the stairs and onto the tarmac. They were greeted at the bottom by a handful of officers. Penny rose up on tiptoes when she saw the blonde curls. The too-thin woman at the back of the line looked somewhat like her old friend, but the angles of her face were sharper, the set of her mouth different. Her face was turned away, though. Penny wasn't sure.

She called out the name. "Eleanor!"

The woman in the Navy uniform turned at the sound of Penny's voice. Stopped in her tracks as if glued to the spot. Then she dropped her bag and ran to Penny.

They embraced, but neither could say a word. What words were necessary in that moment? They had both wondered if they would ever see each other again. They had both survived the worst that one person could do to another. They had both seen too much death, too much agony, too little compassion. They had both emerged from war and imprisonment and suffering and yet had not been utterly flattened by it. None of that needed to be spoken aloud, however.

When they parted, tears flowing down their faces, they both laughed. Penny winked. "You've lost a little weight."

"I could say the same about you." Eleanor smiled as she wiped away her tears. "How are you still here? I thought you went home weeks ago."

"I waited for you. There's something I have—"

"Lindstrom!"

They turned to see Laura Cobb waving them over.

"There's going to be a reception inside and then we're headed to Oak Knoll Naval Hospital. Bring Penny if you like, but we have to go."

Eleanor looked at Penny, imploring. "Stay?"

"Of course."

Penny waited through another reception, another debriefing—though far less intense than the last. But when Laura finally led the nurses back outside toward the idling bus at the curb, she asked if it was okay if Eleanor rode in the cab with her.

"We'll follow right behind. I promise."

For a moment she was certain Laura would refuse. But she nodded and said, "Stay close."

Penny linked her arm and led Eleanor to the cab that waited beneath the shade of a red flowering gum tree.

"I'm still having trouble believing I'm here." Eleanor looked at the bright petals. She slid into the back seat. "I mean, I know I'm back in the U.S. and I'm out of harm's way, yet I still can't quite believe that I'm sitting here with you and that I'm clean and I had breakfast this morning and it wasn't a measly handful of hulls dotted with insect carcasses."

They both laughed when the driver looked at them with alarm in the rearview mirror. He pulled away from the curb and Penny instructed him to follow the bus.

"The thing is," Eleanor continued, "*this* is what I wanted all along. And yet now that I have it, it almost feels like it doesn't belong to me."

Penny reached for her friend's hand. "But it does belong to you. And me. And Lita, too, even though she's far away."

"I saw her before I left. Just for a few minutes. But it was a gift. And I'm so grateful. I could have easily missed her if we hadn't crossed paths at Bilibid."

"I can't tell you how glad I am that you two connected, even if it wasn't for long."

Eleanor cleared her throat. "Lita told me something else, Pen."

"She did?"

"She's not coming to America."

"Of course she is. We talked about it. I'm going to help her immigrate. I'm all set to—"

"She changed her mind," Eleanor interrupted. "She plans to tell you in a letter. She decided to stay in the Philippines. She *wants* to stay, even after the war. You saw the country, what has become of it. There is so much that needs rebuilding, and she feels she has to be there for that. Also to help care for some children who depend on her, she said."

Penny sat back against the seat of the cab, envisioning the orphans they had rescued on that terrifying night. She also recalled the adoration in Lita's eyes when she looked at them, the same as they held for her. She couldn't blame Lita a bit for not leaving, though Penny would miss her friend dearly.

"We *will* be together again someday, though," Eleanor continued. "I know we will. I promised her we would."

Penny sighed. "I guess all of us are finding out where we belong now that we are free again." She thought of the letter, and the few minutes remaining to them in the taxi. "Which reminds me, El. I have something for you." Penny took a deep breath, reached inside her purse, and pulled out the letter.

It took a moment for everything to register, for Eleanor to read the return address and the date on the postmark. She looked up at Penny in astonishment. "It's from John," Eleanor said.

"Yes."

"How—"

"It was delivered to Santo Tomas the day before we were liberated. It'd been found in the ruins of the Cavite post office."

Eleanor turned the envelope over, noting its broken seal. "It's been opened?"

"The letter arrived like that, Eleanor. It wasn't mine to read, but it was mine to deliver. *This* is why I waited here for you." She pressed the letter into Eleanor's hand.

Eleanor Lindstrom took one long, shaky breath before she lifted what was left of the flap and pulled out the two crisply folded sheets of paper. Penny watched her face—not the scenery—as she began reading. She watched the surprise and confusion roll across Eleanor's face but did not interrupt her. Finally, after several minutes, her hands fell to her lap and she looked at Penny, baffled.

"Is everything okay?"

"I don't know."

"Well, what did he say?"

Eleanor held out the papers.

"Are you sure?"

She nodded and Penny took them from her hand.

November 5, 1941

My dear Eleanor,

   I have spent many a night wondering if I should write this letter to you. I don't know what you will think of me when you hear what I have to say, and that alone has been reason enough for me not to send it. But I've prayed and pondered this and I believe you should know the truth. I pray you will not think less of me when you hear it.

   I did not marry Karin. After you left to go back to the Twin Cities, I wanted to proceed with my plans for the wedding, but I could not stop thinking about you and I knew that was wrong. I couldn't understand why you kept filling my thoughts when I was just months away from marrying a woman I had already proposed to and whom I thought I loved. But the fact that I was thinking about you and what you told me concerned me. I realized that I was fond of Karin, but we had met when we were college freshmen—only eighteen years old—and in the seven years since, we had changed, grown up. We were still good friends, but I did not love her like I should and I knew I needed to call off our wedding. It was utterly unfair to Karin to marry her hoping I would begin to have the same feelings for her that I so quickly had with you.

   Needless to say, it was a cruel thing to do to her and I upset a great many people, not only Karin and her family and friends but in Silver Lake too. The deacons had expected me to bring in a new bride. They were very concerned that I called off my engagement, especially when I told them it was because I had feelings for someone else. I did not tell them or anyone else that it was you. They did not like that I broke a young woman's heart and had romantic feelings for another woman during my engagement, and of course my jokes in the sermons had already upset a few. I could tell it was their wish that I resign my post. The probationary period wasn't even up yet, so it was easy enough to do, and I knew I could not minister in a place where I had no one's trust. Before I left, I checked the church secretary's files for church members serving in the military and found your address in Manila. I wrote it down and took it with me.

I am now the principal at a Lutheran school in St. Paul, and I'm loving my new position very much. I had forgotten how invigorating and exciting it is to be around children and young people all day long. It's a good place for me to be right now.

I can't help feeling that your joining the Navy and moving so far away was because of me and the hurt I caused you, and for that I am so profoundly sorry. I know I do not deserve anything from you in return, and I will understand if you have moved on after the pain I caused you. But I hope you have not moved on from me. It is my ardent prayer every day that you have not.

I understand this letter will have to travel a long way to you and any answer you write will have to travel a long way, too, but I will wait for it, Eleanor. I will wait for you to decide what you will do with me. I will wait for your answer no matter how long it takes you to decide if you will give me another chance. Even if the answer is no, I will wait.

I promise you. I will wait.

Yours always,
John

Penny looked up. She had expected the contents of the letter might be troubling—that someone in Eleanor's home church had died or that John Olson and his wife were having a child—but this possibility never crossed her mind. "What are you going to do?"

"I'm not sure." Eleanor turned to the window and looked up at the peaceful blue sky. "All this time I imagined him married. To her. I kept telling myself I had to forget him. I *tried* to forget him. I even met someone at the prison camp and I *wanted* to forget him."

"But you didn't?"

Eleanor brought her gaze back to the envelope. "No. But it feels different now."

"Because of this other man?"

"Maybe. Yes, I think so." Eleanor blinked back shimmering tears as she dropped her gaze from the world outside the window. "David Mathis was a good man, Penny. The best, actually. And a wonderful friend. I think perhaps I was starting to fall in love with him, but then he was killed. The guards at our camp shot him for sneaking out to get food for the children."

"Oh, I'm *so* sorry."

"The day David died was the worst day of my imprisonment. And yet . . . I think I learned something from loving and losing him." Eleanor stared down at the papers in her hand. "This letter from John is wonderful and so unexpected, but I'm thinking now that love is something that grows. It can start as something powerful, of course, but it still begins small. I think my love for John began that way, but I didn't nourish it because I didn't think I could. And now that perhaps I can, I want my affection for him to grow like his apparently has for me. It should if we are meant to be together. I won't know if we are until I go back home and see him." Eleanor looked up at Penny. "Wait. You didn't go home."

"No. Not yet."

"But your parents . . ."

"I'll see them in a few days. I wanted a bit of space between war and them. I needed time to think as well."

Suddenly everything was occurring to Eleanor at once. "What about Charley? And that little girl in the STIC? Where are they? And MacArthur! They said he met with you all at Santo Tomas. Is that true?"

She answered the easiest question first. "It is. MacArthur came to camp right before they sent us to Leyte. Gave us field promotions of one full rank right on the spot." Penny grinned. "You are looking at *First* Lieutenant Penny Franklin."

Eleanor smiled. "Congratulations, my friend."

"Newt is back with her parents. And Charley is out there"—she waved a hand at the window—"somewhere. I haven't heard anything yet."

"Oh, Pen. Are you okay?"

She'd been asking herself the same thing for weeks now. And it had taken that long for her to find the answer. "I went to Manila robbed of everything. My daughter. My husband. My parents. I had no real friends before I met you and Lita. Then the war came, and I found Newt. She gave me back a little bit of what I'd lost. Just enough to believe that I might have been a good mother after all. That maybe one day I *can* be."

Penny took a deep breath and blew it out between pursed lips. "Charley helped me understand that it's possible to love more than once. God, I hope he's okay, and I hope there's more to that story. But if not, he gave that back to me and it *has* to be enough for now. Maude and Father Domingo—well, maybe it sounds silly—but they reminded me what it's like to be loved. Just because. And I do know my parents love me, El. But I hurt them, and they hurt me, and I'm headed home to deal with that soon."

The bus in front of them slowed and pulled to the curb before Oak Knoll Naval Hospital, and the taxi followed suit. "This war took so much from all of us. But it gave us something too. *Each other.* I never would have met you or Lita otherwise. I never would have known what true friendship feels like. We didn't lose four years; we gained the world." Penny pulled Eleanor into one last hug and whispered, "Goodbye."

When Eleanor looked up, her eyes held a tiny glimpse of the light that had filled them before the war. "Goodbye," she said with a smile. "For now."

Eleanor stepped out of the taxi and Penny watched as she walked up the steps of the hospital and through the front doors. Then she slumped back against the seat and sighed.

"Where to?" the driver asked.

"The bus station."

———◆———

It was raining when she got home one afternoon, three weeks after the bus pulled into the depot in Houston. And not just cats and dogs either, but every other kind of animal as well. It was raining an entire barnyard as she sat in her car, already soaked to the skin, in front of her porch, waiting for it to stop.

Driving felt weird after being out of practice for so many years, but her car was still there and in perfect working order thanks to her father who had—without her knowledge—come to her house once a week and driven it around the block. He had also mowed her grass and trimmed the bushes while her mother dusted, vacuumed, and ran the taps. It was easier than writing, they'd said.

Easier than apologizing was what they meant, but there was enough of that to go around, and Penny had apologies of her own to make. She'd been making them consistently ever since she got home, calling her parents every time she made some new discovery about the way they'd cared for her house during her time at war. Mouse traps in the attic. Tulip bulbs in the flower beds. Fresh paint on the shutters.

It was a start and in a little while she would go over for Sunday dinner. Not too long. She never stayed long. Just a couple of hours. It was a way to ease into knowing them again, this once-a-week ritual. But there was something she wanted to do first. If the rain would let up, that is.

Penny craned her neck and looked at the flagpole she'd asked her father to install last week. The Stars and Stripes hung at the top, sodden and flapping in the wind. She'd forgotten to bring it down before the storm hit. To be fair, her mind had been on a different flag.

The one in her purse.

Penny pulled out the U.S. quartermaster's flag and spread it across her lap. She'd come from the seamstress and had gotten drenched as she ran to the car, hunched over to protect the silk fabric. Penny ran her thumb across the new copper grommets she'd had the seamstress install. She could fly the flag now. But not too often. Only on Sundays. She didn't want it to get tattered. How would she ever explain that to Charley?

Penny tried to gauge the distance to her front porch and saw the rocking chair shift back and forth. But not in the wind. A man was sitting there, watching her.

"Dad?"

She couldn't make out his face, but the size and build were right. Penny folded the flag and carefully set it back in her purse before she threw open the car door and bolted for the house. Her head was down, water dripping in her eyes by the time she made it up the steps and beneath the overhang.

"I was headed over soon." She stomped her feet. "You didn't have to come for me."

"But I promised I would."

She froze. Penny knew that voice. Knew it and missed it and even now with those words hanging in the air between them was afraid to let herself hope. So she screwed her eyes shut lest the man in front of her not match the voice.

But it was Charley Russell and he spoke again, closer now. "Unless you're expecting someone else?"

She shook her head, unable to utter a single word.

"Look at me, then."

Penny felt a finger trail along her jaw, and she opened her eyes. Charley stood there, crooked grin on full display. Older. Thinner. Graying a bit at the temples. But still, it was undoubtedly him. He took another step forward and she noted the limp, the way his body leaned hard to the right.

"I believe you have something that belongs to me, Lieutenant Franklin," he said with a formal nod and a teasing light in his eyes.

Her voice cracked with emotion when she answered. "That's *First* Lieutenant Franklin to you."

Penny wasn't sure who stepped forward first, but in a heartbeat he pulled her to his chest and tucked his face into the crook of her neck.

"How?" she whispered. "How are you here?"

"Same as you. Liberated, patched up, and sent home." He rubbed his nose against the soft skin of her throat. "Besides, I made a promise."

"I didn't believe you'd keep it."

"We're gonna have to work on that." He pulled away so he could look at her. Charley pushed the wet hair away from her face. His hands dropped to her shoulders, and he drank in the sight of her face as though this was his last chance.

"I have something for you," she said.

Even as his eyebrow lifted in question, his gaze dropped to her mouth. "Is that so?"

Penny shifted out of his embrace and pulled the flag from her purse. She unfolded it and showed him the new grommets. "I was waiting for the rain to stop so I could run it up the pole."

"You were going to fly it?"

She shrugged, suddenly embarrassed, and stared at the second button on his shirt. Penny slid her hand into the pocket of her skirt. She felt the eight of hearts and decided to tell him the truth. "I thought it might help you find me."

Captain Charley Russell—a man she'd once hated and now feared she could not live without—pulled her close, bent his head, and took the kiss he'd come for. Then he took another. And another. He kissed her until they were both dazed and breathless. He kissed her until the rain stopped.

EPILOGUE

Manila
August 1951

The islands far below Eleanor looked like postcards of paradise tossed onto a blue satin tablecloth. She had pondered many times what it would be like to see the Philippines again from an airplane window. The last time she'd seen them like this, she was still getting used to freedom and the horrors of imprisonment were clinging to her. Seconds earlier when the pilot announced the approach to Manila, Eleanor fully expected her pulse to start racing, but as she stared down at the verdant archipelago on the other side of the glass, she felt only a sense of calm.

This was a surprise. Reclaiming her life after the war had been a challenge in ways her outprocessing from the Navy hadn't prepared her for. After the initial media coverage of her release from the prison camp at Los Baños and the grand welcome back home in Silver Lake, there had been a strange feeling of severing, the pain of which had made no sense. Eleanor hadn't wanted for one second to go back to being a prisoner nor even a Navy nurse, but once she was neither anymore, the fact that no one back home was able to understand what she'd experienced had been a dull but constant ache. It was almost like being isolated and held captive again, but in a prison of her thoughts. Why had she and the others been imprisoned like that? Why did so many have to die? What if the rescue had been delayed by just a day? What if when the Americans had finally arrived she and every other prisoner at Los Banõs had been lying in that monstrous ditch, their bodies bullet ridden? How could people do to one another what she had seen them do? How had she witnessed all of this and not been completely undone by it?

Over the past six years she'd climbed out of that bizarre fog of unanswered questions and she hadn't wanted to fall back into it, as much as she ached to see Penny and Lita again. She now breathed a sigh of relief that seeing the islands, finally an independent nation and not a U.S. territory, hadn't felt like a sharp tugging back to that bleak place.

"You alright?" John asked from his seat next to her. He reached out a hand and laid it gently on her arm. The sleeping toddler nestled on his chest and held by his other arm stirred slightly.

Eleanor turned, leaned toward her husband, and brushed a curl from their sleeping son's closed eyes. "I'm okay."

It had been John's idea to name their little boy David.

"He was a hero in the truest sense," John had said when she was still pregnant and they'd started talking about names. "And he was your friend. I think, in a way, he brought you back to me. That makes him my friend too."

Of all the people back home, John was the only one in whom she'd confided fully about everything that had happened in the Philippines, and he was one of the few who seemed to understand how complicated it had been to recover from those experiences.

Eleanor had waited until she'd been home for three weeks to contact him. She hadn't known how best to do it, but after thinking it over, she asked to borrow her father's truck and drove the two hours to St. Paul, unannounced. Her parents had assumed she was going up to the Cities to have lunch with her nurse friends from Abbott Northwestern. A few of them had already been to Silver Lake to welcome her home, and they encouraged her to come up whenever she felt ready for an afternoon out with all the crew.

It felt wrong not to correct her parents as they waved goodbye to her, but her real mission was one she'd only told two people about—Penny and Lita—via letter. The matter between John Olson and her had seemed intimate and private and certainly would've taken much explaining.

Most of the snow had melted but winter still had its grasp in mid-April as she took to the main road leading north. No tree had started budding, the robins had not yet returned, and Eleanor hadn't known if John Olson had indeed waited for her.

She drove to the school where she knew he was still the principal—she'd called under the pretense that she had a school-age daughter and was looking at educational options—and sat in the parking lot for several minutes before summoning the courage to go inside. Eleanor wondered if John would've changed much in the four years since she'd last seen him, but when he emerged from his office behind the reception desk, he looked exactly the same.

He hesitated for only a second before closing the gap between them and embracing her, telling her he'd heard she'd been rescued and had seen her name in the *Minneapolis Star* as having been one of the Minnesota service members recently rescued from a POW camp. He'd been so relieved to hear of her liberation and to know that she was home, safe and sound. The embrace had been one of perhaps a friend to a friend, and she'd been unsure if he still felt the same way about her.

It wasn't long after settling into his office to talk that she found out he did.

"*I told you I would wait to hear from you, and I meant it,*" he'd said. "*I knew what had happened in Manila. I knew not to expect to hear from you while you were held captive, although I hoped I would. But even so, I never stopped waiting. I never stopped praying. I never stopped thinking about you, Eleanor. I still think about you. All the time. If you hadn't come today, I would've written to you at some point. I didn't . . . I just wasn't quite ready to hear that perhaps you'd moved on from me. I'm not sure I'm ready to hear it today either. I hope to God that is not why you've come. To tell me that.*"

She smiled. "*That's not why I've come.*"

They took their courtship slowly, which they found to be exactly what they both needed. She and John realized quickly that they both had idealized perceptions of each other; images of the perfect soul mate that their imaginations and mutual attraction had allowed them to invent and then treasure during the long years of the war and their separation.

The time they allowed themselves to truly get to know each other had gifted Eleanor some of the sweetest moments of her life up to that point.

She had gotten her job back at Abbott Northwestern after her separation from the Navy Nurse Corps, and she and John dated for a year and a half before marrying. And now they had this beautiful little boy, two-year-old David, who enriched their world in the most amazing ways.

But Eleanor still sensed a perpetual incompleteness about her new life. The need to see Penny and Lita seemed to overwhelm her at times. She felt guilty about it. Weren't John and the baby enough?

"It's because the three of you made a promise to see each other again," John said when she finally talked to him about it. *"I know all about making a promise that you fully intend to keep. And I want to help you keep this one."*

She and Penny and Lita had been corresponding by mail since the end of the war, but as the ten-year-anniversary of their first meeting at the Army Navy Club was approaching, it seemed like the right time to finally make the reunion happen.

And now here she was getting ready to land on a Manila tarmac. The promise made between the three friends was about to become real.

Eleanor was not the same person she'd been when she left the Philippines after three years as a prisoner, but neither was she the same person who'd arrived on a hot August afternoon in 1941, desperate to set a new course for her life.

This is the dance of life, isn't it? she mused to herself. *As the music changes, the steps change, and so then does the dancer. But the people we choose to dance with, well, they remain as close to our beating hearts as we will hold them, don't they?*

Thank heaven they do . . .

———◦———

Penny stood outside Manila International Airport, eyes closed, face turned to the sun, and breathed in the warm, fragrant air. It smelled of frangipani and jasmine. Of wet earth and humidity. Freshly mowed grass and the brine of distant salt water. Not at all what she remembered.

She waited for the other odors associated with this place to assail her:

diesel exhaust, gunpowder, and sweat. The wet-rock scent of deep, dark caves. The stifling air of small, crowded rooms. Unwashed men. Frightened women. Rotten vegetables. Illness. Blood. She had worried about those smells—and their associated memories—on their long red-eye flight. They had leapfrogged from one city to another, each hop bringing them closer to the Philippines. Houston to Los Angeles. Los Angeles to Honolulu. Honolulu to Manila.

Funny how it used to be the *sounds* that rattled her. Now it was the smells.

Six years ago, Manila had reeked of death. But today, the only aroma she could detect was paradise. And that was a mercy. Penny let out a long breath and opened her eyes.

The airport—little more than a single runway and a low building that served as a passenger terminal—used to be part of the United States Air Force base. It was transferred to the Philippine government after the war but had not yet undergone any sort of major renovation. They'd deplaned right onto the airstrip and walked two hundred feet to the terminal, shifting from the cool plane to the hot tarmac, then into the air-conditioned terminal, and out again into the humid August air to find a cab.

Someone grunted behind her, that universal sound of male curiosity.

Penny turned and looked at her father. "Not what you imagined?"

He set an arm around her shoulder and dropped a kiss to her temple. "I hope you'll forgive me, but I tried very hard not to imagine it at all," he said. "I couldn't wrap my head around how my little girl was in the middle of a war."

Years. It had taken them *years* to work through the pain they'd inflicted on each other. But the honesty helped. And that was the rule they lived by now: just tell the truth. So when she'd asked her parents if they would like to accompany her on this reunion trip, they said yes. They wanted to see the place that had changed their daughter.

"You know, I don't think I've ever seen a sky that blue," her mother said, joining them at the curb. She'd made a beeline for the restroom once they landed and, now relieved, was surveying their surroundings with her usual critical eye. "Blue, yes. But not *that* blue."

"We're closer to the equator," Penny said. "It makes everything more intense."

Her mother was watching her with a gimlet eye, as though Penny might disintegrate right here on the curb.

"Stop," Penny told her with a huff. "I'm *fine*."

"You don't feel—"

"I feel the same as I did yesterday. And the day before."

A row of cabs waited in a neat line not far away, their shiny black hoods reflecting the sun. Other passengers drifted through the terminal doors and fell into two categories: the seasoned traveler who knew exactly what to do, and the baffled tourist, turned upside down by jet lag and confusion.

"How does this work?" Her father squinted at the closest cab. "Am I supposed to whistle? Wave?"

Penny laughed. "I imagine they're waiting for us to get our bags."

"Oh." He turned back to the terminal. "Maybe I should go check?"

"No need," Penny told him as Charley pushed a luggage cart through the door.

"But . . ."

"Dad, he will smack you with that cane if you so much as offer."

Charley's limp hadn't been temporary. Nor was it easy to fix: two operations to remove the shrapnel in his hip. Penny had insisted on watching both surgeries from the observation deck at the Texas Medical Center. The doctors hadn't liked it, of course, but it wasn't like she grew faint at the sight of blood. Besides, her Bronze Star and battle ribbon spoke for themselves. As did being Mrs. Charley Russell, former officer in the U.S. Army Nurse Corps.

The wedding was small. Just her parents and his, six months after he'd found her in Houston. A backyard ceremony. A love-drunk week in Galveston Bay on honeymoon. And then the real work began. The patching of two broken souls now bound to each other. But they understood the damage and how it played out on any given day. How the backfiring of a car sounded like a gunshot and could send you diving for cover behind the couch. How the smell of rubbing alcohol could turn your stomach. How you could drift off midconversation and stare at your dinner plate for fifteen

minutes, swallowed by some memory that had been triggered by an innocent mention of coconut. Or something equally benign.

They understood.

And that was enough.

"Ready?" Charley reached them at the curb.

"Yes," she said, then looked around. "Wait. Where is she?"

"In the bathroom." Her mother scowled. "Applying *lipstick*. You know,
I didn't let you wear that nonsense until you were eighteen."

"Well, I'm not her mother. Am I?"

Ellen Briscoe, otherwise known as Newt, had spent one week with
Penny every summer since they arrived back in the United States. She was
seventeen now and newly graduated from high school, but one would never
know it. By all appearances the girl looked twenty-two. Short and curvy,
fond of flared skirts and kitten heels, she sashayed out of the airport with
all the sass you'd expect from a girl who had experienced more in less than
two decades than most people did in an entire lifetime. Newt still wore the
gold-nugget necklace. And she still looked at Penny as though she was her
own personal true north. Charley she tolerated, but that was to be expected.
God help anyone who took the lion's share of Penny's affection.

"What are you all standing around for?" Newt demanded. "I thought
we had somewhere to be?"

As if on cue, as if he was her real grandfather—and honestly, you could
never convince the man otherwise—Penny's dad stepped into the street, put
his fingers to his mouth, and whistled loud enough to summon the dead. A
cab pulled forward obediently.

Today was August eighth. Ten years to the day since Penny had that
first drink with Lita and Eleanor at the ANC. She couldn't wait to see them.
They'd written, of course. And there had been the occasional phone call on
Christmas Day or New Year's. Once or twice on a birthday. But it wasn't
enough. Her friends had been an anchor during the war. And she wanted
them to know this version of her, the Penny who had rebuilt her life despite
everything.

Her father situated their luggage in the trunk, and her mother slid into
the front seat beside the cabdriver. She was already peppering him with

questions, asking how long it would take them to get to the hotel. Newt took her seat in the back beside the window. All of it made Penny want to cry.

And Charley knew that, of course. He understood. Which was why he pulled her close and whispered into her ear, "Are you okay?"

She pushed the tears away with the heels of her hands. "I'm fine."

"That's not what I meant." He rested his hand on the swell of her belly.

This was the last chance they'd have to travel before Penny was so far along in her pregnancy that it wasn't safe. Seven months. Farther along than the first time. She set her hand on top of his and felt the baby give a strong kick.

"I've never been better," she said.

———•———

Ironically, Lita was grateful for the unfortunate news.

The cake she'd ordered had been dropped by the baker's new assistant, and the shop was racing to finish the replacement. At the profuse apologies that greeted her, Lita smiled and assured them it was but a small problem—because compared to all she'd lived through, it was. And besides, the brief delay gave her a chance to sit on a bench outside the shop, watch the sunlit bustling of Manila pass by, and simply pause for a moment.

The day had been a busy one, full of food preparations and anticipation of the late-afternoon festivities. She'd hardly slept the night before, given her excitement. And her nerves—though that did seem silly. The trio's unique bond from wartime combined with updates through posts, as regular as those she traded with her sisters, had long solidified Lita, Penny, and Eleanor as family. Through handwritten letters, they'd shared the ups and downs of normal life, the frustrations and joys. Lita's tears from happiness stained more than a few of the pages she'd received bearing news of proposals and weddings and babies.

Of course, she had shared tales of her own children as well. Not born of her womb, mind you, but ones who made her a mother all the same. As predicted, the war had left many a homeless, parentless child. With the nuns' help she'd taken them in and cared for them at the convent, where she worked tirelessly to reunite them with any relatives who'd survived. Of the others, sixty-seven remained with her to this day, housed in a lovely new orphanage compliments of U.S. military leaders who'd conceded to her incessant requests. Clearly they'd detected in her manner she wasn't about to give up.

She'd gained that from the war.

And from others she held dear.

The thought brought her hand to her skirt pocket, from which she drew out the letter that had arrived just that morning. This, in truth, was another reason she was glad for an opportunity to sit with her ponderings.

Dear Lita, it began. No matter how many years, even decades, would pass, she imagined the sight of Lon's handwriting would forever cause a slight hitch in her chest. The missive was relatively brief yet friendly, like each of his annual letters he sent normally at Christmas, at which point she always responded in kind. The fact this one came in August had worried her until she discovered the reason.

She reread his words now, skimming through his typical update of life in Chicago and the rigors of medical school—the limits of his capabilities to help wounded soldiers during the war, once home, had driven him away from a flashy banker's career and toward his true passion of becoming a surgeon.

Again she slowed upon the phrase: *I'm engaged.*

Lita knew, even direly hoped, he'd eventually meet the right girl. He deserved that and so much more. It was a sign of fully moving on, a good thing. Still, this didn't stop tears from moistening her eyes, even as she smiled at the bittersweet news.

"Here you go!" The woman's voice in Tagalog pulled her gaze upward. Standing over Lita, the aproned baker appeared with a brown box and flushed cheeks. Lita slipped the letter back into her pocket, to later store away with keepsakes from her past.

"Oh, that's splendid," she replied in her native tongue, rising to accept the replacement. Coconut cake with mango filling. Just like she and her friends had enjoyed at the ANC.

"Thank you for your patience. I do hope it proves worth the wait."

"I can already tell you—it's perfect."

With care yet purpose, Lita strode back toward the café. Motorcars and bicyclists zipped past the moving crowd. Vendors hollered to reel in customers. Gasoline fumes and the scents of street food swirled in the humid air. One might think it seemed no war had occurred here at all. Evidence remained, however: in the mounds of rubble from buildings not yet restored, in pockmarks on walls left from bullets, in old, dark stains on the streets that could pass for oil, unless a person knew better. The country was still healing, like its people.

Like Lita.

Even after six years, there were times while turning a city corner when she'd flash back to a vision of a Japanese soldier wielding a bayoneted rifle; or passing a city square, she'd gasp seeing Dr. Alvarez kneeling on a platform. She would sweat and tremble as reality returned. Then, collecting herself, she would forge on and combat the memories as best she knew how: by helping to rebuild what had been destroyed. She'd lend a hand where she could, raise funds when able, including for her village. A repayment she was proudest to provide.

Thankfully today the quarter-mile walk delivered her back to the café without incident. It was a path she knew well from when she and Reyna had roomed upstairs, and from all their family gatherings held there since.

Closed for private event, the sign on the door read in Tagalog. Thanks to Reyna's doing.

A light breeze from fans greeted Lita's entry. Spread among the otherwise vacant space, the tables were set with white linens and centerpieces of jam jars filled with colorful orchids. She set down the boxed cake on a long table that would soon host a buffet of her favorite Filipino dishes, then she stretched her hands, which still often stiffened for the same reason her headaches some days would come and go. They were minor inconveniences considering what could have been and what so many others faced.

She checked her watch. A half hour until their four o'clock arrival.

A fluttering rose within her just as Reyna emerged from the kitchen. "Ah, there you are! I need to dash out, but the daiquiris are in pitchers and ready to pour."

Lita was about to thank her and explain how the cake had held her up, but the sight of Reyna's flared dress, pinned-up hair, and makeup diverted her. "I thought you just had errands to run." She shot her gaze toward Reyna's outfit while raising a brow.

Reyna corrected, "I said I had things to see to, which I do."

"Such as?" Lita blocked her from passing, seeking an admission of what she'd suspected for several weeks. "Come on. Spill already."

Reyna rolled her eyes. "Look. I'll tell you about him when there's something to tell."

Lita exaggerated a gasp. "So there *is* a him!"

A blush crept into Reyna's face. "You're annoying," she muttered and swerved around Lita to bolt away. "Be back later tonight."

"Feel free to bring him along," Lita called out as the door shut. Chances were high he was a fellow at the hospital, where Reyna spent the majority of her time. She'd been promoted to head nurse, a fitting rank for her pride in patient care—and her knack for ordering people around.

Right then laughter burst out, and Lita followed the sound into the kitchen, where her two main helpers among the café staff were putting the finishing touches on the food. With no shortages or rations these days, there was kare-kare stew and chicken adobo and lumpia Lita had personally made, in her mother's signature style. There was even catfish she'd caught herself, from her latest night-fishing outing insisted upon by Reyna—the girl was nothing if not the embodiment of tough love.

But that was what sisters were for. Including those made so by law.

"What's so funny in here?"

Jun-Jun, sweet and mischievous as ever at ten, was grinning while standing beside Reyna's brother—Lita's husband of two years, Cesar—who shook his head. "Trust me, honey, you don't want to know." Cesar's chestnut eyes glimmered, and he touched her lips with a tender kiss that warmed her. She often marveled at the gentleness of his soul. If not for the smattering of scars on his back and chest and the occasional nightmares she'd calm him from—the same as he did for her—she'd have no inkling he spent years in the jungle fighting for his life and their freedom. And for a country that was now truly theirs.

She watched him now, laughing and razzing Jun-Jun in a fatherly way over the kid's eagerness to meet Newt—her photographs from Penny had spurred a crush despite the age gap. And who was Lita to squash a boy's dream?

In that moment a question returned to her.

After a recent visit by her sisters, along with her many nieces and nephews, Cesar had whispered as they snuggled into bed at night, "Should we finally start a family, Lita? One of our own?"

"Maybe," had been her answer, as she was well aware she was considered ancient by some standards. Plus, it wasn't as though they weren't already helping the nuns and other orphanage staff raise dozens of children as it was.

Suddenly, though, whether from Lon's letter releasing a faint, lingering tie or from a full circle of healing that would surely come from today's long-awaited reunion, she sensed that the next time they lay in bed and he posed the question, her reply wouldn't be "Maybe."

"Well, I'd say you're all set here." He wiped his hands on a towel. "I'm going to check on the builders and get cleaned up." With the expansion of another classroom at the orphanage, there were always details to confirm, and he wasn't due back here for at least another hour.

It was Penny's idea, and a good one, for her family and Eleanor's to settle at the hotel while the three friends met in private before the rest joined in as a beautiful but chaotic circus. Lita was surprised Penny and Eleanor hadn't met up in the States over the years. When she'd remarked as much in her letters, they'd said life simply got away from them, and that really it didn't seem right to meet without her.

Selfishly, Lita savored that reason.

Just minutes until four, she set out a plate of appetizers on the long table, then smoothed her hair for the hundredth time, her nerves buzzing.

That's when the tinkling of a bell announced the door opening, and she turned.

Two figures walked in, and the world went quiet. With eyes alight and faces beaming, Penny and Eleanor were lovely as ever and, incredibly, here. In person. In this room.

Through their brief collective breath, a sudden calm flowed through Lita. For as the three of them stood there, on the cusp of hugs and tears and ramblings of stories, it was as if a lifetime had passed—and somehow no time at all.

AUTHORS' NOTE

O f the many things we would like to elaborate on in the following pages, two must be established up front:

First, if you have not yet finished *When We Had Wings*, may we gently suggest you do so before reading any farther? Spoilers abound below and your reading experience will be greatly enhanced if you are not given answers to questions you haven't yet had the chance to ask.

Second, though inspired by the real Angels of Bataan and Corregidor, Eleanor, Lita, and Penny are figments of our imaginations. In essence they are amalgamations of the many nurses—Army, Navy, and Filipina—who faithfully served during World War II. More information about these women, real and fictional, is included below.

This book exists because of a surprise email that showed up in our inboxes in the spring of 2020. Like most of the world, we were all at home, a bit dazed and confused by the sudden onset of a global pandemic, when an unexpected but intriguing opportunity was presented to us by Amanda Bostic, the publisher of Harper Muse:

Did we have any interest in writing a collaborative novel set during World War II?

It is a subject we are all quite fond of and familiar with. Of the more than two dozen novels among us, nine take place in or around the Second World War. As longtime colleagues and friends, we were extremely interested in tackling such a creative project together. The only difficulty was finding a subject that none of us had covered and that all of us agreed was fresh and compelling. Once Susan Meissner suggested the Angels of

Bataan, one evening and a single documentary made us fall in love with them.

It is worth noting that there's a primary reason we hadn't heard of these nurses in all our years spent researching and writing in this genre: the United States government forced these women to sign papers saying they would not discuss their experiences after the war.

Well.

That didn't sit right with us. It was their story after all. Shouldn't they be able to tell it? Not according to Uncle Sam. Thankfully, by the time we were introduced to this bit of history, a handful of biographies had (finally!) been written about these extraordinary women. This was due in part to the fact that, as members of the Greatest Generation, many had passed away.

Here is the truth: General Douglas MacArthur allowed these women to be taken captive. He had an opportunity in April 1942 to evacuate all Army and Filipina nurses from Corregidor and out of the Philippines, but he chose to take other military personnel instead. As a result, the nurses were imprisoned by the Japanese and spent more than four harrowing years in various camps. The U.S. government could not explain the general's choice, so they hid it instead. The fact that every one of those nurses survived the war and came home is nothing short of a miracle.

For the related benefits of vital research, we owe a huge debt of gratitude to *We Band of Angels: The Untold Story of the American Women Trapped on Bataan* by Elizabeth M. Norman, *The Indomitable Florence Finch: The Untold Story of a War Widow Turned Resistance Fighter and Savior of American POWs* by Robert J. Mrazek, and *This Is Really War: The Incredible True Story of a Navy Nurse POW in the Occupied Philippines* by Emilie Le Beau Lucchesi. In these books, we discovered stunning accounts and invaluable details that inspired the characters of Eleanor, Lita, and Penny. Even though our nurses are fictional, the hardships the women endured are not. Here are a few instances where we drew from real life in developing their interwoven tales:

Penny's aversion to the sounds of war stemmed from an account in *We Band of Angels*, described by Dr. Alfred Weinstein, who inspired the grandfatherly character Dr. Thomson. Though Captain Charley Russell is also fictional, a quartermaster on Corregidor did in fact ask one of the Angels to smuggle out the U.S. Army Quartermaster's flag and keep it for him. She succeeded, and the scene in which Penny saved the flag from a Japanese guard in Santo Tomas did indeed happen. Many of the details surrounding the young war orphan who attached herself to Penny are also real (though her name and proclivity toward pickpocketing are fictional). It made sense to us that Penny—in all her brokenness—would be the one to care for this little girl. In real life, a child bonded with the nurse Helen Cassiani, or "Cassie" as she was known to her friends, who also appears in our novel and whose impressive reveal of a bottle of Johnnie Walker Red at her twenty-fifth birthday party in the jungle was too fun not to include.

One of our greatest frustrations in researching this novel revolved around our inability to find accurate resources detailing the experiences of the Filipina nurses during the war. Unfortunately, many biographers treat these women as an afterthought. It is for that reason that we relied so heavily on *The Indomitable Florence Finch* to help flesh out Lita's experiences during the second half of our book, sadly confident that the shocking accounts of Ms. Finch (who also battled bigotry as a mestiza) weren't uncommon. Her time in the Kempeitai headquarters was particularly horrifying, as were her descriptions of the Manila Massacre. (How on earth had none of us heard of this ghastly occurrence before?) After her liberation from the Women's Correctional Institution and subsequent evacuation to America, Florence enlisted in the Coast Guard as an SPAR. The war ended before she could secure her desired post in a Pacific war zone, but her sheer attempt to do so after all she had been through exemplifies the profound fortitude, bravery, and unbreakable spirit of the Filipino people.

Because the Army and Navy nurses were separated so early in the war, most of our information regarding the Navy nurses and their time at Los Baños prison camp was found in *Rescue at Los Baños* by Bruce Henderson and *This Is Really War*. From these books we gleaned tales of the famed baseball game between American and Japanese soldiers and the heartbreaking details of what Eleanor endured during her time at this POW camp.

In case you are wondering, Maude Davison, Laura Cobb, and "Mama Josie" Nesbit were also real. These women led their nurses through literal hell and should be household names. It is a travesty that their stories are mostly hidden in dusty archives. Ida Hube, as inexplicable and convenient as she may seem, was not only real but gave the Angels myriad supplies through several traumatic years. She provided resources, and thus power, at a time when they would have otherwise had none. Father Domingo, on the other hand, is fictional. The same goes for Lon McGibbons, Reyna Delos Santos, and David Mathis—though, of course, they feel just as real to us as the authors.

Should you be interested in reading more about the Angels of Bataan (and we highly suggest doing so), we recommend reading the books previously listed, as well as *Angel of Bataan: The Life of a World War II Army Nurse in the War Zone and at Home* by Walter M. Macdougall and *What a Way to Spend a War: Navy Nurse POWs in the Philippines* by Dorothy Still Danner.

Writing a full novel as a team is a wonderful if challenging, confusing, yet delightful experience. (We will all miss our daily email and text threads!) From the ups and downs of our journey, it feels as though—to a comparatively far safer extent—we have waded through a war together, driven by a shared passionate cause, and forged lasting bonds. All to say, we are very proud of this book, and we hope it helps shed light on some of the countless stories of astonishing women that have been hidden for much too long.

ACKNOWLEDGMENTS

First and foremost, our heartfelt gratitude goes to our incomparable agent, Elisabeth Weed of The Book Group, to whom this book is rightly dedicated. There are no words to fully convey how much your support, in every way, means to us all. We are also enormously thankful to our wonderful editors Kimberly Carlton, Julee Schwarzburg, Jodi Hughes, and publisher Amanda Bostic, along with the rest of our fantastic team at Harper Muse.

We send loads of appreciation to Ben Major with the World War II U.S. Medical Research Centre for his research assistance, Natsu Tabata for her help with historical Japanese language, and Filipina nurse Jing Ignacio for reading a good portion of the manuscript to provide invaluable input. For help with Filipino character names, cultural references, and traditions, as well as our use of Tagalog, we thank Jovy Gill and Angerene Aldridge, whose mother, Angelita Delos Santos, has long been like a *tita* to Kristina and whose leche flan and lumpia will forever be among her beloved childhood memories.

We are also grateful to you, the reader, and to everyone behind the scenes who helps spread our stories and enables us to do a job we love so much: the booksellers, librarians, bloggers, book champions, and, most of all, our (extremely patient) families. Thank you—thank you for everything.

DISCUSSION QUESTIONS

(Spoilers included)

1. Penny, Lita, and Eleanor become fast friends upon meeting and maintain that bond despite their years of separation. What do you think binds them together before, during, and after the war? Can you relate to their steady friendship?

2. The nurses were forced to transition from a paradise assignment to dealing with the worst elements of war. How did each one learn to cope? Have you ever had your world turn so quickly upside down?

3. Eleanor falls in love within weeks of meeting John Olson and initially believes the feeling is mutual. What do you think she found most compelling and attractive in him? Do you think they ended up with a good marriage? Why or why not?

4. Penny's parents chose to break communication with her at a time when she probably needed it most. Discuss possible reasons why. What emotions do you think her family members were struggling with?

5. Lita's goals for her life were shaped largely by her family, driven by practicality then guilt, and ultimately by a true sense of purpose. What most contributed to forming your own life goals? How have they evolved over time?

6. What were Penny's strengths? Her weaknesses? How about Lita's? Eleanor's?

7. How was Penny changed by her relationship with Newt?

8. A romance sneaks up on Lita when she's least expecting it. Why do you think she was truly avoiding any courtship? Have you ever had similar reasons for doing the same?

9. Early in the story, much of Eleanor's sustaining hope for survival centers on her concept of home. How does this hope change as the war progresses and the situation grows dire?

10. What do you think is the difference between duty and compassion? How much were these two virtues in play for the three nurses?

11. For release from Bilibid Prison, the Filipina nurses sign an oath of allegiance to the Empire of Japan. Would you have done the same? Would the decision have been difficult?

12. In the latter part of the book, Penny reflects that "mercy is always power." What do you think she means by that? Do you agree?

13. If David had lived, do you think Eleanor's future would have taken a different path? How did he most impact her life?

14. What did you find most extraordinary about the roles of Penny, Lita, and Eleanor during their imprisonment? Do you think their courage and resolve are unique?

15. How has this fictionalized story of the real Angels of Bataan affected you? What did you find most surprising? Most touching?

ABOUT THE AUTHORS

Ariel Lawhon is a critically acclaimed, *New York Times* bestselling author of historical fiction. Her books have been translated into numerous languages and have been Library Reads, One Book One County, Indie Next, Costco, Amazon Spotlight, and Book of the Month Club selections. She lives in Nashville, Tennessee, with her husband and four sons. Ariel splits her time between the grocery store and the baseball field. Visit her online at ariellawhon.com; Instagram: @ariel.lawhon; Twitter: @ArielLawhon; and Facebook: @ArielLawhonAuthor.

Photo by Kristee Mays Photography

Kristina McMorris is a *New York Times*, *USA TODAY*, and *Wall Street Journal* bestselling author of two novellas and seven historical novels, including the million-copy bestseller *Sold on a Monday*. The recipient of more than twenty national literary awards, she previously hosted weekly TV shows for Warner Bros. and an ABC affiliate, beginning at age nine with an Emmy Award–winning program, and owned a wedding-and-event-planning company until she far surpassed her limit of "Y.M.C.A." and chicken dances. She lives with her family in Oregon. Visit her online at kristinamcmorris.com; Instagram: @kristina.mcmorris; Twitter: @KrisMcmorris; and Facebook: @KristinaMcMorrisAuthor.

Photo by Holland Studios

About the Authors

Photo by Stephanie Carbajal

Susan Meissner is a *USA TODAY* bestselling author of historical fiction with more than three-quarters of a million books in print in eighteen languages. She is an author, speaker, and writing workshop leader with a background in community journalism. Her novels include *The Nature of Fragile Things* (starred review in *Publishers Weekly*), *The Last Year of the War* (named to *Real Simple* magazine's list of best books for 2019), *As Bright as Heaven* (starred review in *Library Journal*) and *Secrets of Charmed Life* (Goodreads finalist for Best Historical Fiction 2015). Susan attended Point Loma Nazarene University and lives in the Pacific Northwest with her husband and their yellow Lab, Winston. Visit her online at susanmeissnerauthor.com; Instagram: @susanmeissnerauthor; Twitter: @SusanMeissner; Facebook: @susan.meissner; and Pinterest: @SusanMeissner.